KAINE'S REBELLION

SHATTERED EMPIRE

D.M. PRUDEN

Ebook ISBN 978-1-989341-16-2

Print ISBN 978-1-989341-17-9

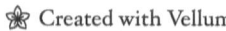 Created with Vellum

A NOTE TO THE READER

Thank you for purchasing a copy of Kaine's Rebellion.

This is the fourth book in the Shattered Empire series, and I have tried to make this novel self contained so it isn't strictly necessary for a reader to be familiar with the previous three books. That having been said, however, having read the preceding material will answer some of the inevitable questions that remain unaddressed within this volume.

If you have not read the previous volumes but wish to pick up a discounted copy of any of the books, you can do so at this link: https://books.bookfunnel.com/shattered-empire

Hayden Kaine has evolved in unexpected ways since I conceived him in 2018. He has grown from a cocky, but insecure young man concerned with the preservation of his own skin into a maturing man who's known pain, loss, and the nature of sacrifice for the benefit of others. I'd like to think that is the path that we all journey as we grow older and wiser.

Of course, like all of us, Kaine still has much to learn.

I hope that you enjoy reading Kaine's Rebellion as much as I enjoyed writing it.

Pax et Caritas,
Doug Pruden
February 22, 2022 (20220222)

"Diplomacy is the art of telling people to go to hell in such a way that they ask for directions."

—Winston Churchill

SALT AND CLAY

Hayden awakened on his belly, the earthy aroma of salt and clay filling his nostrils. Something tickled his hand. He opened his eyes to a strange, six-legged cross between a lizard and a beetle crawling up his arm.

Disgusted, he shook the creature off and watched it scurry away and dig itself into the sand.

He peered around, confused, until he gradually realized he was in the middle of a desert.

His head and ribs hurt, and his face felt burned. He passed his hands over his torn and scorched uniform searching for any other injuries. Finding none, he sat up.

A synthetic body lay five metres away, face down and inert. He crawled over and rolled it to its back. Its artificial skin was burnt away, revealing the mechanism beneath. The body's torso and limbs showed extensive damage as well, with one leg missing.

Confused, his eyes followed a path of disturbed earth leading to a small crashed ship, half-buried in a dune and tilted on its side. Smoke rose from the blown hatch. The hull exhibited heavy carbon scoring, suggesting it had been fired on.

Kaine struggled to piece together his fragmented memories.

They'd been in a battle, and there was an explosion. He recalled being strapped into the emergency escape pod.

Squeezing his eyes shut, he tried to recall more through the dull throbbing in his head. He vaguely remembered a screaming noise, the rush of air around him, and violent shaking.

His gaze returned to the scorched hull of the vehicle to confirm his recollection. Who would do such a thing?

Grasping his head, he shut his eyes to try to remember more.

Pavlovich ordering the ship abandoned was the only reason he could imagine why he now found himself here. His eyes were drawn to the damaged synth.

He recalled one of Cora's synths entering the bridge.

His eyes widened at the realization that the one he now stared at was her.

With his heart racing, he examined the android, calling out to her, but she gave no response.

Desperate to save her, he painfully stood. Gripping his bandaged ribs, he realized Cora must have administered first aid to him before she collapsed.

He stiffly walked to the burning pod. After tearing a strip from his shirt to tie over his mouth, he entered the blown hatch. Locating the extinguisher, he put out the smouldering fire in the control console.

The smoke stung his eyes, and he couldn't breathe as he searched the wreckage. Finding what he sought, he exited the vehicle and dropped to his knees in the sand, coughing.

After taking a moment to recover, he rose and hurried back to the fallen android with his prize. He turned her over and inserted the portable storage module he'd retrieved into the back of the machine's head, hoping he wasn't too late. The unit's display indicated something had transferred, but he couldn't verify if he got everything.

He needed to find a proper computer interface to find out, but smoke still billowed from the destroyed ship, so he had no choice but to wait before he could enter again to determine if anything remained functional aboard.

After putting the storage module on the dog-tag chain around his neck, he sat in the sand and assessed his surroundings. The pod's survival pack was next to where he awoke, and its medical kit lay open beside it. Tears ran down his cheeks as he imagined Cora devoting her last moments to his care.

He looked out to the surrounding desert, flat and dun-coloured, broken by red rock outcrops worn into tortured shapes by aeons of wind and blowing sand. The air grew cooler as the sun began to vanish behind the distant mountains.

In the fading light, the smoke coming from the ship was diminishing. Rummaging through the pack, he found a flashlight.

Returning to the wreckage, he confirmed his fear. The fire had destroyed everything inside. A steadily beeping distress beacon sent out an automated signal, so he still hoped he might be rescued by the locals.

He swallowed the lump in his throat.

What happened to *Scimitar*? What provoked the attack?

They were not strangers to the suspicion they encountered in other systems they visited. The isolation imposed on every planet in the Confederation following the failure of the jump gate network served as the perfect spark to ignite decades of built-up discontent into conflict. But fifteen years had passed since the collapse, and most of the former colonies had long since resolved their issues in one manner or another. The ongoing open hostility here was exceptional.

His ribs ached, and from the way the skin on his face felt, he'd suffered radiation burns. He dug through the medical kit to find antiradiation drugs and ointment for his skin.

He didn't know where he'd crashed; he wasn't sure which planet he was on. *Scimitar* was on approach to the inner colony world of Oberon when the attack happened.

Fatigue suddenly overwhelmed him. He found an old imperial jacket in the survival pack, giving him an idea of when the last time was that anyone performed maintenance on the ship. Too tired to retrieve the survival gear and rations from the undamaged exterior storage compartment, he decided to retrieve what he needed in the morning.

Pulling the coat's collar up against the chill, he used the bag as a pillow and settled in for the night inside the smoke-tinged cabin. A shrinking part of him hoped *Scimitar* survived and Pavlovich was searching for him. But his spirits wavered. The captain would not have launched the escape pods unless the situation was dire. The chances of *Scimitar*'s survival were not good.

Concern for his friends and worry he might be found by the same people who shot him from the sky kept his mind buzzing. But exhaustion and the pain medication began to make him groggy, and he drifted into a deep sleep.

Pavlovich should not have been there, and yet to Hayden it seemed natural for him to be.

Scimitar's bridge configuration was wrong. People he knew to be dead for many years occupied the stations. His own workstation was in the wrong location, against the bulkhead instead of beside the helm station.

Bizarrely, a waiter entered and deposited a plate of food before each of them. Pavlovich grinned at him and said, "Shall we share a philosophical conversation over dinner?"

From thin air, their server produced a clay tureen and proceeded to fill their plates to the brim with a spicy tagine. Hayden searched but could find no utensils.

He asked, "What are we going to discuss?"

Pavlovich gestured to the front screen of the bridge. The vista of the galaxy's core illuminated everything as if it were daylight. Nearer to the ship, brilliant flowers bloomed from nuclear explosions hurled between battling fleets.

Confused, he looked at Pavlovich. "Are we at war with someone?"

"We've stepped into one," said Pavlovich. His appearance changed. His beard became streaked with silver and his once black eyebrows were almost white. Lines around his mouth and beneath his eyes testified to a lifetime of worry.

He spoke in Cora's voice. "Can war be justifiable, Hayden?"

"What? What are you talking about?"

"I ask you a simple question. Is it possible to engage in a just war?"

He turned again to the view outside. Debris from destroyed ships and frozen bodies floated in the void as *Scimitar* passed by them.

Pavlovich/Cora continued, "Augustine said cases existed for a justified war."

"Who?"

"Saint Augustine; under certain conditions, he said, one could conduct a war of justice. Do you agree?"

"I...I don't know. I don't think any war is justifiable."

"Even against someone who commits atrocities? "

The plates and the waiter vanished, along with most of the bridge. Pavlovich remained in his command chair. Hayden stood before him, his hands in shackles.

"Am I on trial for something?"

In his heart, he knew the answer. He was guilty of something, but for the life of him he could not recall what.

"We are all being judged," said Pavlovich.

His appearance had again altered. Instead of a uniform, he wore a robe cinched at the waist with a golden rope. Sandals were on his feet, and his hair was white. A faint halo glowed around his head.

"You began this conflict, Hayden. How can you justify your actions?"

"I don't know what you are talking about. I didn't start

anything. We stepped into the middle of this battle; don't you remember?"

"Not this one; all of them. Before this, even before the destruction of the jump gate. Everywhere we've ever visited is tearing itself apart from the seeds you sowed. Being isolated created cleansing chaos, can't you see?"

"How can I be responsible for the situation in this system?"

"Billions of people perish. Do you not feel any remorse for your responsibility?"

Hayden's heart banged in his chest. The Pavlovich figure was not angry or judgemental. He showed genuine concern and compassion.

"Why are you asking me this? What happened?"

"How do we know when we are on the right side? I need to know what I am fighting for."

"We're not on any side. Don't you remember? We are fugitives, on the run from Robert Thomas. We have nothing to do with these people tearing themselves apart."

The patriarchal being gazed at something in the distance. They were outside the ship now, floating in the black of space. All the stars were gone, and the husks of destroyed ships and the bodies of the dead surrounded them. They increased in number and pressed in on him to the point where he couldn't breathe.

"Your sins are coming for you, Hayden Kaine. Are you prepared to atone?"

Panic rose in him, and he screamed.

He shot up to a sitting position. Cold sweat drenched him, and his heart pounded furiously.

The darkness disoriented him. His searching hand fell upon the survival pack. The rough fabric against his fingers grounded him.

"Stupid nightmare."

He inhaled deeply, held his breath for a few seconds, then blew it out, trying to bring his pulse down. Shivering, he pulled the jacket's collar up. The stench of burnt circuitry assaulted his nostrils.

Rubbing the sleep from his eyes, he looked through the open door of the escape pod at the first rays of morning light peeping over the horizon.

He sighed and fell back against the pod's bulkhead.

"I never thought I'd be relieved to see this place," he muttered.

As his head rested against the cold metal, he wondered what his next steps should be. Nobody came during the night, so he surmised the emergency beacon was damaged.

He dragged the bag onto his lap and dug inside until his hand fell upon a ration bar. Pulling it out, he peered at it in the dim light.

"I wonder how long this thing's been here."

He tore open the wrapper and took a tentative bite, surprised by its freshness. He gobbled it up and pulled out one of two sealed water canisters.

He hadn't drunk anything since the crash, and his throat was as dry as the desert outside. Aware of the preciousness of the resource, he rationed himself to a few sips. The warm liquid vanished inside his mouth as fast as he sipped, but he resisted the temptation to take gulps. He could live for weeks without food, but without water death would come within a couple of days at best, and he doubted he might find more when this ran out.

Hayden let his head bump back against the bulkhead.

Maybe someone nearby saw his ship come down and had dispatched a rescue team. Perhaps they picked up the homing beacon before it died out prematurely. There was no way to know. The biggest question now was what to do next.

He could remain with the pod and hope someone came looking for him. But what if no one did?

"Can't think like that. Stay focussed on the positive."

His hand went into the backpack and felt for the outline of the storage module.

If *Scimitar* was destroyed, this was the only part of Cora he could save. If he recovered a complete copy of her, it held all of her memories and knowledge, as well as her personality. He didn't want to contemplate another scenario.

It had taken Hayden a long time to become comfortable with how she could fragment her persona and occupy various locations throughout the ship simultaneously. Only his encounters with her in virtual reality helped him remember her as she was when they met years before: a wide-eyed, bright young engineer.

He longed to speak with her now. If anyone could help him rationalize what to do next, she could.

The landscape shone brilliant magenta in the morning light. Lazy heat waves already rose on the horizon and distorted the orange globe of the sun.

It was going to be a scorcher.

Hayden had crashed late in the day, long after the peak midday temperature. The desolate wilderness surrounding him and the baked and eroded stones of the outcrops nearby testified to the harsh environment. Aside from the weird creature crawling up his arm earlier, he'd seen nothing alive.

He tried to recall what he knew of this world. A central desert occupied most of Oberon's largest continent, stretching for hundreds of kilometres.

He could've crashed anywhere in the vast wilderness. If he was closer to the coast, he could be a few days hike to a more temperate environment or a settlement. But in which direction? He could set off randomly to any point of the compass and never be sure if he headed into the core of the desert or away from it.

With access to the navigation record that the pod would've made on entry, he might be able to determine his location. But those records had burned up, along with anything else of potential use to him.

"What am I going to do?"

He lay still, enjoying the relative cool of the shade offered within the pod's interior. He wished he could store it to use against the heat he knew was coming. One thing became clear: without rescue, he would be dead in days.

A distant whine disturbed the silence. As it became louder, he thought he recognized the sound of a turbine. An aircraft?

Exiting the pod, he shaded his eyes and squinted against the sunshine as he searched for the source.

In the distance, something hung above the horizon. Distorted by the rising heat waves was an aircraft, and it appeared to be coming in his direction.

Hayden let out a loud whoop.

He grabbed the pack and scrambled to the top of a nearby dune for a better view and to reassure himself it was real. The ship was close enough for him to identify it as a K-15 recon airship. The distinctive engine noise grew louder as it approached.

He dropped the pack and raised his arms to wave. Hayden couldn't believe his luck.

A hundred metres in front of him, the desert blossomed with twin rows of sandy geysers that advanced toward him. Not certain he believed his eyes, he hesitated before instinct kicked in. He grabbed up the pack and slid down the protected face of the dune as the bullets strafed over where he'd stood. The ground vibrated beneath him as the gunship roared past only a few metres overhead, trailing a cloud of fine dust blown up by its jets.

Still dumfounded, he stared at the ship as it began a lazy turn to make another run.

Hayden scrambled down to the desert hardpan and sprinted to a nearby outcrop. His feet sank ankle-deep into the loose sand at its base, making it a struggle to climb to the formation.

As he ducked behind the rock, bullets tore into the remains

of the escape pod before they pummelled the wall of rock protecting him.

The ship followed and roared past him.

As it began its turn, Hayden slogged through the sand to put the outcrop between them once more.

A rocket flare bloomed on the ship's hull, and a second later, the pod exploded in a violent eruption. Hayden covered his head to protect himself from flying shrapnel, grateful nothing more than sand sprayed over him.

He crouched, poking his head up to see the approaching aircraft slow and stop to hover thirty metres away. His eyes never left the vessel as it slowly approached the smouldering crater where the pod once stood.

Staying hidden, Hayden watched the pilot scan the surroundings in search of survivors. Half buried to his waist in the wind-drifted sand, he cowered as the roaring turbines drew nearer.

He dug himself deeper into the sand and piled as much as he could over himself. He prayed his ruse would work, because the pilot would finish him with gunfire or another missile if he was spotted.

Time slowed to a crawl. Dust and the earthy, salty scent of the desert tickled his nostrils. Pinching his nose to stifle a sneeze, he remained motionless.

The whir of the engines grew louder, and he felt the thin veneer of sand covering his legs shift in the draft blown up by the jets.

After the longest few seconds of his life, the engine's pitch rose, and with a roar, a cloud of dust blew up as the ship departed back to where it came from.

Hayden lay motionless until he no longer heard the aircraft. Then he struggled to exhume himself from his makeshift camouflage and stood to brush off his clothes. Sand and dust cascaded down his back. The blue morning sky greeted him as if nothing unusual had happened.

He surveyed what little of the escape pod remained.

Whoever that was must have been with the people who shot him down. Someone didn't want witnesses.

Hayden decided to search the wreckage for anything useful that might help him survive. He found the remains of the pod's weapons locker, but the pistol was damaged and useless. Everything was gone, including the survival gear, emergency rations, and water supply he hadn't yet retrieved from the storage compartment.

He still had the two bottles he'd found in the pack. Their contents wouldn't keep him alive for very long.

The attack eliminated all other options. All he could do was try to find a settlement before he died from the heat or someone else came by to kill him.

Looking in the direction the aircraft came from, he surmised its base must be there. It may or may not be inside his range, and it was the only hint as to where some semblance of civilization lay. It was probably not a good place to go.

Staying here to wait for someone less hostile to come by was an option but also a long shot, given what just happened. It also felt like he'd be giving up.

He scanned the horizon in a 360-degree turn. Some hills lay in the distance in the opposite direction from where the aircraft had come. He guessed they might be within a day's walk.

Having decided where to go, his only remaining question was when he should leave. He'd crashed in the evening, when the air was cooling. He didn't know what the peak temperature would be, but he had no doubt it would be hellish. A search group being launched in the morning suggested to him they wanted to complete their patrol before the heat of the day climbed to the point where nothing would be moving worth shooting at.

Evening, then.

He would hunker down and stay in the shade of the outcrop for the day and set out toward the mountains at sunset.

Recalling the coolness of the sand as he lay beneath it, he searched the debris field for a piece of the fuselage to use as an improvised shovel. He intended to dig himself a burrow to wait out the heat and start his journey before sunset. He hoped there wouldn't be any predators prowling at night.

He recalled his basic survival training. They'd been forced to spend five days surviving in the wilderness with nothing but a knife and a bottle of water. At least there'd been tree cover and plenty of game to hunt and streams to drink from. He never opted to take the advanced harsh environment survival course and now regretted his decision. Common sense would have to guide him, but staying hydrated enough to think straight and make sound decisions might become a problem. He didn't like his chances.

As he reviewed his surroundings, he doubted anything else qualified as a better choice. If the desert didn't end up killing him, some of the locals had already demonstrated their willingness to do so.

Taking his makeshift shovel, he trudged back to the outcrop and began to dig.

THIRST AND DEATH

The hills in the distance were much farther than Hayden had first estimated. After rising an hour before sunset, he'd started off toward them. The light from the planet's two moons illuminated the surroundings so he could keep his goal in sight for most of the night. But by the time the dawn light began to peek over the horizon, he was crestfallen to see his destination was still perhaps another day or two's walk.

He'd rationed his water through the night, keeping his sips small and infrequent, but one bottle was almost empty. At the rate he was going, he'd run out before he reached his goal.

Even after he arrived there, he had no guarantees he would be able to locate more, and panic began to gnaw at him.

Stopping, he surveyed his surroundings in the quickening daylight. The ground beneath his feet was desiccated and cracked. He was walking across a once vast lakebed, the realization of which made him aware of his thirst. Scanning about, he spotted a rock formation about half a kilometre away. The rocks were a short deviation from his intended direction, but they would provide him with the only shelter possible once the sun climbed higher.

He took a longer look at the mountains in the distance. He

could identify trees on the lower slopes. That gave him some hope there might be water, if he could reach them.

Hayden realized he hadn't given any thought to the possibility of rescue since his departure from the escape pod. His heart faltered as he continued to search the vast emptiness around him. The prospects of being found grew remote.

He arrived at the outcrop as the temperature started to warm. Already, the distant horizon was distorted with rising thermals, and a wavering reflection gave the false impression of a lake or sea between them. He was grateful he still had his wits about him and wasn't tempted to head off in that direction to slake his thirst.

But it wouldn't take long for him to approach such a state when the last of his water was gone. He needed a way to remain cool in the heat of the day.

The soil here was dry clay. It would be more difficult for him to burrow under than the sand at the crash site, but he decided to try regardless, since any insulating cover might save his life in the heat of the day. Desiccation cracked; he knew enough geology to understand it had once been the bottom of a deep still body of water.

He set down his pack and removed the makeshift shovel. As he dug, the dry clay surface disintegrated into a powder. But after reaching a depth of half a metre, digging became difficult as the soil became cooler and denser. The distinct odour of wet earth rose with every shovelful. Pressing some of the dirt between his fingers, he was surprised when it stuck together.

Water must lie somewhere beneath him, percolating up from the water table and saturating the soil.

With newfound energy, he quickened his pace until he'd excavated a metre-deep hole. At the bottom of the pit, the earth stuck together in clumps.

Pausing, he sat on the edge of the hole and wiped his brow with the back of his hand. He was perspiring too much and couldn't afford to lose precious moisture to the dry air. But there was water out of his reach; he knew it.

Tearing a strip from the fringe of his shirt, he used it to mop up his sweat. He wrung the salty contents from the cloth into his parched mouth. It wouldn't slake his thirst, but at least he'd retain some moisture.

As he repositioned his feet, he became excited when they stuck to the bottom of the hole. To his delight, a small amount of water began wetting his footprint.

With renewed enthusiasm, he grabbed his makeshift shovel and fell to his knees in the hole to dig. After uncovering another few centimetres, he was rewarded with the sight of a small amount of water at the bottom of the pit.

He tossed aside his tool and used both hands to scoop up a small amount of muddy liquid into his palms. Without any fore-thought, he lapped up his hard-won prize, only to gag at its saltiness.

With disappointment on the verge of despair, he stared at the modest trickle of water seeping into his well. It was too brackish to drink.

On the verge of tears, he collapsed and sat in the bottom of the hole. He'd spend half the morning digging, expending energy when he should have been resting, and all for nothing.

Too busy remonstrating with himself, it took him some time to realize that his pants were soaked from the accumulated few centimetres of water in the hole.

Bending down, he scooped up handfuls of water and poured it over his head. The cool relief it gave from the desert heat was the most glorious sensation he thought he'd ever experienced, and he continued to bathe until his clothes were soaked.

He couldn't drink it, but it might yet save him from death by dehydration in the blazing sun that was reaching its zenith.

Digging his jacket from the pack, he soaked it thoroughly. Curling up in the bottom of the hole, he covered his head with it to wait out the heat of the afternoon.

Hayden awoke from a dreamless sleep with a start. The jacket covering his head was bone-dry and stiff with encrusted salts. Muscles stiff, he rose to his feet. His pants crackled, and dried powder cascaded from them. Fine dust encrusted his hands and arms. Reaching up, his hair and face were gritty with a brittle crust that flaked away when he rubbed at it.

He looked down at the dry pit he'd fallen asleep in. The brackish water was now long gone.

The sun had fallen to within a few degrees of the distant horizon. There were, perhaps, three hours remaining before sunset.

The air around him was scorching, with no hint of a breeze.

His stomach growled.

He pulled over his backpack and fished out one of two remaining emergency ration bars.

Like Solomon, he weighed the wisdom of how to portion his remaining food before he split it and returned half to the pack.

Sitting on the edge of the hole, he savoured every chew, aware this could be one of his last meals. Sparingly, he sipped at his remaining water and made a mental note of the amount remaining before he sealed it up and returned it to the bag.

He eyed the distant mountains. They were much closer than the day before, but he was unsure if he could reach them before sunrise. In his weakened condition, he wouldn't be able to match the pace of the previous night.

As the afternoon sun beat down on him, he regretted not putting some of the brackish water in his empty bottle. He wouldn't be able to drink it, but it would help to keep him cool. He didn't think it wise to expend energy deepening his hole to find more.

He decided it was probably just as well he hadn't saved any. In a dehydrated delirium, he might be tempted out of desperation to drink it.

Deciding there was no further advantage to delaying, he gathered up his belongings and threw the pack on his back. He knocked the stiffness out of his jacket and draped it over his head.

Selecting a lonely peak on the distant mountain range, he resumed his journey.

When the sun rose again, he was not yet at the mountain range. But he was near enough to make out individual trees on the beginnings of a broad and gently rising piedmont.

The going was tougher in the rising temperature as he struggled to climb the gently sloping eroded sandstone. The trees, he noted when he drew close enough, looked like saguaro cacti, except that they possessed a dozen arms spreading away from the trunk instead of upward. Between the trees grew a thick, thorny undergrowth that became denser as it ascended the ancient mountains.

He sat on an eroded boulder that had once rolled down the hillside and took out his bottle. With disappointment, he noted there were only a few centimetres of water remaining, despite his efforts to ration it overnight.

He needed shade and water, or he wouldn't last the day.

Eyeing the nearest cactus, he dismissed any notion of cutting into it to find water.

When he was a boy of ten, he'd spent a week with his cousin, Philip, who was a year or two older and lived near the Sonoran Desert on Earth. They'd spent the previous evening watching old cowboy movies and were fascinated when the lost hero lopped off the top of a barrel cactus and drank the liquid inside to save his life.

The next morning, he and Philip headed out into the nearby wilderness to try out their newfound survival technique. The result was a day of puking their guts out and a stern lecture from his uncle about the stupidity of what they'd done.

The following day, he took the two boys back into the desert and showed them the proper way to look for water, repeatedly drilling into them the importance of not being caught in the desert without the precious resource.

Smiling at the memory, he began to scan the hillside. Hayden was aware the flora and fauna were not the same as on Earth, but he counted on the importance of water for any organism's survival to be universal and for geological processes to be a constant everywhere.

One thing to look for was green trees like willow or aspen, which needed water to survive. Hayden was aware neither species would be found on this world, but he hoped to find an analogue for them, like the cacti. It was a long shot, but he was running out of options.

He ducked when something flitted past his head.

A small, birdlike creature flapped its wings as it darted from cactus to cactus.

There was water nearby, or at least there would be if he was on Earth with his uncle.

He sat and studied the small creature after it settled on the top of a cactus to preen itself with its blunt beak. Instead of feathers, it was covered in a thick coat of long dark hair, which made it look like a tiny kiwi. A long, barbed, snake-like tail waved behind it, plucking at the cactus as if hunting for insects, which it would transfer to its mouth.

A second, smaller pair of vestigial wings, devoid of hair, were perched on its shoulders above the larger, covered wings used for flight. The spindly little appendages flapped as if trying to cool the creature's balding head in the intense heat of the sun.

Startled, it froze and turned its head from side to side before it suddenly took off again. Hayden lost sight of it as it disappeared over a nearby ridge.

He scanned his immediate surroundings, looking for whatever had frightened the creature away. He couldn't see anything, but that didn't mean a venomous or otherwise dangerous creature didn't lurk nearby.

Rising from the rock, he searched for a way to reach the rocks where the bird-thing had vanished. The other side of the ridge would be in the shadows for most of the day and one of the places his uncle had taught him water might be found.

He picked his way through the underbrush until he found a narrow, well-worn animal path and followed it to a notch between the ridge rocks.

Hayden stood at the top of the hill and gazed down into a shadowed coulee carved into the sandstone as if by a giant knife. Halfway down, in the deepest recesses of the small canyon, green, leafy branches waved in a cooling breeze blowing up from below. More of the strange little birds flitted from branch to branch.

Feeling as if the weight of the universe had been lifted from him, Hayden laughed aloud.

Somewhere, down below, hidden in the day-long shadows, was his salvation. Now all he had to do was find it.

He picked his way down the steep slope. Slipping on loose gravel, he caught his balance as the small pebbles clattered downhill. He thought he heard splashing from behind the squat, thickly growing vegetation below him.

Reining in his enthusiasm, he worked his way down. As he neared the undergrowth, the familiar gurgling of running water became unmistakable, and he pushed through the waist-high branches to find the source of the happy noise. When his boot splashed ankle-deep into a trickling stream, he stopped and stared down in disbelief.

As if not wishing to trust his eyes, he bent down and tentatively touched his fingers to the cool flow.

He dropped to his knees in the middle of the stream and scooped up hands full of water to splash on his face. Touching it to his lips, he risked a taste; it was a little salty but otherwise drinkable.

Hayden let loose a whoop of joy before he palmed water into his parched mouth. It almost hurt to swallow the cool water, but it did not restrain him from drinking until he could swallow no more without fear of vomiting it back up.

He threw down his bag and pulled out both water bottles. The small amount that remained in the one he poured over his head in celebration. He filled both to the brim and put them in his pack, returning to scoop more water into his mouth with his hands at a less frenetic pace.

So engrossed was he in slaking his thirst that he failed to hear the noise of something approaching until it was almost upon him.

He reached for his bag, prepared to make a run for it, when he slipped on the slick stones and fell, gashing his knee.

The bushes parted in front of him. A young boy of about ten stared, wide-eyed, at him. Both froze in place, startled until the boy's eyes fell on Hayden's discarded jacket lying next to the stream.

An expression of pure terror replaced his surprise, and he turned to run back the way he'd come.

Overcoming his shock, Hayden grabbed his jacket and pack and followed the boy into the brush.

"Wait," he called out in Standard. "I won't hurt you. I just want to talk to you."

The fading sound of disturbed branches told him the boy was not going to stop.

Cursing, Hayden listened for the direction the boy was going and followed the sounds of his panicked rush to escape.

Hayden emerged from the thick underbrush and stepped onto a dry landscape like the one on the other side of the ridge. The blazing morning sun peeked over the hill behind him, and its warmth on his back was uncomfortable after the cool shade.

A hundred metres ahead of him, scurrying along a worn path, ran a young boy. On the ground behind him lay a full waterskin, discarded because it weighed down the youngster and impeded his escape. He must have been terrified to drop such precious cargo.

Kaine picked up the heavy bag and walked after him. The boy had not appeared tired or sweaty from a long journey, so he reasoned wherever he was running was not far.

The path followed an abandoned arroyo at the base of a broad valley, walled by steeply rising, weathered red rocks.

About half a kilometre farther along, he came to an array of squat buildings. As he neared them, he noted most were built from mortared stone matching the rocks from the surrounding hillsides, though a few were ancient, prefabricated shelters. The fleeing lad had long since vanished into the small village, which appeared to be abandoned.

Hayden followed the path as it broadened into a wide dirt street running through the middle of the settlement. The only sound on the still air was the scuff of his boots.

He stopped and called out, "Hello? Is anyone here?"

There was no reply, though he got the distinct impression eyes followed him from behind drawn curtains.

"You dropped this," he said, raising the waterskin.

He looked around him, hoping to see a curious face in a window or doorway, but the village appeared abandoned.

Hayden decided to press farther on in the hope of encountering someone. Warily, he continued down the street until he came upon a central square. In the centre was a low, circular wall. Four weathered stone pillars rose from the ground around it to support a broad roof, providing respite from the scorching sun now high in the sky.

Around the plaza tall trees, like palms, rose to about twenty metres. Many of them appeared to be dead, the broad, leafy fans drooping from their crests brown and brittle.

After scanning the surrounding buildings for any sign of life, he approached the roofed area and peered over the edge of the waist-high wall. It surrounded a deep pit sunk into the earth. As Hayden leaned to peer down, he couldn't see the bottom, but the cool air rising from it was moist. Several muddy buckets were arrayed around the wall, each tied to a neatly coiled rope.

This was the village well, he realized, but it appeared to be almost dry. The dead trees around the central plaza supported his conclusion. It explained why the young boy had trekked so far to obtain water from the stream.

Hayden was certain he was being watched. He continued to scan the surrounding buildings as he set the waterskin down beside the well. Sitting on the low wall, he slipped off his pack and removed a water bottle.

As he drank, he realized these people feared him.

Did the airship that attacked him have anything to do with their mistrust? The boy's eyes almost popped out of his head when they fell on Hayden's old Confederation jacket. Could that be the reason they were afraid?

He returned the bottle to his pack and placed it at his feet. Rising, he stepped out into the sunlight and raised his hands high.

"I'm not armed," he called. "I mean you no harm."

From behind him, a gravelly voice said, "Just keep your hands up, and don't move."

Footsteps scuffed as someone approached. Hayden turned his head to catch a glimpse of the man.

"I said don't move."

He snapped his head forward. "I'm unarmed. I'm just looking for shelter."

"Put your hands on top of your head and get on your knees," said the man.

Kaine swallowed and slowly knelt, careful to keep his arms raised.

Two sets of hands grabbed and pulled his arms behind his back. A coarse rope was tied around his wrists. A man holding an ancient rifle stepped around and presented himself. His face was deeply tanned and weathered, attesting to a life lived in the desert. He wore a burnoose that fell to his ankles, and the hood was pulled up over his grey hair to protect him from the sun. Keeping the gun barrel trained on Hayden's chest, he appraised his captive.

"Why are you here?" The man's Standard was accented but understandable.

Hayden recalled his diplomatic training and forced his facial muscles to relax so he didn't appear confrontational or as afraid as he was.

"I told you; I'm just seeking shelter."

"Where are the others?"

"I'm alone. My ship's escape pod crashed in the desert two days walk from here." He gestured with his head in the rough direction from where he'd come.

The man appeared confused by Hayden's story, then the grim determination returned to his face.

"The rebels destroyed your ship?"

Kaine slowly shook his head. "I have no idea who attacked me."

Anger flared in the man's eyes, and he aggressively pushed the barrel into Hayden's chest.

"Bullshit."

Kaine felt his confident façade collapsing. "I'm telling the truth; I'm not from this system."

"You're imperial," said the man.

"I was. A long time ago."

Hesitation entered the man's dark eyes. "You wear the uniform."

"Yes, but I can explain that."

Behind him, the footsteps of the men who'd grabbed him shuffled in the sand. His captor looked up at them before returning his attention to Hayden. He narrowed his eyes.

"All right; talk."

Kaine sighed with relief. He worked up enough spit to swallow and wet his throat. "As I said, I'm not from this system. Our ship arrived during a battle. Both sides began to fire at us and..."

"What do you mean 'arrived'?"

Hayden paused as he realized how absurd his story must sound. These people had been cut off from the Confederacy ever since the light gate system collapsed.

"Listen, a lot has changed in the past fifteen years. Our ship possesses a faster-than-light drive. That's how we got here. We popped into the middle of a battle over the planet. We took heavy fire from both sides. I came down in an emergency escape pod."

The gun barrel pressed harder into Hayden's chest. "Even if I believed you, your story makes no sense. If you're imperial, why would your people shoot at you?"

Hayden shook his head. "I...I can't answer that."

His captor studied him for several seconds. "So, they destroyed your ship, you say."

"I...I don't know. I was knocked unconscious, and when I came to, my pod had crashed. I wasn't able to contact my ship —"

"Why didn't you stay with the pod and wait to be rescued?"

Hayden stared at the man and debated if he should tell the truth. "Because I was attacked by an airship. The pod was destroyed, along with all my emergency rations and survival gear. I escaped with my life."

"Why did you come here?"

Kaine chuckled. "Dumb luck. I picked a direction and started walking."

The man was hesitant about something in Hayden's story.

"Your ship; what's she called?"

He said, "She's called *Scimitar*."

No sign of recognition came to the man's face. "Never heard of her." He looked up at his companions. "You?"

"No," replied a man at Kaine's back.

"Would Krellig know?"

"Maybe. He's not due back until tonight. What shall we do?"

The man with the gun returned his eyes to Hayden and studied him. Then he addressed his companions.

"Lock this one up in the storage shed. Krellig can decide what's to be done with him."

Hayden was pulled to his feet and directed to a small, prefab building on the edge of the square. One of the men pulled a set of keys from his pocket, and the door was unlocked and opened. They gestured for him to enter.

Inside were stacks of fertilizer and bags of grain with faded writing on them marking them as colonial supplies, but they appeared to be years old.

As one of the men untied his hands, the man with the gun told him, "We'll keep you in here with the rest of the useless shit the Confederation sent us."

"I told you, I'm no—"

"Yeah, yeah." The man waved a dismissive hand. "Krellig will decide whether you are or aren't."

He gestured toward the stacks of grain. "Make yourself comfortable. You'll be brought food and water. We're not the ignorant barbarians you people treat us like."

"Thank you."

"Don't thank me yet. You may wish you died in the battle if Krellig doesn't like your story."

"Who is Krellig?"

"You can ask your questions of him. In the meantime, get comfortable."

The man turned and left. The door closed behind him, and keys turned in the lock.

The dim interior was cooler than being in the direct sunlight. Slivers of light peeked in around the edges of the locked door, casting the surroundings in a dull grey. Already the sweat trickled down his back beneath his shirt, and he wondered how hot the place would become as the day progressed. The air felt stuffy, and accumulated grain dust tickled his nostrils, prompting him to sneeze.

With nothing to do but wait, he pulled a bag of grain from the pile to use as a cushion. He sat down, leaned against the wall, and pondered his fate.

UNWELCOME GUEST

Hayden woke with a start, drenched in perspiration. Unsure of where he was, his heart raced. The scent of dust and grain forced recollection of his situation. It was almost pitch black in the storage shed, and the air was still hot from the heat of the day. Any slivers of light that had crept between the cracks of the door were gone, so he assumed it must be nighttime.

He went to the door and pressed his ear against it. Men's muffled voices conversed. Then footsteps drew closer to the door.

He moved back and sat on the grain sack. Someone fumbled with the lock, and after a few seconds the door opened outward, revealing the silhouettes of two men against the bright, starry sky. A brilliant light shone in his face, blinding him.

"Get up," ordered one of the voices. Kaine stood, and two men grabbed him by each arm.

As they escorted him across the plaza and past the central well, he noted several lights in the windows of buildings that appeared abandoned only a few hours before. People were out in the cool evening, socializing. Children scurried around the plaza, kicking a ball. It made sense for the evening to be when people were out and about.

Across the plaza, people turned to stare. Some expressions were curious, but others betrayed open suspicion bordering on hostility. Whatever the Confederation had done on this planet, they blamed him. Not a good way to start a meeting with any of them.

But there was the curious animosity the man with the rifle had displayed for those he called the rebels. It didn't sound like they held a favoured place in these peoples' hearts either.

Hayden was led to one of the larger stone buildings where two men stood guard before a set of double doors. The small group was waved inside.

Inside what appeared to be a dining hall, dozens of people milled about rows of long tables, laughing, joking, eating, and drinking.

These men and women were not villagers, Hayden suspected, but an occupying force. All were dressed in some sort of military clothing, though they shared no common uniform. Some wore standard imperial garb, while others' dress was less distinct. A collection of weapons leaned against one wall, but he noted that many of the celebrants still retained sidearms.

At the head of the long table at the head of the hall, a muscular bearded man held court. His uniform, if that was what one could call it, consisted of a flak vest, beneath which he wore no shirt so that his muscled shoulders were displayed prominently. They were covered with various tattoos favoured by the Special Forces branch of the military. His long black hair was slicked back and draped behind his ears, exposing his broad, creased forehead. Heavy black eyebrows hovered over menacing dark eyes, and white, strong teeth glistened behind his jet-black beard. He reminded Hayden of a young version of Pavlovich.

He presumed this man must be the one they called Krellig. He was flanked on both sides by a small group of men and women, each of them similarly garbed and each displaying similar tattoos, attesting to a career in the military. The way they laughed and jostled about attested to a camaraderie Hayden knew could only be acquired and nurtured through years of shared strife.

He was pushed forward until he was about three metres from Krellig and his group. Hands held him while he awaited acknowledgement from the leader.

The burly soldier looked up from his interrupted joke and glared at Hayden for several seconds before he signalled for the guards to bring him forward.

At a nod from him, one of the others at his table stood up and pulled out his chair, offering it to Hayden. Hesitating for only a second, he straightened his back and sat.

Krellig sat again and returned his attention to the dinner on his plate, ignoring Hayden. After a few mouthfuls, Krellig called over one of the servers and gestured for him to place a drink in front of his new guest.

"You're probably thirsty after a day in the hotbox," he said before he returned his attention to his half-finished meal. Kaine wasn't sure if it was a rhetorical statement, so he picked up the mug of beer and took a healthy gulp to slake his thirst. After replacing it on the table, he swallowed the bitter beverage and wiped his mouth with the back of his hand.

"My name is Hayden Kaine."

The man raised an eyebrow but continued to focus on his plate. "Is that supposed to mean something to me?"

"I wouldn't think so," Hayden lied. "I presume you are the one they call Krellig."

A grin spread on the man's face as he leaned back in his chair and extended his arms in the presentation of himself. "In the flesh."

"I'm afraid I've not heard of you before today." The words were out of his mouth before he realized how impertinent they could be interpreted.

Instead of anger, Krellig laughed. "Well, perhaps you are new to this system after all."

His laughter died, and he fixed a cold stare on Hayden. "Or, perhaps, you are a convincing spy D'Ville sent to kill me?"

Hayden smiled and gestured with open arms. "I'm hardly in a position to do that, am I?"

Krellig took a bite from a something resembling a chicken leg and smiled around chews. "Unless you're on a suicide mission, with some kind of explosive concealed on you."

"Your men searched me before they brought me here."

The other man nodded, entertaining a different thought. "Perhaps I should avoid all risk and have you taken out and shot."

Despite his precarious position, Hayden began to enjoy this fellow. He smiled and said, "Perhaps that is my plan; maybe I'm being monitored from orbit, and when my heart stops a ship will unload its payload on this location."

Krellig chuckled and shrugged. "Then I suppose it would be better to let you live long enough to move you to another location—or is there a failsafe for that case?"

Hayden shrugged and smiled.

Krellig studied him for several long seconds before he burst out in laughter. "You're good, Kaine, I'll give you that. Now let's dispense with this fencing bullshit and get down to business."

"Sounds good to me."

"Why are you here?"

"Like I told your man this morning, just dumb luck."

"Pretty good luck if you ask me. You could have wandered anywhere else. This is the only settlement for a hundred klicks."

Hayden nodded. "I can understand your suspicions, but I'm telling the truth. These hills were the closest thing to my escape pod, and they were in the opposite direction of where the ship that fired on me appeared to come from. I'm curious about one thing, though."

Krellig smiled. "You want to know if it was one of my ships that fired on you."

"It would be a handy thing to know, you must admit."

His host picked up his mug. "Trust me, Kaine, if I had access to airships like those, I'd have far better uses for them than blowing up crashed escape pods." He punctuated his statement with a long swig of beer.

"Who do they belong to?"

He returned his mug to the table and fixed Hayden with an icy stare. "You seem to be confused about who is interrogating who, Kaine."

Not waiting for a reply, he signalled for the men who brought him to the hall to come forward.

"I'm returning you to the hotbox. I'll have some supper sent to you. In the morning I will dispatch a scouting party to confirm your story. I don't have to tell you what will happen if they return empty-handed, do I?"

"No," said Hayden as he stood. "I think the consequences are perfectly clear."

"I hope we have a chance to continue our conversation, Kaine. You amuse me."

He nodded to the guards, and Hayden was taken away.

An hour or so later, the lock on the shed door rattled and a young boy entered. He carried a lantern in one hand and a bowl covered with a napkin in the other and appeared to be struggling with concealing his nervousness.

"I won't hurt you," said Hayden. "You can put the bowl down by the door if you'd prefer."

The boy straightened and tried to harden his expression. "I'm not afraid."

Hayden shook his head. "I didn't think you were."

They stared at each other for several heartbeats before the boy turned to place the food on the floor by the door.

"You're the boy by the creek, aren't you?"

The lad appeared surprised to be recognized and nodded, his nervousness reasserting itself.

"My name is Hayden."

The boy looked at the floor for a moment. "I'm Reilly."

"It is a pleasure to meet you, Reilly. Thank you for bringing me some supper."

"I...I'm not supposed to talk to you."

Hayden nodded. "I understand. Thank you anyway."

Reilly found some courage, and his chest puffed out. "I'm almost twelve, you know."

"I thought you were at least thirteen."

"No, not yet; but when I'm old enough, I can join the militia."

"I believe you'll make a fine soldier."

The boy beamed and turned to leave. He hesitated as his hand reached for the door latch, then he turned back to Hayden. "Are you a soldier?"

"Me? No, I'm the first mate on a starship."

Reilly stared at Hayden with awe in his wide eyes. "Really? You've been to other planets?"

Hayden nodded. "Many."

The boy's brow wrinkled in thought. "My dad said the doorway to other worlds was closed before I was born."

"That's true; it was called the jump gate, and it connected all of the star systems in the Confederation."

Reilly scowled. "They say you are with the imperials."

"I used to be, but not now. Everyone was before the jump gate system collapsed."

"Why aren't you with them anymore?"

"They wanted to do things I didn't agree with, so I left."

"In your starship?"

"Yes, it's called *Scimitar*."

Reilly frowned as he worked out a problem. "If the jump thing was broken, how did you get here?"

Hayden smiled. "You are a very sharp young man, Reilly. You're correct; I didn't come through the jump gate. My ship has a special engine that allows us to go wherever we want, like this." He snapped his fingers.

"Like magic?"

Hayden chuckled. "Almost."

"Does anyone else have one?"

Hayden's smile faded. "I'm afraid they do."

"I think I would like to visit other worlds."

The door behind Reilly opened, and a man stepped through who did not appear pleased. "I told you not to talk to this man."

Reilly cowered. "I'm sorry, Papa."

The anger faded from the man's face, and he placed a gentle hand on the boy's shoulder. "Go and help your mother."

The youngster nodded and departed. The man faced Hayden. "You shouldn't fill his head with nonsense."

"You were listening. Everything I told him is true."

"We're not backwater hicks who will easily believe a stranger's fanciful tales. I worked at gate control when the system went down. I know what is possible and what is not."

"My ship has an FTL drive. I wish I could prove it to you."

The man turned to leave but stopped before he reached the door. With his back to Hayden, he asked, "How did you acquire this technology?"

"It is alien, from a race called the Glenatat."

He turned to face Hayden and stared at him for several long seconds. Relaxing, he said, "I can normally tell when I'm being bullshitted, but you're very good at this."

"That's because I'm not lying. My ship, the *Scimitar*, encountered them on a mission to Mu Arae, almost fifteen years ago."

"Isn't it a quarantined system?"

Hayden nodded. "For good reason. Did you ever receive a warning about the Malliac threat?"

He shook his head. "No, what was it?"

Hayden lowered his head as the memories flooded back. "They were the reason for the collapse of the jump gate system. After that happened, they swarmed across most of the star systems in the Confederation, destroying everything in their path like a relentless swarm of locusts. We barely managed to stop them as they converged on Earth."

"How many systems were lost?"

Kaine shook his head. "I'm not sure. Some estimates go as high as eighty percent."

Blood drained from the man's face. "We've had no news from anyone for so long." His expression hardened. "Why were we spared?"

Hayden shrugged. "This system is on the fringe of Confederation territory, not on a direct path to Earth for the Malliac."

The man was visibly shaken. He shook his head. "This all sounds too fanciful."

"What reason would I have for telling you a lie?"

He scowled at Hayden. "That's the thing about con men; if you can see through them, they aren't very good."

"I don't know what I can say to convince you." He pointed to the covered bowl on the floor near the door. "Do you mind if I eat now?"

The man frowned before he picked up the bowl and passed it to Hayden. Without another word, he turned and left.

KRELLIG

Having slept through the day, Hayden spent his time pondering what he'd avoided thinking about since his crash: What happened to *Scimitar*?

The aggression they encountered on entering this system was nothing new or anything their modified ship couldn't handle—or so he had once imagined. His last recollection aboard the ship was it taking a hit from a nuke, something its augmented armour should have shrugged off. His next recollection, though, was of awakening in the sand outside of his crashed escape pod. Try as he might, he couldn't imagine a scenario in which Pavlovich would order him stuffed into an escape tube and ejected from the ship unless things were dire. The fact that Cora's avatar accompanied him, or more likely carried him into the pod and launched with it, disturbed him more.

The worrisome question gnawed in his belly. Did anyone but him survive?

He, Pavlovich, Cora, and the rest of their small crew only had each other when they'd fled Earth and the wrath of the new president. Politics, or, more specifically, his desire to stay uninvolved, drove them away, forcing him to leave behind his friends and surviving relatives. He didn't worry about them because they were either in the correct political sphere or not in any position to endanger Admiral Thomas's plan to consolidate power within what remained of the Confederation.

Hayden found himself on the wrong side of the admiral when he refused to become the public face of humanity's narrow victory over the Malliac. It was something he couldn't bring himself to do, given his own culpability in the collapse of the jump gate, and that was what sealed his fate.

Left little choice, he fled with Pavlovich, no friend of Thomas either. Now fugitive vagabonds, they'd hopped from star system to star system in the search of... He wasn't sure what they'd been searching for.

At first, it was to find a home, a place they could vanish to live out their lives. It turned out to be a very difficult thing to do given their possession of a unique, enhanced starship capable of interstellar travel.

Everywhere in what remained of the Confederation they encountered the same drama. Systems like this one tore themselves to shreds in the aftermath of being cut off from the empire. The destruction of the light gate system had seeded chaos everywhere. None of the few surviving systems they'd visited since their exile had remained untouched by the struggle for power. Nature, it seemed, abhorred the vacuum left by being cut off from Earth. None of it was a worthy testament to humankind's expansion into the local galactic arm.

And there was nothing but strife to come. Faster-than-light technology was now in Thomas's hands, and as he rebuilt his decimated fleet, they would return to every surviving system to reassert authority. Thomas was obsessed with rebuilding the Confederacy, and it was apparent to Hayden from his travels that few wished to return to the old ways.

No one, especially Hayden, had understood how tenuous the empire's hold was on its territories until the local governments lost their ability to call in ships and troops to quell local unrest.

The entire civilized galaxy became a pot boiling over. He'd come to realize most people hated the Confederation.

That revelation was a shock to him at first. He'd grown up on Earth, nurtured and raised as a political scion, all but destined to become president. Though expected of him, it was a role he didn't covet, and nobody was gladder than him when circumstances took that cup from his lips and gave it to Thomas. But he'd never hated the regime, and he didn't know anyone while growing up who expressed the sentiment.

The problem was, he realized, his narrow point of view as a member of the ruling class. It wasn't until he journeyed to the colony systems that the true nature of Confederation rule became apparent.

His musing was interrupted by someone unlocking the door. As it swung open, the morning brightness blinded him.

"You're to come with us," said a man's unfamiliar voice.

Blinking as his eyesight adjusted to the light, Hayden rose to his feet.

Instead of manhandling him out of the shed, the man turned and walked out, expecting to be followed. Overcoming his surprise, Hayden walked after him. Two armed men who'd been waiting outside on either side of the door fell into step behind them. He noted with some relief that their weapons were slung over their shoulders and not pointed at him as they'd been yesterday.

He was escorted across the square, which was coming alive at the end of a hot day. Shopkeepers were opening their kiosks. A cluster of preteens stopped kicking their ball to stare at him as he was led into the same building where he'd met Krellig.

The armed escort waited outside as the man who'd come for him led him across the empty hall to where Krellig waited in the same place he'd been the previous evening. He looked up and smiled, then nodded a dismissal to the man who'd brought Hayden.

"Sit down, Kaine, and have some food."

As he spoke, two men wearing aprons entered the hall from a side door, each carrying a tray. After placing plates before the two seated men, they departed, leaving only them alone in the vast, empty dining hall.

"Dig in before it gets cold," said Krellig as he shook open the table napkin and placed it on his lap. "I'm certain it's been a few days since you've had a decent meal."

Hayden waited for his host to begin eating before he picked up his fork and examined the contents of his plate. A light greenish patty with the consistency of scrambled eggs rested on a bed of rice.

"It's a local delicacy," said Krellig as he chewed. "The children go into the hills to collect the eggs from nests."

Hayden asked, "Birds or lizards?"

"Hmm...not sure about that; the creatures share features of both. It's tasty, though, when seasoned. Give it a try, because it's all we have to feed you until the supply caravan arrives."

Hayden suddenly realized how ungrateful he must seem and shovelled a forkful into his mouth. Surprised at how sweet it tasted, he cleaned up his plate. His host was smiling at him as he finished.

"Sorry, I didn't realize I was so hungry."

"It is I who owes you the apology, Mister Kaine."

"Your men found my ship?"

"What remained of it; I'm impressed you managed to walk the distance here."

"Basic survival training helped—or as much as I could recall. It took me two nights."

Pushing his empty plate to the side, Krellig leaned on his elbows on the table and studied Hayden. "They also found something curious that I hope you can shed some light on."

"What's that?"

"They uncovered the remains of a synth; pretty much destroyed, but there was enough of it to confirm what it was."

There was something guarded in Krellig's voice that told Hayden to be cautious about how he answered the unasked question.

"It was one of my ship's medical synthetics. It must have dragged me into the escape pod because I don't recall much about how I got stuffed into one and launched."

Krellig nodded. Hayden didn't believe him to be nearly as sincere as he appeared and decided to remain cautious.

"Tell me what happened to your ship; the *Scimitar*, isn't it?"

Hayden nodded. "As I told your people, we aren't from this system—"

"Where are you from?"

Hayden swallowed the morsel he was chewing. Not everyone reacted favourably to his story. There was still a lot of anger over what happened after the destruction of humanity's only means of interstellar travel. He decided to remain cautious until he had Krellig figured out. "*Scimitar* is—was a patrol cruiser assigned to the outer rim systems in sector four."

"That's a long way from here. You must have transited to a system closer to home before the gate collapsed."

"Ah, no."

"Oh, that's right. You told O'Connor your ship has an FTL drive that you acquired from some alien race you encountered out by...Mu Arae, wasn't it?"

"Um, yes, that is correct."

Krellig nodded. "He also mentioned something about a different threat that overran most of the colonized worlds between that system and Sol. The Malliac?"

"Yes; they were stopped at Earth, but the cost was high."

"You'll have to forgive my scepticism, Kaine, but we don't get much news from the inner systems since the collapse."

"I know it all sounds fantastic; I don't know what I can say to convince you I'm telling the truth."

"Well, showing me your ship would be a nice start. Where is

she?" Krellig's expression was hard, and Hayden felt his eyes boring into him.

Hayden frowned. "I really can't tell you."

Krellig's face softened, and he leaned back in his chair. "Right, you said you were unconscious when they launched you. Tell me about what happened when you arrived in the system— before your pod was launched."

"Um, okay... We jumped into this system from Canopus."

Krellig leaned forward, his eyes eager. "Using your FTL drive."

"Yes..."

"You just...popped into existence from a star system sixteen light years away."

Hayden chuckled. "Yes, that is how it would appear."

"So, one moment the long-range scanners showed nothing, and the next your ship would have appeared. That must have been a shock to see."

It was now obvious to Hayden that Krellig knew more than he was telling and trying to catch him in a lie.

"That sounds familiar to what we've encountered elsewhere."

"I can imagine, given the isolation we've experienced for the past few years, your sudden, unannounced arrival near a system jump-gate node long thought dead might cause quite a stir."

Hayden smiled. "I didn't say anything about arriving near the jump gate."

"Oh, didn't you? I just assumed; force of habit and all—but please, go on."

Hayden was now certain Krellig already knew what took place.

"Within an hour of our arrival, a patrol approached. We contacted them to let them know we weren't hostile."

"It sounds like you've done this before."

"After a few bad situations in the past, we came up with a protocol that works most of the time."

"And it worked this time? Nobody fired on you."

Hayden nodded. "We were ordered to stand down to be boarded, which we complied with."

"Who did you encounter?"

"Three ships with active Confederation ID beacons. The codes matched what was in our records, and aside from caution, they showed no open hostility toward us, so we had no reason to suspect they were anyone but imperial forces."

"Because you're always friendly with the local governments, right?"

Hayden's brow creased. "*Scimitar* was once a Confederacy ship and still looks like one. It is only logical for us to acknowledge that when we contact the local regime on our arrival until we establish what has happened."

"There's unrest in other systems besides this one?"

Hayden nodded. "In almost every colony we've visited there is unrest. In some cases, the local authority has retained control, but in others, they are in open conflict with—" He stopped himself from saying rebels. "With freedom fighters, like yourself."

"So, you play both sides of the fence until you determine who to side with."

"We never know what the situation is when we arrive, so we're cautious until we can learn what's happened."

"What do you do if you're not welcomed as part of the big, happy Confederation family?"

"We are fired on, occasionally. Usually, diplomacy prevails when we explain who we are."

"And when diplomacy fails?"

Hayden smiled at Krellig's clumsy trap. "We leave."

"You don't fight the enemies of the empire?"

"We don't have a dog in their fight, so we go."

Krellig rubbed his chin. "Let me get this straight. If you arrive and are accepted as a member of the Confederation, you stay; if not, you turn tail and run. It sounds to me like you are

stay; if not, you turn tail and run. It sounds to me like you are still a part of the empire, despite your story."

The rebel leader was right. The way Hayden explained their mode of contact, they indeed appeared to be friendly to the Confederacy.

"We are independent and don't have a quarrel with anyone."

"Why do you travel from system to system? Are you spies, trying to ascertain how much control the empire holds over its former territory?"

"We aren't spies."

"Then what are you?"

Hayden's face fell. "We are refugees, looking for a place to call home."

"You mean to say that you are deserters with a stolen starship which happens to possess the only FTL drive in existence."

Hayden hesitated. He'd never thought of himself in those terms. "I suppose it appears that way."

"If you're telling me the truth, why have you never settled down anywhere? Why do you jump from colony to colony?"

"Curiosity, I suppose. We have the means to discover what transpired since the light gate network was destroyed."

"Why? From what you tell me, the empire is shattered. Why do you keep jumping unless you are trying to make an inventory of where the Confederacy still rules?"

Hayden's eyelids narrowed, and he struggled to regain his composure. "People deserve to know what happened; to learn why things are happening to them. For many, like here, there has been no news from the outside. They are ignorant of the Malliac or what is happening elsewhere; all people know is that the jump system no longer functions, and their lives have been turned upside down. New governments have risen, open rebellion is raging, or the old regime still rules through brutal suppression of dissent."

Krellig's brow was furrowed. He crossed his arms over his

chest and studied Hayden. His expression softened. "Tell me what happened after you were boarded by the patrol."

"That never happened. Before we could rendezvous with them, another force appeared on our scopes, vectoring to our position at high speed."

"Who was it?"

Hayden shook his head. "They weren't friends of the patrol ships. They accused us of leading them into a trap. Before we could say anything, they opened fire on us."

"Your ship was damaged, then?"

Hayden hesitated. *Scimitar*'s enhanced armour, courtesy of the Glenatat race, shrugged off their missiles. But something told him he shouldn't let Krellig know. It was a gamble to keep the information secret, since the rebel leader already seemed to be familiar with what occurred.

"*Scimitar* took some significant hits, yes, but our drives were undamaged. We decided to run."

"To where?"

Krellig appeared too eager.

"We needed time to spin up our FTL drive, so we decided to head to the outer system."

"With the imperial ships in hot pursuit?"

"Yes, and the rebel ships as well."

"So, you had everyone on your tail."

"It seemed that way, but there was also a good chance the second group was coming to our aid. We took a gamble and changed course to intercept them, in the hope that our pursuers would break off."

"Did it work?"

Hayden shook his head. "They began to fire at us as well. Maybe they thought we were a decoy, who knows?"

"What happened?"

Krellig was like a little kid listening to the story and anticipating the end.

"We got caught in the middle, both sides firing at each other and at us."

"It sounds horrific. Did you defend yourselves? Why didn't you turn on your FTL drive and jump away?"

"The drive needed time to recharge. We tried to defend ourselves and escape, but ships from both sides closed in on us."

"So you fired your weapon."

Hayden sat up straight and glared at Krellig. "You were there, weren't you?"

A sly smile turned up the corner of Krellig's mouth. "What was that weapon you fired? I've never seen anything like it."

"If you were there, tell me what happened to my ship."

"Of course; first answer my question. What kind of weapon did you use to destroy those ships?"

"Ships?" Hayden rubbed his temples. He couldn't recall anything after Pavlovich ordered him to fire the dark energy cannon and make a hole for them to escape through.

"Don't play dumb, Kaine. You're right, I was there. I witnessed with my own eyes the destructive power of your weapon as it shredded two of our vessels and one of the empire's. What is it?"

"What happened to *Scimitar*?"

"Tell me what I want to know. Is it alien technology?"

Hayden struggled, unsure of how much to reveal. If *Scimitar* were destroyed, knowing about the cannon would do Krellig no good. Pavlovich must have escaped. Krellig could not have indicated his intentions more if he had written them on the table in crayon. He wanted *Scimitar*'s dark energy weapon.

"She jumped, didn't she?"

Krellig sighed and stood. He called out, and the armed men who had escorted him from the shed appeared.

"Take him back to the box."

The soldiers walked up behind Hayden as he rose from the chair. There was a mixture of frustration and admiration on Krellig's face. They stared at each other for a few seconds before

Krellig waved his hand and Hayden was escorted out of the hall and back to his cell.

As the door was locked behind him, Hayden couldn't contain his smile.

Scimitar must have jumped.

But if she was able to spin up the FTL drive and jump, where did she go?

He sighed and examined his surroundings. The late afternoon sunshine leaked between the slats of the shed's wooden roof, lighting up the dusty air with sunbeams. Sweat trickled down his cheek and back.

Hayden surmised the only reason he still lived was that Krellig viewed him as a means to possess *Scimitar*'s technology. His hand squeezed the pendant hanging around his neck. He couldn't let him know about Cora, but he had to find some way to talk to her. Krellig had said his people discovered the remains of her avatar in the wreckage. Maybe they'd brought it back with them. If there was some way for him to get to the synth body—

His shoulders sagged, and he sat on a sack of grain. Dumb luck had gotten him into this situation, and it was beginning to look like dumb luck was the only way he would get out of it—or maybe not.

Something came to him he hadn't thought of in years, something his professor told him on the first day of his class in diplomacy. Hayden smiled at the recollection of Professor Hammond, a portly former diplomat dragged out of retirement to teach a bunch of new cadets. At the time, Hayden was sure the only reason he'd agreed to such a menial job after an illustrious career was because he was bored and wanted to have fun making miserable a few students who thought they could cut it in the diplomatic corps.

He recalled the first lecture the old fossil gave.

"Diplomacy is like any other sales transaction. By that, I mean once you uncover what your counterpart wants, you have discovered his point of weakness. The fates of empires have turned on awareness of such insights."

It was obvious what Krellig wanted and why. He coveted the weapon he'd seen cut down three warships as if they were made of paper. Somehow, Krellig was his key to finding *Scimitar*, as he was Krellig's means of obtaining the dark energy weapon.

There was no choice.

He rose to his feet, brushed the dust from his trousers, and went to the locked door. After pounding on it with his fist, he shouted, "Tell Krellig I want to talk."

As he waited for his message to be delivered, he leaned against the door.

He decided what Hammond had taught was only partially correct.

Diplomacy is the art of letting someone else have your way.

This time the rebel leader came to him.

Krellig's face betrayed no emotion when Hayden told him.

"A dark energy weapon, you say." He smiled. "Why didn't you tell me that when I asked?"

Hayden shrugged. "Every time we revealed our ship's technology, nothing good happened."

"Because only a fool would not have a use for such a weapon. What changed your mind about telling me the truth?"

"Can we have candour?"

Krellig considered the question, then nodded.

"Cooperating with you is my best chance at surviving. It is obvious you know what happened to my ship and may have the means to reach it. I want to get back to my people, or at least learn what happened to them."

Krellig's smile broadened. "So you have no moral objection over how we will use the weapon once we find it."

"I told you, I have no love for the Confederacy. If my ship

was destroyed and salvaging her technology for you is my only chance, then I'll take it."

"What makes you so sure we haven't already recovered the wreck of your ship and possess the weapon?"

The words cut through him. Hayden's heart tried to pound out of his chest. He inhaled and tried to rein in his galloping emotions. Forcing a smile, he said, "I thought we agreed on candour?"

Krellig nodded. "Very well, we believe we know the location of your ship, but we can't recover it presently, since it is in government-controlled territory. We need your cooperation when we reach it because we won't have the time to search for what we need. We require your knowledge of the ship for that."

"Where is it? What is her condition? Did the crew survive?"

Krellig held up a hand. "Slow down, Kaine. All I know is an approximate location at present. As to her condition or the fate of your crewmates, I'm afraid I can't tell you anything."

Despite his training, Hayden allowed his face to betray the fear in his heart.

"In due course, you'll be told the details. Now, it is enough to know that *Scimitar* is deep within Federal territory, and as far as our spies can determine, her presence is still unknown to them. We have time to make a recovery plan."

Hayden nodded. "What can I do to help?"

"It is good to hear you ask that, Kaine, but I'm no fool. I believe you are sincere about wanting to find your ship, and while it would be useful to have your aid, none of us is prepared to trust you. Some are advocating for your execution."

"I get it, you fear I am a government spy leading you into a trap. Given how I arrived here, I can understand that. Let me prove otherwise."

Krellig laughed. "Just the thing I'd expect a spy to say."

Hayden extended his hands in surrender. "So, assign me a mission that will let me persuade you I'm not working with your enemy. Test me, and if I fail, you can still execute me. Just give me a chance."

Krellig's expression was unreadable as he considered the proposal. "All right, I'll let my council vote on it."

He turned to leave the shed but stopped on the threshold and turned back. "Try to get a decent night's rest. If you see the morning, it will mean we've voted in your favour."

As the door shut behind Krellig, Hayden muttered, "Sleep? He must be joking."

PROVE YOURSELF

Hayden was roused from a deep, dreamless sleep. The room was pitch dark, and a bright flashlight shone in his face, blinding him.

"Get up and come with us," said a male voice.

He tried to swallow, but his mouth was dry. "Why? Have you decided to execute me?"

"I was told only to come and get you. Just get up and follow me."

Hayden rose from his makeshift bed. He assessed his chances of overpowering the fellow and making a run, but blinded by the torch in his face, he knew that was an ill-considered plan. Grabbing his jacket, he followed the man outside, where they joined a woman. Neither of them was armed, and they both dressed in well-used imperial body armour. In silence, they escorted him from the shed and into the plaza.

The sky overhead was filled with stars, and Hayden longed to be once more travelling among them. A faint glow on the horizon heralded the approach of dawn.

They led him past the great hall to a small stone building, where they directed him inside.

Entering, he was greeted by a short, bespectacled, balding man who introduced himself as Yuri, the quartermaster.

Without any further discussion, he handed Hayden a stack of clean clothing, some toiletries, and a small backpack.

"What is all this for?"

Yuri handed him desert boots. "Looks like you're going out. These should fit you, but if they don't, I'll see if I have anything else. We're a bit pressed for supplies now."

Hayden examined the footwear. The boots appeared to be new.

"Mine are in good shape," said Hayden as he tried to pass them back to Yuri.

The quartermaster glanced at Kaine's feet, then pushed the boots back toward him. "You'll need these where you're going. The others are waiting for you through there." He pointed to an opened door.

Hayden picked up his kit and went through the doorway. Six others waited for him in the small, windowless room. Krellig stood at the far wall beside a tactical display screen that had seen better days.

Arrayed before him in a semicircle, three men and two women sat in mismatched chairs. One empty seat remained, presumably for him.

"Good morning, Mister Kaine, please join us."

"What's this?" asked Hayden as he sat.

"We're taking you up on your offer," said Krellig. "We have decided not to kill you, yet. "

"Much obliged."

Ignoring Hayden's sarcasm, Krellig addressed the group. "This is a quick in-and-out raid. Kaine here is going along for the ride. You may use him as you see fit, but unless he really screws up, make sure he gets back here in one piece."

The soldiers chuckled.

"M'gomba is mission leader," said Krellig as he indicated the man sitting beside Hayden. The dark-skinned soldier was muscled and over two metres tall, as far as could be guessed from his sitting position. He nodded at Kaine, who returned the acknowledgement.

"I've authorized him to shoot you if you get out of line," said Krellig.

"I won't be any trouble; tell me what you want me to do."

M'gomba's laugh was deep and resonant. "You may regret saying that."

The others joined him in laughing at the private joke.

Krellig turned to the display screen, which came to life, showing a satellite image of a settlement.

"For Kaine's edification, this is Sittot, the regional capital. Its population hovers around ten thousand."

"Less than that after we visit them," said one of the women. The group chuckled.

Krellig smiled before he gestured for them to settle down. He directed his comments to a close-up that appeared on the screen.

"This is the base that launched the airship that destroyed your pod, Kaine. Your story inspired me and pointed out something we have needed for a long time. The mission is simple: I want one of those ships. You are to infiltrate the base, acquire one, and destroy the remainder. Any questions?"

"Why only recover one of them?" Hayden asked.

The group was stunned into silence for a few seconds before they burst out in laughter.

"I'm sorry, but did I say something funny?"

Krellig said, "M'gomba, how many pilots do we have?"

"None, sir."

The rebel leader fixed his eyes on Hayden. "This will be a short mission for you if you tell me you cannot pilot one of those crafts."

Kaine glanced at the five others in the room, who all studied him closely with hungry, predatory eyes.

He swallowed and forced a smile. "Of course I can."

Krellig said, "I presumed as much. Let's continue."

As he resumed the briefing, M'gomba nudged Hayden with his shoulder and said, "We will learn soon enough if you lie."

When the briefing was finished and the group rose to prepare for departure, Hayden approached Krellig.

"If you want my help to locate *Scimitar*, there's something I need."

"Oh?" Krellig raised a questioning eyebrow. "Go on."

"I require access to the synth you recovered from my pod's wreckage."

Krellig remained expressionless as he said, "What makes you think we brought anything back with us?"

"Come on Krellig, neither of us is a fool. You and I both know that particular model is not standard imperial construction."

"Assuming I did have it brought back here, why do you need access to it?"

Hayden frowned. "Look, we agreed on candour. Like the weapon on my ship, most of its other technology is alien. Probably the biggest reason you should bring the synth back is because it's more valuable in your hands than leaving it to be covered by sand or recovered by your enemy. I can make use of its technology to get you what you want. "

Krellig regarded him for several seconds. "All right, we did bring it back. I'm forced to admit my people are stymied. The metallurgy of some of the components is nothing they've seen before. But there wasn't a heck of a lot of it left, just some scattered components: an arm, part of the head module, and the lower torso. I don't understand why it is so important to you."

Hayden was shocked by the other man's report of Cora's condition. When he last saw it, her synthetic body, except for some significant damage to the torso, was intact. He suspected that was the condition Krellig's people found it in and that they had disassembled it.

"May I see it?"

"How will it help find your ship?"

Hayden swallowed the lump in his throat, hoping his prepared story was convincing. "Certain components of the synth are quantum-coupled with corresponding equipment aboard *Scimitar*. If the ship still exists, I should be able to locate it."

"That assumes the coupled component on the ship wasn't destroyed."

Hayden shook his head. "Normally, as far as Confederation technology is concerned, that would be the case. Glenatat tech is too difficult for me to adequately explain. Let's say for the moment that any piece of *Scimitar* that still exists will be linked to the synth."

Krellig's eyebrows rose. "Impressive, if you're telling the truth. That suggests there is an interdimensional transposition capability for the alien technology."

Hayden was impressed. Krellig was more than a military grunt leading a ragtag group of rebels. This man had extensive postgraduate physics knowledge to come up with that idea.

"In a way, you are correct. It is how the FTL drive functions. Honestly, only our chief engineer understood the workings of the Glenatat modifications to our ship. I could barely follow her when she tried to explain any of it." Hayden smiled faintly at the memory of Cora. His hand reached for the pendant beneath his shirt. Realizing what he was doing, he stopped himself.

Krellig nodded. "Very well, I will grant you access to the synth after you have completed this first mission. If you are killed, my people will have to figure out how it works on their own."

Realizing he could not push for more immediate access, Hayden covered his disappointment with a smile. "I should probably avoid dying."

"Probably a wise choice," replied Krellig.

He excused himself to go to speak with M'gomba.

Hayden went to the display to study the satellite image of

their target. From what he could tell, the base they intended to raid was well defended. More important, though, it was a major outpost of the loyalist government the rebels were fighting.

If *Scimitar* was within their territory, as Krellig had told him, then he had ended up on the wrong side of the war. This mission was an unbelievable stroke of good luck for him. They were going to transport him right to the doorstep of the people who could really help him find *Scimitar*.

Within the hour, they were climbing into the back of a tracked transport vehicle. The sun was poking over the mountain when they set off from the village. The early hour did not deter many villagers from seeing the task force off on their mission.

The compartment Hayden and the others rode in was more like the back of a wagon. The only protection from the rising sun and the heat of the day was a thin, composite cap over the rear bed of the vehicle. A canvas covered the back, keeping most of the dust raised by their tracks out of the compartment.

Ancient air conditioning units whined as they fought to keep the temperature in the vehicle within a tolerable range. Still, Hayden thought it was bloody hot, and the perspiration ran down his back and dripped from his forehead.

One of the women of the group passed a bottle of water to him. "Stay hydrated. We can't afford to have you bonking at a critical moment."

"Bonking?"

She grinned. "It's not what you're thinking. It's an old athletic term. It means to run out of energy because of a drop in blood plasma volume due to dehydration."

One of the men called out, "Can you tell that Chang is our medic?"

"Be nice to me, Caldwell, or I'll let you bleed out next time you're shot."

The others jeered.

She shook her head and spoke to Hayden as she passed him a small packet. "Take these, they will keep your electrolytes in balance."

"It sounds like you have a lot of desert experience."

She laughed. "You think this is the desert? This is nothing." She pointed to the view outside. "To the south of us, over those mountains, the real desert extends for two thousand klicks past the equator. This is the garden spot of Capula until you get to the pole or far enough west to the coast."

"Capula? I thought this planet was called Oberon."

"You really aren't from here, are you?"

"Nope, I literally fell from the sky."

She grinned. "Yeah, I heard that about you. Capula is the name of this continent. It is the largest one on the planet. Most of it is arid, except around the coast. That is where most sane people live if they can."

"Where are you from?"

"Me? I grew up in Argent." When she noticed the incomprehension on his face, she added, "That's the village we just left."

"So, would that make you insane?"

She raised an eyebrow and fixed him with a critical stare.

Hayden blushed and said, "Sorry."

She continued to glare at him for several seconds until she smiled once more.

"That was a good one."

Deciding it best to change topics, he said, "I didn't have time to study the regional map before we left. Where are we going?"

"The regional capital, Sittot."

"You mean 'Shit-pot,'" said the one named Caldwell. A couple of the others laughed before they returned to their own private conversations.

"How long have you been fighting the local government?"

"Since I was eight or nine. Shortly after the jump gate went down."

"It must have been frightening."

The smile faded from her face. "We weren't supposed to be here. My dad was being transferred from Ceti Alpha to Aldebaran. We were on a stopover for our ship to recharge her jump gate engine when everything went down."

"How did you end up in Argent?"

"When it became apparent the gate wasn't coming back online, my parents looked for local work. Dad was a military hydro-engineer, so it made sense for him to get a posting somewhere his skills were needed. We ended up in Argent."

"When did the rebellion reach your village?"

Her wistful expression told Hayden he'd touched a sensitive topic.

"It's hard to recall, it was so long ago. Maybe six or nine months after we arrived. Before that, I knew something wasn't right because of my parents' hushed conversations when they thought I wasn't listening."

Seeing her pained expression, he said, "What happened?"

"Our village wasn't involved in the insurrection, but the loyalists came anyway, searching for rebels. They arrested anyone who was able to aid the uprising and took them away. My father was among them. Then they poisoned the well and departed."

"Are you serious?"

"I think they intended to deprive any rebel force of a potential outpost by taking away the village's ability to support them."

"It didn't work."

She shook her head. "A few weeks later, the first rebels arrived. They brought rations, fresh water, and equipment to drill a new well."

"The government drove you into the arms of the rebellion."

Chang nodded. "Argent became their base of operations and has been ever since."

"Does the loyalist government in Sittot know where this base is? Why haven't they wiped you from the map?"

"They tried, at first, but we were better organized than them and fought off air and ground raids from defensive batteries in the hills. Krellig is a former strategic planning officer. He knew all the weak points in their supply chain. Within weeks, he brought the local government to its knees. They couldn't focus on hunting Krellig because they were too busy suppressing food riots in the capital."

"How long ago did this happen?"

"They replaced the local commander five years ago. It took time, but they have systematically regained complete control of Sittot. They've pushed us back and reclaimed most of the territories they lost. Argent is one of the few places they haven't been able to retake, but they are mounting pressure. Only last week an air raid destroyed one of our defence batteries in the mountains. That is the closest they've come to attacking Argent since it all started."

"Forgive me for this, but if they were intent on crushing you, it would make more sense for them to make an orbital strike or use surface-to-air missiles. Fighting a primitive ground war with you for the last five years makes no sense."

"It is not so strange if you consider the extent of the uprising, and we are not a big enough problem for them to throw resources at. This conflict is system-wide, not only happening here on Oberon. Until very recently, almost every night, if you looked up at the skies, you could see battles in orbit."

"What's changed?"

"News is rare, and we only hear what Krellig tells us. He returned from a strategic meeting with the rebellion leadership. His mood is significantly darker than when he left. I think the war is going badly for our side."

"That would explain why the local government finally is getting the resources to take you on seriously."

Hayden also now understood Krellig's almost desperate urgency to obtain *Scimitar*'s weapon.

Chang's face was ashen, and she lowered her voice to a whisper. "I think it is only a matter of time before they get around to wiping out Argent and every other rebel outpost from orbit."

"Chang." M'gomba scowled at her. "What are you doing? There is to be no unnecessary conversation with the prisoner."

"Uh..."

Hayden grabbed a tube of ointment from her open medical bag on the floor and held it up. "She was telling me how to take care of my sunburn."

"Well, finish up and get over here."

"Yes, sir," she replied.

When M'gomba turned away, she plucked the tube from Hayden's hand and gave him a different one.

With a smile, she whispered, "Thanks, but that was haemorrhoid cream."

Hayden grinned back and nodded his appreciation before she rose and joined M'gomba.

Hayden turned to gaze out the dusty window. He brushed the dust from his trousers and sat back. His smile faded as he realized he had not shared that kind of conversation for a very long time.

Guilt bubbled up when he realized he had not thought of Stella since his crash. Even though she had been dead now for almost four years, it still hurt when he remembered her. Whether it was a defence mechanism or simply the natural way a person lets go of a lost one, he wasn't sure, but he'd been recalling her less often over the past few months.

He had been a wreck after her death. Not to the point of being suicidal, but almost. The only thing that had kept him going and not falling into a black pit of despair was the knowledge of how she would respond if she found him mourning her after this long.

Stella gave her life for him. For everyone. The only reason this foolish, insignificant rebellion was happening was because of her sacrifice in drawing the Malliac to their doom. Only a select few knew it was Stella who had made not only humanity's victory possible but also the continued existence of this universe.

That knowledge of the significance of her sacrifice had made it difficult for him to mourn her. It almost seemed that doing so was an affront to the life of every living being.

So, he'd tried remembering as much of the joy and the good times as he could. He recalled her smile, the gentle tone of her voice and imagined conversations with her, very similar to the kind he had just shared with Chang.

That, of course, intensified the guilt he felt at neglecting to remember her for the past few days.

Stella, of course, would be furious with him for taking on any guilt. He could imagine her telling him to get on with his life and that she still lived in his heart, but he had a very difficult time believing that.

He had found it more difficult with each passing day to recall her face. He had a mental image of her, and in his mind he knew her by sight, but if he were asked right now to describe her features, he didn't know if he could.

The only person he found he could turn to during those early days after Stella's death had been Cora. That, when he thought of it, was weirdly ironic, given that for all intents and purposes she had perished long before Stella.

He smiled as he recalled the bright, smiling face of the petite blonde engineer who had befriended him when he first arrived aboard *Scimitar*.

Now she was disembodied, a part of the ship. She kept everything running and was the only reason *Scimitar* could get by with a skeleton crew.

Now, of course, the only time he experienced a visual representation of the real Cora was when he visited her in virtual reality. Over time, he'd seen a change in her. Still his friend, she grew more distant with each passing day, as if she had forgotten her humanity and become part of the alien technology she occupied.

The visits with her in VR were the only time he thought of

her as anything like who she was when they first met. She always appeared as the same young, petite woman, but recently the avatar she presented him had become more idealized; less human.

He grasped the pendant beneath his jacket. If *Scimitar* was destroyed, the memory module around his neck was all that remained of his friend. He couldn't allow her to perish. He'd lost Stella and maybe Pavlovich and the others. The only one who remained might be Cora, and he had to do everything humanly possible to preserve her and restore her.

He didn't know if she remained sentient within the module. Was it a self-contained environment in which she could thrive, or was she stored as static alien code that needed technology to reanimate? The thought caused him to wonder if she was ever alive or merely a facsimile programmed by the Glenatat. It pained him to think he might have lost the two most important people in his life.

Cora was his mission now. He had to do everything possible to restore her. If that meant he had to betray these people so he could gain access to *Scimitar*, then so be it. He wasn't a part of their fight. He had his own issues with Thomas and the version of the United Earth Federation the old man was intent on restoring to a new entity he called the Grand Terran Confederation. He couldn't care less about the fate of the petty dictators who had seized power in system after system. Restoring the Confederacy was Thomas's goal.

It wouldn't be too long before he arrived, using his version of the Glenatat FTL engines. When he did, he would come in force, and it wouldn't matter who won this little war in this insignificant system. Thomas would restore his authority, set his own puppet in charge, and move on to recover the next system on his list.

What these people fought for was meaningless.

He didn't have the heart to tell them their rebellion was doomed no matter what.

His path was clear. At the first opportunity, he would escape and go to the regional commander. It pained him that he might be forced to sell out these people, and the innocent ones back in Argent, but this wasn't his fight. If he didn't take care of his own, nobody else would.

He leaned back against the wall and closed his eyes, not wishing to make eye contact with anyone. It would be best to remain aloof and not strike up any friendships. He already regretted the familiarity he shared with Chang, but he couldn't afford to be distracted from what he must do to save those he loved.

If that meant everyone else on this mission perished, so be it.

He felt sick to his stomach.

DECISION AND CONSEQUENCE

The drone of the engines, the gentle rocking of the vehicle, and the heat the day took their toll on Kaine. He dozed, periodically roused by a bump or a burst of laughter from the soldiers in the transport. In that place between dreams and wakefulness, he was barely conscious of the transport stopping and cutting its engines.

A poke to his shoulder pulled him awake, and his eyes opened to a scene of intense activity. M'gomba thrust a pack into his arms and said, "Get up and get moving."

"What is happening?" he asked, but M'gomba had moved toward the back of the transport. All the soldiers were on their feet and assembling their gear, fixing their helmets and prepping their weapons. Still dazed, he searched for some clue as to what had stirred them. Before he could ask Chang or any of the others, the commander's resonant voice ordered everyone out of the transport. Hayden fell into the flow and joined the others on the desert floor.

Moments after stepping from the transport and into the blazing sun, its oppressive heat started to sap his energy. Chang approached and pulled the helmet from Hayden's pack, which he'd dropped at his feet. "Put this on."

She didn't wait for him to comply before she hurried along the ranks to assume her place. A rough push from behind by M'gomba informed him he was to follow her. Picking his pack up and throwing it over his back, he jogged to catch up with the squad dashing to a nearby hillside. As they reached the rocks and scrambled for cover, Hayden asked one of them, "What is happening?"

"Airship coming," the man named Caldwell answered briskly as he prepared his weapon.

All the soldiers had now managed to conceal themselves within the craggy hollows of the rock formation. Two of them assembled a portable missile launcher. Before he could ask any more questions, the roar of the transport's engine caught his attention. The vehicle started spinning in place, its churning tracks throwing a thick, obscuring cloud of fine dust in the still air.

The transport vanished into a dust devil like those he'd seen on his trek to the mountain.

When the drone of an approaching aircraft rose above the noise of the transport's engine, Hayden understood what had happened.

He crouched lower to conceal himself in the shadows of the rocks as an airship approached.

Hayden wished he had a weapon with which to defend himself.

The menacing aircraft hovered over the hillside, the pilot searching for something. With no warning, it tilted its wings and slowly moved toward the cloud of dust thrown up by the vehicle.

Only when the pilot's attention had turned did the two soldiers with the missile launcher expose themselves. With practised efficiency, they set the weapon in place and within a second launched two short-range missiles at the unsuspecting aircraft.

Both projectiles hit home. Flames accompanied by a massive double explosion enveloped the airship.

Cheers from the soldiers rose above the noise as the burning aircraft tried to maintain altitude and turn its guns toward its assailant. The aircraft listed to the right and spiralled to the desert floor half a kilometre away, crashing with a massive explosion that destroyed it.

The soldiers scrambled down the hillside. Spirits were high, and they clapped each other on the shoulder in congratulations. The wreckage burned as M'gomba stepped up beside him. He turned to the veteran, saying, "You drew him into a trap. What made you think he'd fall for it?"

M'gomba shrugged and said, "Sometimes they are overconfident. This time we got lucky. Must have been a new pilot."

"And what if it hadn't worked?"

M'gomba raised a sardonic eyebrow. "Then we would be walking the rest of the way."

He called to the group and ordered them back to the vehicle. As Hayden fell in line with them, he caught sight of something in the distance where the aircraft had come. A plume of black smoke rose hundreds of metres into the air. He tapped M'gomba on the arm and pointed.

The commander's self-satisfied smile faded as he stared toward a distant site. One by one, the rest of the squad turned to see what had attracted their leader's attention.

Before Hayden could ask, the black man ordered everyone into the transport, double time. Hayden fell in with the others and clambered aboard. M'gomba was the last aboard as the tracks began to turn. The vehicle revved its engine and sped toward the smoke in the distance.

Chang's face was ashen as she turned from the window. He moved to sit beside her. "What is it?"

She faced him, disbelief still on her face. "There is only one settlement in this direction. Bantry is the village we intended to use as our forward operations base."

It took a moment to register what she was telling him. He stood and tried to peer in the direction they were going, but the cloud of smoke was no longer visible from his vantage point. He turned to Chang. "You think that airship attacked the village?"

"Kaine."

He turned to see M'gomba frowning at him.

"Sit down and shut up."

They all stared at him like he'd broken a taboo. He pressed his lips together and sat back on the bench to ride in silence for the remainder of the trip.

Twenty minutes later, the vehicle began to slow, and the mood in the cabin grew tenser. He thought he could smell their fearful anticipation in the air.

The vehicle rolled to a stop, and everyone remained seated, afraid to learn what was going on outside.

M'gomba stood and strode through the vehicle toward the door. Pushing it open, he jumped outside into the brilliant sunshine. Hayden listened to his footsteps crunching on the sand as he walked away from the transport.

Seconds passed without hearing anything from outside. Caldwell stood and followed the commander from the vehicle. One by one, the other soldiers stood and walked to the door. Finally, Hayden joined them.

What he saw when he stepped on the sand froze his blood.

They were in what remained of a village square.

Burned out buildings smouldered.

Bodies of men, women, and children lay everywhere. Many were bullet-riddled and unrecognizable. Others were burned beyond recognition. Nowhere could he see any soldiers.

"What the hell happened here?"

The soldier he had asked looked at him before he walked away to check one of the buildings. The rest scattered to other structures.

Hayden went to Chang, who knelt beside the body of a small boy of about six. His chest was blown open by a large-calibre weapon like the kind that would have been fired from the airship.

He knelt beside her to put a hand on her shoulder as she wept.

The team was sullen and silent as they gathered in an operations room beneath the remains of the largest building in the village. Armoured and shielded, it had withstood the attack. None of the villagers were fortunate enough to be in the room when the attack began.

M'gomba cleared his throat to get everyone's attention. "This is a...setback, I know, but it doesn't change our mission."

Caldwell spoke up. "I'm sorry sir, but I don't agree. Our support was to come from here. As of right now, we are a bunch of underprovisioned grunts in a tracked vehicle. We will never get close to the airfield without the access codes. There is no way we can complete this mission."

The others muttered agreement.

"Maybe there is," said Hayden after much consideration.

"Excuse me?" said Caldwell.

"I think we can get our hands on one of those airships."

Caldwell and the others started to jeer at him.

"That's enough," shouted M'gomba. "What are you talking about, Kaine?"

"Well, the airship that killed this village is the same one that attacked us, right?"

"Yes, and we killed the bastard," said one of the men.

"That's my point. The pilot would have reported his mission completed after he finished—"

Hayden stopped when he saw the stricken look on Chang's face, as well as a couple of the others.

"What I am trying to say is he hasn't returned to base or reported in since then."

"They will send someone to look for him," said M'gomba, realizing where Hayden was going.

He nodded. "That's right. All we need to do is locate the emergency transponder in the wreckage and set up an ambush for whoever comes looking for him."

"But we need to capture an airship, not shoot another one down."

"We can fake a signal; make it appear like the pilot is wounded and holed up in, well, anyplace we choose."

"Here," said Chang. "Make it be here. We can't bring back any of our friends, but we can make a statement about what it cost to kill them."

M'gomba studied Hayden, weighing his plan. "It won't be easy. They will send more than one ship. How do you propose we six, or seven if we include you, pull this off? One airship might land, but they will keep one or more flying cover and blow us out of existence the moment we poke up our heads."

"It won't take six or seven," said Hayden. "Only one. Me."

"You've spent too much time in the sun without a hat."

He shook his head. "Please hear me out. I'm the only one wearing an imperial uniform, remember? I'm proposing that I pose as the downed pilot."

"That won't work. They'll know the guy."

"Not if they find him wearing a helmet and unconscious."

"Idiot, the minute they take of your helmet they'll see you're not their man and shoot you."

"That's where you come in. You will conceal yourselves around the location where I'll be with the transponder. The minute they exit the ship to recover me, you start shooting, and they won't have time to do anything but grab me and run back to their ship. Once I'm aboard, I'll surprise them and take them out, giving us one airship."

"That is insane. The support ships will target us," said Caldwell. Turning to M'gomba, he said, "Commander, this is nuts. I vote we turn around and return to base while we can."

"And tell Krellig what? That we failed our mission? How do you think that will sit with him?"

"He'll understand. He—"

"Stow it, Caldwell."

"Commander, you can't be seriously considering this insane plan," said Chang.

"You shut up too. All of you pipe down. I need time to consider this." Fixing Hayden with an intense stare, he said, "Are you sure you can pull this off, Kaine?"

"Listen, M'gomba —and the rest of you, too—this may be your last opportunity to get an airship before Argent is taken out from orbit. I've taken on worse than what these guys can throw at me. I'll make it work, but not unless we work together."

Hayden lay face down on the sandy ground beside the smouldering wreckage of the downed aircraft. M'gomba's team had recovered both the emergency transponder and the scorched helmet and flight suit of the dead pilot, neither of which fit him. At first, he was uncomfortable about wearing a dead man's equipment, but he soon realized doing so was the best way to make his plan work. The rescue team had to believe he was the surviving pilot.

His arm covered his nose and mouth so he wouldn't breathe dust as he waited, sweating in the hot sun, for a recovery ship to come. The pistol concealed under his jacket dug into his stomach.

He'd argued with M'gomba about the need for him to have a weapon. In the end, the leader realized that without it the plan could not work, but that didn't mean he trusted Hayden with one. The small-calibre gun held two rounds. If more than two men were on the rescue ship, that would be problematic, but it was as much as the commander would compromise his better judgement.

Waiting while observation satellites confirmed him as a

possible survivor needing rescue, Kaine had plenty of time to reconsider his real plan.

He'd had always planned to defect to the government forces at the first opportunity after they arrived at Sittot. With that mission scrubbed, he'd thrown out the first idea that came to him and was shocked when M'gomba accepted it. Logically, he shouldn't have, although by same argument, Krellig should have ordered him shot instead of sending him on this ridiculous mission.

Maybe he was being given enough rope to justify Krellig's suspicions of him being a federal spy. He had no doubt he was in the sights of six weapons now.

The question was, did they believe there was a chance he was on their side and could obtain an aircraft for them? It was the only reason he could think of to explain his current situation. If that was the case, Krellig must be truly desperate to get his hands on one. Why else would he risk six lives on the outside chance that Hayden would not betray them? M'gomba may have realized Hayden's plan was an opportunity for his team to further reduce the number of aircraft available to the federal forces in an ambush.

The whine of aircraft turbines in the distance broke his chain of thought. With M'gomba's team concealed among the rocks, the trap was set, and he was the bait.

He risked a glimpse over his arm. Three ships approached the crash site. Two were combat raptors, like the downed ship. Hayden's heart skipped a beat when he realized the third airship was a small troop transport. If it carried a task force, the plan was pooched, and M'gomba's men would shoot him before they could reach him.

The raptors rose to a higher elevation to provide cover while the transport ship settled to the ground in a cloud of dust.

The side door slid open, and two people emerged. Behind them, nobody else occupied the passenger cabin.

He lowered his eyes and pretended to be unresponsive when

a man and woman arrived at his side. The man stood guard, cradling a short-nosed automatic weapon, while the woman produced a medical kit.

"He's alive," she shouted over the din of the aircraft's engines.

Playing it up, Hayden moaned.

"Hey buddy, can you move?"

He feebly nodded and shifted his legs, hoping it was enough to demonstrate that they could risk moving him.

"We have to get him out of here," said the man.

"Help me lift him."

They grabbed him under his arms and hoisted him to his feet. Kaine made a show of having no strength to walk, forcing them to carry him to their ship.

As they struggled under his weight, he looked up to see a thinning cloud of smoke in the distance where the last fires in the village burned themselves out.

He couldn't get the sight out of his mind of Emma Chang weeping over the mangled corpse of the dead child. The two people who carried him had good intentions for his welfare, but only because they believed him to be one of their own. Did they share the attitude of the pilot he now pretended to be? Did the people of that village have no value except as practice targets?

Hayden had a difficult time imagining what kind of monster could do such a thing. An action like that would only happen if sanctioned from higher up the chain of command. Were these the kind of people he was prepared to side with?

The idea nauseated him.

He'd intended to play the role of the injured pilot until they got him back to their base. Then his crude plan was to identify himself and try to reach the commander, finding a yet to be determined way to locate *Scimitar*. It was a half-baked idea. The only thing that drove him to conceive it was his intuition that the government forces would provide him with a better opportunity to find his ship. If necessary, he'd been prepared to give up intelligence about Argent, if it might gain him the necessary trust.

Now, he questioned what he'd set in motion.

Did he want to align himself with a regime that was capable of such an atrocity? What would Stella say?

She'd be ashamed of him more than he now was of himself.

They reached the waiting aircraft and hoisted his limp form onto the floor of the cabin.

He rolled over and kicked the surprised woman in the jaw, knocking her to the floor. In the same motion, he pulled his pistol and shot the man point-blank in the face.

The pilot turned to check on what the commotion was. Kaine shot him as he fumbled to draw his holstered weapon.

The woman ran from the ship, waving at the guarding raptors above. She fell, shot dead by one of M'gomba's men.

Realizing all hell was about to break loose, he rushed to the helm, stepping over the body of the pilot. A missile launched from the rock formation and exploded against one of the gunships overhead.

As it spewed smoke and spun out of control, its companion unleashed its own missile at where the rebel fire had originated.

Hayden searched the console until he found the already active gunnery interface. Grabbing the control, he fired the thrusters and pushed the ship into the air, hoping the other pilot would assume he sought to escape under cover.

Five metres off the ground, he turned his ship, locked on to the raptor, and opened fire with both anti-personnel guns.

Bullets tore into its fuselage as the shocked pilot was slow to react to the surprise attack. The critically damaged raptor returned fire.

Hayden ducked behind the console as holes were ripped through the hull. Alarms went off, and the ship pitched sideways. He tried to regain control but realized the attack had destroyed the helm.

He gripped the seat, his eyes wide with terror as the ground spun and rose at him.

The ship slammed into the desert floor. Hayden bounced off the shredded console. Only the ill-fitting helmet saved him from cracking his skull. Still, he saw stars as he lay, stunned, and sprawled on the deck.

Smoke filled the cabin. He rolled to his hands and knees. Covering his nose and mouth, he stumbled to the rear cabin and jumped through the open side door.

A thundering boom shook the ground beneath him. Without looking for the source of the explosion, he stumbled from the downed ship and ran toward the nearby rocks.

Two of M'gomba's troops emerged, their weapons trained on him. He stopped in his tracks, pulled off the helmet, and raised his hands high.

"Don't shoot. It's me, Kaine."

On returning to Argent, Hayden was escorted from the transport to meet with Krellig. Instead of being taken to the great hall, he was led past it and down a narrow alley. It was evening, and the sun had dropped behind the mountains, taking with it the heat of the day. A cooling breeze blowing down from the hills was whipped into a gust in the narrow space between the buildings.

He followed his escort into a nondescript building and up a narrow flight of stairs to a small room. There, he found Krellig standing beside a kitchen table. The place was a single-room apartment with a rudimentary kitchen and enough space for a single bed in the corner. It was compact but clean.

When his escort left, he said to Krellig, "The mission failed. We didn't get your aircraft."

"I heard that. I also heard about what happened to Bantry. I..."

Krellig averted his eyes. When he looked up again, he had regained control over his wavering composure.

"It was a ballsy thing you did, Kaine. I'm impressed and grateful for your effort."

Hayden paused to consider the wisdom of his reply.

"You took a big risk on me. What made you so sure I wouldn't defect to the federal forces?"

"I wasn't sure about you at all."

He studied the rebel leader. "You knew about the attack on the village before you sent us out there."

The other man's reply was a self-satisfied smile.

A wave of unexpected anger stirred inside Hayden that he was cautious to keep under control.

"Did anyone else know?"

Krellig slowly shook his head. "Only M'gomba."

"Your people won't be pleased with you."

"I doubt you'll tell anyone; you're too smart for that."

Hayden raised an eyebrow and offered a half-smile. "Am I?"

Changing the topic, Krellig said, "I thought you might be more comfortable here than in the shed."

He surveyed the room. "Thank you, this will be much more comfortable. "

Something on the table caught his attention. Noticing his interest, Krellig stepped aside. "I thought you might want to see this."

Arrayed on it were sundry bits of technology that comprised the remains of a synthetic's torso. Hayden smiled and reached out to stroke the battered head as if greeting Cora in person, rather than her empty shell.

"This is all we could recover," said Krellig, "or at least all we could find amidst the wreckage. I hope there is enough here for you to work with."

"Absolutely," said Hayden, his attention still focussed on it. He glanced up and added gently, "You realize I can't guarantee you will get what you want? If the ship is intact and my captain still in command, or if the government salvaged her, it will be almost impossible."

Krellig nodded. "I know."

"Why are you doing this, then?"

"I'll answer you with another question. What did you learn out there with my people?"

Hayden felt the quiet rage he'd kept a lid on beginning to rise. "The people who perpetrated the massacre are... monstrous."

He glared at Krellig as if he was somehow responsible.

The rebel nodded slowly. "We intercepted a report from the assault team last night. The recon mission was to confirm our worst fears."

"But that was a civilian target. There were no combatants, no military hardware. As far as I could tell, it had no strategic value besides its location."

"This is what we fight against," said Krellig. "Do you think this level of oppression is a new development? There has always been a malicious disdain for the people in this region by this governor."

"But what possible reason could there be for that?"

"I believe it goes back to the early colonization of Oberon; a holdover animosity from a grudge everyone forgot. The group that curried favour with Earth in the beginning retained power over the decades. They became entrenched in the belief they were the natural rulers of this world. Earth did nothing to discourage it—in fact, there is evidence they encouraged it to keep a firmer grip on the planet. That way a more democratic form of government arising that might give them problems was avoided."

Hayden shook his head. "No, you are mistaken. That would never happen. The Confederation promoted the democratic process on all colonial worlds."

"That may be what they told everyone back on Earth, but I assure you, nothing like that happened here since anyone can remember."

"There must be some reason Earth didn't know of this. The local government must have deceived their superiors."

"Are you really so naive, Kaine? Even if, as you suggest, the local government was run by despots who took great pains to suppress the truth, why did word of it never leak back to Earth? If it had, they would have sent investigators and cleaned house. Wasn't that the way the system was supposed to work?"

"Yes, but—"

"No network is so leak-proof that some word wouldn't get out, given the degree of space traffic between here and the inner systems at the time."

Hayden's stomach ached. "No, something would have gotten out."

"Assuming it did, and seeing that nothing was done to correct the situation, what is the obvious conclusion?"

Hayden scowled at Krellig but could find no words.

"Kaine, your idyllic belief of how the Confederacy functioned was the product of a constructed myth. It was fed and nurtured by every president who held power."

"No, I can't believe that. It must have been supported and concealed at a lower level of government, within the bowels of the bureaucracy."

"Why?" Krellig said, "What was there for a bureaucrat to gain by such a subterfuge?"

"Payoffs; their silence was bought."

"For five generations? Because that is how long this has been going on here. I know of three other systems where the exact same thing occurred. The corruption was systemic, and it went all the way to the top."

Hayden's mind whirled. If what Krellig said was true, it meant anyone remotely connected to the political elite was culpable. His own father and grandfather would have been aware of the corruption. It was too much to believe.

He had no love for the version of the empire Thomas sought

to create, but what he witnessed here today had no resemblance to the society he believed he grew up in as a loyal citizen. "The Confederation was never intended to be like this."

"Maybe what you experienced on Earth was more idyllic. Out here in the colonies, things have always been different. Governors have always sought to carve out their fiefdoms far from the oversight of central command. They've always ruled this system with an iron fist, and I would be shocked if it didn't happen in most other places. The Confederacy gave birth to the filth such people thrive on. They sent out the dregs to govern in the furthest regions, and massacred villages like Bantry are the result."

Kaine's mind was awhirl. It required all his effort to force himself to hear Krellig out.

"Out here, far from Earth, monsters were only constrained by the threat of being replaced if they created too much chaos. When the gate network collapsed, there was nothing to hold them to account, and what you see here is the result."

Hayden could not look at Krellig. The man's words were too difficult to accept. "I can't believe things were this bad."

"You can, perhaps, understand why nobody wanted much to do with your ship when you arrived."

For the first time, he understood the hostility *Scimitar* had experienced in every system it visited. When the gate system collapsed, they'd experienced for the first time what it was like to have control of their own destiny. When they arrived out of nowhere, it must have been frightening to realize that the technology existed for the empire to be reestablished.

"There is something you should know," he said. "Your rebellion doesn't stand a chance in hell of achieving permanent change. As I speak, the Confederation is rebuilding its fleet and equipping all its new ships with FTL engines. Thomas, the man who took power on Earth, is determined to rebuild an empire. He is sending fleets to every surviving system to retake them. He will put his own people in charge, and that will be the end of any dreams you have of living lives out from beneath the heel of the Confederacy."

Krellig's face darkened, and he leaned against the table. "I feared something like this. How long do we have?"

Hayden shrugged. "Weeks or months...perhaps years at the outside, but they will arrive here. Their construction program was just starting when we left Earth."

The rebel leader stared at the floor for a long time. When he looked up, his arrogant expression was gone, and there was help-lessness in his eyes. He studied Hayden for several seconds.

"We need your help, Kaine. If what I've described—what you've seen—offends your sensibilities in even the smallest way, you must agree that something must be done. We can't permit the present oppression to continue. Even a brief victory will give our people hope."

Hayden gently shook his head. "Krellig, even if you can lead your rebellion to victory, whatever you replace it with will fall when Thomas arrives. He will have the numbers, the ships, and technology that you will not be able to resist. It will be for nothing."

Krellig's eyes flashed with anger. "You are saying we should lay down our arms and stop opposing murderers."

"I'm not suggesting your struggle isn't just. I'm pointing out that any victory you achieve will be short-lived—a few years at most."

"It will plant the seed of hope for another generation. A victory, no matter how short-lived, can inspire and show our chil-dren that oppressors can be overthrown. Is that not worth the effort of resisting?"

Hayden's thoughts went to the young boy he met in the wilderness, Riley. It was for him and his generation Krellig and his people fought, not for themselves. And if all they accom-plished was to keep one small spark of hope alive against the next oppressor, perhaps that would be enough to change some-thing for their children's children.

"Of course it is worth it," he said.

Hayden looked at the damaged synth on the table. Reestablishing a link to Cora might be the only hope these people had. It wasn't much, even if he succeeded. In his wildest imaginings, the best that might be achieved would be to get Krellig his weapon. With it, his rebels might have a small chance of defeating the monsters who ruled this system. They might even be able to put up a brief and noble fight against Thomas's fleet when it arrived.

But the chances of that dead-end outcome were slim to nonexistent.

All he knew was he would never be able to view the old Confederation with the same complacency. Everything he'd ever believed or worked toward in his career was based on deception. He could fool himself into the delusion that had he remained and succeeded Thomas as the old admiral wanted, he would be better than what came before. But in his heart, he knew the truth. Had he remained to take his "rightful" place, nothing would have changed for the people in this system or any other.

Absolute power breeds absolute corruption. It had gone on before his eyes while growing up, and he never had a clue what was happening; never recognized the decay festering beneath the shiny veneer of the Confederation. Any hope that he would have been somehow better than what he replaced was unrealistic.

"I'll help you," he said. "I can't guarantee I will succeed, but I will do my best."

With a broad grin, Krellig clapped his hand on Hayden's shoulder. "You're doing the right thing."

Hayden returned a half-hearted smile. "Then why don't I feel much hope?"

"Hang on to that sliver of it, Kaine. Hope is a potent fuel, and a small amount can burn hotter than the sun, given time."

AWAKENED

After Krellig left, Kaine worked through the night to try to rebuild the interface on Cora's synth. His knowledge was nowhere up to the task, but he'd spent a great deal of his time aboard *Scimitar* assisting Cora. The trouble was that he never understood half of what she tried to teach him about Glenatat technology, and he now regretted not being a more diligent student.

At the time, there seemed to be no need for him to do so. Cora's disembodied presence was ubiquitous throughout *Scimitar*. She could far more easily insert herself into the equipment from within and execute repairs with efficiency and delicacy that the nimblest fingers could never achieve. The Glenatat components seemed to respond like living things to her prompting. There was very little she couldn't do, being part of the ship, but for the few tasks requiring a physical, human touch, he was more than happy to assist her with them.

He smiled at the recollection. As the first officer aboard a regular ship of the line, it was only necessary for him to be familiar with the intricacies of how his ship functioned, leaving the actual repairs and maintenance to far more competent people.

But when he and the others decided to flee the Confederacy, their crew was the bare minimum needed to operate *Scimitar*. Cora was the only one intimate with how the human technology interacted with the vessel's alien augmentation. The ship was not designed to be a Glenatat ship, and constant adjustments and compensations for the natural limitations were required.

He saw less and less of Cora in her synth body as the increasing fragility of *Scimitar*'s human-built systems demanded her constant attention. But there were limits to her omnipresence, so the responsibility fell on him to assist her where he could.

He removed the memory crystal from around his neck and connected it to his jerry-rigged device.

Breathless, he stared at the inert equipment, hoping he hadn't made some ignorant mistake. As first one minute passed, and then five more with no response, he despaired, fearing that recovering Cora was beyond his ability.

What if she was in a state she couldn't be revived from? He didn't want to call it death—her physical body had been dead for years—but what if there was a different kind of mortality for her? Nobody, including Cora, really understood what the Glenatat artificial intelligence responsible for her present state did to her. All that remained of his dear friend was her humour and compassion. She was smart, too. The cleverest engineer he'd ever met, but her translation into whatever she was now had augmented her native intelligence by orders of magnitude. He sometimes wondered if it was an effort for her to dumb things down so he and Pavlovich could understand her.

Exhaustion overpowered his despair, and despite his desire to stay awake to try again, his eyes grew heavy. Before long, his head rested on his arms as he leaned on the table.

"Hello? Is anyone there?"

Hayden's head jerked up; the fog of sleepiness was gone. His heart pounded as he scanned the room. He was certain he'd heard someone, but he was alone in the dimly lit apartment.

He blinked the sleep from his eyes and examined the inert interface on the table before him.

"Just a dream," he whispered.

He stood and stretched the stiffness from his back. A flash of light caught his attention, and he realized the sun was up and poking rays between the drawn curtains. He walked to the window and opened the drapes upon a bright morning. The radiated heat from the windowpane caressed his face. It was not yet midmorning, and the day promised to be another scorcher.

He worked his sandpapery tongue over dry lips and went to the kitchen for a glass of water. Leaning against the counter, he savoured the sensation of the precious liquid sloshing over his tongue as he swished it between his cheeks.

Wiping his lips with his hand, he realized he hadn't shaved in many days and wondered if there was somewhere he could shave and shower. He probably stank, and people had been too polite to complain.

A quiet hiss from the table seized his attention. He stared at the android skull and the arrayed components, expecting something to move.

"Hello? Is anyone there?"

Hayden rushed to the table and grabbed the synth's head. "Cora? Is that you?"

"Hayden?"

Sobs burst from him as he pressed his forehead against the synth. "Yes, it's me. Oh god, I thought I'd lost you."

"Where...where am I? It's dark; I can't see or feel anything."

"I downloaded you into a Glenatat memory crystal."

There was perplexed silence from the speaker.

"I don't understand what you're saying. What happened?"

Tears ran down his cheeks. His voice cracked as he answered her. "After the crash, you dragged me from the wreckage. You were damaged, and your power core was failing. I transferred you, but until now, I didn't know if I botched it."

"What crash? Hayden, I don't know what you're talking about."

Emptiness formed in his gut. He sniffed and wiped his nose with the edge of his sleeve before he found his next words. "Cora, what is the last thing you remember?"

Several seconds passed.

"I...I'm not sure. I have a vague recollection of something called...*Scimitar*. I remember you...and someone else, but I don't know his name."

"Pavlovich?"

Another pause.

"Yes...yes, that's him. Is he with you?"

Panic crawled up Hayden's spine as he stared at the damaged components on the table.

"Hayden?"

"I'm here. No, Pavlovich isn't with me."

"Where are you?"

"I'm on the surface of the planet Oberon. I came here with you in one of *Scimitar*'s escape pods. We crashed. Don't you remember?"

"No. Hayden, what's happened to me? Why can't I see or feel anything? Did I break my spine in the fall?"

"What fall?"

"I...I remember an accident...I think I was injured. I remember a flash—a panel exploded. I think I was working on the ship's fusion regulator...it's all so fuzzy and unfocused. Almost like it's not my memory but someone else's. Do I make any sense, Hayden?"

He sat back and stared at the synth's remains in horror. Those were her last human memories before the accident that nearly killed her, years ago. His voice cracked. "Yes, Cora, the memories are yours. You've told me that story before."

He regretted his careless reply.

"Before? It just happened, didn't it? How long have I been out of it?"

Something sounding like a gasp came from the speaker.

"I remember you weren't there when the accident happened. Oh, Hayden, we thought you were dead. Thank God you're all right. But I'm confused...when did you find us? What's happening?"

They were separated by half a galaxy when the accident that changed her occurred.

He and Stella, believing they were *Scimitar*'s only survivors, settled on the only habitable moon in the Mu Arae system. It took ten years, but from somewhere across the cosmos, Pavlovich returned for him in a transformed *Scimitar* and this new incarnation of Cora.

Desperation clung to his heart like a lamprey thirsting for his last remnant of hope. Pushing back the tears, he struggled to steady his voice. "Cora, are you certain you can't recall anything more?"

"I don't know what you mean."

"Is there anything at all you can remember, even if it seems strange? Please try."

There was a long pause. "I...I vaguely recall some weird dreams."

He said, "Tell me about them."

"It's nothing I can describe. Just a strange feeling, like I was outside of my body. You and Pavlovich were talking to me like I was present, but I wasn't. It was as if I was part of the surroundings—it doesn't make sense; just a strange dream."

Hayden gasped and covered his mouth. Her recent memories might still be there, hidden somewhere inside the crystal's alien matrix. Maybe it was fragmented, but the fact she seemed to be in touch with them in some way gave him a glimmer of hope.

A red light began to blink on the device.

"Oh, no."

Hayden scrambled to his feet and searched the room. Spotting his pack by the bunk, he rushed to it and dumped the contents onto the bed.

"Hayden, are you still here?"

He called back over his shoulder, "Yes, I'm still here. Give me a moment."

"I feel strange. So sleepy..."

Desperation strained his voice. "Stay with me, Cora. Don't go to sleep."

He spied the flashlight. Seizing it, he pried it open and dumped the battery into his hand. Cursing, he tossed it onto the mattress and scoured what remained of the bag's contents.

"I...don't think I can stay awake..."

"Fight it, Cora, please."

He rushed to the kitchen and threw open the cabinet. Pots and pans tumbled to the floor as he pulled them out.

"Hayden? What's happening to me?"

"A few more seconds, Cora. Stay with me."

Spying the toaster on the counter, he grabbed it and started to pry it open. After a few seconds, reason came to him. He looked at the disassembled appliance in his hands. "Shit."

He returned to the table. "Cora, sweetie, I have to disconnect you. I'm running out of power, and I don't know what will happen if the battery dies while you're hooked up to this thing. I'm afraid you might not—"

He stopped himself. Cora wouldn't understand.

"You're not making sense, Hayden."

Tears welled up and trickled down his cheek.

"I know. Close your eyes and get some rest. I'll talk to you when you wake up later, okay?"

"Okay. So sleepy. Thanks for being here with me, Hayden."

He sniffed. "I wouldn't be anywhere else, Cora."

The flashing light grew dimmer with each pulse. Closing his eyes, he shut down the interface and disconnected the memory crystal before the power was exhausted.

Clutching it in his hand, he leaned on the tabletop and covered his head with his arms. He couldn't stop weeping.

Cora was alive, and for that he was grateful. But he feared for her. Was she still conscious without the power connected, alone and afraid in whatever dark, empty reality she occupied? Or was she suspended, disconnected from time and reality until the next trickle of power that would restore her?

He banged his hand on the table until it hurt.

He should have thought of the power requirement before he started. He'd been in such a rush to see if she was still alive, he didn't check the state of the synth's battery. It wasn't one in the conventional sense. Like Cora, it was uniquely Glenatat in design. He didn't know if anything in human technology could recharge the dark energy battery powering Cora's matrix. He didn't know if a substitute was possible to construct.

He feared what would happen if the battery's power was exhausted; didn't know how much longer it would last, or if it would recharge on its own, or if there was any way to recharge it at all. The technology was so totally alien, only Cora understood it.

She was alive, and that was the most important thing, but there might not be any way to ever recover her. He was trapped in a horrible feedback loop. Without Cora, there was no way to locate *Scimitar*, and without the technology on the ship, he didn't think there was a way to help her.

Hayden spent the next hour sitting at the table and attacking the problem from every angle he could conjure.

The Glenatat battery required charging, but the details of its unique power requirements were only known to one person, and that was Cora. He had spent enough time assisting her aboard *Scimitar* to have a rudimentary understanding of how the alien technology worked, but that was it.

The problem he faced was akin to an early Palaeolithic human trying to invent gunpowder after seeing how a matchlock rifle worked.

As he considered that analogy, he chuckled. It was more like that caveman being asked to build a fusion reactor after teaching him how the sun was powered. It was a practical impossibility.

And yet he was far better equipped to tackle the problem than any other human. He'd seen firsthand how the Glenatat technology worked and experienced what it was capable of.

As far as his education was concerned, Cora had done far more than explain how it worked. She had spent many hours trying to teach him the math. He couldn't follow half of it, but he was far from ignorant.

The fact was, he knew just enough to fail spectacularly. All he needed was to find the courage to risk it. If he failed, Cora would be lost forever.

He didn't know that for certain, but he had to consider it a major risk in his calculations. Far more was at stake than Krellig's rebellion or finding Pavlovich.

Children's laughter pulled him from his thoughts.

Curious, he went to the window.

Outside, Riley and his friends played a modified version of football. He was surprised to see a couple of Krellig's soldiers kicking the ball around with them, laughing like kids themselves when the youngsters tackled them for no apparent reason.

He found himself smiling. It was a long time since he'd heard children laughing, and he drifted to thoughts of Stella and the dreams they once shared of starting a family.

Fate had other, far crueller plans for them, however. He was not destined to be a father. Her loss impacted him more than any regrets about never being a parent.

He couldn't recall his own father ever playing with him. His dad had considered quality time to be more cerebral. To him, the hours spent tutoring his son on the intricacies of politics were a far better use of his infrequent and short visits home.

Hayden never thought he'd missed anything, though. He had plenty of friends—perhaps too many, recalling his father's admonitions about neglecting his studies to spend time with them.

Still, it was only he and his friends who ever played. None of the adults ever joined in—not like this.

His brow crinkled.

Why did that observation seem so profound to him?

He returned his attention to the adults, who continued to gather around the improvised playing field. Some joined, spelling off those who needed a breather, but most were content, even happy, to stop their daily routine to cheer and enjoy the spectacle.

He marvelled at how a children's improvised game could become a community event. Even Krellig had joined in the contest, which had somehow transformed into a wild rumpus. The ball was soon forgotten as children piled on the grownups, hanging on to legs and arms, climbing onto backs until adults were dragged to the ground to be piled upon by a squealing mass of children.

Hayden laughed as Krellig struggled to walk with six or seven small adversaries clinging to him. It was a battle he didn't mind losing.

Finally, the melee died out, and dust-covered children joined their parents to leave the square as the morning heat became less tolerable.

Krellig, his trousers and tunic caked with fine sand, stood and waved to them as they departed. When the square was emptied, he brushed off his clothes and walked to the walled well. There he wiped his brow and took a deep drink from a bucket of water resting on the ground.

There was a satisfied expression on his face, almost contentment, as if he treasured the moment with gratitude.

Then he did something that caught Hayden off-guard.

He leaned down and picked up a pulse rifle that had been leaning against the wall before striding toward the great hall.

Hayden blinked, not sure if he should be shocked or impressed by the slack attitude that permitted such a destructive weapon to be left there during the game.

Krellig was not alone in his apparent carelessness. Several of his soldiers were retrieving their weapons without a second thought.

The surreal transposition of the casual manner they returned to being soldiers after spending time with their loved ones was something Hayden had never seen.

For him, a military career was something kept separate from family life, hidden away from innocent eyes to keep them ignorant of the violence their parents might perpetrate in the line of duty. On Earth, it was unheard of for children to see, let alone have casual access to weapons.

Here, it was a normal course of life for the two to be juxtaposed. These adults appeared to hide nothing of the reality of the world from their offspring.

He wondered if a similar scene in Bantry hadn't been disrupted by the attacking government ship. How many people on this planet lived like this, playing with their families in one moment, only to be called to fight off an invading force in the next?

It was not just the idea of leaving weapons lying around that struck Hayden, but the destructive power of those firearms.

They were pulse rifles, weapons powerful enough for a single one to bring down a shielded aircraft at up to one kilometre.

An idea suddenly came to him, one that had been fermenting in his subconscious since he'd first noticed what the weapons were.

Hayden let out a whoop.

There might be a way to recharge the Glenatat battery. All he needed to do was persuade Krellig to give him a pulse rifle.

He smacked his forehead.

"Dummy!"

Why would Krellig trust him with such a weapon? They hadn't even trusted him with a fully loaded sidearm. He was certain Krellig had ordered him watched—he'd be foolish not to do so, and Krellig was no fool.

It was one thing for the rebel leader to trust Hayden to find a way to point him to *Scimitar*. Krellig had a lot to gain from his cooperation, but Hayden didn't for a minute believe the leader trusted him with free rein. Not enough to provide him with one of the most powerful weapons in his arsenal.

Right now, the only thing it cost Krellig to pretend to give Hayden the illusion of being trusted was access to a destroyed synth and some clever words. In fact, more than once it crossed his mind that Krellig might be far less generous or trusting than he appeared. The effort he'd made to gain Hayden's empathy for his cause could be a means to gain his cooperation.

No, it was a hopeless dream to expect Krellig to hand over one of the weapons.

But he didn't need a rifle—only a power core. Unfortunately, that wasn't a distinction that would garner approval, any more than asking for the firearm. There were multiple ways to rig a power core to use as a bomb. It was one of those things taught in advanced weapons training at the academy.

It would be far easier for Krellig to suspect mischief. As far as Hayden knew, there was no understood way of using the core as an alternate power source. He wasn't sure if his idea was possible.

It was more likely that he would blow the village off the map than succeed in draining and regulating the power to transfer into Cora's battery.

But it was the only means he could think of to get the task done and free her from her imprisonment.

There was only one way for this to work. He would have to tell Krellig the truth about the Glenatat technology. It was risky, and he couldn't give any hint of Cora's existence.

The lack of trust ran both ways, and despite how powerful a weapon *Scimitar* could potentially be for Krellig, it would be useless without Cora.

TIME FOR SOME CANDOUR

When Kaine was brought to him, Krellig sat at a desk in his quarters, a place that also appeared to serve as his office. The desktop was cluttered with reports, and a pile of unread ones was perched on the corner, awaiting the commander's attention.

He looked up from his reading. The single lamp on the table cast ghoulish shadows on his tired face.

He addressed the guard who accompanied Hayden. "What is it?"

"He insists on speaking with you. I tried to tell him—"

Krellig waved the man to silence, then leaned back and rubbed his eyes. After stretching his arms above his head with a disconcerting crackle, he eyed Kaine for a few seconds before dismissing the soldier.

After the man closed the door, he indicated the empty chair in the corner. Hayden pulled it to the desk and sat.

"What do you want, Kaine?"

Hayden hesitated, questioning the wisdom of using what he'd come to bargain with. But since it was the only currency at his disposal, he said, "There are a few things you should know about *Scimitar*."

The rebel leader raised an eyebrow. He placed the datapad down and spread his hands, palms down, on the desk. "I'm all ears."

"I have to warn you; you might not believe me."

Krellig leaned back in his chair. "Kaine, with the kind of day I've had, I can use some entertainment. Let me hear what you've got."

"All of the advanced technology aboard *Scimitar*...well, it wasn't designed or built by humans."

"I'd guessed as much. Where did you get it?"

"From an ancient race of super beings."

Krellig smirked. "That is almost funny, Kaine."

"It's also the truth. We were sent to Mu Arae to recover a xenoarchaeologist who was studying the ruins they left behind aeons ago."

"You mean like those we've found throughout the galaxy over the past century?"

"Yes. They were all outposts for a once vast empire ruled by a race called the Glenatat. The scientist managed to interpret some of their writings that showed where they'd gone and how to reach them through an artificial wormhole."

"So, your captain just decided to become an explorer and go look for them?"

"Not exactly." Now committed, Hayden sighed. "When we first encountered the Malliac—"

"They are the invaders you told me were finally defeated at the Sol system."

"Yes. Let's say we came out on the poorer end of that initial encounter. Our ship was damaged, and with the jump gate down, we were sitting ducks for another assault. We took a gamble on the theory and found the wormhole."

"You were trapped at Mu when the network went down?"

Hayden swallowed. It was too easy to let Krellig believe that instead of having to explain the truth. "Yes."

"And where did it take you?"

"I honestly don't know, but the theory was correct. We found the Glenatat."

Not batting an eye, Krellig said, "What did they look like?"

Hayden hesitated. "The ones I encountered were disembodied brains floating in a tank."

"You're dead serious, aren't you?"

Hayden kept his expression neutral. "I couldn't be more serious."

Frowning, Krellig studied him for several seconds. He slowly shook his head and said, "Well, I said I wanted to be entertained. Fine, keep talking. I want to see where you are going with this... story."

Hayden tried to swallow, but his mouth was as dry as the desert he'd crossed. He'd taken things down a path that was becoming dangerous. If Krellig learned the truth about what happened at Mu Arae—about Hayden's role in the collapse of the jump gate network, things might go badly for him. He could find himself facing a firing squad or be branded a lunatic and locked away for the rest of his life.

He'd been a fool to disclose as much as he had. Krellig was already having difficulty with the truth. He had to tell the rebel leader something believable—something that would corroborate what he had already witnessed—something about *Scimitar* and its weaponry.

"The Glenatat repaired our ship and upgraded us with adaptive self-repairing hull armour and a dark energy cannon to defend ourselves against the Malliac. They also gave us the data to invent our ship's faster-than-light engine. We jumped back to Terra to warn them about the threat. Since the Malliac only possessed sub-light-speed technology, we had ten years to prepare defences around Terra. With the jump gate network down, there was no way to warn many of the outer colonies."

He paused, hoping Krellig would swallow his modified version of the truth.

The rebel stared at him for several long seconds before his

expression softened, and he nodded. "That explains the amount of firepower your ship withstood. We were probably just as astounded as the feds when the nuke they threw at you didn't even dent your hull."

Hayden was grateful that his smile of relief was interpreted as pride in his vessel. "Yep, she's a tough little ship."

His expression sobered. "But even *Scimitar* isn't indestructible. We took on a lot of damage. I was knocked out in the blast and was fortunate enough to have been put in an escape pod; otherwise..."

His thoughts drifted to Pavlovich and the others, and he wondered how many of them had survived.

They sat in silence.

Krellig drummed his fingers on the desk. When the quiet grew uncomfortable, Hayden said, "Well?"

Krellig sniffed and broke eye contact. "I'm not saying I believe everything you've told me, but I witnessed your ship in action, so I'm willing to be open to the possibility you're not lying."

Hayden sighed his relief.

"What made you decide to tell me, Kaine?"

"I wanted you to know what is at stake if she falls in the wrong hands. Her technology will be a game-changer for either side, but I think you have already considered that."

Krellig smiled but said nothing.

"Anyway, after seeing what you're fighting against, I wanted you to understand what you are asking me to help you recover. You must appreciate we couldn't interface our ship with the alien tech without a specialized AI. Whoever finds *Scimitar* will need that to make anything recovered work."

"And I suppose you are going to tell me you have access to such an AI."

He nodded. "The synth you recovered was linked to the ship's AI. I've gone over the components, and the interface is intact—at least enough that I think I can repair it."

"All of this is wishful thinking. We don't know where your ship is."

"The interface is linked to the Glenatat systems aboard *Scimitar* on the quantum level. If we can get it working, it can tell us where the ship is."

Krellig's expression was unreadable. Hayden hoped his own poker face was enigmatic.

"And what do you need to repair it?"

"I have to recharge the Glenatat dark energy power cell."

Krellig raised an eyebrow. "I don't suppose we can plug it into a fusion generator?"

Hayden chuckled. "I'm afraid not. I need something I can phase-regulate the quadrature—"

Krellig raised a hand to stop him. "I trust you know what to do. What do you need, Kaine?"

He swallowed. "I need a charged phase rifle power core."

Krellig stared at him. "I did not see that coming."

"It's the only source that can break the Coulomb barrier and—"

"I said I trusted your expertise, Kaine, but that doesn't mean I trust you. You must understand why I can't hand one over to you. Even if I decide you don't present a risk to us, my senior officers would be within their rights to question or even countermand my order and lock me up."

"I know I'm asking a lot of you, but it is the only way."

Krellig sat back in his chair and stroked the stubble on his chin. "Leave it with me to consider, Kaine. If I think your case has merit, I will discuss the matter with my advisory council. That's the best I can give you."

Hayden nodded and stood. "I understand, General."

"Thank you for being candid with me, Kaine. At least, I hope you were, and this wasn't some bizarre con job."

Hayden smiled weakly. "It's not a con. I want to find out what happened to my friends, and if by doing so I can help your cause, so much the better."

"I wish I could believe you, Kaine."

"How can I help that process along?"

Krellig considered the question. "Leave that with me, too."

Hayden leaned against a wall and watched the sun sink over the hills. The paving stones of the village square were still hot with radiant heat. A hint of the cooling breeze preparing to blow down from the mountains was already on the air, but it wasn't enough to disperse the pungent scent of cooking cabbage coming from the kitchen in the main hall.

The square was coming to life. People emerged from the buildings, and merchants opened their shops to set their wares out for the evening's anticipated commerce.

M'gomba emerged from the building that housed Krellig's quarters. Spotting Kaine, he strode toward him. The way his jaw was set told Hayden that whatever his mission, he was not happy about it.

"Kaine, you're to come with me."

Not waiting for a response, the man walked past him toward a narrow passageway between two buildings. Hayden shrugged and followed.

M'gomba led him to the school building Krellig's soldiers used as a base for their operations. He was taken into the room he'd been in only a couple of days before. Among those present were most of the soldiers he'd accompanied to Bantry, but he didn't see Chang among them.

Turning to M'gomba, he said, "You could have told me where to come."

M'gomba's nostrils flared. His gaze remained fixed on Hayden as he announced to the room, "Sit down and pay attention. We have got a lot to cover, and I don't want any screw-ups."

Kaine shrugged and took a seat while M'gomba walked to the head of the room. He stopped to examine the day's algebra lesson scrawled on the ancient blackboard before he used his sleeve to wipe it clean.

Facing the soldiers, he said, "We have another opportunity to relieve the feds of some equipment we require."

He turned his back to them and began to draw a diagram on the board. Kaine looked at the others, whose attention was locked on M'gomba as they made notes on their datapads.

He returned his attention to the front of the room, puzzled why M'gomba wasn't using a holo-display and beaming the information to the soldiers' individual cortical implants.

It struck him that since his arrival, he'd seen no evidence of anyone using their LINK. His was removed years before, when it became defective, and he'd never replaced it. He flagged the observation to discuss with Krellig later and returned his full attention to the briefing as he pulled out his own pad.

"The general needs an orbital flyer, since he is still grounded. Since Kaine failed to acquire us one the last time, we are giving him another chance."

"It was hardly my fault," muttered Hayden.

"What was that?"

"I, er, was just wondering where we're going."

"If you'll shut up and quit interrupting, I'll tell you."

"Right. Sorry. Please continue."

For an instant, M'gomba looked like he was about to explode. He smiled. "Thank you so much, Mister Kaine."

Hayden clamped his lips together and bit his tongue to keep from uttering the smart-ass rejoinder that popped into his head.

As the briefing resumed, Hayden relaxed and considered why he disliked M'gomba so much. Part of it was a reaction to the soldier's surly nature and unmasked disdain for him. M'gomba reminded him of a drill sergeant who'd taken a dislike to him when he was a cadet at the academy. Wallis was his name. Hayden hated the man as much if not more than the old veteran did him. He'd made that year a living hell for Hayden, singling him out to make an example for every minor infraction. It felt personal, but he had no idea how it could be so. No member of his family had ever served in the military, so there was no connection there; his father and grandfather were both career politicians. The only thing he could think of was that Wallis resented him for his entitled pedigree. Hayden was used to such treatment from other training officers, but Wallis's dislike for him was disproportionate, almost pathological.

Of course, in those days, he was not one to take such bullying lying down. He'd learned long before that any complaints would fall on deaf ears unless what was done to him caused physical injury, and Wallis was careful not to cross such a line.

He organized some of his friends, and together they began to pull retaliative pranks on the sergeant. The old soldier had convinced himself that Hayden was behind the childish and annoying hazing, but Kaine and his crew, as they were known, were careful to cover their tracks, leaving no damning evidence that would get them expelled.

One day, an unknown drill instructor replaced Wallis. When asked the reason, the woman explained that the sergeant had suffered a heart attack the previous evening.

It was later learned someone had put a hallucinogen in his coffee that had triggered the heart attack. An inquiry board was convened to investigate the matter, but there was insufficient evidence to implicate anyone, though it was an open secret among the cadets that Kaine and his crew were the ones responsible.

Overwhelmed by guilt for what he'd done, he suspended his association with his friends and spent the rest of the semester as a model cadet officer.

Wallis never returned, and Hayden often wondered what became him. Several times he made plans to check in on the old soldier but could never work up the courage to face him.

"Kaine!"

M'gomba's voice echoed off the walls of the small room. Hayden mentally kicked himself for his wool-gathering. He wracked his brain for anything his divided attention had actually paid attention to. Scanning his scribbles on his datapad, he vaguely recalled M'gomba talking about the flyers they were going to target.

He took a gamble and said, "They sound a lot like E-14 Raptors, I think."

M'gomba narrowed his eyes and huffed. "Are you familiar with their operation?"

"Uh, yeah, I suppose so. I trained on E-16s, but the fourteen is just an older model."

"So, you can pilot one."

"Of course."

"Why the hell didn't you say so? Please pay attention, Kaine. Lives depend on you getting this right the first time."

He glanced about the room at the others. Some glared at him with unconcealed contempt, while one or two shook their heads in amusement.

Hayden's cheeks warmed as he directed his gaze at his datapad and resolved to give his full attention to the remainder of the briefing.

Thirty minutes later, M'gomba dismissed them with instructions they were to meet for departure in two hours. Hayden waited for a few minutes after everyone departed. As he stood to go, a woman's voice from behind startled him.

"Don't let M'gomba rattle you."

Chang leaned against a table, smiling.

He returned her smile. "You've been there the whole time?"

"Pretty much."

He joined her at the back of the classroom. "I'm pretty sure he hates me."

"I wouldn't take it personally; he hates everyone."

Their laughter died into an awkward silence.

Hayden cleared his throat. "Are you joining us on the mission?"

A silky strand of black hair escaped her ponytail as she shook her head. "No, Taylor is the designated medic for this one."

"So why put yourself through that excruciating briefing?"

She tucked the loose hair behind her ear and shrugged. "I had nothing better to do."

Another brief silence fell between them before she said, "Have you eaten?"

"No, the smell from the hall kitchen wasn't appealing."

"Yeah, I don't recommend Cookie's cabbage rolls. I was thinking of a better option, if you're game."

Hayden raised an eyebrow. "M'gomba is expecting me to be ready to go in two hours."

She checked the chronometer on her wrist. "One hour and fifty-four minutes." Looking up at him, she smiled. "The village isn't that big. You'll have plenty of time to eat and get ready. The alternative is going out hungry, unless you want to risk eating with the others."

He wrinkled his nose. "I'm imagining what the transport is going to smell like. Whatever would compel him to cook that before a mission?"

She laughed. "It's Thursday. Cook doesn't give us a lot of variety."

"Maybe M'gomba could have delayed the mission for a day. What's served on Friday?"

She shook her head. "A really bad version of French onion soup. Trust me; the cabbage is better."

Hayden inclined his head. "In that case, I'd love to join you for dinner."

She laughed as she pushed herself away from the table. "Good choice. Follow me."

She led him across the now bustling square to a small kiosk from which the delicious smell of barbecuing meat emanated. Chang greeted the old man behind the counter with a peck on the cheek before holding up two fingers.

The man's eyebrows rose when he saw Hayden. He beamed as he nodded at her.

She shook her head. "It's not like that, Ummo. It's Thursday, remember?"

Ummo's nose wrinkled. "Phew. In that case, I'll give you both extra for tomorrow too."

She laughed at the old man's joke and produced a handful of coins from her pocket. He shook a finger at her. "You know your money is not good here, Emma."

He glanced sidelong at Hayden.

Kaine awkwardly patted at his pockets. "I'm sorry, but I—"

Ummo frowned and waved his hand. "No, no. Emma and her friends don't pay."

He turned to the rotating spit behind him and carved off thin slices of meat, which he wrapped in flatbread along with some vegetables. After rolling them closed, he topped each with a sauce and presented them proudly to Chang.

She bowed as she accepted them, then led Hayden to a nearby table on the edge of the square.

They sat opposite each other, and he gazed over her shoulder at the star-bedazzled sky and the second of the moons rising over the hills.

"It's a beautiful evening," he said.

Chang put a plate in front of him, then licked her fingers and smiled. "Most evenings are like this in the winter months."

"This is winter?"

She nodded as she lifted her flatbread to her mouth.

"How hot does it get in summer?"

She shrugged. "Hotter than this; nobody comes out in the summer."

"Even at night?"

She shook her head as she chewed. Nodding toward his plate, she said around a mouthful of food, "It's better when it's warm."

He smiled and took a bite. "Wow! This is delicious; probably the best thing I've eaten in a long time."

"Well, the best since you crashed on Oberon, I expect."

Hayden shook his head as he chewed another mouthful. Seeing her quizzical expression, he swallowed and said, "I mean, the food on *Scimitar* was okay, but I can't remember the last time I tasted real meat. What is this?"

"Choya."

"I'm sorry?"

She chuckled. "Oh, I suppose you wouldn't know. It's a desert animal—like a gila monster from Earth, but larger and with hair covering most of its body. They are a cross between a reptile and a mammal—the one with the pouch that hops around."

"A kangaroo?"

"Yeah, that's it."

Hayden considered the meat-filled wrap. "I saw some odd flying creatures when I first arrived. I don't know why, but I was surprised by them. For some stupid reason, I was expecting birds like on Earth. My brain must have been addled by the heat."

She nodded as she chewed. "Those are achatos. They were the first engineered food source made when Oberon was settled."

"They aren't native to this planet?"

She laughed. "Oh, no. Oberon didn't have any fauna besides some poisonous insects. Every animal here was genetically engineered to survive in this climate. Now, they are abundant enough to provide a supplemental source of protein for most of the population outside of the cities."

"What about cows or chickens?"

"None of the original livestock from Earth survived. New species needed to be developed or the original settlers would have starved."

"Wouldn't it have been easier for everyone if they had adapted domesticated livestock?"

She frowned. "Easier for who? Not the animals enslaved for food."

"I'm sorry, I didn't mean to offend you."

Chan shook her head. "I'm not offended. I keep forgetting what Earth is like—I've never been there. Here, my ancestors had a certain philosophy regarding animal husbandry. They thought it better for all involved if we had to work for our food."

"Better for the animals because they have a sporting chance to avoid being a—sorry, what was this called?" He held up the last of his tortilla.

"Aquentaca." Her laughter was music to him.

Hayden grinned and popped the last morsel into his mouth.

They fell into an easy silence, and Hayden allowed his attention to drift to the star-filled sky. Sadness rose as he recalled *Scimitar* and all the friends he may have lost. He felt guilty for taking time away from repairing Cora and locating his ship, but there was little more he could do without a power source. To have any hope of gaining Krellig's trust, he had to fulfil his role in the upcoming mission.

Emma's voice interrupted his musings. "Is something wrong?"

"What? No, I was thinking of the mission. Why does Krellig need access to an orbital flyer? I mean, shouldn't his focus be on the struggles on the planet and not above it?"

She studied him for a few breaths. "How much do you know about him?"

He shrugged. "Not much, I admit."

"Well, he was once a general in the planetary forces. One day, he received orders to send troops against a rebel group in the arctic region. The government had severed their supply chain, and they were out of provisions and freezing to death. While travelling to capture the rebels, he received orders to wipe them out instead."

"Let me guess; he refused the orders."

She nodded. "When he returned to base with prisoners instead of corpses, he was arrested and thrown in the same prison that housed several rebel faction leaders he'd been responsible for capturing."

"The government hoped he'd be murdered in prison so they wouldn't have an untidy mess by executing him themselves."

"But the opposite happened, and Krellig became allies with his former enemies. When a mission was mounted to break the rebels out, they took him with them."

"They trusted him?"

She laughed. "About as much as he trusts you. Like you, he was required to prove he wasn't a spy."

"And how did he do that?"

"He gave us a space fleet."

Hayden's jaw dropped. "How?"

"He was familiar with a number of other disaffected officers who were upset by his arrest. Through a series of missions, much like the one you are going on, enough ships were captured for Krellig to mount an attack on the orbital hub. They managed to capture three patrol corvettes."

"They just walked away with them?"

"I told you, Krellig had friends, and some of them were in the Admiralty. Their crews were loyal to their captains, so capturing the ships was not a problem."

"Keeping them would have been. Where was the fleet?"

"Sheridan—she was the governor then—had deployed ships near the jump gate. There was still a strong hope at the time that it would come online again, and she wanted to control traffic entering and leaving the system. Krellig sent his ships to the outer system as a precaution in case that happened, and the Confederation sent reinforcements. When it became obvious the gate would never reactivate, things sort of cascaded into a larger civil war. More ships defected to Krellig, and before long he had a fleet to challenge the loyalists."

"So, with all those resources, why is he stuck down here?"

"He maintains close ties to all the rebel factions on the surface. Our little group is special to him, since we were the ones who broke him out of prison, and he visits often when he returns to the planet for meetings with the other leaders. Krellig was trying to unify us for a final offensive against the capital. But things went badly."

"What happened?"

"Krellig was in orbit, coordinating an attack on the government fleet. Their mission was to remove the threat of our surface forces being bombed from space during our planned ground assault. Something happened during that battle that turned the tide in the government's favour. Our fleet suffered heavy losses. Krellig's ship was destroyed, and he barely escaped. He went to ground here because we are one of the few safe places for him to hide. Like you, he is marooned on Oberon, unable to establish contact with whatever remains of the fleet. We don't know how many of them survived or where they are."

"So, you're telling me Krellig isn't the real leader of this group."

"No. M'gomba is, but he defers to Krellig because of his rank and reputation."

"And how does that sit with M'gomba—losing command, I mean?"

"Hard to tell. I think he's okay with it because he's always been one of Krellig's admirers. They served together a long time ago. It was M'gomba's plan to break Krellig and the others out of prison."

"What became of the surface assault plan?"

"It never took place. Once our leadership learned what happened to their orbital support, they cancelled it. Every faction has been hiding since."

"How long ago did all of this happen?"

"A little before you showed up. That's why you haven't been trusted. We thought you came down in an escape pod from one of the government ships. Your ship must have arrived in the middle of that battle when it was attacked."

Chang had got most of the story right. *Scimitar* was attacked by both sides. But what she didn't know—and what Krellig hadn't told anyone—was *Scimitar* was probably the reason the rebel fleet was routed.

He couldn't recall how many ships they destroyed in their bid to escape the conflict. *Scimitar*'s dark energy cannon must've torn through enough of Krellig's ships to inadvertently turn the tide in favour of the government forces. *Scimitar* was the reason the rebel forces were in disarray across the planet and being hunted. If their arrival had been better timed, they might have been greeted as friends instead of foes by two sides.

Krellig wanted to get off-planet to reunite with what remained of his fleet. He was also desperate to get his hands on the dark energy cannon because, having seen it in action, he smelled victory, even with a much smaller fleet.

The pending arrival of Confederation forces would complicate matters terribly for both Hayden and Krellig. Once Thomas completed his consolidation of power in this system, he didn't see how the rebels could prevail, even with the dark energy cannon. Thomas had *Scimitar*'s FTL technology and a reverse-engineered prototype of the cannon. For all he knew, they'd tested it and all the Confederation ships now had one installed.

Thomas wanted all of *Scimitar*'s Glenatat technology. With knowledge of its adaptive armour alone, he would become invincible. Without Cora, he'd never be able to take advantage of most of the ship's systems, but there was still some technology aboard that he could replicate.

Hayden was running out of time.

Emma cleared her throat and stood. "Your mind is already on the mission," she said. "I'll leave you to get ready."

He rose as well. "Um, thanks for the meal. It was delicious."

She smiled. "Maybe we can do this again after your return?"

Feeling his cheeks warm, he said, "I'd like that, but next time I'll buy."

She laughed. "With what? I thought you didn't have any money."

Hayden grinned. "I suppose I'll have to find a job."

"I think, if this mission succeeds, you will be too busy for that."

"Then I'll just insist to Krellig that he put me on salary."

Her smile softened. "Make sure you come back, okay?"

He nodded. "Sure thing."

She walked across the square and disappeared into a building.

He shook his head. "What the hell are you thinking, Kaine? She's too young."

He checked his chronometer.

He still had an hour to prepare for the mission. Best to focus on that if he wanted any chance to repair Cora and find *Scimitar* before Thomas's people arrived.

SHOW YOUR METTLE

With Chang not part of the mission, Kaine had no one to talk to in the transport. Not that M'gomba would have approved if he did. The stern-faced commander insisted on focussed silence during the journey, so Hayden allowed himself to succumb to the drone of the engine and the transport's irregular rocking. He drifted off into uneasy slumber.

The abrupt halt of the vehicle snapped him back to full alertness. On M'gomba's order, the squad of twelve men and women poured out of the back of the transport with their packs and weapons. Hayden was disappointed but not surprised he wasn't trusted with a firearm.

With both moons set, the star-filled sky provided the only faint illumination. He could discern the outline of the high hills surrounding the parked transport. He recalled from the mission briefing that they were in a narrow gully that fed into a dry riverbed. About a hundred metres beyond, swallowed by darkness, was the other side of the valley.

As the team assembled, he donned his helmet and turned on the IR display. As he did, Caldwell sidled up to him. He was a head taller than Kaine and ten years younger. Assigned as Hayden's babysitter, he was not pleased about it.

Maintaining silence, M'gomba walked up the line, taking a visual roll call. At his order, everyone activated their combat armour stealth fields, and the team set out into the dry riverbed.

In single file, the small group trekked four kilometres up the valley. The surrounding walls grew higher and the riverbed narrower as they gained elevation over the gentle slope.

The wind-blown desert sands underfoot gave way to stream-smoothed rocks, making the going tougher. A misstep by one of the team sent a clatter of stones rolling. As one, the group froze, weapons at the ready as everyone scanned the surrounding hillside. Their stealth fields would shield them from casual observation, but if someone pointed a tactical field scanner in their direction, they were screwed.

Everyone was aware of the exposure their position placed them in. It had been one of the most intensely discussed aspects of the briefing and the one that caused the most discomfort for everyone. But alternate plans had been considered and dismissed as riskier. As foolhardy as it seemed, travelling up the valley to their target under cover of darkness was the best of several poor options.

The hidden airbase they approached still lay a kilometre upstream and another fifty metres above them. It was perched on the edge of a broad plain that ancient glacial runoff had carved into a broad valley system.

A cavern near the top of the cliff had been modified as a hangar for two E-14 attack raptors, capable of atmospheric and orbital operation. They were a formidable weapon, even if they were older models of the ones Hayden had trained on.

A direct assault on the base would be suicidal, so the team's objective was the entrance to a cave system connected to the hangar cavern. The intelligence Krellig's people relied upon indicated the engineers who built the hangar had not discovered it. Of course, the biggest risk of the mission was that the intelligence reports were faulty and that the cave system was monitored to prevent what M'gomba's team attempted.

After sufficient time to assure him their noise had not attracted attention, the signal was given to proceed. Hayden was grateful he hadn't dislodged the stones, and he paid extra attention to where he placed his feet as he continued.

Five minutes later, the group halted near the coulee wall. Six soldiers established a defensive perimeter while the remaining advanced to a two-metre-tall rock perched against the hillside. Four of the men strained in silence against the boulder. As it rolled aside, a small cave opening was revealed, large enough for one person to crawl through.

One at a time, three of the soldiers removed packs and pushed them into the opening before flattening on their bellies and crawling in behind. As they did so, a man and a woman whose names he hadn't learned left the defensive group to continue up the valley. They each carried pulse rifles.

A heavy tap on his shoulder by Caldwell indicated it was Hayden's turn. With a sigh, he dropped his pack to the ground and pushed it ahead of him into the claustrophobia-inducing tunnel.

There was a time he would have suffered a panic attack on being asked to enter such a confining space. His time aboard *Scimitar*, assisting Cora with maintenance inside even more confining access tubes, had acclimated him to tight spaces. He still felt a pang of anxiety when called upon to do something like this, but it was now easier to ignore the paralyzing emotions that once controlled him.

The tunnel was only about ten metres long, and soon Hayden emerged into a wider space. Though still in darkness, his IR display gave him sufficient illumination to feel like he hadn't entered his own grave. The space was small; he and the others were still forced to stand hunched beneath the low ceiling, but he was grateful it no longer felt like he struggled to exit a birth canal.

Caldwell and M'gomba crawled after him into the rocky vestibule. As they emerged, Hayden brought up the map display of the cavern system on his HUD. The team had been warned it was incomplete, and many of the tunnels remained unexplored.

M'gomba shouldered past him and took the lead. Hunched over, Hayden and the others followed into the depths of the earth with only their helmet VR displays to guide them along their intended route. If the map was wrong, they could enter an uncharted tunnel and become lost.

The going was slow. They were forced to crawl through the tight tunnels that connected different caves. Some of the caverns were immense, with three-metre-high stalagmites rising from the floor to meet with stalactites descending from the high ceilings. Others were only large enough for a single person to occupy.

As they moved deeper into the cave network, Hayden fought to keep his claustrophobia from reasserting itself. He was grateful his only visual feedback was through the VR display. It permitted him a degree of disassociation from the reality of his surroundings.

Nearing the end of their journey, they moved in single file through a relatively wide connecting tunnel when the line came to a halt. The soldier who had relieved M'gomba in the lead spoke over the radio.

"It's blocked."

At the words, Hayden's heart rate seemed to double, and the panic he'd kept at bay until now redoubled its effort to overwhelm him.

He consulted the map. They were very close to the end of their route. A few metres ahead, the tunnel system should connect to the deepest recesses of the cavern-cum-hangar.

M'gomba squeezed by the others to join the soldier in the lead.

After a few moments, which felt far too long to be minutes, M'gomba said, "We're here."

Hayden asked, "Why is it blocked?"

He regretted breaking protocol, but instead of remonstrating, M'gomba said, "Because the people who knew about these caves must have hidden this opening when the Feds discovered the cavern on the other side of this wall."

Reining in his growing anxiety, Hayden struggled to recall the details from the briefing about this possibility.

Two of the soldiers removed their packs and dug through them for the required equipment. Drills were produced, and after squeezing to the front of the line, one of them proceeded to bore into the wall and set an anchor. He moved to where the opening should have been and repeated the procedure.

When finished, his companion passed him two pulleys, which he fixed to each of the anchors. The operation was repeated two more times before a thin, carbon-fibre rope was strung between the pulleys. The bundled ropes were passed back, and everyone grasped hold of them.

At M'gomba's command, as one, everyone put their backs into pulling.

"One, two, pull. One, two pull."

With each heave, the rock on the blocking wall began to crumble. The defined outlines of a square-cut door appeared on the stone face.

"One, two, pull. One, two, pull."

Over his radio, Hayden heard the laboured breathing of everyone as they put their strength into dragging open the hidden door.

A line of light broke through the crack. It dawned on Hayden how long they'd been navigating the tunnel system, and he realized it must be midmorning. On the other side of that door lay the hangar-cavern.

They'd done it.

M'gomba signalled for the pulling to stop. Everyone collapsed against the walls of the tunnel to rest. M'gomba's voice came over Hayden's headset.

"Kaine, get up here."

He released the rope and squeezed past the exhausted soldiers, with Caldwell on his heels.

As he arrived, one of the men threaded a fibreoptic cable through the small crack. A second later, Hayden's HUD presented him with a view of the hangar on the other side.

Two E-14 raptors took up most of the space. Both looked prepped and ready to be launched at a moment's notice. Aside from a few maintenance people moving about performing routine jobs, nobody else was in view.

"We're in luck," M'gomba said. "I don't see anyone in there who is armed."

Suddenly, from the other side of the doorway, a klaxon started to blare.

Shit, thought Hayden, *they're on to us.*

"Quiet," hissed M'gomba.

Everyone froze in place as the alarm pulsed. On his HUD, Hayden saw a flurry of activity. Armed soldiers in combat armour appeared, running across the deck and toward the opening hangar doors.

"The alarm isn't for us," said M'gomba. "Something is going on outside."

Hayden listened as the commander tried to reach the teams that remained outside the cave. After several unsuccessful attempts to reach anyone, he said, "The cave might be interfering with the signal."

"Or they may all be dead," said Caldwell.

"No," said M'gomba, "it doesn't sound like that. There hasn't been any gunfire yet. They've been spotted."

As if to prove his point, a distinctive whine, familiar to Hayden, rose in volume beyond the door.

"If they aren't dead, they will be soon," Kaine said. "That's one of the raptors starting up. They're launching it to deal with our team outside."

"Shit," said M'gomba before he repeated his attempt to communicate with them.

"We're screwed," said Caldwell. "After they finish them off out there, they'll have eyes and ears all over that valley. It will only be a matter of time before they find the cave entrance. We're trapped."

Nobody said anything. The entire team retained a professional demeanour. Even Caldwell's comment, though reactive, had been delivered as a fact rather than an exclamation of rising distress. Hayden was impressed by their discipline and was forced to reconsider his initial opinion of Krellig's people. He was ashamed he'd prejudicially viewed them as nothing more than a rag-tag group of locals. These people were all professionals.

"The mission is pooched," said M'gomba. "We'll have to fight our way out through the hangar while we still have the element of surprise and their attention is elsewhere."

Hayden couldn't believe his ears. "You're going to leave your people outside to be torn up by that raptor so you can make your escape."

"It is the only way their deaths will be meaningful."

"That's cold, M'gomba."

"It's war, Mister Kaine."

"Fighting our way through that hangar is crazy. We will be outnumbered and outgunned."

"If we take the initiative while it's available, some of us may get to safety."

"Or we will all be hunted down by the raptor when it is finished shredding the others."

Ignoring Kaine's objection, M'gomba unshouldered his weapon and announced to the team, "Check your firearms and your stealth field generators. We will pull that door open enough for us to squeeze through one at a time. With our stealth fields active, we will make our way along the wall toward the hangar doors. With luck, we won't be spotted until we get to the opening."

As M'gomba relayed his plan, Hayden racked his brain for an alternative.

"Wait," he said. "I have an idea that can save most of us."

M'gomba's men turned to him.

"I'm listening," said M'gomba.

Before replying, he checked the HUD visual of the hangar interior to confirm he hadn't missed something.

"They are only launching one of the raptors. Nobody has boarded the second one, and it is unattended. We can adapt our original plan. It may be easier, in fact, since everyone's attention is directed outside."

"In case you haven't noticed, we've lost the element of surprise," said M'gomba. "They are on high alert out there. Even if you make it to the raptor unseen, the minute you fire up the engine, they'll know something is up. You'll never get that thing off the ground before they open fire."

Kaine shook his head. "For at least fifteen to thirty seconds, most of the deck crew will assume the ship is being launched to support the other one. By the time they figure things out, I'll have engines at full power and the guns primed. Any weapon they have to bring that thing down is directed at the canyon. I will cover everyone's exit with the raptor. I might be able to go after the other one and take it down before it gets to our people in the valley."

M'gomba paused to look at him before saying, "Remove your helmet, Kaine."

"What?"

"Your helmet; take it off."

Confused, Hayden undid the chinstrap and did as he was ordered.

M'gomba removed his own and, for several long seconds, stared through narrowed eyes at him.

Finally, he relaxed his gaze and said, "I wanted to look for deception in your eyes, Kaine. I see none. I believe you are sincere about wanting to help us."

"And?"

"We shall proceed with your proposed plan, with one addendum."

"What's that?"

M'gomba took in a deep breath, then surveyed his men before replying. "You will steal the raptor as you've described, but you will leave with it under our protective fire. You will fly it directly back to Argent."

"What? No! That's crazy; you'll all be killed."

"Obtaining this ship is our primary objective, no matter how many of us it costs. Mister Caldwell will accompany you to ensure you do not deviate from my orders. Am I understood?"

Kaine stared at the commander and knew no argument would change M'gomba's mind. He glanced at the others. Their body language betrayed their commitment to the success of the mission, even if it meant their deaths. He'd never witnessed such fanatical devotion.

He had no other choice. He couldn't make a break with the rest of them. Without a weapon, he'd be little more than a target. Once the raptor finished off the men in the valley, it would return and make short work of this group. Taking the raptor was his only chance of staying alive.

"Okay," he said, "but I think you are selling your lives needlessly."

"Our lives have already been bought and paid for."

With nothing to say in return, Kaine donned his helmet. He moved to the opening, and Caldwell came to stand behind him.

On M'gomba's signal, the others heaved on the ropes and pulled on the door until it was open wide enough for them to squeeze through.

M'gomba stopped him and said, "Caldwell will shoot you if

you deviate from my orders. Get this raptor back to Krellig at all costs."

Hayden swallowed and glanced back at Caldwell. "Understood."

M'gomba released him, and he squeezed through the opening. Stepping into the hangar, he flattened against the stone wall and activated his stealth field so he would blend into the rock face. Seconds later, Caldwell joined him.

Nobody was near the raptor; everyone's attention was focussed elsewhere.

Crouching, both men ran across the deck to the back of the ship. Hayden was relieved to see the access ladder was already down. After checking that they remained unnoticed, he dashed to it and scrambled up, with Caldwell on his heels.

The space inside was cramped. The raptor was a small, manoeuvrable combat flyer capable of orbital and atmospheric flight; basically, a flying engine equipped with a pressurized cabin large enough for a pilot and one passenger.

Kaine ordered Caldwell to raise the ladder and close the hatch as he made his way to the cockpit. He removed his helmet, strapped himself in, and took a moment to become reacquainted with the controls. He was relieved to find the interface did not differ from the more advanced models he'd trained in.

Caldwell came forward to join him.

"Strap in and keep quiet," said Hayden. "I need to focus; it's been a while."

Pulling off his helmet, the other man said, "I thought you said you can fly this."

"Did I?"

As he heard Caldwell's gasp, he smiled and activated the engine. Outside, people nearby turned in surprise. As the whine of the engine rose, the confusion on their faces changed to concern. Then the interface lights turned green and, as Hayden predicted, the observers realized what was happening. He glanced toward the hangar doors. Some of the armed soldiers were running back toward the ship, their weapons raised.

He wasn't concerned. The raptor's armoured hull would stand up to anything short of a pulse cannon at close range.

As bullets bounced off the fuselage, Hayden pushed the throttle. The wind from the vertical thrusters knocked some of the closer bystanders over. The raptor lifted to hang two metres above the deck, engines screaming.

A phalanx of soldiers gathered between them and the doors. To his dismay, two field pulse cannons were among them. But no one's attention was on him. Something behind the raptor captivated their interest.

Seconds later, one of the men carrying a pulse cannon dropped as M'gomba's men laid down cover fire. In the distance, the hangar doors were slowly closing.

Soldiers scrambled for cover behind crates and vehicles.

Hayden activated the weapons system and locked the targeting interface on one of the hangar doors.

Caldwell shouted, "Kaine, watch out."

He looked through the canopy at the unfolding chaos outside. The surviving soldier with a pulse cannon was completing his set-up. In a few seconds, he'd have the raptor in his sights, and their chances would be next to nothing.

Hayden brought the repeating guns online, and without taking the time to sight them, opened fire. He rotated the hovering raptor and raked the guns across the enemy troops. Bullets ripped through crates and ricocheted off the rock walls of the cavern. The man with the pulse cannon vanished in a cloud of blood and bone fragments, as did several of those who were near him.

Deactivating the guns, Hayden turned the raptor back toward the now blocked hangar entrance and reacquired his target.

The ship jerked as its missile launched, and a second later a fireball ignited against the closed hangar doors.

When the smoke and flames dissipated, Hayden was dismayed to see that, though severely bent, and blackened, the doors remained in place.

His pulse quickening, he launched a second missile. This time when the smoke cleared, one of the doors dangled from a single hinge, and the other, though still in place, looked like crumpled aluminum foil.

The raptor lurched as heavy ordnance struck the ship. Hayden's control panel lit up with warnings, but as he scanned them, he was relieved to see they hadn't suffered any significant damage. He looked out the cockpit to see one of the pulse cannons had been recovered and was in the process of charging.

He applied the forward thrusters and directed the ship toward the still partially blocked opening. As the ship accelerated, he fired a third missile.

The raptor flew into the expanding fireball. Hayden's restraints dug into his shoulders as the ship crashed into the remains of the doors.

Then they were airborne and rocketing away from the cliffside with nothing but blue sky overhead.

Kaine exhaled his held breath.

"Holy shit," said Caldwell from behind.

"Yeah," replied Hayden as he turned his attention to the panel lit up like a Christmas tree.

"She's a tough little ship, though. No major structural damage."

"Wow. It's no wonder we haven't been able to bring many of these things down."

"Get in touch with M'gomba," said Hayden. "Tell him to retreat inside the cavern and close the door."

"What?"

Hayden banked the ship. "Tell him to signal when they're inside."

"What are you doing, Kaine?"

"Just do it, Caldwell. I'm trying to save their asses."

He heard the click of a pistol safety being released and glanced back at Caldwell's sidearm pointed at his head.

"You will follow the commander's orders, Kaine."

"Or what? If you shoot me, this thing will crash, everyone will die, and Krellig won't get his precious ship. Put that stupid gun away and let me try to save your friends."

The soldier's eyes darted to the cockpit window. Black smoke billowed from the hangar opening in the side of the cliff. Finally, Caldwell nodded and holstered the gun.

"I owe M'gomba my life a half dozen times over. He can get as mad at me as he wants if we make it through this."

Hayden grinned and returned his attention to the controls.

As they approached the hangar, Caldwell informed him M'gomba and his men were safe.

Kaine slowed the raptor until it hovered outside the blackened maw they'd just escaped from. He reactivated the ship's guns, only now there was time to program the firing computer. With the location of every living thing in the hangar identified by the ship's AI, he gave the order for the computer to fire the weapons.

With deadly precision, the guns fired a short, five-second burst. When they fell silent, Hayden checked the sensor readout and confirmed nobody had survived.

With a rock growing in the pit of his stomach, he said, "Tell M'gomba it's safe to come out."

Turning the hovering ship, Hayden directed it down the coulee in search of the other raptor. He was anxious because enough time had passed for it to have been recalled. He'd anticipated having to engage it when he'd blown through those hangar doors.

He didn't get far when he saw a plume of black smoke rising from the canyon below the hangar entrance.

With his remaining missiles hot and his guns at the ready, he slowly circled downward to investigate, keeping one eye on the perimeter sensors.

As he drew nearer the source of the fire, his worry of being attacked by the other raptor diminished. It evaporated when he finally got a clear look at what lay below.

Resting in a crumpled heap on the rocks at the bottom of the coulee were the burning remains of the other raptor. Embedded in its midsection like an axe in a log was the hangar door Hayden had blown away.

"Damn," said Caldwell, breaking the silence.

Hayden swallowed the lump in his throat. "Yeah."

He pushed the power on the thrusters and pointed the raptor down the valley toward the cave entrance.

As he crept the ship forward, he scanned the rocky floor below, searching for any sign of M'gomba's men. His heart fell when he found what remained of them.

Much as Hayden had done to the soldiers above, the downed raptor's guns had torn the rebels apart.

"I'm sorry, Caldwell."

"The poor bastards never stood a chance."

With nothing to be done for them, Hayden flew farther down the valley. After he confirmed the transport was still there, untouched, and the survivors had a way to return home, he pushed the thrusters and rose into the sky to deliver their prize to Krellig.

TRUST AND FRIENDSHIP

G etting the raptor past Argent's defence network proved more challenging than Hayden anticipated. Even with advance warning to the rebels of their approach by Caldwell, surface-to-air missiles were locked on them from the instant they entered rebel airspace. They were ordered to set down in the desert, twenty kilometres from the village.

It wasn't until the success of their mission was confirmed by the returning M'gomba that Hayden was granted permission to bring the raptor to Krellig.

The ship set down outside of the settlement in a billowing cloud of dust. After Kaine and Caldwell exited the ship and their identities were confirmed, a squad of specialists went over every centimetre of the vessel to confirm there were no bombs or booby-traps aboard.

Only when the safety of their prize was confirmed did Krellig appear, beaming from ear to ear.

"You did it, Kaine. I am very impressed."

"I'm saddened we lost people getting this thing."

Krellig nodded as he approached the raptor. He placed his hand on the fuselage as if confirming it was there. "Everyone knew the risk when they volunteered."

"I was drafted."

A conspiratorial smile turned up the edges of the general's mouth. "Really? I was informed otherwise."

Asshole, thought Hayden.

Noting his disquiet, Krellig said, "I appreciate what you did to save my people. M'gomba wants your head for disobeying him, of course, but let me deal with him. A lot of families owe you a debt of gratitude for bringing their loved ones home. I doubt your glass will be empty during this evening's celebration."

He wanted to inform Krellig that receiving the power core he'd requested was the only appreciation he needed, but he sensed this wasn't the time to bring that up.

Instead, he inclined his head. "I look forward to celebrating with everyone tonight."

The festivities in the village square were still ongoing when he decided to call it a night. The predawn glow of the pending sunrise outlined the hills as he stumbled home. The cool desert air on his face refreshed him and counteracted the effect of too much alcohol in his system.

Hayden turned to the colourfully dressed villagers whirling and laughing as they danced to a song he didn't know. It was a catchy tune, though. Almost enough to make him want to return and ask Emma for one more dance.

He shook his head and whispered drunkenly to himself. "No, that's not appropriate; she might get the wrong idea."

Humming along to the music, he stumbled toward his apartment.

He slept until late afternoon and was only woken from a deep slumber by the persistent knocking on his door.

When he opened it, a soldier snapped to attention and presented a package wrapped in a rough burlap cloth.

"From the general, with his compliments."

After Hayden accepted it, the man turned with perfect military form and strode away.

Smiling to himself, Kaine closed the door and took his gift to the table he was using as a workbench. He glanced at the expressionless face of Cora's synth and said, "What have we here?"

He undid the wrapping and was pleased, but not surprised, by the sight of a pulse rifle power core.

Hayden set to work to confirm by its gauge that it held a full charge. When satisfied it did, he retrieved his tools and removed the casing to expose the internal energy source. On seeing it, recollection of his previous failure came to him.

Realizing this might be his only chance to revive Cora, he resolved to be extra cautious and plan his tinkering more carefully this time. He didn't wish to risk anything while still hungover.

He reattached the cover and set the power core aside. Finding his datapad, he sat down to work out his methodology before he attempted anything.

He worked well into the evening, taking a break only when his stomach reminded him of the need to eat.

It was well past midnight, and many of the merchants in the village square were in the process of shutting down their stalls. Hayden searched among them until he located Ummo's kiosk.

The old man smiled as Hayden approached.

"Good evening, I hope I haven't come too late."

"Not at all," said Ummo, who began to take out the things he'd just finished putting away. "I'm afraid I can only offer you the same thing you had the other day."

Hayden smiled. "I'd like that; it was delicious."

As Ummo prepared the meal, Kaine looked around at the other merchants. "Everyone seems to be closing early tonight."

"We only received word. We are going home to pack."

Hayden frowned. "Pack for what?"

Ummo raised his eyebrows. "You didn't hear? The order came from the Big House that we are relocating."

"The village is being evacuated?"

The old man nodded as he passed Hayden's food to him. "We weren't told why. I suspect it has something to do with that flying machine you stole for Krellig."

Kaine turned again to watch the last of the merchants fold up his storefront.

Facing Ummo, he said, "Where is everyone going?"

He shrugged.

"Well, aren't you concerned?"

Ummo waved a dismissive hand. "This isn't the first time, and it won't be the last. Whatever is happening will blow over, and we'll be permitted to return. Please excuse me, but I must close as well. Can I get you anything else?"

"Uh, no, thanks. I'm afraid I can't pay you for this yet."

The old man smiled. "I told you, Emma's friends don't pay."

"For what it's worth, I'm sorry to be responsible for this."

"Oh, don't waste energy on worry. You did what was necessary, and now we must do the same. Everyone has a duty to the cause, and this is mine."

He gently grasped Hayden's wrist. "Take care of yourself, young man. I can tell Emma is fond of you."

Kaine thanked him and departed to allow him to pack up. He looked at the abandoned square. If an evacuation was underway, it was happening quietly. Perhaps Ummo was confused and there was some other explanation.

He considered going to Krellig but realized even if he'd been the hero of the moment the previous evening, the general didn't owe him any explanations. The power core had been the fulfilment of an implied promise. Krellig only honoured it because there was something in it for him. He did not strike Kaine as a person who let sentimentality influence his decisions.

In a way, he admired Krellig's commitment to the cause he fought for, even if he detested the man's manipulative methods. He cynically wondered what value these villagers held for him that he would go to the required lengths to evacuate them. It didn't make sense. Either Ummo was mistaken, or Hayden did not understand Krellig at all.

Deciding he'd be told what he needed to know when it became necessary, he returned to his apartment to continue working. If there were a planned evacuation, Krellig would not leave him behind; he was the only person who could operate the stolen raptor.

———

A rap at the door broke Hayden's focus. He checked his chronometer to see it was approaching dawn.

When he opened the door, the same soldier who delivered the power core snapped to attention. "Sir, the commander sent me to fetch you."

Without waiting for a reply, the man turned and headed for the stairs. Hayden grabbed his jacket and followed the silhouetted figure lit by torchlight toward the square. He was led past the Big House and down an unfamiliar street to the only building with a light on behind drawn curtains.

His night vision improving, he saw two shadowy figures lurk outside the door and caught glimpses of shouldered weapons in the torchlight of his escort.

The man stopped before the door and gently knocked. The door opened a crack, and whispers were exchanged inside. Then, the door was pulled open, and M'gomba appeared in the opening, gesturing for Hayden to enter.

He crossed the threshold, and the door was shut and locked.

"Krellig is in there." M'gomba pointed to the kitchen. Hayden started walking but paused when the other man didn't follow. He turned back to see M'gomba pulling on his combat jacket. As he slung his pulse rifle over his shoulder, he said, "He wants to speak to you alone."

Without waiting for any kind of reply, he pulled open the door and disappeared outside.

Puzzled, Hayden turned and walked to the kitchen.

Inside, Krellig sat at the small table, intently studying a datapad. He looked up, grim-faced.

"Please take a seat. I'll be with you in a moment."

Krellig returned his attention to the device.

Hayden glanced at the kitchen. Unwashed dishes were piled haphazardly in the sink. Several cupboard doors were open, their interiors empty except for an odd cup or container.

In the corner, a suit of combat armour was draped over the back of a chair. A rifle leaned against it next to an overstuffed backpack.

Hayden pulled the chair out from the table and said, "Going somewhere?"

"The village is being evacuated," said Krellig without looking up. "You and I are the last to leave."

Hayden's heart jumped into his throat. "What about the villagers?"

"Gone; about three hours ago."

"I didn't hear a thing."

A wry half-smile appeared on Krellig's lips. "This isn't their first evacuation."

Kaine wanted to ask why they hadn't told him but was fairly certain of the answer.

As if sensing his question, Krellig put down the datapad and looked up at him. "I'd like you to come with us."

Hayden raised an eyebrow. "I take it you aren't going with the villagers."

"They've gone to hide in the caves nearby. My troops and I are retreating to our backup stronghold."

"What's happened?"

Krellig's forehead creased. "We intercepted a dispatch... several, actually. Vissani's troops are on the move."

"Who is Vissani?"

The general frowned. "The regional administrator, and he is mobilizing all of the troops at his disposal."

"Why?"

Krellig shook his head and smiled. "I guess I've been a bigger thorn in his side than I thought. The comm chatter makes it clear he wants my head for a trophy to take to the governor; he needs something to show for the resources he's expended chasing after us. They are preparing a major offensive against us; something our defence network can't repel."

Krellig, sat back, his hands resting palm down on the table. He regarded Hayden for several seconds.

"I owe you an apology, Kaine."

A small smile tugged at Hayden's mouth. "For locking me in a shed?"

Krellig coughed a short laugh. "I suppose I owe you one for that, too. No, I'm sorry I didn't believe your story about your ship, or the Confederacy, or anything."

Hayden's eyebrow rose. "You accepted my story enough to demand *Scimitar*'s dark energy cannon."

The general wagged a finger. "I told you I wanted your ship's weapon because of what I saw. I never actually believed your story about it being alien technology. I thought it was some new kind of rail gun the imperials thought up."

"So, you thought I was one of Vassani's men?"

Krellig nodded. "Sorry, but I was stringing you along in the hope you might drop some intel."

"Even after the things I've done for you?"

The general shrugged. "The incident at Bantry could have been designed to establish our trust in you."

"And the raptor?"

"That one surprised and confused me somewhat. Sending you was a test designed to force your hand. Instead, you took out an entire airbase. It almost seemed too easy, but I was starting to become convinced you were who you claimed to be; but not quite. It is a horrendous thing to believe Vassani might sacrifice a raptor and an entire airbase just to gain my trust, but it isn't beyond him. Truth told, when we learned his troops were on their way here, I was prepared to order your execution."

Hayden swallowed the lump in his throat. "What changed your mind—I presume you've changed it."

Krellig sighed. "The channels have been full of chatter for the last twelve hours. The government isn't even trying to encode anything. What you told me would happen has."

Hayden's eyes widened. "Thomas has arrived?"

"I don't know if he is here, but a large fleet popped up on the long-range sensor net sixteen hours ago. They were met in a manner like how you described you were. Except that this time, the patrol ships dispatched to greet them were promptly blasted to atoms. The capital received orders to surrender control to the Confederation fleet admiral. The governor and every senior administrator, minor clerk, and soldier on the planet have been recalled to swear allegiance to the Confederacy or face the consequences."

Hayden's blood ran cold. "Shit."

Krellig swallowed as if he had more bad news to convey. He held the datapad toward Kaine.

"What's this?"

"News about your ship."

Hayden snatched the device from Krellig's hand. He scrolled down, skimming most of the text, until *Scimitar*'s name appeared.

He read, then reread the short passage, unable to believe what he read.

"Destroyed?"

"I'm sorry."

"It says she burned up entering the atmosphere."

Krellig spoke quietly. "Whatever survived reentry crashed in the ocean off the coast of the northern continent. They swept the site but found only a few fragments of debris."

Hayden's hands shook as he tried to continue reading through tear-filled eyes. He put the device down and wiped his cheeks with his sleeve.

"The only reason we intercepted this report is that one of the first questions the Confederacy fleet commander asked was about your ship. This is what was transmitted."

He stared at the datapad, only looking up when Krellig's hand rested on his shoulder.

"You are welcome to come with us. I don't know what else to offer you. I can't promise you'll live much longer than if you stay, but I suppose you can take your chances here. I suspect, however, your capture or death might mean a lot more to Vassani than even mine."

Hayden's voice was hoarse. "What will you do?"

Krellig shrugged. "Go to ground. We're good at it. With any luck, there will be confusion when whoever the Confederacy puts in charge arrives to reorganize, and we might be forgotten for a time."

He gestured to the armour and equipment on the chair. "That is for you, regardless of your choice. I wish I could do more for you, Kaine."

"What about the raptor?"

Krellig smiled sheepishly. "I lied to you. I have plenty of excellent pilots. I just didn't have anything for them to fly."

Hayden shook his head, smiling. "I should have guessed."

Krellig nodded curtly. "We are leaving in ten minutes if you're interested."

As the general departed, Hayden grasped the pendant hanging beneath his shirt and wondered how he would be able to tell Cora about *Scimitar*.

Alone in the kitchen, he sat at the table, stunned.

A transport engine starting up outside roused him. He stood and shoved the datapad into his back pocket. Going to the chair, he picked the suit of light armour up off the chair.

Stripping off his torn trousers, he pulled the snug suit on and slipped on the boots. After throwing the pack on his back, he grabbed the heavy rifle and the helmet and followed Krellig out the door.

As he walked toward the transit, a thought nagged at him. Arriving at the vehicle, he was met by Krellig. His men were already aboard.

"Decided to throw your lot in with us?"

He tried to force a smile but could only manage a weak grimace.

"Give me one minute, please. There is something I need from my room."

Krellig frowned.

"Please? Everyone else had more warning than I got."

"What could you possibly need?"

Hayden opened his mouth to explain, but Krellig waved a hand. "Be quick. You have one minute, then we are gone."

Hayden turned and dashed across the square.

Bounding up the steps, he crashed through the door to his apartment and stood on the threshold long enough to locate what he wanted.

Grabbing his improvised interface and the new power core, he threw them in the pack and rushed back to the awaiting transport.

He climbed aboard as the vehicle was pulling out.

Krellig shook his head at him.

Hayden replied without being asked, "Yes, it was worth it."

He went to the only available seat, shoved the pack under it, and sat down.

Through the window, he tried to watch the village of Argent as they departed, but the darkness swallowed up everything outside. Having grown fond of the place, he wanted to bid it farewell, and he hoped the government troops would spare it for the villagers to return to.

A MISSION

A vibrating surge shot up his arm, and Hayden's hand was jolted back by an invisible force.

Tingling from fingertip to shoulder, he stepped back from the workbench and eyed the responsible device.

"Shock yourself?"

There was more amusement in Chang's voice than concern.

Not turning to her, he replied, "It shouldn't have done that."

"Do you even know what you're doing?"

She stood next to him and joined him in his study of the Glenatat interface.

When he didn't respond, she nudged him with her elbow. He jumped at her touch as if shocked a second time.

Hayden stared at her for a second, then shook his head. "I thought I did. It was...weird."

Chang's brow furrowed, and she looked at him. "Maybe I should take you back to medical and check you out."

He shook his head and forced a gruff guffaw. "I'm fine; it just caught me off guard."

"Why are you rubbing your arm? Can you move it?"

Hayden frowned as he released his shoulder and raised the affected arm to flex his fingers in her face. "All good—see?"

"Hmph, there might be other brain damage."

He smiled. "None that wasn't there before I met you."

She shrugged and turned her attention back to the work-bench. "What are you working on anyway? Hey, is that a pulse power core?"

Hayden interposed himself between her and the bench.

"Is there some reason you're here, Ms. Chang?"

After a second, she gave up trying to peek around his back and looked up at him with a mischievous twinkle in her eye. The scent of her shampoo conjured memories of Stella, and he unconsciously tensed every muscle.

Seeing his expression, she took a half step back. "Sorry, I didn't mean to pry. You weren't at breakfast or lunch, so I thought I would check up on you, but you're busy."

She started to turn to leave.

"You're not prying." He softened his expression and forced a smile. Stepping aside, he allowed her to examine what he'd been working on.

Cautiously, she stepped toward the bench. Pointing at the power core, she said, "Isn't that dangerous?"

The core's casing was removed, and soldered wires connected it to the Glenatat device. Cora's memory crystal lay on the table next to it.

"Not if you know what you're doing," he said.

She looked at him and raised a questioning eyebrow.

He blushed. "I'm not an expert in this sort of thing."

She nodded and returned her attention to his work. He was grateful she resisted the temptation to tease him about his apparent lack of competence.

"What are you trying to do? Is this alien technology?" She pointed at the crystal.

He sighed. "Yes. I'm trying to establish a connection with it, and I needed the power core to jumpstart the interface."

She bent closer to examine the crystal without touching anything. "Is it a weapon?"

"No, it's a..." He frowned. How could he explain Cora to her in a way that wouldn't generate a thousand questions—even prompt her to run to Krellig to shut him down?

"A database, then?"

Hayden let the building tension fall from his shoulders. He leaned forward and picked up the crystal to show her. "I suppose part of it is a database. I'm interested in accessing its interpreter."

Her eyes lit up. "Oh, it's an AI. Why didn't you say so?"

He nodded. "Yes, an AI; that's right. An alien one."

"The Glenatat you mentioned are who built it?"

"They are."

She smiled and then turned back to admire what was in his hand.

"Did you meet them? Where are they? What are they like? I'm sorry if I'm asking too many questions, but the idea of an alien intelligence existing out there fascinates me."

He laughed. "Whoa, slow down. The Glenatat are an ancient race, a disembodied intelligence. They live in some region near the galactic core—or in an alternate dimension. I'm not really sure about that."

"What do you hope to learn from talking to it?" She pointed at the crystal.

His face fell, and he swallowed. "My original hope was to use this to find my ship."

Silence fell between them.

He blinked back tears and cleared his throat. "Now, I suppose I just want to see if it can help us with anything in its database."

That was the cover story he'd given Krellig.

When he first heard of *Scimitar*'s fate, it felt like a punch to the gut. He was too stunned to think of anything. Only Krellig's prompting gave him any sort of direction. Without it, he might have wandered off into the wilderness until thirst claimed him.

Only the thought of Cora prompted him to recover the

interface from his room. While the loss of *Scimitar* and Pavlovich was devastating, the additional loss of her would have been too much. He'd grabbed the items with no idea how he would make it all work, only the need to make it so.

Cora might, of course, be able to access her memories to invent something to help Krellig and his rebels, but that was secondary. He just needed to know she lived in some form.

"Well, we can sure use anything to give us a chance at surviving," said Chang, bringing him back to the present.

"I can't promise any kind of success."

"As long as you don't blow us all to kingdom come..." She winked. "It's just important to us you are trying, Hayden."

Her hand rested on his shoulder. "But you need to feed yourself. I expect to see you at supper."

He smiled. "Yes, ma'am."

She returned his smile and left the room.

He didn't know if her concern for him was because of her role as a medic, or if she genuinely cared. It didn't matter to him, since he had no intention of forging any bonds with these people. They were a safe shelter in a storm; that was all. His real family—or what was left of it—was all he needed. That, of course, presumed he could reconnect with Cora. If he couldn't find a way...

No, he thought. *Mustn't think like that.*

He turned his attention to the workbench. Hesitantly, he reached for the power core. When it didn't shock him, he relaxed and picked it up to examine.

He frowned at the power readout. It was half drained.

"What the hell?"

He looked at the hand that had been shocked. The jolt he'd received had been a few volts at best. Little more than a big static zap. It was not enough to drain a power core capable of outputting five hundred megawatt hours.

Placing the core on the table, he bent down to examine the Glenatat crystal. The only place that power could have gone was into it, but there was no way to tell. It was possible the core Krellig gave him had a faulty readout and was never fully charged. He wished he understood the Glenatat technology enough to know what was going on.

He picked up Cora's memory crystal. He wished he knew what he was doing.

He rubbed his temple to ease the building headache. At the same time, his stomach growled, and he realized the penalty he was paying for his obsessive focus over the last few hours.

Slipping the crystal in his pocket, he decided he would think better with some food in him. Perhaps he could talk the cook into giving him a snack to hold him until supper.

"There you are, Kaine."

Krellig entered the kitchen and sidled up next to him on the bench.

"Don't let me interrupt your meal," he said, "I can wait."

Hayden nodded his appreciation and swallowed what was in his mouth.

"It's okay. I can multitask."

Krellig smiled. "How is your experiment coming?"

Hayden shook his head. "Not sure if I'm on the right approach. I'm afraid it may be some time..."

The commander shook his head. "That's not why I'm here." He regarded Hayden expectantly.

Taking his cue, Kaine set his fork down and pushed the plate away. "We can talk now."

"Great! I can use your help with an opportunity that has presented itself."

"Sure; what is it?"

"I want you to lead a raid."

"You recall until a couple of days ago I was a prisoner you considered executing?"

Krellig waved away the argument. "I was never going to shoot you. Besides, you're all-in with us now...." He grinned. "Ready to prove yourself and all that, right?"

Hayden sighed. "You have a mission you don't want to risk your people on."

"Kaine! You *are* one of my people."

Hayden nodded, confident in his reading of the other man. "What do you want me to do for you?"

Krellig cocked a questioning eyebrow.

Realizing his error, he amended, "I meant to say, 'for us.'"

The commander's smile returned. "Exactly." He exhumed a datapad from his pocket and placed it on the table between them. "We keep getting a lot of unfiltered chatter. This morning, this came to my attention."

He turned the pad and pushed it toward Hayden. After studying the document, he looked up at Krellig.

"It says the local detachment is to have its commander changed. So what?"

"Did you read who is replacing her?"

Hayden reexamined the information, then shrugged. "Never heard of her. So what?"

"Neither have I, and I know every officer above the rank of second lieutenant."

Hayden frowned. "You think her replacement might be from the Confederacy fleet?"

"It would make sense, wouldn't it? Put new officers in place with a few trained rangers under their command. It would help to ensure a more orderly transition of power."

Hayden shrugged. "Sure, I suppose so. Why is this news so important?"

"Because, my friend, it implies the new guard doesn't trust the old one to obey them. They are replacing anyone in a position to cause them the smallest amount of trouble."

Kaine nodded. "It's a sound tactic."

"I see it as an opportunity for us."

Hayden frowned. "What is the mission?"

"This particular detachment is the one chasing us. They are camped about fifty kilometres from here, looking in the wrong place. I need someone to go on a little spy mission."

"Sorry?"

"It is possible this intel, and a lot of the other stuff flying around, is bullshit broadcast for our benefit. I need to verify this is a real thing."

"How will this help? It might be staged to support the false intelligence."

Krellig shook his head. "Kaine, you don't understand. This is one of literally thousands of communiqués being transmitted between the Confederation fleet and the capital every hour. And although our little group has been an annoying thorn in this regime's paw, that's all we have been—annoying. If they had the resources to devote to snuffing us out, along with the other dozen groups like ours around the planet, they would have long ago sent more support to the local governors."

"You're saying you aren't important enough for them to resort to a trap."

"Especially when they have bigger worries of how to keep their own heads right now."

Hayden nodded. "So, if we can confirm this is taking place, then it will mean everything you intercept is probably legitimate."

Krellig beamed. "Precisely so—and I like how you used the word 'we' just now."

"Did I?"

Krellig slapped him playfully on the shoulder, prompting Hayden to smile.

"Fine, what do you want me to do?"

"Just a recon mission, only; not a raid. I don't want to put any spotlight on us for now. Find the detachment camp and watch for what happens."

"If the Confederation sends a replacement, we'll know what's really happening. Sure, sounds simple enough. What kind of support do I get?"

"I'm sending two of my best with you, Caldwell and Hashido."

"Only the three of us?"

"It's reconnaissance, remember. Fewer chances of being detected."

Hayden nodded. "Okay, when do we leave?"

"After sundown; in the dark with stealth shields to mask your thermal signal, you won't be easily spotted from orbit. You should get something to eat and prepare your kit."

"Aye-aye." Hayden saluted, then with a smirk, he turned to go. He stopped and called back to Krellig. "By the way, the charge indicator on that power core you gave me is faulty. It only had a partial charge."

"Really? Sorry about that; I'll get you another one when you return."

Kaine departed with an uneasy feeling the reason the power core wasn't as advertised was that the rebel leader didn't yet trust him. Hopefully, this mission would change that.

The sand itched beneath his armour, and he couldn't scratch.

Beneath the broiling midday sun, Kaine and the others lay on their bellies, peering over a ridge.

"I count thirty regulars," whispered Caldwell. "Oops, make that thirty-one."

A soldier emerged from behind a transport vehicle, zipping up his trousers.

"Where's the commander?"

"Probably waiting inside the vehicle where it's cool," replied Hashido with a chuckle.

Hayden longed to wipe away the sweat tickling his eyebrows, but the closed visor prevented any such indulgence. Even wearing the thermally controlled armour, he was uncomfortably warm. He wondered how long a person would last without any protective gear this deep in the central desert.

Hayden said, "Why are they here, of all places?"

Caldwell shifted position to look at him. His armour's camouflage field flickered subtly as he did so. Hayden couldn't see his expression behind the visor. "What do you mean?"

"Aren't they supposed to be searching for us? They seem to be going in the opposite direction."

"That tells you how good their intelligence is," said Hashido.

Hayden didn't believe the government troops were that incompetent. "Look around us. This dune is the only elevated point for kilometres, and it is barely able to conceal us."

"Count your small blessings, Kaine. We were damned lucky they stopped near it," replied Caldwell. "Otherwise, we would have to watch them from over there."

He gestured toward the distant volcanic ridge kilometres away.

Hayden frowned. "My point is they are exposed. They haven't set up any kind of perimeter. Tactically, it is the stupidest thing they could do. It doesn't make sense."

"They're waiting here to meet with their new commanding officer," said Hashido. "It's probably what they were ordered to do."

"Hmph," said Caldwell. "More like a hostage exchange than a change of command."

Kaine agreed with Caldwell. The isolated location provided no position for gunners to conceal themselves from an orbital scan. An approaching dropship would have an unimpeded view of the surrounding terrain and some assurance they wouldn't be ambushed after landing. It spoke volumes to how little the invaders trusted in a peaceful transition of power.

He was grateful for the limited stealth technology built into his armour. It wouldn't protect them from a detailed scan, but it would be sufficient to conceal them from a routine survey if they didn't move unnecessarily.

His heads-up display popped to life, indicating a fast-approaching ship.

"Here they come," he said.

The troops around the transport scrambled to obey their sergeant, who yelled at them to make themselves presentable and gather in ranks. From the vehicle, the local commander emerged, strapping on her helmet. Her shoulders were slumped, as if in defeat.

A shadow crossed over them, and everyone except the now assembled troops looked up at the landing dropship. A thick cloud of dust kicked up under the roar of engines as the craft elegantly settled in place twenty metres away.

"Holy shit, that's big," whispered Caldwell.

"I've never seen anything like it," said Hashido.

"Antilles class, from a heavy cruiser," said Hayden. "It's a new design," he added after recalling how long his companions had been isolated from the rest of the Confederation.

Neither of the men responded. Their attention was captured by what was taking place only a few dozen metres away. The dropship's door opened, and a ramp extended. Before it contacted the sand, five armed and armoured troops descended and formed a defensive phalanx. The squad commander appeared to evaluate the troops assembled in front of them, and after a few seconds, he turned to beckon someone to join them.

"Are those Rangers?" Hashido asked.

"Yes," said Kaine.

"Shit, I have never seen any before. Will you look at the size of them; all over two metres tall, and they look mean."

A uniformed officer descended the ramp. Something about the man's manner struck a nerve. The way he carried himself, flaunting—not his rank, but the authority he represented; the authority of a long-absent parent who'd come home to a mess the children were responsible for.

But it wasn't only that. Hayden was raised on Earth, where the air of superiority adopted when dealing with anyone from the outer systems was second nature to many. It hadn't been until he was sent away to serve under Pavlovich that he'd realized it was as much a part of him as it was with the strutting peacock who now marched past the assembled men and zeroed in on their commander. It took a lot of time and patience on Pavlovich's part, but over time the captain affected a change of the ingrained prejudices of his headstrong young first officer.

The replacement commander imperiously approached the commandant. He stopped two metres away and waited to be saluted before he returned the courtesy. Only then did the fellow's self-satisfied expression turn to condescension as he began to address his counterpart.

"What do you think he's saying?" Caldwell asked.

"Hi there. Lovely day. Sorry to be sending you to the gulag and all," said Hashido.

Hayden slipped the pulse rifle from his shoulder and began to inspect it.

Caldwell hissed, "What are you doing, Kaine? Our orders are to observe and report, nothing else."

Finished checking that his weapon was charged, Hayden lowered it and turned to face the others.

"When do you imagine another opportunity like this might present itself? Between the three of us, we have enough fire-power to take out everyone down there before they could locate us and get a shot off."

"Kaine," said Hashido, "those are Rangers. I have heard stories of what one of those guys can do. There are five of them."

Hayden turned and checked the scene. After two seconds, with his eyes still evaluating his intended target, he said, "Look at them."

With obvious reluctance, Caldwell and Hashido followed his gaze. The Rangers seemed relaxed as they casually cradled their weapons. One or two of them shifted their weight. They reminded Hayden of bored teachers supervising children at recess, impatient to return to another duty they considered more significant.

"They came to put on a show, fly the colours and use their presence and reputation to intimidate the locals. No one else down there is armed."

That wasn't exactly true. The commandant and the sergeant both wore a holstered sidearm, which would be ineffectual against anyone wearing even minimally rated armour.

"Those Rangers are not taking it seriously. We can easily get the drop on them."

"They're wearing combat armour," said Caldwell, his tone rising.

"We have three fully charged pulse rifles. Also, let's not forget that missile launcher you bitched about carrying all this way. If you had no intention of using it, why did you bring it?"

"In case we encountered another aircraft."

Hayden shrugged. "So, use a rocket on the dropship while it's grounded."

"Kaine," said Hashido, "even if we agreed with your suicidal craziness, Krellig would have our balls for breakfast. He specifically ordered us to only watch. What part of that do you have the most difficulty with?"

Hayden sighed and shifted his position to look directly at them both. "Since I met you, the only thing I have seen Krellig do is to retreat or send out parties with no mission other than gathering information or stealing shit. If this is a rebellion, when was the last time you guys saw any action?"

Hashido shrugged. "I dunno, a few weeks."

"Thirty-six weeks," said Caldwell. "We've done nothing but hunker down and avoid patrols since the disaster at Vinarra."

Hayden said, "What happened there?"

Hashido said, "We got really bad intel and walked into an ambush. Krellig managed to get most of us out, but we lost fifteen, and over half of us were wounded. Since then, he hasn't trusted any intelligence."

"So, what is he waiting for?"

"Damned if I know."

"I think it scared him," said Caldwell. "You should have seen his face when I told him what we found at Bantry; he looked like someone had stepped on his grave."

Hayden turned to check on events at the transport. The imperial officer was droning on, apparently fond of his own voice. Returning his attention to his companions, Kaine said, "Look at them down there—not the Rangers. Everyone else is demoralized and cowed."

He gave them a few seconds to check. "The same thing is happening all over the planet. The Confederation would love nothing better than to restore their authority without so much as a single complaint from the locals. It makes their job so much easier and allows them to finish up and move on to the next system. What do you think will happen to your rebellion once they've installed their own officers?"

He didn't wait for them to answer. "They will lower the hammer on you so fast, you guys won't know what hits you. These troops specialize in suppressing uprisings."

"So how will attacking change any of that?" said Hashido.

"For starters, it will slow things down; send the message this planet will not be the doormat they believe it to be."

"How will that help us? They will see us as a more urgent threat."

"Not if they're busy clamping down on the local forces first. If we get this right, nobody will suspect us; they'll believe these guys killed each other."

"What about the dropship?"

"It's a sitting duck right now, especially for those rockets."

"This is crazy," said Hashido. "You will just make things worse by attacking them."

"And how will things get better if we don't act? You guys are supposed to be fighting a rebellion, and you're all afraid of getting a bloody nose. If you don't have the stomach for it, why did you even join Krellig?"

Both men avoided his gaze.

"The government deported my parents to a labour camp on Camden," said Hashido. "The only thing they were guilty of was having the wrong friends."

"I was in the same prison they broke Krellig out of," said Caldwell. "I couldn't go home, so I decided to join him. The general was different back in those days; surer of himself."

He looked up at Hayden. "What I don't get is why you're so keen to stir up the pot. What's in this for you?"

Kaine imagined *Scimitar* plunging through the planet's atmosphere to its doom, and his blood ran hot.

"Me? Let's say I've had an epiphany about the Confederation. I also know the new president well enough to only expect things to get much worse for anyone who doesn't agree with him. Besides, the son of a bitch wants me dead, so if I see a chance to kick him in the balls, I'll take it."

Both men stared at him for a few seconds before Caldwell said, "I dunno about this."

Hashido jumped on him. "Are you seriously considering Kaine's goofy idea?"

"He makes a good point, Hash."

"You two are nuts. We are going to follow orders."

Hayden couldn't see either man's expression through their visors, though the way Caldwell compulsively regripped his weapon suggested he might yet be persuaded to act.

Kaine said, "Why do we have these weapons?"

"Self-defence—that's it," said Hashido firmly.

He nodded. "That's what I thought."

He rolled to his belly and brought the pulse rifle up to look through its sites.

Hashido hissed, "What the hell are you doing, Kaine?"

Without taking his eyes from the gun site, he said, "Get ready to defend yourselves, boys."

Hayden told himself he wasn't being irrational. Still, he hesitated. So much could go wrong. If he were more objective, he'd agree with Hashido that his idea was insanely risky, but he couldn't get the thought of the burned-out village or of *Scimitar* out of his head.

His life was all gone. Everyone he loved was dead. Stella, Pavlovich...even Cora. He had no idea if he could restore her. Maybe she was better off remaining dormant in that crystal than being revived, only to have no recollection of what had happened to her in the past ten years. The shock might drive her mad.

If he was going to be forced to start building a new life, he didn't want it to be under the boot heel of Thomas and his new empire. He would rather die here and now. Better that fate than to hide like vermin until he was captured and turned over to the president.

Part of his attention was on his companions. What would they do?

Shoot him in the back, for one thing.

He didn't care. Let the chips fall where they may.

He zeroed in on the Ranger commander.

Hashido and Caldwell crawled up on either side of him, their guns aimed at the troops below.

Hayden smiled to himself. "I've got the Ranger leader. Caldwell takes out the two on his left; Hashido goes to the right. Aim for the joint in their armour at the neck."

"Got it," said Caldwell.

"Yes sir," said Hashido with no sarcasm in his voice. Both men seemed to accept Hayden's assumption of command.

He swallowed the last of his hesitation and said, "Let's make some history."

"Un-fucking-believable!"

Krellig paced back and forth before Caldwell and Hashido. Both men had removed their helmets but stood at rigid attention.

Arms crossed over his chest, Hayden stood separate from them, leaning against a table. The commander had elected to vent at his own men before he dealt with him.

"Caldwell—tell me your version of what happened."

The soldier swallowed nervously. Keeping his eyes forward he spoke loudly and clearly.

"Sir, at approximately eleven-hundred hours we engaged with—"

"Stop!"

Krellig glared at him. "Why do I get the feeling you are about to tell me the same bullshit story Hashido did?"

Caldwell stiffened further. "Sir, it's the truth."

The commander stepped closer until their noses almost touched. "You expect me to believe that after you three had remained effectively hidden for the better part of an hour, you were suddenly detected and fired upon?"

"Yes, sir."

"And what do you think gave you away? Did one of you fart?"

"I don't recall, sir. My stomach may have rumbled."

Hayden snorted, quickly covering his mouth to hide it. Krellig glared at him for a few seconds before returning his attention to Caldwell. He stepped back, rubbing his temple.

"So, if I'm to believe this fairytale, after one of you farted, or belched, the Rangers began shooting at your position."

"Yessir."

"And under heavy enemy fire, from a crack squad of Rangers, no less, you three managed to take them all down."

"Using pulse rifles; yes, sir."

Krellig nodded and replied slowly, "Pulse rifles...right. After this, you continued to defend yourselves from the assembled ground troops who had somehow managed to conjure weapons... is that correct, soldier?"

"Sir, I don't know how they came by firearms."

"Maybe that's because this whole story smells like complete and utter BULLSHIT!"

Krellig didn't give Caldwell time to respond. "Not only that, but you three supermen also managed to destroy the ground transport and a state-of-art gunship."

"I believe it was Antilles class, sir."

Krellig's eyes widened, "Oh, Antilles class, was it? It must have had shit for armour if you took it out without resorting to your rockets."

"Um, I guess we got a lucky shot or two in, sir."

Krellig stared at him. Sighing, he waved them away, saying, "Go, get something to eat and clean yourselves up. I'll deal with you both later."

"Yes, sir," chimed both soldiers in unison before they quickly exited the room.

Krellig watched them leave before he turned to Hayden.

"Those two..." He shook his head. "Please tell me this was your idea."

"They're good soldiers, Krellig."

"I knew that already. I also trusted them to obey my orders, so I can only imagine it was something you said that conned them into disobeying. You're the one I should be furious with."

Hayden arched an eyebrow. "You're not?"

Krellig studied him for a moment. "I really should have you taken out and shot as an example."

"Why haven't you?"

Krellig narrowed his eyelids. "Listen to them."

The distant sounds of celebration could be barely heard from somewhere in the complex.

"They think they are being discreet," said Krellig.

"Can you blame them? From what I've been told, this is the most significant military victory you've had in months."

"You mean *we've* had, don't you?"

Kaine shook his head slowly. "This hasn't been my war, General. Until today, that is," he said with a mischievous grin.

Krellig frowned. "Get the hell out of here before I reconsider assembling a firing squad."

CORA'S SECRET

Hayden thought it best to avoid Krellig to let him cool off. Over the next few days, the fallout from his unsanctioned action began to manifest. Initial indications from the monitored chatter were that tensions between the planetary government and Thomas's forces increased by the day. Both sides accused the other of instigating the altercation. To everyone's surprise, there was no mention of possible rebel involvement.

Krellig reminded everyone that didn't necessarily mean they weren't suspected of being involved, only that the local government couldn't prove it. The incident had slowed down the transfer of power, which was good news to the rebels because it gave them more time to regroup.

Three days after the incident, Krellig departed for a meeting with the rebel leadership to determine their next course of action. With M'gomba in charge, Hayden took the opportunity to make himself scarce by staying in his quarters to work on recharging the Glenatat battery.

Hayden's first problem was to determine if Krellig gave him a depleted power core. Given the rebel leader's mood, he didn't think it wise to press the matter, so he waited until the general departed before he invited Emma to join him in his quarters after dinner.

She arrived at his door wearing a fresh uniform. Her skin glowed, and she'd applied some makeup. He invited her in, and as she passed near him, the smell of shampoo caressed his nostrils.

Worried he'd given her the wrong impression of why he'd invited her, he decided to be direct. He went to the workbench and picked up an object wrapped in an old cloth.

Returning to her, he unwrapped the package to reveal the depleted power core.

She was confused. Embarrassed, he blurted out his request. When he was finished, she appeared crestfallen.

"You want me to steal a power core for you," she said.

Hayden winced. "An exchange would be the more appropriate way to describe it."

"Okay, you want me to swap this depleted core for a new one."

"Preferably one you can verify holds a full charge."

Frowning, she accepted the device from him and weighed it in her hand as she studied it.

She looked up, and they stared at each other for a few seconds before she broke off. "What makes you think I won't tell M'gomba what you're up to?"

"Because you are fascinated by the Glenatat and their technology. This is the only way to show you how it works."

Her face lit up. "Do you mean that? You'll show me?"

He smiled. "You bought me supper; I owe you."

Her elation faded, and her brow creased as she regarded the power core again.

"It won't be easy, but I think I know of a way." She looked up at him. "Give me a couple of hours."

He nodded soberly, not wishing to ask her what she planned, and she didn't appear to want to tell him.

She wrapped the power core in the cloth and went to the door. There, she paused and turned around. Her cheeks were red.

"I'm sorry I misinterpreted your invitation."

"No, Emma, please; it's my fault. I had no intention of giving you the wrong idea, and I apologize for embarrassing you; if I were ten years younger—"

She smiled wanly. "Can we...can we pretend this didn't happen?"

Hayden felt himself blush. "Of course. Thank you for agreeing to help me."

Her smile broadened. "I'll be back as soon as I can. Don't start without me."

With that, she was gone.

He stared at the closed door for several seconds, then shook his head and thought, *Kaine, you could have handled that a lot better.*

Stella and Cora would probably both have sharp words for him about his obtuseness. He should have clued into how Emma felt a lot sooner and put a stop to it before it came to this. While she seemed to bounce back from her embarrassment, he could see she was hurt.

He promised himself to make it up to her. He'd show her everything he could about the Glenatat. If things worked out, he'd introduce her to Cora; he was certain they'd like each other.

He hoped things would work out. He had no idea what he'd do if they didn't.

After Emma returned, triumphant, with the prize, Hayden got to work.

For the first hour, she sat at the table that served as Hayden's workbench, watching everything he did. As time went by, she interrupted his concentration often with questions. He did his best to answer them in the simplest way possible, but as they continued to interrupt his train of thought, he more than once squelched a sarcastic response that would betray his growing annoyance.

But when he found an error in his logic when forced to restart a process she'd interrupted, he realized her questioning had prevented a disaster. Afterward, he didn't mind answering her queries in as much detail as possible, since it made what he was doing all the clearer to him.

After a few hours, out of the corner of his eye he saw her yawn.

"Tired?"

She stretched her arms over her head and straightened her back. "Mmm, my shift starts in a few hours. I should go."

He could tell those words came reluctantly, so he said, "You can grab some sleep on my bunk. I'm too engrossed to quit until I'm finished."

Her brow crinkled. "You're okay with that? You don't want people to get the wrong impression about us?"

Hayden smiled but retained his focus on the delicate connection he worked on. "I'm okay with it if you are."

"You mean that?"

He put down his tools and looked at her. "I've found that people will believe what they want. Whether you stay or go only depends on what you want them to believe of you."

She became thoughtful. "In that case, I think I'll return to my quarters. I don't want anyone to think of you like a dirty old man who seduces young women."

Taken aback, he stared at her until she broke into a broad smile. Then they both laughed.

"I deserved that," he said.

"Damn right you did."

She stood and put on her jacket. When she reached the door, she said, "Promise you'll call me when you get this stuff running, okay?"

"Are you sure? It may only be a couple more hours."

"I'm sure. Promise?"

He nodded. "Yes, I won't start it up unless you are here to see it."

"Great."

She cracked open the door and peeked outside before she smiled her goodbye to him and slipped out.

Hayden smiled to himself as he returned his attention to the delicate task at hand.

After what seemed like a few minutes later, he heard noises in the corridor. Checking his chronometer, he was shocked to see he'd worked through the night.

He rubbed his eyes and stretched the stiffness from his shoulders. Fortunately, he had no active duties and was free to sleep whenever he wanted.

He turned to admire his work, proud of himself. All that remained to do was to connect the Glenatat battery to Cora's crystal. He hesitated, recalling his promise to Emma.

She would be starting her shift in the infirmary in a few minutes and wouldn't be available until it was over.

As eager as he was to turn on the apparatus and speak to Cora—assure himself she was all right—he was also fearful.

What if she wasn't all right? What if the unthinkable had happened and she no longer existed? Did he want to face that disappointment alone? Emma was the only person who knew about Cora or had an inkling of what she meant to him.

He realized he wanted her support in case things went badly.

He picked up his datapad and sent her a message before he collapsed on his bunk and fell into an uneasy sleep.

"Cora? Can you hear me? It's Hayden."

Both he and Emma leaned on the table, eyes fixed on the glowing crystal that contained all that remained of *Scimitar*'s engineer.

Emma's arrival had roused him from a fitful sleep, interrupted by vivid dreams of Cora and Pavlovich. Before activating the interface, he had spent another hour double-checking and testing the delicate connections between technologies with little in common.

Yet, despite his worst fears, the Glenatat battery brought the makeshift interpretive interface to Cora's crystal to life once more.

Now all that remained to cap his success was for Cora to respond.

But she was silent.

Failing to control the rising panic in his voice, Hayden called again.

"Cora, are you there? Please answer if you can."

He and Emma waited, both seemingly afraid to move lest the rustle of clothing cause some unfathomable disturbance that would sabotage their efforts.

Each passing second took with it a little of the hope that remained in his heart.

"Is it you, Hayden? I still can't see anything."

He leaned closer to the interface. "Yes, Cora, it's me. Thank God you're still there."

"Where else would I be, silly? I've been talking to you this whole time."

He frowned. "Do you remember getting sleepy?"

A pause.

"Yes, but I feel fine now. Did I doze off?"

He nodded. "I suppose you did."

"I'm so sorry; that was rude of me. How long did I sleep?"

Hayden wiped away the tear forming. "Not very long; you were tired, so I thought I'd let you rest."

"I guess I needed it. I feel great now, but I don't know why I can't connect to any of my visual feed links on the ship. Did something happen?"

Hayden frowned, puzzled. "What is the last thing you remember?"

"Hmm, that's odd; my memory seems to be fragmented. I recall our arrival in the Oberon system—oh, yes, the ship was hit by...wait, we were under attack, weren't we?"

Kaine almost laughed with delight. "Yes, that's right, we arrived in the middle of a battle. Do you recall anything else?"

"Umm, no. What happened? Is *Scimitar* disabled? Oh, God, I'm sorry. Here I am sleeping on the job when I should be making repairs and—"

"Cora, wait."

Hayden's joy at Cora having most of her memories was extinguished as he searched for the words to tell her what happened. Only when Emma grasped his hand did he remember she was there. He looked at her, feeling helpless.

"You sound upset, Hayden. What happened?"

He cleared his throat.

"Um, we took a hit from a nuke. It fried most of the systems. Pavlovich gave the abandon ship order—"

"He did what?"

"We'd lost all control and were under heavy fire. I was knocked out, and Pavlovich ordered you to put me in an escape pod. Um, it was attacked and shot down. Your avatar was damaged, so I downloaded you into a memory matrix. I've only just managed to awaken you."

There was a long pause.

"I have no recollection of any of that. Where are the others?"

Tears ran down his cheeks. "I don't know."

"Hayden, what happened to *Scimitar*?"

He struggled to swallow. "Uh, I was told a few days ago she'd crashed—well, uh...shit! She burned up in the atmosphere."

Silence settled on the room like a funeral shroud over a casket.

"Cora?"

"I'm still here, Hayden."

"I'm sorry."

"Did anyone else escape?"

"I really don't know."

Another long silence fell over them.

"So, it's just us then."

"I'm afraid that may be so."

"Hayden, are you certain *Scimitar* burned up? Did you see her go down?"

"Well, no, but I was informed by a reliable source—well, I think he's reliable."

"Hayden, I think you were misinformed. I'm pretty sure *Scimitar* is in one piece."

"Cora, I want to be as hopeful as anyone, but—"

"No, you misunderstand me. I don't hope *Scimitar* is intact. I know without a doubt she is."

Hayden's heart was in his throat. "How do you know?"

"Because I'm talking to her right now."

Agape, Hayden turned to Emma.

She said, "What does it—I mean, she, mean?"

"Hayden, who is that?"

"Uh, Cora, this is Emma Chang. She's a friend. Are you sure you're talking to *Scimitar*? Is she intact?"

There was a pause.

"Yes, she's hale and healthy, considering what she's been through."

"You're speaking as if the ship is alive," said Emma.

"Hayden, should we be having this conversation with someone else around?"

"Cora, do you still trust me?"

"Implicitly—you know that."

"Then trust my judgement. Emma helped me to get you back online."

After another pause, Cora said, "I'm pleased to meet you, Emma Chang. Please pardon my rudeness. You haven't caught me at my best."

"Uh, that's understandable, and it's nice to meet you too."

"To answer your question in the simplest possible way, *Scim-*

itar is not alive in the manner you would understand. Neither am I, for that matter. The Glenatat technology that runs throughout the ship is made from material that exists in an excited multidimensional quantum state, meaning they are interconnected, even across vast distances."

"So, you're saying you are in contact with those components now because your crystal is made of the same material."

"Precisely; you are catching on to this quicker than Hayden did at first."

He frowned until he noticed Emma smiling at him.

"So you can determine if the ship is intact from that connection," he said.

"Yes, she's in one piece and functional."

"Where is she?"

"Uh, that part is a bit harder to know. I can feel *Scimitar* across the interdimension connection, but I can't tell where she is in our space/time."

Hayden rubbed his temples. He had no reason to doubt what Cora told him. But what did it mean?

"*Scimitar* obviously survived her fiery entry into Oberon's atmosphere," he said, "but the ship wasn't designed to set down on a planet, so where is she?"

Emma said, "The reports said she came down near the northern coast. What if the ship crash-landed on a long stretch of beach or something?"

"Those same reports said Federal forces didn't find any significant debris," said Hayden.

"But would they broadcast they'd found a sophisticated ship like *Scimitar*? Wouldn't they want to keep it a secret?"

"They might have seen her weapons in action, but they'd have no way to know of her Glenatat enhancements. There would be no reason to conceal they'd found her intact; in fact, finding her whole would cause a big enough stir, they probably couldn't conceal it if they tried."

"She was damaged," said Cora, "and Pavlovich would need to

park her somewhere to fix her hurt."

"Is that possible?" Emma asked. "You'd need some kind of shipyard for that, wouldn't you?"

"*Scimitar*'s Glenatat infrastructure is self-healing. There are a few of her original structural components that would require physical repair, but not enough that would prevent her from being spaceworthy."

"Still, the ship would need time to repair herself," said Hayden. "She was damaged in the atmosphere and unable to set down on land. What would Pavlovich do?"

Emma said, uncertainly, "Put it in the water?"

Hayden stared at her for a few heartbeats.

"How about it, Cora? Can *Scimitar* be safely submerged?"

"Theoretically, there is no reason she can't. Nobody has ever done that with a starship before."

"And Pavlovich is a brilliant tactician—please don't ever tell him I said that. That is what the son of a bitch probably did. He put her in the ocean to hide her while the ship repaired herself."

Emma said, "So what are you going to do, now?"

"I'm going to take this to Krellig."

"What can he do?"

"He can give me men and equipment to go find *Scimitar*," said Hayden.

"The general has his hands full," said Emma. "He is meeting with the other leaders to come up with a plan. Everyone is talking about the possibility of a coordinated offensive being planned to take advantage of the current state of confusion. What makes you think he'll give you any resources to pursue this?"

"He's desperate to get his hands on *Scimitar*'s weaponry. He'll listen."

Emma looked at Cora's glowing crystal on the desk.

"Didn't you promise him that tech before you believed your ship was destroyed?"

"And he was interested enough in it to keep me alive. Now, if there is the possibility of recovering a functional, advanced, Glenatat-enhanced starship—"

"Hayden, promising a rebel leader salvaged components is a different thing than offering him a functional vessel," said Cora. "Captain Pavlovich will have something to say about sharing *Scimitar*'s technology."

"Even Pavlovich can't turn a blind eye to what is happening here. I'm certain he can be persuaded to help these people resist Thomas."

Hayden swallowed as a thought came to him. "Pavlovich and Chin were the only two on the bridge. We must face the possibility that neither of them is still alive. Maybe it was you who put the ship in the water, in which case, *Scimitar* is on the bottom of the ocean waiting for someone to salvage her. I'd rather it be us than Thomas."

"Wait a minute," said Emma. "How could Cora have put the ship in the ocean if she has been here with you?"

"Hayden is referring to one of my segments. I am capable of dividing myself to be in several places aboard *Scimitar* at once."

"Cora is the one who operates *Scimitar*. The rest of us are just passengers, really."

Emma frowned and addressed the crystal. "Then which of you is the real you?"

"It's complicated. When segmented, we can appear to act as independent entities, but we are connected and operate as a cooperative being. Only one of us—me—is dominant. But that only works when we are distributed throughout *Scimitar*, which, in a way, is our—my body. When I become separated from the others like I am now, we become independent beings, cut off from the collective others. The others act like me but operate according to learned behaviour. They are only capable of limited independent thought. When I return, we merge again and share our separate experiences."

Emma said, "That's..."

Hayden said, "Alien?"

Emma smiled. "I was going to say, 'creepy,' but I like your word better."

He returned her smile. "I did promise you the full Glenatat experience."

She nodded. "Yes, you did. Thank you for this, by the way."

"Hayden, I don't feel right about what you propose."

"Right now, Cora, I'm not proposing anything except soliciting Krellig's help to find *Scimitar*."

"I'm more concerned about what you may have to promise to secure his help. What if the price he asks is not possible to pay?"

"I don't have all the answers, Cora. Hell, I don't have any. All I know is I've been marooned on this dustball for months, believing everyone I know is dead. If there is a chance to find Pavlovich and the others, I have to take it. At the very least, I have to confirm if they are still alive."

"You may not get a chance to ask Krellig," said Emma. "When he returns, if he even comes back, he'll be engrossed in organizing the offensive."

"What do you mean that he might not return? Where would he go?"

She lifted an eyebrow. "Do you remember that raptor you stole for him?"

Hayden smacked himself on the forehead. "His fleet; of course. He'll have to coordinate orbital support."

"You could talk to M'gomba. He would make sure Krellig returns to listen to you."

"I'm pretty sure M'gomba hates my guts. He won't listen to a thing I tell him."

"He's the only one with a channel to Krellig right now," said Emma. "You need to persuade him if you want to find your ship. I don't think there is any other way."

Hayden considered her for several long seconds, weighing her words.

"You know him, Emma. What can I say to convince him?"

"He's a good man, Hayden; a man of integrity. Be honest with him."

"Do you want to talk to him for me?"

She smiled. "I'm just a medical tech. Despite what you may believe, M'gomba respects your rank, if not you personally. Appeal to his sense of duty. It's the only way you can ensure your plan is heard."

Hayden looked at the crystal. "What do you think, Cora?"

"I think Emma is a very intelligent woman, and you should swallow your pride and take her advice."

"Ouch. That was candid."

He smiled as he regarded Emma again.

"It seems I've received my marching orders. To M'gomba I will go."

"I told you when you called me, Kaine," said M'gomba, "I don't know when or if Krellig is returning. Why is it so important to know?"

Hayden stood across the desk from the seated M'gomba. It was the first time he'd seen Krellig's second in command out of uniform. The big man was dressed for bed and had fitted Hayden in at the end of a long work schedule.

Getting M'gomba to agree to speak with him had been a challenge, but he'd followed Emma's advice and was upfront with what he wanted. To his surprise, M'gomba agreed to a late-night meeting in his quarters, which also served as an office. The desk that dominated the small room and a cot against the wall were the only furnishings in the spartan space.

He considered how much he should risk telling M'gomba, or Krellig for that matter. Emma's advice had worked to get him a meeting with the commander, and he had no reason to deviate from her instructions. But despite her high opinion of him, Hayden neither liked nor trusted him enough to share Cora's existence with him. She would be an invaluable prize and could very well end up enslaved if he misjudged who he told about her. He still found himself questioning the wisdom of revealing her to Emma.

He decided to keep Cora a secret.

"I have some key intelligence—something that could make the difference for the rebellion's fortunes."

M'gomba laid the datapad on the desk and gave Kaine his undivided attention.

"I'm listening."

He swallowed, then steeled himself, stood straighter and looked M'gomba in the eyes.

"I've restored power to the alien data crystal. It has detected my ship, and it did not burn up in the atmosphere. She is still intact."

M'gomba's expression didn't change. "So?"

Scowling, Hayden was annoyed to be forced to connect the dots for the man. "*Scimitar* has technology and weapons that can win the rebellion."

To his surprise, M'gomba smiled. "Yes, Krellig mentioned your vessel's formidable weapon."

"All we have to do is recover her before the federal forces do."

"Where is the ship?"

"Um, I don't know—yet, but I have a way to find her."

M'gomba stared at him. "Why do you waste my time, Kaine?"

"Let me talk to Krellig."

The commander shook his head as he picked up the datapad and started reading. "I'm busy."

Hayden fought to control his temper. "M'gomba, this is important."

He didn't look up as he replied. "Mhmm, as is this report I'm trying to read."

"Finding *Scimitar* will save lives; it could very well end the rebellion. Please hear me out."

He looked up at Hayden, fatigue etched on his face. "Go to

bed, Kaine, and let me finish my work so that I may do the same. Krellig may indulge your flights of fancy, but I have no time for them."

Kaine's own lack of sleep was catching up with him, and he had trouble controlling his growing anger.

"What the hell is your problem, M'gomba? You've only given me grief since I arrived here. I saved your life, for god's sake, what else must I do before you take me seriously?"

"That's your problem, Kaine; you're entitled. You want to be rewarded for doing a decent thing. There always must be something in it for you, doesn't there?"

"What the hell are you talking about? I've put my life on the line for you people more than once."

"So has everyone else here, but you seem to be the only one who views your effort as currency. The rest of us just try to make life on our backwater planet a little bit more tolerable for our children. But you, you are doing it as a means to an end: find your ship so you can get the hell off of this planet and no longer be bothered concerning yourself with our meaningless existences."

"That's not fair—"

"There, that's exactly what I mean. You think life is a game with rules intended to make things equal for everyone. Admit it or not, you were born privileged, and you will die that way. People like you never change."

Hayden was dumbstruck. He always realized he was born into privilege; how could he not, given his upbringing and the constant reminders of what his family expected of him? But he didn't choose that life. In fact, he'd turned his back on it. His conflict with Thomas was because he didn't wish to follow that destiny.

Yet the truth of M'gomba's words stung sharply. He did view his cooperation with Krellig as a currency. He had an opportunity to get off Oberon, even if it was becoming more remote with each passing day. Never once did it enter his mind to make a life here with these people; to become a part of their community or to embrace their struggle as his own.

Hayden stormed out of M'gomba's quarters.

He wanted to hate the man, but his only transgression was to be direct and say things no one else would. M'gomba's world was binary with no room for grey areas. A person was good or evil. It was a childish way to view a not-so-simple world. Hayden considered his own perspective to be more encompassing, able to distinguish the nuances M'gomba and others like him missed.

And yet, as far as the Confederation was concerned, which of them had got it right? Hayden understood the politics of governing were not simple; good leaders made poor decisions that harmed people, and despots could do things that benefited the populace they oppressed. Neither had the monopoly on absolute good or evil. He had always seen the system from the inside and accepted the empire as it perceived itself: a flawed but beneficial government that brought democracy and prosperity to all its member star systems.

But what he'd learned on Oberon shook his worldview to the core. If what Krellig told him was true, then the Confederacy had never tried to live up to its own values. Long ago, corruption took root and spread until the whole system became rotten. Things would have continued that way if the destruction of the jump-gate network hadn't disrupted the status quo.

Hayden realized he'd only ever seen what he wanted to. The signs of the rot had always been there, even before the collapse. The very fact a military was required to keep the peace within a supposedly united confederacy spoke to the inequity that lurked beneath the surface of their perfect society. Even after the collapse, the strife he'd witnessed in the dozens of systems spoke to an almost universal desire for change. With the collapse, people throughout the once vast Confederation saw an opportunity to change their lives for the better, while those in power who'd benefitted from the system resisted.

He'd considered the destruction of the jump-gate network as

a tragedy when it had been, in fact, a unique opportunity to reshape thousands of societies, or at least make the attempt. At the very least, it put choices into the hands of ordinary people who had never had any. The old system had failed them—no, it had exploited them and made them slaves to a distant Earth that was no longer a home to them, but an alien world. Krellig's people, and the trillions of others like them in other star systems, saw an opportunity to determine their own future.

Hayden had chosen not to see that. He had viewed the conflicts he'd witnessed in a dozen star systems from the same lofty, privileged position he'd enjoyed back on Earth. It wasn't the people he saw, but power factions battling to fill a political vacuum.

M'gomba was right about him.

An icy weight settled in his stomach as he acknowledged his growing sense of shame. He could no longer afford to detach himself from these peoples' struggle, not if he wanted to preserve his soul. There was a diminishing chance he'd ever locate *Scimitar*. Even if he did, he could never go back to flitting from system to system and lamenting how things were unravelling. That old life was over. He needed to get his head around this reality.

He'd fooled himself in his obsession to revive Cora. He'd sincerely wanted to help his friend live again, but she would not have approved of his transactional attitude to accomplish that goal. Her well-being would always remain his top concern, but that didn't mean he couldn't do more to help Krellig without considering how it benefitted his own agenda.

He wondered if he should thank M'gomba for his shocking insight but dismissed the naive notion. It was one thing to claim an epiphany and something else to amend one's attitude and acts. M'gomba, or Krellig for that matter, cared not a whit for how Hayden felt about their struggle. Actions mattered more than philosophies. He would have to demonstrate that he could make a difference.

UNJUSTIFIABLE SURRENDER

Hayden's sleep was restless. He'd been unable to shut off his mind as he struggled with thoughts of *Scimitar*. Where was she? Was Pavlovich with her, or was he dead? Had she been discovered by the federal forces?

He'd finally fallen asleep when a sharp rapping on his door jerked him awake.

He rolled from the bed and stumbled to answer the insistent knocking.

Opening the door, he was greeted by Krellig.

"You look like shit, Kaine."

He blinked and rubbed the sleep from his eyes.

"You came back. What time is it?"

"I arrived an hour ago. The base is still on nightshift; the time is 0400, if you must know. M'gomba told me about your ship. May I come in?"

"Uh, yeah, sure."

Hayden stepped aside to admit him, then went to retrieve his shirt and trousers from the floor and pull them on.

As Krellig waited, he wandered to the table and perused Cora's glowing crystal.

"I'm glad the power core worked for you. I'm presuming it is how you came to be convinced that your ship is intact."

"Yes."

"Do us both a favour and keep the information under wraps for the time being, okay?"

"Sure. Why?"

Krellig sat on a chair and pulled out the other one with his foot for Hayden.

When Kaine was seated, Krellig exhaled noisily.

"You know I was meeting with the rebel leadership?"

He nodded.

Krellig smiled. "Yeah, trying to keep a secret in this place is a challenge."

"What's happened?"

The general paused before answering. "The leadership decided to surrender to the Confederation forces."

"What? Why the hell would you do that?"

He shook his head. "It wasn't an easy decision, but we had to take lives into account, and we think the new Confederacy will offer us better terms than the planetary government. Two days ago, one of the towns that openly supported us was destroyed in an orbital kinetic bombardment."

Hayden's mouth fell open.

"Twenty-thousand men, women, and children are dead; there were no survivors. The government made it clear that it was only the first of many unless we surrender. I presume D'Ville wanted to present the Confederation with a prize to demonstrate his worthiness to continue governing under the new regime."

"D'Ville?"

"He's been Oberon's governor for the past thirty years. He's always been ruthless, and now he wants to play nice with his new bosses to keep his ass safe."

"Shit. I...no words can express my sorrow or my anger."

"Thank you, Kaine. As you can imagine, my hands will be full over the next few days as we try to break the news to our people and negotiate our surrender. It's unfortunate the information about your ship arrived too late for us to take advantage of, but such are the fortunes of war."

"You seem very philosophical about this."

Krellig smiled weakly. "I suppose I am. I guess I'm still in shock over how badly we all underestimated the depths D'Ville would stoop to defeat us."

Hayden shook his head. "Yeah, but to bomb your own populace is monstrous."

"He's Terran and was installed by the old empire. I don't think he's ever thought of himself as one of us. He'll be pissed as all hell if we can cut a deal with Thomas's people and make him appear foolish. It sounds petty, but it's the only course for revenge available. Maybe he'll be tried for war crimes, but I doubt it."

They sat in silence for half a minute.

"Anyway," said Krellig, "I wanted to warn you, so you have some time to decide what you'll do. I imagine that everyone in the Confederation believes you to be dead. I've arranged for you to take the flyer you acquired and disappear—perhaps help that belief along to become permanent. Maybe, after everything eventually dies down, you can find transportation under a new identity back to Earth or somewhere. Or maybe you'll consider staying to make a life here—but I wouldn't recommend that. I don't expect things will improve here in the near term."

"I don't know what to say."

Krellig stood. "You should leave as soon as possible. I can give you a list of facilities like this that are still secret. There will be some holdouts using a few of them, but you shouldn't associate with them for longer than necessary. It's the best I can offer you, and I'm sorry I can't do more. You've been a big help."

"What will happen to you?"

Krellig's eyebrows lifted in surprise, suggesting he hadn't considered the matter. "I don't know. If I'm lucky they'll toss me back in prison, I suppose."

"Why don't you come with me? Together we can maybe locate *Scimitar* and— "

"And what, Kaine? Fight off an empire? That is what we will be facing. I think if you are fortunate enough to be reunited with your ship and crew, you'd be wise to use that FTL and go anywhere else. There is nothing left here to save, and to try will be a waste. Maybe you can still prevent Thomas from getting the tech he lusts after."

Krellig extended his right hand, and they shook.

The general turned and went to the door. "I'll send word when your supplies and ship are ready. Your window for departure is not large, so make use of it. Oh, and please don't share this news until I inform my people."

Hayden nodded. "Of course. Thank you for everything you've done for me, General."

Krellig's weak smile died. He left, closing the door behind him.

Hayden stared after him for several seconds as he reflected on what happened. He wondered if he should have introduced him to Cora. Perhaps meeting her and seeing firsthand the potential of Glenatat technology would have convinced him that finding *Scimitar* might still carry the rebellion to a less ignominious fate.

Then he recalled how defeated Krellig had appeared, like a man whose last hopes were dust—much like Hayden had felt when he'd believed *Scimitar* was destroyed.

Would offering him even a glimmer of hope only be cruelty? Krellig could not continue his resistance alone. The weight of the many lives he was responsible for and had fought for was heavy on him. He had the best interests of the populace to consider. Hayden didn't think he had the right to offer something that could not be realized except as a dream.

He retrieved his pack from under the bed and started stuffing his few belongings in it. When he picked up Cora's crystal, he realized he hadn't even considered asking her how she felt about going into hiding. Would she agree with him that their best hope for survival was to avoid being found by Thomas's people? The admiral would likely kill him, but Cora would be the jewel to complete his treasure. With her enslaved, the little Glenatat technology he already possessed would become more dangerous. He couldn't prevent Thomas from locating *Scimitar*, but he could take the key to use it from him.

But it had to be Cora's decision.

He pushed the power button on the battery. It no longer had any use, but he and Cora had agreed it could serve as a signal when he wished to speak to her.

"Hello, Hayden. I wondered when you were going to consult me."

"You overheard everything, did you?"

"I didn't want to give you the impression I was eavesdropping, but I pretty much hear everything that goes on in here, even your snoring. I'm sorry if I'm being creepy, but I really don't have much else to occupy myself with."

"No offence taken, Cora. What do you think we should do?"

There was a long pause. He picked up the crystal, wondering if something had gone wrong.

"I'm still here, Hayden. Um, may I talk with you about something?"

"Anything; you know that."

"Um, actually, it will be easier to show you in VR."

Hayden glanced at the combat helmet sitting on the table. He'd recently completed modifying it for virtual reality interfacing with Cora, but they hadn't yet tested it.

"Sure, if you want to."

He put on the helmet, lay down on his bunk, and flipped the switch to enter Cora's domain.

Unlike Cora's preconstructed VR environment aboard *Scimitar* that had been based on a real place, in this instance Kaine found himself inside a black void.

A grey floor materialized beneath him, but he couldn't feel his weight and was unsure if he stood on it or floated above. Near him, it appeared as a solid surface, but off in the distance, it became less distinct as it merged to become part of the condensing, formless cloud surrounding him.

"Cora, are you here?"

An indistinct humanoid form emerged from the fog and drifted, rather than walked, toward him. As it neared, it changed, becoming more human. A lump formed in the middle of the face that extruded into an upturned nose. At the same time, eyes, ears, and lips took shape. A face started to resolve, and by the time a mane of long blonde hair materialized, the apparition was recognizable as Cora.

She appeared as the young woman he remembered meeting in the real more than a decade before when he first joined *Scimitar*'s crew. But the avatar was incomplete, more like a painted portrait. All her features were present, but her skin lacked the subtle vibrancy that her virtual avatars on *Scimitar* did.

"I'm sorry about the simulation quality," she said, her mouth not quite syncing to her voice.

He tried to smile, but without feedback, he didn't know if his avatar mimicked it. "Processing capacity of this system is limited."

The Cora image glitched as she shook her head. "No, that isn't the reason. Hayden, I have a problem, and I don't know what to do."

He felt his throat tighten. "Please tell me how I can help."

"I...I can't remember things, details. They just aren't coming to me."

"You've spent a long time in suspension."

"That shouldn't matter. The problem is that I'm losing my

long-term memory. Even my short-term and functional, er, is...I can't think of the words. See what I mean?"

"This is an unusual situation, Cora. I'm sure you will adjust, and everything will come back to you."

She flickered as she glitched again. "I'm not sure. I think I started to show signs of this before we came here."

He recalled the battle they stepped into on their arrival here. Cora forgot the name of the targeting system. She'd dismissed it as a processing limitation, and the situation was too crazy to question her explanation. But he also remembered other, subtle signs she'd shown months earlier. Having to be reminded about systems that needed her attention was only one example he could recall. It was typically human behaviour that everyone displayed on occasion, but Cora was no longer human.

"How long has it been going on?"

"I'm not sure. I was forgetting little things about three months ago."

He searched his memory of the past year for any hint of a clue to the source of the problem.

Hayden shook his head. "I can't think of anything that happened to us then. Our last significant interaction was when those pirates fired on us at Trappist-1, but that was almost a year ago."

"Eleven months, six days and twenty-one hours; I can remember some stuff but forget the name of something as simple as a sock."

"That happens to everyone, Cora."

"Let's be honest here. I'm not like everyone. But I haven't told you the scariest thing that's been happening."

Hayden swallowed in the real, but his avatar didn't mimic him. "What is it?"

"I don't only forget the names of things. I lose my place in time. Sometimes, like now, I'm in the present, but at other times I'm back in the past...I think. I can't be sure because my memories are all jumbled. I am getting so that I can't distinguish reality from memory. Hayden, I'm frightened."

"Do you have any idea what is causing it?"

"I started to formulate a—oh, what do you call it—a theory! Yeah, that's it. I started to form a theory that it was somehow related to how my human engrams are imprinted on the Glenatat computer storage wafers."

"You mean, like the technology in the memory module I downloaded you into?"

"Yes, it's a limited version of the same tech aboard *Scimitar*. I'm not sure how it works exactly, but..."

"What? I thought you knew everything there is to know about Glenatat hardware."

Cora's avatar smiled, the first emotional expression it had displayed. "No, Hayden, I just acted like I knew everything. There is an enormous amount I'm ignorant about. I am constantly learning new things every day."

"So, what is your theory?"

"My engrams form bonds with the atoms in the Glenatat memory wafers. As they are accessed, they alter the structure and connection between molecules of the hardware in a way similar to how a human brain creates neural pathways. Entirely new and unique elements are created in the process as electron-sized connecting fibres."

"I think I follow you. Where is the problem happening?"

"I'm not certain, but because the Glenatat system wasn't originally designed to accommodate human engrams, some of the new elemental fibres being formed contain unstable isotopes."

"You mean to say that parts of your neural network are decaying into daughter products, and those unintended elements somehow interfere with your memory?"

She smiled again. "You paid attention to what I taught you."

He shrugged. "Some of it occasionally sinks in. So, how do we fix it?"

"I'm not sure we can. If I was still integrated into *Scimitar*, I could isolate the contaminated systems and reroute my network, because the entire ship is essentially my brain—at least the Glenatat components distributed through the hull are. It wouldn't solve the problem, but it would take a lot longer before it disabled me. I'd have time to find a workaround."

"But you're not on *Scimitar*. You are contained in a single memory crystal."

"It is a dense structure, but still very limited compared to *Scimitar*'s capacity. Also, the crystal is cracked, which further inhibits my ability to create alternate memory pathways. I fear that if I remain in here, my time is limited before the damage is too extensive. We are already seeing the—what's the word?"

"Consequences."

"Results, but that's a good word too."

"Will you be okay if I can get you to *Scimitar*?"

"You mean, would my dementia be permanent? I don't know. Syncing with any surviving secondary instances of me will mitigate long-term loss, so maybe. There is no way to be sure."

"But we know for certain what will happen if you remain confined to this crystal. How long do we have?"

"For what? I can't remember what we were talking about."

Hayden shook his head. "It's not important. Can you tell me something?"

"Sure, what is it?"

"What happens to you—to your neural net activity—when your crystal is not connected to a power source?"

"I go into a kind of stasis; a coma, I suppose. All thought activity is suspended."

"So, no further damage will happen."

"What are you talking about, Hayden? Did I miss something?"

Hayden was glad the VR interface would not mimic the disappointment he felt. "No, Cora; it's okay. I was thinking aloud."

"Sure. Thanks for visiting me during your duty cycle."

"What?"

"You know how annoyed the captain gets when you use VR for personal visits during working hours."

In the real, Hayden felt his heart drop into his stomach.

"Yeah, well, he was in a good mood today and had no problems with me stopping by to visit you."

He wasn't sure he could maintain his composure and didn't know how much of what he felt was being displayed by his avatar.

Not wishing to upset her, he said, "Um, I have to get back. You know Pavlovich."

"Yes, I do. Please tell him that I'll be back on duty soon."

"I will. Goodbye, Cora."

He disconnected the VR helmet and removed it.

Tears ran down his cheeks as he looked at the glowing alien crystal lying on the table.

He had to get Cora back to *Scimitar* at any cost.

Hayden walked down the bustling corridor.

Glum and angry soldiers elbowed past him carrying bundles of equipment or personal items, all destined for the transport vehicles assembling in the compound's underground garages.

He turned into a less busy passage and continued until he located the quarters he searched for. The door was ajar, so he peeked in on Emma. Her back faced him as she laid out her belongings on the bunk in preparation for packing them up.

"Knock-knock," he announced as he pushed the door open a little farther.

She startled and turned. Her cheeks were wet and her eyes red. When she saw it was him, she blushed and stood, wiping her face with her hand.

"Hello, Hayden," she said, her voice throaty from crying. "How can I help you?"

He shook his head as he entered. "I just came to check up on you."

"Thank you. I'm okay, I guess," she said, forcing a smile. "Disappointed with how things turned out, but..." She shrugged. "It's probably for the best."

Hayden nodded. Unsure of what to say, he picked the safest topic that came to mind.

"Where will you go?"

"We are supposed to transport into Sittot to be processed and debriefed. It sounds like Krellig intends to negotiate a pardon for most of us who aren't in the leadership. I suppose I'll go back to Argent for a while. After that, I don't know."

Hayden didn't like the sound of that plan. Processing the rebels might mean identifying, registering, and releasing them, or it could be something far more sinister. Krellig might believe Thomas's people to be more reasonable than D'Ville, but he knew better.

"I think Krellig and the others are making a mistake," he said. "I'm not the only one who does."

"Nobody wants this. There are some who—"

Emma's eyes widened and her hand covered her mouth.

Hayden nodded. "I suspected that might be the case. Can you tell me any names?"

Her brow knotted. "Please do me a favour and pretend I didn't say that."

"I don't want to get you into trouble, Emma. But if there are some who are not ready to expose their bellies, I'm eager to speak with them."

"This was never your fight, Hayden. Why would you be interested in...?" She glanced over his shoulder at the opened door and then lowered her voice to a whisper. "You know."

He went back to close the door. Then, returning to her, said, "There is something wrong with Cora."

Emma gasped. "What's happened?"

He swallowed, finding it hard to give words to what had occupied his thoughts for the past several hours. "She is dying. Her only chance is to return to *Scimitar*."

"But you don't know where the ship is."

"No, I don't. But Cora can still find it with access to the right equipment. The fight went out of Krellig, but if there are disaffected soldiers who aren't ready to surrender, I have a plan that can save her and give the resistance a powerful weapon against D'Ville and the Confederation forces."

"Assuming you can reach your ship after you locate it."

He nodded. "There is a lot of risk and plenty of ways this can go wrong. In fact, it will probably fail, but I have no choice. I can't let Cora die without trying. You understand, don't you?"

Emma's brow furrowed, and she studied him. "I shouldn't tell you this, but there are a few who don't trust the Confederacy not to execute every single one of us, regardless of the general's assurances."

"They believe Krellig is being naive?"

She shook her head. "No, but he is being calculating. There are far more civilians at risk from more orbital bombings than there are rebel soldiers. Even if they were to shoot every one of us who turns ourselves in, it will save many times more lives if it suspends the bombardments."

"I can't believe he is intentionally buying peace with your lives."

"I don't believe it either, but if it's true, some don't want to sell their lives cheaply."

Hayden narrowed his eyes. "Are you trying to tell me some people are planning a suicide attack of some kind?"

Emma pressed her lips together and shrugged.

"Holy shit," said Hayden.

She touched his shoulder and whispered, "If you are being truthful about the capabilities of the alien technology aboard your ship, I know some who might be willing to help you find it."

"You've seen it for yourself."

"Not the weapons."

Hayden studied her. There was far more to Emma than the seemingly innocent young woman she'd presented. He wondered if she hadn't been playing him the whole time to get a first-hand glimpse at Glenatat technology. Was it possible that Krellig had put her up to it?

"The general saw our weapons in action," he said. "Why not ask him?"

Her face lost all expression, and she took a step back from him. Then, to Hayden's utter shock, she winked.

"I will arrange a meeting," she said. "Go back to your quarters and wait."

"I'm supposed to depart within the next two hours," he said.

A wry smile turned up the corners of her mouth. "You may have a choice to make, Hayden Kaine."

Kaine sat in the chair, impatiently tapping his foot as he faced the closed door of his quarters. He'd given up pacing long before.

On his bunk was his backpack containing everything he owned. Around his neck, hidden under his shirt, hung Cora's crystal.

Three hours had passed since the end of the window given him by Krellig. The corridor outside had grown quiet with the departure of the last scheduled transport.

He muttered, "What the hell is going on?"

Cora spoke into his earpiece. "Was that question rhetorical?"

Hayden chuckled. "Sorry; I forgot you were listening."

"I can turn off the connection if you're feeling self-conscious."

"No, that isn't necessary. I'm glad you're with me again."

"Sort of like your conscience?"

He frowned. "I was thinking more like guardian angel."

"Aw, you're such a sweet talker, Hayden. I'll bet you say that to all the cyber-women you meet."

He smiled.

A shuffled footstep outside the room wiped the expression from his face, and he sprang to his feet.

The handle turned, and the door pushed inward. Hayden was not surprised when Emma poked her head inside. Like him, she wore black fatigues beneath an all-weather jacket.

"I'm glad you're still here. Get your things and come with me."

Obediently, he grabbed his pack and threw it over his shoulder. When Emma turned to lead the way, he zipped up his jacket and checked that the subtle bulge of the crystal beneath his shirt was concealed from view. Then he followed her.

The only sound in the abandoned corridor was their echoing footsteps. Emma maintained a brisk pace, and her demeanour did not encourage conversation. He was grateful that his waiting was finished.

She led him into a section of the complex he'd never seen, and after a twisty journey through hallways that all looked alike, they entered a conference room.

Five people were at the centre table, all dressed in black.

Hayden wasn't surprised M'gomba was at the head of the table. He was pleased Caldwell and Hashido were present as well. The other two grim-faced soldiers were a man he didn't recognize and a petite woman named Aubrey Martini he'd met after his arrival here.

M'gomba gestured to an empty chair. "Please take a seat, Mister Kaine."

Hayden dropped his pack by the door and sat down while Emma sat next to the other woman.

"I want to make one thing clear," said M'gomba. "The only reason we are having this meeting is that Chang advocated for you. Given a choice, I would have let you rot in your quarters, but we are out of options."

Hayden swallowed. "I understand and appreciate this opportunity."

"It isn't an opportunity, yet. It's more of an interview, really. We will listen to your proposal and then discuss it among ourselves. If we like what you say, we will engage with you further about details."

"And if you don't like it?"

"We will shoot you. We can't risk knowledge of this cell leaving this compound. I'm sure you understand what is at risk."

Hayden looked in turn at each person around the table, ending at Emma. He turned to M'gomba and said, "Then I suppose I'd better be persuasive."

Caldwell chuckled, earning him a sharp look from M'gomba.

Emma spoke up, her formal manner making Hayden uncomfortable.

"You can begin by introducing us to Cora."

Hayden glanced at the others and then nodded. He reached up, removed the crystal from around his neck, and placed it on the table.

"Cora, please introduce yourself to these nice people."

Her voice came over the speakers in the ceiling. "Hello, I was once Cora Symes, chief engineer aboard the UEF *Scimitar*. I won't bore you by reciting a ship registration number you won't recognize."

The woman named Aubrey spoke. "We've been briefed that you were once human and that you are somehow integrated with alien technology."

"The technology of an ancient race known as the Glenatat preserved my memories, personality...my soul or essence, if you prefer."

"Frankly, this sounds ridiculous."

"I realize that you are all sceptical about what you have been told about me. In the interest of making this inquiry brief, I suggest another method to demonstrate the nature of Glenatat technology. I detected that you all possess active cortical implant devices. I am going to do something that is not possible for human technology."

Everyone tensed up at the mention of their implants.

The man Hayden didn't know said, "What do you propose?"

"I will access your cortical LINKs and converse with you individually, answering all of your questions in detail, and in less time than this clumsy oral method."

"That isn't possible," said the man.

"Then, if I succeed, will you allow yourself to be convinced I am who I claim to be, or at least possess technology beyond what you are familiar with?"

Cora didn't wait for anyone to reply. Their bodies went rigid. As one, their eyes closed and their eyeballs twitched beneath their lids.

He didn't know that this was within Cora's capability. Long before her conversion, when he first encountered the Glenatat and their enemy, the Malliac, he had deactivated his implant, as did all of *Scimitar*'s crew. He'd never missed it until now. He wondered what the experience was like to communicate with Cora using his mind.

The trance didn't last long. Emma was the first to open her eyes. Agape, she looked at him and shook her head as if she couldn't believe what had happened to her.

One by one the others came back to the present, all with reactions like Emma's.

The last person to emerge was M'gomba. Something was different about the way the man looked at him, but he couldn't put his finger on what he saw.

"That...that was extraordinary," he said. "I did not believe your story until now, Mister Kaine."

Hayden tried to remain gracious. "Frankly, M'gomba, I would have had trouble believing me. I take it you are all ready to hear my plan."

Everyone nodded, but M'gomba held up his hand. "Please,

explain it to us. That experience was...intense and not something I wish to repeat."

Hayden wondered what had transpired between him and Cora to affect the man so deeply.

"Cora and I arrived here three months ago on our vessel, *Scimitar*. The greeting we received was less than hospitable. She and I were ejected in an escape pod, which you all know. From intercepted reports, we think our ship came down somewhere along the northern coastline. We don't believe she's been found, yet."

M'gomba said, "That is deep within the federally controlled territory, and the coastline is almost a thousand kilometres long. Even if we could get there, finding the ship will be impossible unless you have a way to specifically locate it."

Kaine indicated a device in the middle of the table. "May we access your holo-display?"

"I don't believe your friend requires my permission to access anything within this base. Please proceed."

Hayden suppressed a smile and reached across the table to activate it, though he wondered now if that was even necessary after seeing what Cora could do.

A ghostly image of Oberon as seen from space appeared and floated above the centre of the table. The view zoomed closer until a space station appeared. The facility consisted of three concentric rings independently rotating at different rates about a central axis.

Multiple ships were docked at various points around the outermost ring that were recognizable as UEF battle cruisers. Hayden realized the station was at least a kilometre in diameter.

Cora's voice filled the room. "This is the *Xury Baecher* orbital docking platform. It monitors all surface activity via a network of interlinked observation satellites. Normally, these would have detected a downed ship, but *Scimitar*'s hull renders her undetectable. I, however, can use the data from this grid to locate *Scimitar*'s unique signature."

"Why can't you just access the station from here, as you've done with our equipment?"

Cora's chuckle sounded eerie coming over the speakers.

"The docking platform's security is slightly more sophisticated than what you've put in place here. There is also the problem of proximity. In my current limited incarnation, I must be within a few hundred metres of equipment to access it remotely. To find *Scimitar* I will need to physically link with the satellite computer."

The man Kaine didn't know scowled. "Infiltrating *Xury Baecher* is impossible, and if it could be done, the odds of breaking through the security—well, I don't understand why we are even listening to this."

"Thank you, Xander," said Emma. "I think we all recognize the difficulties involved."

"Calling them difficulties is an understatement," said Aubrey. "We all signed on to continue the fight and make a significant blow against the federal forces. We must make them appear weak so that D'Ville is removed from power. Everyone around this table and the others not here are committed to giving our lives for this. But we must be pragmatic and pick a target where we have a reasonable chance of succeeding. The orbital dock is too well defended. We would perish before we got off the surface."

People spoke over one another, and the discussion soon devolved into multiple side conversations.

Finally, M'gomba's booming voice silenced the room.

"Before everyone gets too twisted off over details and reasons why this won't work, why don't we allow Kaine to tell us what the prize is?"

Shocked, Hayden regarded the commander like he was someone he'd never met before. The experience with Cora had changed something about M'gomba's attitude toward him.

"Thank you." He cleared his throat. "General Krellig understood *Scimitar*'s significance for the rebellion. The ship has a powerful weapon, a dark energy cannon. Its destructive power is beyond anything you've seen."

Cora spoke to him privately through his earpiece. "Why don't I just show them, Hayden?"

Nonplussed, he covered his mouth and turned his head to reply, "How can you do that?"

"I had to occupy myself with something over the past few days, so I looked through all the files in the computer system. I found a visual record of Krellig's encounter with us."

Hayden whispered into his hand, "We are going to discuss limits, Cora."

Her giggle reminded him of when he'd first met her.

Looking up, he addressed the others. "We have something to show you." He directed their attention to the holo-display.

It was strange for him to witness *Scimitar* from the perspective of another vessel.

The ship was in high orbit over Oberon. Three ships approached it from different directions, and he recalled that two others were near the ship that made the recording.

Missiles exploded against *Scimitar*'s armoured hull, which, after the flare dissipated, showed not so much as a scratch to the shiny finish.

Then, a blinding flash overpowered the image as a nuclear warhead struck *Scimitar*. When the view was restored, his ship remained, apparently unscathed, though Hayden recalled the minor damage reports that scrolled across his console on the bridge. He remembered how they were desperate to get away from the conflict and were the target of multiple attacks.

The memory of Pavlovich reluctantly giving the order to use the cannon to clear a path for their escape was still clearly etched on his brain.

As if on cue, a deep violet lance of energy erupted from *Scimitar*'s forward weapon. It collided with one of the attacking ships, which seemed to waver and ripple like a reflection in a pond disturbed by a pebble. As the distortion wave subsided, explosions ripped through the other vessel until only fragments remained.

An audible gasp arose from everyone on seeing the cannon's awesome destructive power unleashed.

The image winked out, and the room was as silent as deep space.

"That your ship survived that kind of sustained bombardment was amazing enough," said Xander, "but that weapon. I've never seen anything like it."

"Can you imagine what we could accomplish with such destructive capability?" Aubrey said. She looked at Hayden, awe still written on her face. "A prize like this will change everything."

She turned to M'gomba. "We must acquire it at any cost."

The others agreed, and all turned to wait for M'gomba to speak.

He addressed Hayden. "Mister Kaine, it seems there is a raid to plan."

RECOVERING HOPE

H ayden's plan was ambitious and reckless, but the situation was desperate, and everyone agreed the prize was worth the risks. If they pulled this off, they could redeem what they all viewed as a disastrous decision by their leaders to surrender. Finding and taking control of *Scimitar* would give a key asset to the rebellion that could help them not only derail the ignoble surrender but also give the rebels a fighting chance to depose D'Ville. At the very least, they would make him look bad enough for the incoming Confederation to replace him. There was no guarantee, however, that his replacement would be any better.

The best scenario for the people of Oberon was if D'Ville could be defeated. Then the rebel leadership could negotiate directly with Thomas's representatives about the reestablishment of Confederacy rule. It was the best way to improve the lot of the population and right some historic wrongs.

All of that was moot, however, if their leaders surrendered. That could not be allowed to happen. *Scimitar* must be found, and soon.

For Kaine's plan to work, they had to transport a team to the orbital platform. Once there, they would avoid station security long enough to find an access point to the central computer.

Then it would be up to Cora to match wits with the system's AI and use the planetary surveillance network to locate the ship on the planet's surface.

Of course, reaching it would be a separate operation that couldn't be considered until they knew where it was.

The first part of the plan was the simplest and defined the size of the team.

Krellig had left behind the raptor Hayden stole. It was certainly capable of reaching the space dock, but its shortcoming was passenger capacity.

The small ship was designed to accommodate two. In a pinch, two more could squeeze into the narrow space behind the cockpit, but something had to be rigged up to keep them from bouncing around the cabin.

There was also the problem of the additional weight, especially because they were leaving the planet's gravity well. They would have to remove mass from the ship, and that meant going up without missiles or other weapons.

Hayden saw no problem with removing the raptor's ordnance. If things went bad, they would be outgunned by the orbital's defence batteries anyway. Before it came to that, however, he was concerned that they threatened to push the design limits of the craft with so many aboard.

Caldwell drew the short straw as the only male soldier going along. After their recent exploits, they had come to grudgingly respect each other. Kaine, of course, was the only qualified pilot, and by default Cora's legs and arms. Anyone else who went along would help Caldwell protect him as he attempted to reach an access point for her to work her magic. The solution was to send the women. They were smaller and could squeeze more comfortably than men into the restricted space. Their smaller mass only helped the ship's chances of reaching orbit.

Hayden had no worries about their capabilities. All Krellig's soldiers were well trained, and he'd seen Emma and Aubrey in action on the range and in the gym. Both were much better shots than him and far more formidable at hand-to-hand combat.

To prepare, he and Cora ran dozens of simulations until they found a way to trim every possible extra gram from the ship.

The mass of each person, their clothing, weapons, ordnance, even Cora's crystal, had to be considered. By the time they were finished, the three soldiers going along to protect him were restricted to a single pistol and five bullets each; Hayden would not be given a weapon. Even the amount they ate and drank for the twenty-four hours before launch was an important detail. Emma was required to supply a calculated dose of laxative and diuretics for each of them to ensure their bowels and bladders were voided before takeoff. The situation did not fill Hayden with an abundance of confidence in their already meagre chances of success.

Unvoiced to anyone was his concern about Cora. He counted as a blessing that she'd made it through the briefing without her memory glitching. During the two days since then, however, she slipped more frequently into the past each time he visited with her.

Emma was, of course, aware of Cora's condition, but he'd managed to conceal from her how fast she was declining. He didn't know how long she had before she'd be forever lost in the past.

With her consent, he'd turned off the Glenatat battery powering her matrix, placing her in suspension until the mission started. He hated to do it, but there was no other way. Cora couldn't be allowed to degrade to the point where it was impossible for her to fulfil her role. Without her, the team would be blown out of the skies before they could get close to the orbital.

The riskiest part of the mission would be after they docked. The team would infiltrate the facility, and that could only be accomplished by defeating the security system, which was monitored by the station's artificial intelligence. Their best and the only hope was Cora being able to take over the station's computer.

Once she established a link with it on the raptor's approach, she would then work from inside the network to take command of ship traffic control and the docking ring.

Even if everything went flawlessly to that point and they managed to dock and leave the ship, they were only halfway to their goal. The security AI was an independent extension of the formidable machine intelligence that ran the station itself. It was the entity that controlled access to the surveillance network, among other systems critical to planetary defence, and Cora had to overpower it to fulfil the mission.

Hayden was confident she would be up to the task under normal conditions, but her instability was a significant risk. She might gain access but then glitch and become lost and disoriented. Not even she could predict how that would play out if it happened. The station's principal AI might overpower and isolate her, making her a prisoner within the computer. Or, even worse, control of the entire station could be lost, threatening geostationary stabilization, life support, and a thousand other systems the failure of which could destroy the orbital and kill thousands aboard it, including them.

When the time came for the team to depart, Hayden arrived at the hangar early to go over the ship a final time. Nothing could be left to chance, since the smallest mistake could mean the difference between making orbit or plummeting back to the surface in a ball of fire.

As he finished his inspection and walked around to the front of the raptor, Emma approached. Like him, she wore a government-issued flight suit. Her features were taut, and there was tension in her voice as she said, "Are we ready for this?"

"Are you?"

She looked up at the ship. "I've never been to space before."

"You took the antinausea pill, didn't you?"

She nodded. "It upset my stomach."

"We will only be in zero-gee for a few minutes until we dock with the orbital. You'll be strapped in, so keep your eyes focused outside the cockpit window and take deep breaths. I can find you a barf bag if you want."

"Sounds like a good idea," she said as her gaze returned to the raptor.

Hayden asked, "Are you sure you want to do this?"

Her eyes darted back to him, and her brow furrowed. "I can handle this. Besides, I'm a better shot than you and the lightest person on the team. Your calculations will be screwed up if anyone replaces me."

"You can still change your mind."

She snapped, "I'm going, and that's the end of it."

He raised his hands in surrender, but before he could reply, someone else said, "You don't want to piss off Chang, Kaine. It won't end well for you." Caldwell punctuated his comment with a broad grin.

Hayden said, "Are you speaking from first-hand experience?"

"She's the medic. If you get hurt, she can make you comfortable or let you suffer."

Emma frowned. "You didn't suffer that much."

"I have the emotional scars to go along with the physical ones."

"Well, you shouldn't have been such an asshole."

"Okay," said Kaine, unsure if they were serious. "Point taken; don't piss off Emma."

Chang and Caldwell stared intently at each other for a few seconds before they both burst into laughter and hugged.

"Asshole," she said into his shoulder.

"Bitch," he said as he pulled her closer.

They slapped each other on the back and parted wearing grins.

"Don't let those two fool you," said Aubrey Martini as she and M'gomba approached. "They really hate each other."

Hayden smiled. "Yeah, I can tell."

Aubrey embraced Emma, then Caldwell.

M'gomba said, "They are my family, Kaine. Bring them home safe." He extended his hand.

Hayden accepted it, saying, "I will do my best."

M'gomba seemed to want to say more. Instead, he glanced to Aubrey, who smiled. "I'll keep an eye on everyone. Our plan will work."

Seeming reassured, the commander stepped a pace back. Straightening his posture, he saluted. "Good hunting."

The other three snapped to attention and returned his salute. Hayden hesitated, then joined them.

M'gomba turned and marched from the hangar without looking back.

Hayden regarded the others as they continued watching the door their commander left through.

He cleared his throat. "It's time."

Turning, he led the way to the ladder to board the raptor. When his back was to them, he reached up to touch the outline of Cora's crystal beneath his shirt. Chang and the others shared a bond, as he did with Cora and Pavlovich. He recalled Stella and the pain of losing her. His fear of what could happen to Cora if the mission failed reasserted itself.

Pushing down his anxiety, he grasped the ladder and climbed up to enter the waiting ship.

———

The overhead doors of the hangar parted, revealing the lilac afterglow of a desert twilight sky that deepened with intensity as the sun dropped below the distant mountains.

With a rising roar from its engines and a blast of dust, the raptor lifted to float a few metres above the deck. Then, with a push on the throttle, the craft rose through the opening and into the cooling evening air.

Once clear of the building, Kaine activated the forward thrusters. As he was pressed into the cushioned pilot seat, Caldwell grunted. Hayden eased back the acceleration as much as he dared.

He called back to the others over the noise of the engines, "I'm sorry this will be uncomfortable, but it can't be helped."

"We can handle it," shouted Emma from behind him in her makeshift harness.

"Let's get this part over with," said Aubrey.

"Okay," said Hayden. "Brace yourselves."

He eased into the acceleration and pointed the nose of the ship skyward.

"Activating boosters in five-four-three-two-one..."

He reflexively braced his head against the back of the chair and fired the orbital engines. He hoped the others remembered and applied the all-too-brief training he'd given them to withstand the gee forces.

He thought he heard one of the women gasp, and he was worried something was happening to one of them, but the deafening din made him realize he'd imagined it. They were professionals and had practised their lessons, and since he was in no position to do anything to help if someone was in distress, he was forced to trust in their abilities.

Turning his head, he caught a glimpse of Caldwell in the jump seat. His eyes were squeezed shut, and he gripped his chest harness.

Kaine stayed alert for any warning signs that might force him to abort.

After eight and a half long minutes, the boosters shut down, and Hayden no longer felt his weight pressing into the seat.

Outside the cockpit, the shadow-shrouded night side of Oberon curved away beneath them. A thin band of atmosphere glimmered around the planet's edge like a silver ring catching the light of the setting sun.

Hayden called out, "Is everyone okay?"

"Yup," said Caldwell.

Aubrey replied, "Mm-hmm."

"I think so," said Emma weakly.

Hayden consulted the navigation computer. "We're on the right orbit, so you can undo your harnesses if you'd like to experience weightlessness. Keep a grip on something so you don't run into anything...or each other."

"Ugh," said Emma. "I don't feel so good. I'm staying right where I am."

"Deep breaths, remember? Look out the window at the horizon."

"Mmm...sure."

"Use the barf bag," said Aubrey before Emma retched.

"Hang in there," he said. "Just a few more minutes of this."

She groaned.

Hayden was grateful that her stomach was empty but still felt sorry for her.

Slipping the crystal from around his neck, he hesitated before activating its power cell. If Cora was going to glitch, now was the best time, before they were within the security perimeter of the orbital station.

She spoke in his earpiece. "Hello, Hayden. I presume we made it off-planet."

"Yes, indeed, Cora; our computer is ready for you to take over."

"I'm already linked. The ship is now under my control."

He took his hands away from the instruments and placed them in his lap. Cora sounded like her old self, and he allowed himself to turn his vigilance down a notch.

"That's odd—the station's security AI is hailing us."

"Why so soon?"

"Give me a moment..."

Kaine's heart rate jumped. "What's going on?"

"Don't distract me. This is slightly more challenging than I anticipated..."

Hayden held his breath as his hand moved to the throttle.

"Cora?"

The connection was silent. His eyes searched the instrument panel until they fell on the manual override. There was still time to break off their approach and return to the ground without raising too much suspicion.

"Okay, we're good."

"What the hell happened?"

"It appears that the Confederation already upgraded the station's operating system. It is more complex than the twelve-year-old version they were running. I needed a little time to find a way in, but all is good. We are cleared to dock at berth sixty-one, and the traffic piloting subsystem assumed control to bring us in."

"Are you still good?"

"Are you worried I might glitch?"

"Ah, no, I...er."

"You're a poor liar. I'm fine, Hayden. Sit back and enjoy the ride."

Kaine realized his hands were balled into fists, and he stretched his fingers apart. He wanted to trust Cora's self-assessment. Under normal circumstances, he would never question her capability. She had operated *Scimitar* for years. Piloting a raptor was something she should be able to handle without any thought.

But if she glitched...

He didn't want to insult her by asking her to give him control of the ship, but he could not force the worst case from his thoughts.

The orbital station emerged from the planet's shadow, and the sight pushed every worry from his mind. They were still twenty kilometres away, but the massive structure dominated the view.

He closed one eye and lifted his thumb to block out the two heavy battle cruisers docked to the outer ring. It had been over a decade since he'd last set foot aboard a similar station back on Terra. He'd almost forgotten how awe-inspiring these amazing masterpieces of engineering were.

"Holy shit, that's big," said Caldwell.

"You ever been on one?" Hayden asked.

"No, but I've seen it from the ground. I knew it was huge, but I had no idea."

"Oh, my," said Emma. "How does something that size stay up here?"

Hayden turned to look at her, the answer on the tip of his tongue. She frowned at him.

"Of course, I know how," she said. "It's difficult to believe when you see it."

The cabin became silent as they all fell under its spell.

Cora spoke in Hayden's ear. "I wish I still had my eyes."

He didn't know how to respond. She monitored all the raptor's sensors and could "see" the station across the entire electromagnetic spectrum, in much more detail than human vision was capable of perceiving. And, yet, he couldn't imagine what it would be like to lose his sight and replace it with a stream of abstract data. She always seemed so accepting of what happened to her that the possibility she might miss the simple human sense of sight hadn't crossed his mind.

"Cora, I..." He struggled to find words, but she interrupted him.

"Hayden, do you see her?"

His heart went to his throat.

"Who?"

"*Scimitar*. Is she in view?"

Shit, he thought.

He reached for the manual override. "Everyone strap in; we're aborting."

They all spoke at once.

"Why?"

"What's happened?"

"Are we under attack?"

He shouted over them. "Just do it, now!"

He pressed the button, but nothing happened.

"Cora, please release the controls to me."

"That would be very dangerous. It would set off about a dozen alarms, and I don't control the station's weapons. Why do you want to make us a target?"

He didn't wish to alarm the others who were all scrambling to obey his order to strap in. So far, his conversations with Cora had been over his earpiece, and they had no clue what she'd said.

He whispered, "Cora, please trust me. Give me control of the ship."

"Hayden, I'm not glitching."

"Then, why did you ask me..." He lowered his voice further. "Why did you ask that question?"

"Because I've reviewed the list of ships docked at the orbital. *Scimitar* is one of them."

XURY BAECHER

Kaine stared at the massive orbital station as they neared. His eyes went from ship to ship docked along the visible portion of the outer ring.

He spoke into his mic. "Cora, you're positive *Scimitar* is here?"

"I'm sure a ship by that name is listed as docked here."

His eyes returned to the orbital. "Which bay? Can we see it from here?"

"She is at berth 241, on the opposite side of the station."

"Shit."

"Hayden," said Emma from behind him, "what's wrong?"

He hesitated to answer. What if Cora was glitching and only imagined she'd identified *Scimitar*?

"Some new information is coming in—nothing serious; something Cora flagged. I'm checking it out."

Adjusting his mic and abandoning further efforts to be discreet, he said aloud, "Cora, show me a visual record to confirm."

He winced when she sighed in his earpiece and understood how offended she must be. It couldn't be helped.

The communications screen on his panel came to life, and a

comprehensive readout of all the vessels, outbound, docked, and inbound scrolled across it. Every ship's name, registration number, assigned berth, time of arrival and departure, and a half dozen other details were displayed. Scrolling down, he spotted *Scimitar*.

"This lists only her name and berth—no other information."

"That is the complete record, Hayden."

"What is the significance of it being in red?"

"It is in a restricted section. Probably why the full record isn't available."

It was also another clue suggesting the mystery ship was their *Scimitar*.

"Can we take a tour around the station to confirm?"

"Not without drawing suspicion from anyone monitoring the traffic patterns. I can control the AI, but not what people see."

"Damn."

He weighed the problem for a few breaths.

"How far away will we be docking from berth two forty-one?"

"It is on the outer ring, where the larger ships are docked. We are being directed to a bay on the innermost one. And before you ask, I can't reroute us to anything closer."

He exhaled noisily. They would have to make their way through the station to reach it.

"What's going on, Kaine?" Caldwell asked.

He sighed and rotated his chair so he could address everyone.

"We believe *Scimitar* is docked in a high-security section of the station."

"You believe?" Aubrey said. "You can't confirm it, though."

He nodded. "Naturally, this complicates our mission."

"If true, then yes," she said. "Our abilities are taxed with what we came to do. We can't change our objective."

"Hayden," said Emma. "What if it is another ship with the same name? What if Cora is mistaken?"

He frowned and pointed to the readout. "Nothing is wrong

with her ability to read. Yes, a distinct possibility exists that it isn't our ship, but if it is…"

He let the thought hang for them to process.

Caldwell said, "So, what do you propose?"

"We can ignore this new information and complete our mission. Our tactics are rehearsed, and our exit strategy is established. As planned, it is risky but achievable."

"And potentially pointless," said Emma. "Our planning and objective assumed the government hasn't yet located the ship. If *Scimitar* is docked here, we may never get another opportunity to seize it."

"I like her," Cora said into Hayden's ear.

He suppressed a smile.

Caldwell looked out the cockpit at the now looming station. "How long until we dock?"

Cora replied over the ship's speakers. "Two and a half minutes."

Hayden said, "Cora and I know what we want to do, but given the significant additional risk, I can't ask any of you to participate. It's up to you three to decide where we go from here."

"What will you do if we vote to abort the mission?" Aubrey said.

He smiled. "None of you can pilot the ship to return. I won't abandon you here."

"Aubrey," said Emma, "we were all prepared to give our lives rather than surrender. I think it's worth the risk to confirm *Scimitar* is here and find a way to steal it out from under their noses."

Cora again spoke in Kaine's ear. "I really like her, Hayden."

Caldwell blew out his breath. "Kaine, you have a way of shaking things up, but you haven't disappointed me yet. Emma is right, I vote we try."

All eyes turned to Aubrey. She studied each of them before saying, "I'm in."

After Emma finished hugging her, she said, "All right, Kaine, what's our new plan?"

Cora still controlled the station's security AI after they docked. She disabled the surveillance recorders, and Hayden and the others exited the raptor unobserved.

He approached the biometric scanner at the end of the docking bridge and placed a hand on the panel. Cora overrode the rejected scan and opened the door while entering him into the station's personnel database. He stepped across the threshold and onto the metal grid on the floor, teeth gritted for the sound of an alarm if something went wrong.

Nothing happened, and he walked through and into the corridor.

After the others followed him in turn, he said, "Where do we go now, Cora?"

"The principal AI is in control beyond this point," she answered in his ear. "I need an access port to talk to it, just like in the original plan."

Hayden consulted the map displayed on the datapad embedded in the sleeve of his flight suit.

He started to whisper to the others but stopped himself when he spotted two people coming around the curving corridor. They were engaged in a conversation and hadn't yet seen them.

Straightening, he cleared his throat and pointed in the direction the pair came from. "It's this way."

He started walking, and the others fell in step behind him. As he neared the couple, one of them glanced at him. Hayden offered a friendly nod and continued walking.

Anxiously, he counted his steps, and when he'd gone about ten metres, he looked back. They were still engrossed in their discussion.

Blowing out his held breath, he checked the map and quickened his pace until they reached the indicated junction. He continued down the short side corridor until he came to a door marked, maintenance.

"Place your hand on the reader like before; you should be in the system."

He whispered, "Should be?"

When Cora didn't reply, he wasn't sure if she was pissed at him for questioning her competence or because she didn't really know.

He glanced back the way they'd come, then pressed his palm against the scanner. The red light turned green, and the door slid aside into the wall. Beyond was a small room lined with computer interface nodes.

Hayden waved them inside ahead of him. After one last check to ensure they hadn't been seen, he entered and closed the door behind them.

The space was cramped, so he squeezed past the others to reach the access node Cora required.

"The housing is shielded; hold me against it."

He removed her crystal from around his neck and examined it in his hand.

"How are you doing?" he whispered to her.

"I think I'm okay, but we both know I can't tell when I'm glitching."

"Just tell me where we are and why we're here."

"You brought me and a team to the *Xury Baecher* orbital docking platform aboard a stolen raptor. We came to locate *Scimitar*, but now—"

"Okay, you sound like you're fine."

"Can we please get started?"

"Wait, I thought of something. How will I know you've succeeded?"

"Now whose memory is glitching? I will retain a link to the crystal to communicate, remember?"

"I was just checking."

"Hayden, I'm fine."

He swallowed the growing lump in his throat. "Promise you'll come back to me, okay?"

"I promise. My job is easier than our original plan because I don't have to overpower the system AI. I'm just poking around for information, so if I do it right, the intelligence won't realize I'm here."

"Be careful."

He placed the crystal against the nodal housing.

The seconds became a minute, and with every heartbeat, he grew more anxious that something was wrong.

Emma whispered, "What's happening? Is she inside?"

As if to answer her, the door slid open.

Cora spoke in his ear. "I've blinded the station's monitoring system to you, but that is the most I can risk. I'll direct you along the route I've cleared. Go to the corridor and turn left. Hurry, I can't linger too long in here."

Kaine relayed the instruction to the others, and they filed out the door and around the corner. There weren't many people on their level, but as they progressed through the station, those they encountered gave them strange looks.

"Cora, we're getting too much attention in our flight suits."

"Give me a moment...okay, I've got something—a quarter-master's supply room. But you'll need to detour and go down ten levels. There is a lift fifty metres away around the next corner to your right."

Hayden explained the problem as he led them to the elevator.

When they were inside and the doors were closed, Aubrey said, "How the hell are we going to obtain new uniforms without a proper requisition?"

"Cora is working on the problem."

"We're putting a lot of faith in your AI."

"She's not an AI," said Emma sharply.

Aubrey shook her head. "Whatever—all I'm saying is the

deeper we get inside this place, the more dangerous this becomes."

"Which is why we need a change of clothing," said Hayden.

Caldwell unzipped his suit enough to reveal the pistol he wore in a shoulder harness. "Does the quartermaster have anything better than this? A change of clothes won't help us if we're discovered."

Hayden understood his unease and wanted to remind him that if it came down to a shootout, they were doomed. Caldwell and the others were aware they would be more cautious without access to additional firepower. Still, they were soldiers, and he appreciated how naked Caldwell must feel this deep inside enemy territory with only a pistol.

"First things first; we need to get out of these suits."

Caldwell grunted and drew the zipper up.

The doors parted, and they exited into a vestibule. Opposite them was a door labelled prominently as the quartermaster's office. Hayden glanced up at the security camera near the ceiling, and his heart skipped a beat.

As if reading his mind, Cora said, "I control the security feed on this level."

"What about a requisition?"

"It's handled. Hurry!"

Hayden waved the group forward and led them through the door.

Behind the desk was a short man in his late fifties. The epaulette pinned to the collar of his uniform identified him as a sergeant. Hayden guessed him to be an underachiever who was putting in his last few years at a low-stress job before easing into what he believed to be a well-earned retirement. He was the kind of bureaucrat who didn't want to risk his pension by doing anything with a hint of impropriety.

The man lifted bored eyes from his screen and perused them with an expression of annoyance.

He sighed and said, "Requisition."

When Hayden didn't respond, the man lifted an eyebrow and glanced at the palm reader on the desk.

"Well?"

"Right, sorry," said Kaine as he pressed his hand to the device. "It was a long flight."

The quartermaster nodded as he examined his screen. After a moment, he looked up, frowning.

The light on the reader was still red.

Hayden laughed weakly and made a show of rubbing his palms together to warm them before he tried again. In the corner of his eye, he caught sight of Caldwell pulling down his zipper.

He kept his hand pressed against the pad, clenching his jaw tighter with each second the light refused to become green.

Then, when he feared Caldwell might take matters into his own hands, the light changed, and the tension lifted from his shoulders.

The clerk's attention returned to the screen, and he squinted to read the document. Then, after a brief visual evaluation of each of them, he turned and entered the opened doorway behind him that led to the stores.

A couple of minutes later he emerged with a bundle of neatly pressed and folded uniforms, which he plopped onto the desk.

"This is all I have."

"I'm sure they'll be fine," Hayden said. "Is there somewhere we can change?"

The man's eyebrow arched again. "Are you serious? Get the hell out of here."

Hayden glowered at him while pointing to his old lieutenant's epaulette pinned to his lapel. "Is that how you speak to an officer, *Sergeant?*"

The colour drained from the older man's face, and he rose to his feet to try to stand at attention, but stiff muscles did not permit him to do so quickly.

"I'm sorry, sir. I have no excuse for my rudeness."

Kaine wanted to tear a strip off the man. He'd experienced the same attitude far too often during his military career, usually in older officers. It was very rare for such a breakdown of discipline among the enlisted soldiers because of the natural consequences. Morale appeared to be at a low point everywhere within the Oberon military structure.

"If you wish to make it to retirement, you will step aside and allow us to use the storeroom to change our clothes."

The man swallowed hard and moved out of the way. Hayden nodded to the others. "Be quick about it."

As they filed past him, Kaine continued to stare down the hapless sergeant. When the others returned, he took his turn to change. Exiting, he noted that the man had not moved during his absence but cowered under the glare of Caldwell, who sat on the edge of the desk.

Caldwell snapped to attention when he saw Hayden. Kaine fought the urge to smile as the other man struggled to stand and instead motioned for him to remain seated.

"Sergeant, I'm feeling generous today because I'm tired and don't want to spend the time to write you up. It would be in your interest to forget this incident ever took place. Do I make myself clear?"

"Absolutely sir."

Kaine motioned at the others that it was time to leave, and after he turned to follow, he gave in to the insistent urge to smile.

Ten minutes later, they'd retraced their steps and were back on mission. They continued along the route Cora marked on the map, and Hayden was relieved when they didn't attract attention. Thanks to their newly acquired uniforms, they blended in with the rest of the personnel. As they encountered more people on the upper levels, he had less opportunity to speak to Cora over the comm. That bothered him.

When he heard her voice, he could evaluate her state of mind. The radio silence they were forced to maintain made that impossible. He resolved to pull her out the moment she exhibited any minor memory lapse or was at a loss for the right word. He worried what would happen if she became disoriented or forgot who she was.

When the group found themselves at an unoccupied corridor junction, he whispered, "How are you holding up, Cora?"

"I think the station AI is getting suspicious, but so far he hasn't checked the subsystem I'm in. I may have to slip into another one to avoid detection or leave entirely. If that happens, I can't keep you hidden from the security monitors. I'll try to give you ample warning if that appears likely to happen."

"How much danger will you be in? Do we need to pull you out now?"

"If you do, you're all screwed. You won't get off the station because I won't be able to plant false departure documents. Don't worry about me; I'm nimble. If I go offline, assume I'm hiding, and I'll be back when the coast is clear."

"What should we do?"

"Linger in a populated area and act as if you belong."

He wanted to ask her about the other concern but decided she didn't need the distraction. Besides, he'd be surprised if it wasn't already foremost on her mind. The best thing they could do was to hurry and shorten the time she would have to remain in the system.

He reminded himself that Cora wasn't residing inside the station's computer. She was still in the crystal, in as much as she could be anywhere. It was her active consciousness that ran around the orbital's network. He really didn't understand how she did it, but he knew that she couldn't be physically lost to him if something went wrong. It just wasn't clear to him—and she hadn't explained—what would happen to her if she was discovered. That worried him, mostly because Cora hadn't seemed too sure of the consequences either.

He quickened his pace and led the team farther into the station until they reached the end of the route on the map. They were outside one of the docking platforms on the outer ring. This one was marked with flashing red signs as a restricted area.

They strolled past the guarded door and around a nearby corner where they couldn't be seen.

"It looks like we found it," said Emma.

Aubrey said, "Now what?"

He held up a finger to request a moment and addressed Cora. "We're at the entrance to the secure area."

Nothing came back to him over his earpiece.

"Cora, please respond. We've reached the docking area."

There was still no reply.

Emma said, "Hayden, what's wrong?"

He shook his head. "Cora's not answering, but she warned me this might happen if the system's AI started looking for her."

Caldwell frowned. "So, what do we do?"

"We'll have to give her some time."

Aubrey said, "How much time, Kaine? We are deep inside enemy territory, and it won't take very long before someone takes notice of us lurking here. We need a backup plan, right now."

He glanced up at the closest monitoring camera then turned away. She was right. If Cora was avoiding the AI, it would control the security subsystem.

"Let's keep moving," he said.

He forced himself to walk at a leisurely pace, wondering how much time he should give Cora.

They came upon a food court and sat around one of the few empty tables. The din of people sharing conversations over their mealtime break was strangely comforting. Hayden imagined being enveloped by a blanket of noisy anonymity.

Caldwell's attention was on the busy food kiosks a short distance away.

"Damn, I'm starving. Does anyone have credits?"

Aubrey tapped his arm. "You've gone for a lot longer between meals. Besides, you told me you need to drop some kilos."

"Unless someone left loose change in your pocket, none of us has any money," said Emma.

She dug into her jacket and produced a handful of coins. Handing them to Caldwell, she said, "Get us some coffee; we look suspicious sitting here."

Aubrey took them from him. "Relax. I don't want you fainting."

She rose and walked to the nearest kiosk.

Emma said to Hayden, "How long are we going to wait for Cora?"

He didn't know, and he was beginning to worry that she'd been silent for too long. What if she'd glitched and was confused and disoriented? What if the AI found and somehow trapped her? The prospect of losing her terrified him more than the consequences of them being discovered.

Hayden was upset with himself for putting her in danger. He thought they'd both weighed all the risks—and maybe she had and downplayed them—but he hadn't considered the full spectrum of complications Cora's loss would cause.

If she glitched, then she could spend eternity lost in a living hell. Perhaps worse, if caught, she'd be turned over to Thomas, if that were even possible without her crystal matrix. How far could she physically be from it? His hand clutched at the device hanging around his neck.

There was so much he didn't understand about his friend. She'd always behaved and interacted with him like her old self. So much so that he'd never considered her to be anything than the young engineer he met on his first day aboard *Scimitar*.

But the cold reality was that Cora wasn't human in anything but her personality. She was alien—as much Glenatat as anything else. He'd seen indications over the past few years that she was changing subtly. The human part of her was giving way to whatever she was destined to become.

The thought had terrified him, and he'd avoided bringing it up with her because the idea of losing her a second time was too painful to contemplate.

Yet he would lose her if this mission was aborted. He had to find a way to get her crystal to *Scimitar*. He hoped she could merge with or be absorbed by the ship and reunited with the bit of her that was a permanent part of it.

And if by some disastrous outcome, she was lost in her present form, would that be the end of her? If he set foot on *Scimitar*, would he encounter a version of her that was identical in every way to the Cora he knew but ignorant of what they'd experienced together these past few months? He didn't know.

Perhaps the human part of her had been with him all this time. Maybe the part of her that was *Scimitar* was no longer anything resembling the person he loved, but instead just a machine.

Aubrey returned with a tray and placed it on the table. She plucked a cup of coffee from it and offered it to him, but he barely paid attention.

"Hayden," said Emma, "what's wrong?"

"It's been too long."

Aubrey put the cup down in front of him. "Take a drink and relax, Kaine. If your AI friend is as good as you say she is, we should give her more time."

Embarrassed, he forced a smile and took a sip.

"You're right," he said. "She just needs a little time."

Aubrey was right. There was no reason, yet, to panic.

He wanted to remain hopeful, but if Cora had glitched, more time would not help them.

DESPERATE PLANS

Emma's eyes were riveted on Hayden. "How long should we wait?"

He looked back the way they came.

"Cora's not answering; it may mean nothing more than she's avoiding the station's AI and can't talk."

Caldwell said, "Could it mean she's been captured?"

Hayden's eyes were drawn to the security camera mounted on the wall at the far end of the dining hall. "I don't believe so. If that were the case, the AI would impose a station-wide lockdown to search for whoever put her in the system."

"Okay," said Aubrey, "that means there's some time, but we don't know how much."

"Maybe we just need to be patient," said Emma. "If Cora is hiding, she could regain control when the coast is clear."

Caldwell lowered his voice. "Sit here waiting to be captured ourselves? I don't like that idea. We didn't come up here to do nothing."

"Relax, Caldwell," said Aubrey, "we aren't 'doing nothing.'"

"What do you mean?"

"I mean, even if we can't reach *Scimitar*, we are fulfilling our primary mission."

"I don't understand," said Emma.

Aubrey's smile sent a chill down Hayden's spine. She said, "You will soon."

"What did you do?" Kaine asked.

"Something we were all committed to do before we got side-tracked by your ship hunt."

He racked his brain for some idea of what she might mean.

"Are you talking about a suicide attack on the station? That's an insane idea."

"Is it? The loss of this station on D'Ville's watch will end him. It will also galvanize our cowardly leadership into finishing what we started instead of surrendering. If we can strike here, we will show the Confederation how strong we are. It gives us the upper hand to negotiate a real change in government that is in our favour and not that of the empire or its cronies."

"Or it could backfire and bring the full weight of the imperial forces down on this planet," said Emma.

"You were committed to this kind of action before. What's changed?"

Emma's eyes darted momentarily to Hayden.

"Obtaining *Scimitar* would give us a weapon to use against military targets. We would possess an overwhelming advantage, without killing tens of thousands of people."

"But now it doesn't look like we will ever reach Kaine's ship, and the longer we sit on hold, the greater the risk we will be discovered. This plan was never going to work, even before we modified it. It was a convenient distraction to persuade him to bring me here to fulfil my mission."

"This is as much a civilian target as military," said Emma. "Thousands of noncombatants will die if you do what you propose. Destroying this station would make us no better than D'Ville."

"Innocent lives are lost in war, Emma. It's time you and Krellig realize that."

"I'm with Aubrey on this one," said Caldwell.

Hayden said, "Destroying the station will only be regarded universally as a terrorist act and will scuttle any hope for peace. The government will use it as a rallying call to turn anyone who harbours sympathy for your cause. Think—do you want to be remembered for committing an atrocity?"

Aubrey snorted. "Who are you to lecture us about atrocities? You haven't lived under the oppressive boot of your Confederation. They exploited Oberon for generations and bled us through their corrupt governors. Do you honestly believe the orbital bombing was the only such incident?"

Caldwell said, "I lost family to D'Ville and those who came before him. We all have. Our people suffered so the friends of your empire could grow fat off our world's riches."

"I told you about my family," said Emma. "Your people are responsible for so much suffering here."

"I'm sorry for what happened to all of you."

"No," said Aubrey. "You don't get to offer your insincere apologies. You are Terran. You were part of the system; you benefited from the corruption that sucked the colony worlds dry."

"I can't help where I was born. If I knew this was happening, I would not have supported it."

"Even after you became the president? Don't act so shocked, Kaine. I know who your family is and who you are."

Emma said, "What are you talking about, Aubrey?"

"Did he not confide who he really is during your little tête-à-têtes? Hayden Kaine is the chosen one, a scion of the most important family in the empire. They influenced the selection of presidents for at least a hundred years." She pointed at him. "He was destined to become the next one before everything went to shit. He is one of them, Emma. He isn't one of us."

Shocked, Emma turned to him. "Is this true?"

He struggled to find the words. "Yes, but I wanted nothing to do with my family's plan for me. That's why I left."

"But you still joined their military, didn't you, *Lieutenant*?"

The word dripped from Aubrey's lips like a caustic acid. "You were still an instrument of our oppressors, sent from system to system to quell unrest."

"I never participated in a mission like that. As I said, I was ignorant of the corruption. It sickens me that my family was complicit, but even before I learned of that, I turned my back on Thomas and his dreams to rebuild the shattered empire."

"Why are you so important to him that he pursues you across the galaxy?"

Aubrey didn't let him respond.

"Emma, did you know that Thomas wants Kaine to assume a figurehead role in his new Confederation? He is needed to give the dictator credibility with his own people."

"I refused," said Hayden. "It's why I ran."

"Aubrey," whispered Emma, "when did you learn all this?"

"M'gomba told me. It seems, Kaine, you are important enough for the empire to put out a bulletin for your capture the moment they arrived. I don't understand why Krellig chose to harbour you. That was another weak and stupid decision by him."

Emma said, "And where is M'gomba with all of this?"

"He was torn between his foolish loyalty to the general and common sense. He knew all about Kaine but still decided to give him enough rope to learn what his true intentions are. If he did manage to locate his fabled ship, we considered it a bonus to the real operation to bring down this station."

"Why weren't we read in on this?" Caldwell asked.

"Need-to-know. You two were sent for exactly the reason you were told: to protect the asset. If Kaine could locate his ship, we needed to return with the information."

"So, what is your new plan?" Hayden asked.

She shrugged. "I think there is a better way of dealing with an asset like you."

Caldwell said, "What are you thinking?"

"What will Thomas pay if we offer Kaine to him? Something

tells me he is more valuable than his ship is. If we turn him over, we can write our own ticket to govern ourselves. It's worth considering."

She opened her jacket to reveal the pistol in its shoulder holster.

"Aubrey," hissed Emma. "Close your jacket and keep it shut. You're attracting attention."

A few heads turned in their direction, attracted by their intense hushed argument. Hayden smiled and waved at them. With their interest noticed, they became disinterested and got up to leave.

"Station security will come down on us if we're not careful," he said. "Is that what you want?"

Leaning forward on the table, he stared into Aubrey's grey eyes.

"Taking me hostage and negotiating with Thomas won't help you. I know the man. You are being naive if you believe he can be trusted to honour his word."

"It's worth the attempt."

"Your world and every other one he brings back into the fold will learn what real oppression is once *Scimitar* is turned over to him. There is a limited window of opportunity to deprive him of it. Don't be foolish."

"I'm just adapting the plan. Right now, it doesn't appear that your AI girl was successful."

"Give her time. She'll prove you wrong."

"There is no way we can get our hands on that ship—probably never was, even with her help. We don't have the men or the firepower to take on what's behind those security doors, so I'm going to do what is necessary to ensure Thomas doesn't get his hands on it. I'll destroy your precious *Scimitar*, along with everything else on this station."

Hayden's heart tried to beat its way out of his chest. He fought to maintain a calm demeanour. "What, exactly, is your intent?"

"We will sit here and patiently wait for the clock to run out."

"What clock?" Caldwell said.

A sly smile formed on her lips, and in that instant, Hayden understood how he'd been used.

"The raptor," he said. "You did something to it."

"It took some doing, but our engineers rigged the engines to overload. In a little less than two hours a two-megaton blast will take out the inner docking ring and compromise the structural integrity of the station."

"When did you plan to tell us about this?" Caldwell hissed.

"Don't look so butt-hurt," she said. "If we had stuck to our original mission, we'd have gotten what we wanted from the computer by now and be well on our way as planned in the station's emergency escape pods. Discovering *Scimitar* here forced me to improvise in case there was a chance to steal it. It is, as Emma said, a significant prize. It's a shame it will now really burn up in the atmosphere this time."

"Listen, Aubrey," said Hayden. "As long as a security lockdown hasn't happened, I believe Cora can still help us get *Scimitar*. There is no need for this senseless violence. With the ship in your possession, you hold a very strong hand to negotiate a lasting peace on your terms. Do you think you've seen oppression? If you destroy this station, the consequences will be catastrophic for everyone."

"I, for one, am glad the jump-gate collapsed," she said. "It gave us a chance to rise up and determine our own destiny. But we didn't act, and now that window of opportunity is closing. I'm not a fool like Krellig or M'gomba. There can be no peace with your empire. They've already demonstrated their intentions, and I am not naive enough to believe things will improve for us no matter what we do. I will die before I submit to a resurrected oppressor. They need to understand what it will cost them to control Oberon."

Hayden saw something in her eyes that frightened him. Aubrey held no doubts about what she was doing. She was a fanatic, close-minded to the idea that compromise or peace was achievable. In her mind, there was only one course to follow. He wondered how many others like her D'Ville and his predecessors had created.

He cleared his throat. "I could call out for station security and warn them."

She patted her jacket. "You'd be dead before they responded."

"And we would be killed in the subsequent shootout," said Emma. "Don't be a fool, Aubrey. Maybe you want to die senselessly, but neither of us signed up for that."

She glanced at Emma and Caldwell. "Relax, there is still time for us to make it to the escape pods."

Hayden said, "I'm not inclined to participate."

The room began to spin as a wave of vertigo came on him. He shut his eyes until he felt things return to normal.

When he opened them, Aubrey was smiling. "Feeling woozy?"

His eyes shot to the half-empty coffee cup in front of him.

"You drugged me."

"There was no way you would cooperate, so I slipped something into your drink."

He tried to stand, but his legs gave out, and he collapsed back onto the chair. "Relax, Kaine. We'll continue this discussion back on the ground."

He blinked to try to clear his blurred vision. Squinting, he pointed to the far end of the dining hall at some dark figures entering.

"I think they might have other ideas."

As she turned to follow his gaze, he reached up to pluck the comm unit from his ear and palmed it.

Aubrey turned back. "It's nobody, but we're wasting time; we should go. You two help him to his feet."

"We'll attract attention," hissed Caldwell. "What do we say about him?"

"He's diabetic and didn't take his insulin. Don't worry, I can sell it. Grab him."

Hayden's vision dimmed, and the ringing in his ears grew louder as Emma and Caldwell gripped his arms to help him stand.

He touched Emma's hand to confirm it was her, then grabbed her free hand and slipped the earpiece into it.

Then the room grew dark and he passed out.

Hayden slipped in and out of consciousness as they struggled to support him from the dining hall. Aubrey explained to someone that they were taking him to the infirmary.

When he opened his eyes, the corridor became a spinning tunnel. Nausea overcame him, and he vomited the coffee all over his jacket.

Caldwell's voice seemed to come from the bottom of a well. The words were muffled, but he thought someone said something about them being noticed.

Darkness.

Falling.

A heavy blow to his chin, followed by a vague pain along his jaw.

He tried to speak but couldn't form words.

No one held his arms any longer, and a cold surface pressed against his cheek. He struggled to push himself up against it, but everything spun. He collapsed back to his belly as his surroundings rotated about him.

Something plucked at his arms. A shadowy figure seized his hands and dragged him.

He no longer had control of his limbs and could not fight against the demon dragging him into Hell. The storm continued to rage around him as an overwhelming panic gripped him. Every childhood fear of eternal damnation drummed into him seemed to rise at once in his mind.

Someone called his name from a great distance.

Something grabbed under his arms and lifted him.

The ringing in his ears became unbearable. He spun help-lessly in an invisible vortex and felt himself being pulled down a bottomless well.

His fuzzy vision dimmed until darkness enveloped him.

Hayden woke with a start, his heart racing.

He was on his back and stared at a lighting panel in the ceiling. Confused, he scanned the unfamiliar surroundings.

It took a moment to realize he lay on a gurney in a small room.

"Oh, good," said Emma as she entered his field of vision, "you're awake."

Hayden pushed himself up on one elbow. They were alone in a medical examining room. She was dressed in a white medical coat. He squinted to try reading the identification badge pinned to her pocket, but he still had trouble focussing.

"What happened?"

She held up an empty hypo-spray. "I just gave you a stimulant. You were completely out of it. I convinced Aubrey that she'd overdosed you and that you needed immediate medical attention."

"Did I?"

"She definitely gave you more than the recommended dose. You were never in any danger, but she doesn't know that."

Hayden gingerly pushed himself up to sit on the edge of the gurney and rubbed his aching jaw. "Did I fall at some point?"

"Yes; are you hurt?"

"No, not really. Where are we?"

"We brought you to the nearest infirmary.

"Why are you dressed like that?"

She looked at her coat. "Oh, this...we kind of improvised to get you in here. It's a long story that ended up with a doctor and a medical tech being locked in a closet. Aubrey and Caldwell are outside keeping watch."

She opened her hand and offered him the comm unit he'd passed to her. "I've been trying to raise Cora, but she doesn't answer. Why did you believe you could trust me with this?"

He examined the unit before putting it in his ear. "Was I mistaken? You seemed as shocked as I when Aubrey revealed her true mission."

She paled. "I never imagined her capable of such a thing. I can't let this happen, and I am clueless about how to prevent it."

Hayden glanced at the closed door. "What was your plan when you brought me here?"

Emma sighed. "I didn't have one, but I knew there would be no chance to stop her if we made it to the escape pods."

He frowned.

"I'm sorry," she said.

"You did the right thing; she must be stopped."

"Any ideas?"

He looked around the room. "Not really, but give me a moment. What kind of condition will Aubrey expect me to be in when we leave here?"

She blushed. "I sort of convinced her you were dying, so any semiconscious, compliant state where you can walk with assistance to the station's escape pods."

Hayden blew out his breath. "Not my favourite form of transportation."

Spotting his jacket, he asked Emma to pass it to him. He patted it until he found what he wanted and dug the small datapad from the pocket. Turning it on, he brought up a holo-map of the facility.

Emma approached and pointed at a section. "We're here, and the pods we are heading for are here."

Hayden turned the map. "The raptor is in this docking bay."

"That's ten levels down. We should contact station security

and tell them about it. Then we can make our escape in the confusion."

He shook his head. "The station will be put on high-alert lockdown while they check it out. Besides, Aubrey's escape plan was always doomed. Anything approaching or leaving will be blasted to atoms by the defensive grid unless cleared by the AI."

She frowned. "Without Cora, no one is getting off this station. Aubrey always planned to become a martyr."

"That's how it appears."

"Then why the charade of trying to get us off the station with you?"

Hayden shrugged. "To distract you and Caldwell from interfering, most likely. I can't really say."

She snapped at him. "Then why didn't she just start shooting us in the mess hall if she had no intention of escape?"

"A security lockdown would increase the possibility of her bomb being discovered. The longer she can keep things quiet, the better the odds for completing her mission."

Tears pooled in her eyes. "Hayden, what are we going to do?"

"We probably can't stop the overload—maybe with Cora's help it's possible, but..."

He swallowed. "Anyway, the raptor's manoeuvring jets and autopilot are still functional. If I can get to the docking bay, I can program the ship to leave the station."

Emma's eyes widened, and she spoke quickly. "Then the orbital's guns will destroy it. That sounds like an excellent plan."

"Well, I don't know about that; we'd still be trapped aboard."

"But thousands of lives will be saved."

Hayden nodded. "Yes, but I don't expect Aubrey or Caldwell to be very cooperative."

"He is a survivor. We can tell him what will happen if we try to use the escape pods."

He smiled tightly. "Forgive me, but he isn't the sharpest knife in the drawer. I like him, but he is too easy to influence—I've done so myself. Aubrey might have him completely sold on her cause."

Emma's brow creased. "Then we will ensure neither of them gets in our way."

She held up the empty hypo-spray.

"You're going to drug them," said Hayden.

"Damn right I am. Put them to sleep and hide them in here."

"I can't think of anything better." He glanced up at the cabinets behind her. "Do you have the drugs in here?"

She smiled. "I have just the right thing in mind. I'll need a minute to prepare the hypos."

He nodded his approval, and as she turned to begin preparing the anaesthetic, he reached for the comm unit in his ear and quietly spoke.

"Cora? Are you there?"

The seconds ticked by without any reply, and with each one he felt a little bit more despair.

The longer she didn't respond, the more the likelihood that she'd glitched. His stomach knotted at the thought.

They'd gotten so close. *Scimitar* was out of their reach. If he had planned things better, they might have had time before she became lost in her own memories. But they hadn't known the ship was here. There was so much he wished he'd known.

He touched his shirt where her crystal hung beneath it. It was warm from the energy within. Was Cora still inside, or had she become part of the station's computer? He should have quizzed her more thoroughly about the mechanics of the transfer, but she'd been so confident about the process that he'd never thought to question her.

The truth was they were both desperate enough to locate their ship that no danger or argument would have dissuaded them from attempting this mission.

But it had been for nothing.

Worse; now he was burdened with the knowledge that the Confederacy had the ship. Perhaps Aubrey's plan was for the best. Blowing up the station would destroy *Scimitar*. It would prevent Thomas from gaining a terrible weapon to intimidate other star systems into compliance.

But destroying the station would also murder thousands and guarantee that an iron fist would descend upon Oberon. Aubrey, Caldwell, and Emma believed they'd seen oppression, but they didn't know Thomas as he did.

As much as it pained him to do so, he had to let *Scimitar* go. It was lost to him, as was Cora. Unless she merged with the ship, she was doomed. Perhaps she was already beyond even what *Scimitar* could do for her, but he'd never know.

All he could do now was to try to help the people who had saved him. If he could stop Aubrey's bomb from killing so many, the peace process that Krellig and the other leaders were negotiating might succeed. Right now, that was the best chance for Oberon.

WHAT MUST BE DONE

Hayden began to feel normal by the time Emma finished preparing the anaesthetic.

"I only have the one hypo, so we need to coordinate how to handle those two."

"How fast will that take effect?" He pointed at the hypo-spray in her hand.

"Depends on body weight, but even Caldwell will be out after ten seconds."

"Then he should be dosed first. I can probably restrain him for that long. Aubrey is likely to shoot us when she figures out what's going on."

"We will have the element of surprise if we're smart about this. When they come in, I'll get Caldwell to assist me lifting you off the bed—you'll have to pretend you're still a bit loopy."

He smiled. "I think I can handle that."

"You'd better. When he goes to lift you—"

Hayden nodded. "I get it. I'll go limp, and you can stick him with the hypo. What about Aubrey?"

"I can handle her; just keep Caldwell restrained until he passes out."

"You're sure about that?"

She frowned. "We train together; I know all her moves. I'll keep her occupied until Caldwell is out, and then you can restrain Aubrey while I dose her."

"It sounds simple enough."

He had his doubts but swallowed them, since he didn't have a better plan.

Hayden sat on the edge of the gurney while Emma went to the door. Before she opened it, she looked back at him and scowled as she whispered, "You're wearing your game face. You need to look pathetic to sell this."

He nodded and assumed his best sick puppy expression. She shook her head.

"Look at the floor and mumble if spoken to."

He smiled. "Would it help if I drooled?"

"Jesus, didn't you ever pretend to be sick as a kid? Just keep your head down."

He complied and stared at a point on the floor as she left the room.

Her voice was muffled from the other side of the door, and then it opened again.

He listened as footfalls entered the room. Hayden risked a quick glance to confirm it was Caldwell who approached.

"Hang on," said Emma. "I'll give you a hand with him."

"Time is running out," said Aubrey from near the doorway.

Emma went to his other side and put her arm about his waist. "Let's do this together; on three. One...two...three."

Her free hand was in the pocket of her med-coat. As they shifted his weight from the gurney, he let his legs collapse beneath him.

Caldwell grabbed him with both arms to support him.

Emma pulled the hypo from her pocket, but Caldwell didn't anticipate her letting go and lost his grip on Hayden. They lurched into Emma, and the hypo-spray clattered to the floor.

Time seemed to stop as everyone stared at it.

Hayden came out of the trance first and punched Caldwell in the stomach.

The breath went out of him, and his legs gave out, but he retained his grip on Hayden's sleeves and pulled him to the floor with him.

As they began to wrestle, a crash told him that Emma and Aubrey had gotten into it.

The contents of a medical tray were dumped to the floor.

Hayden managed to get purchase and pushed himself on top of Caldwell to deliver a punch to his jaw.

The soldier's eyes blazed with fury as he blocked the blow and responded with a savage elbow to Kaine's cheek.

Stars danced before his eyes as he fell off Caldwell. He rolled to his side as the other man fell on top of him. Meaty hands clutched around his throat and started to squeeze.

His arms flailed at Caldwell's head, but his blows were weak and didn't faze the man. He tried to pry his assailant's hands from his throat, but his grip was like iron, and his full weight pressed down on Kaine's chest.

His vision darkened.

Desperate for air, he let go to push on the floor and try to buck Caldwell off him. As he did so, his hand fell on the hypo-spray.

He grabbed it and brought it up against Caldwell's thigh with a satisfying hiss.

Surprised, Caldwell shifted his weight. It was enough for Hayden to leverage him off him.

The two men rolled on the floor, but this time Hayden managed to get onto the other man's back and press his face into the tiles.

He held him there as the seconds seemed to drag on. Finally, after what felt like an eternity, the soldier stopped struggling and his arms fell limply to the floor.

A cry of pain from one of the women pulled Hayden's attention to their struggle.

On the floor by the door, Aubrey was on Emma's back. With legs wrapped around her torso, she held her in a chokehold.

Coughing as he tried to take a deep breath, he scooped up the discarded hypo-spray from the floor and staggered toward the women.

He grabbed Aubrey by the hair and forced her head to the side. She screamed and tried to bite him as he injected the sedative into her neck.

In far less time than it took for Caldwell, she went limp.

Emma pushed Aubrey off and rose to her knees. She rubbed her throat as she looked at Hayden.

"That could have gone better."

"Ya think?" Hayden painfully lowered himself to sit beside her.

They both laughed.

"What should we do with them?" he asked.

She looked at Aubrey, then Caldwell. "They'll be out for at least an hour. I think we should leave them in here and let station security know where to find them."

He frowned. "That's a bit harsh, don't you think?"

"Spending the best years of her life in a gulag is too good for that bitch. She was prepared to murder everyone aboard this station; might yet succeed if we can't stop the raptor's overload."

"But Caldwell." He turned to look at the soldier lying on the floor.

"He wasn't following orders," she said. "He went off-mission when he sided with Aubrey's plan. They both belong in prison."

"Remind me not to piss you off."

Emma sighed. "I suppose we can avoid calling security. These two can try their luck making it off the station after they wake up."

Hayden smiled. "That's sporting of you."

"Not really; they'll still answer for this when Krellig learns about it."

He stood and offered her his hand to help her stand. "Shall we go?"

She waved him off and pushed herself to her feet.

Hayden retrieved Caldwell and Aubrey's pistols.

Handing one to Emma, he said, "Let's save some lives."

They emerged from the infirmary into an empty corridor. Emma led the way to the nearest junction, where they entered a wide, busy causeway. Dozens of station personnel bustled past them, all preoccupied with their own business.

There was a window set into the curving wall across from them. Kaine weaved his way through the traffic to stand at it and stare out at the view of the station hanging above Oberon's iridescent blue horizon.

Emma tugged at his sleeve. "The elevator is this way."

"There she is," he said.

"What?" Her gaze followed where he pointed.

Half a kilometre beneath them was the edge of the rotating outer docking ring. Connected to it, barely visible behind the curved surface of the station's structure, was the distinctive dorsal form of a UEF cruiser.

"That's *Scimitar*? Are you sure?"

"I'd recognize her anywhere," he said, his eyes glued to the sculpted grey hull. Hayden's mind easily visualized the obscured part of the vessel. He didn't need to see the registration number to know his ship.

With a heaviness that enveloped his soul, he realized how close he'd come to his goal. The ship he'd once believed destroyed was only a few hundred metres away, but it may as well have been on the other side of the galaxy.

His hand touched the crystal beneath his shirt.

So close. If only events went differently, he might have been able to reach it to save Cora. Even if he could get to *Scimitar* now, he didn't know if she could merge with it, or if doing so could save her. Tears misted his vision at the realization that he'd probably lost them both.

"Hayden," said Emma softly. "We have to go."

She was right. Cora might be gone and *Scimitar* beyond his reach, but countless lives were still at risk. He could indulge his sorrow later, but there was still work to be done.

He wiped his eyes with his sleeve and faced Emma.

His voice cracked as he said, "Lead the way."

She squeezed his elbow and smiled reassuringly.

Slipping her hand into his, she led him into the flow of traffic moving along the passage. Hayden couldn't avoid looking out every window they passed, trying to catch one last glimpse of his ship.

They broke from the flow of bodies at a lift station, where they joined three people who waited. The wait was short, and when the doors opened, they followed the others into the lift.

Hayden's anxiety rose as they pressed the buttons for their levels. He exhaled his held breath after the last person selected a level three above the docking bays.

In silence, they rode the lift down to the first level. The doors parted for a man and woman to exit. No one else boarded.

The remaining man glanced at them, an unspoken question on his face.

Kaine realized that the level the fellow was going to must be somewhere the average person was not expected to go. He smiled and reached across to press the button for the docking level.

His suspicions were confirmed when the man appeared satisfied and returned to gazing ahead at the closed doors.

The lift stopped, and he departed. When the doors again closed and they were alone, Hayden let out a long breath and fell back against the wall.

He looked at Emma.

"You seem very calm," he said.

She smiled weakly. "I'm petrified. I don't think I'm cut out for this sneaking about."

Hayden returned her smile. "Me neither, but we do what's required of us, right?"

His weight seemed to increase as the elevator slowed. Steeling himself, he faced the doors.

They opened to the familiar vestibule they had passed through on their arrival.

Going from memory, he led the way out of the lift and into the curving corridor that led to the bay where their raptor was parked.

Stopping before the entrance, he checked the hallway in both directions before he pressed his hand against the palm reader set in the wall.

He was rewarded with the hiss of hydraulics and the door sliding open.

"It looks like I'm still listed in the database. This is a good sign."

"Let's hope our luck continues to hold," said Emma.

He checked the empty corridor again.

"The plan isn't a complex one. I'll slip inside and try to shut down the reactor while you keep an eye open out here."

"And what if you can't shut it down? Aubrey seemed confident about that not being possible."

"In that case, I'll set the autopilot to take the ship out to the defensive perimeter. There it can detonate safely or be blown to bits by the station's guns."

"In either case, alarms are going to sound. Is there an escape plan for us in all this?"

The corner of his mouth turned up into a wry smile. "Shouldn't we have discussed that before we came down here on a fool's errand?"

"Preventing a disaster is the primary goal, so what happens to us was always secondary. I think we both knew that. However, I can't help being open to the possibility of escape."

"There are emergency escape pods back the way we came," he said, "but unless a station evacuation is ordered, launching in one will be a death sentence."

"What you're trying to tell me is that there isn't a way for us to get off this station."

"Not unless we can commandeer another ship or stow away on one."

"Well, that blows."

Hayden chuckled. "Yeah, it does. On the hopeful side, if we are both still registered in the system, we can live incognito until we figure out how to get back to the planet."

"I'm okay with that. Maybe we can figure out a way to get Cora aboard *Scimitar*."

He tried to smile. "Maybe we will, but first, we have to make sure the station survives."

Emma nodded curtly. "One thing at a time; of course."

"If this goes as planned, I should be in and out in about five minutes without anyone knowing what happened."

"And if it doesn't go according to plan?"

He pulled the pistol out of his jacket's inner pocket and examined it. It would do him no good inside the hanger, so he handed it to her. "If I set off an alarm, I'd appreciate you watching my back until I can do what's required."

"If you trip an alarm, that'll screw up our plans to survive, but yeah, I'll buy you whatever time you need."

"You're an impressive woman, Emma."

She locked eyes with him, then grabbed his face and kissed him on the lips.

Hayden froze.

By the time his wits returned, she'd broken off the kiss and stepped back. Her cheeks reddened as she covered her mouth with both hands.

"I am so sorry. I...I don't know why I did that."

The silence between them grew awkward, and Hayden felt himself blush.

"I should go," he said.

She avoided eye contact. "Right, I'll keep watch, as we discussed."

With nothing left to say, he turned and went through the doorway.

LET ME DO THIS FOR YOU

To his relief, Kaine passed through the security grid without incident. Unable to do anything about the security camera, he hurried to the raptor and opened the engine access port. On touching the housing, he jerked his hand away. It was hot; not enough to burn him or set off the infrared sensors in the hangar, but not what he expected. Steeling his nerve, he grabbed the latch and pulled open the panel. A wall of heat hit him in the face and forced him back from the opening.

He slammed the door shut and listened, but no fire alert sounded. He considered the matter and decided that the sensors must be calibrated to allow for the heat of thruster jets inside the hangar. The temperature behind the access door, while uncomfortable for him, was not hot enough to set off the alarm. Aubrey's engineering team had been clever about keeping their sabotage from being detected. He suspected the heat buildup curve was exponential and that by the time things became hot enough for the station's fire suppression system to respond, it would be too late.

After a few seconds of pondering the problem, he removed his jacket and wrapped it around his head. Then he reopened the panel and reached as far inside as he could without touching the edges of the opening.

Everything appeared normal to his untrained eye. He hadn't expected anything obvious to be out of place but thought it was worthwhile to eliminate the easiest solution first.

Closing the cover, he boarded the ship. Inside, the cabin was uncomfortably warm but tolerable.

He went to the helm's instrument cluster and noted the engine temperature, then turned his attention to shutting down the fusion reactor. He tried everything he could think of, but every action proved futile.

His heart skipped a beat when he again checked the thermal readout. The reactor temperature had increased by ten degrees in as many minutes. The buildup was accelerating, and he was running out of time.

He activated the helm and tried to initiate the autopilot, but it wouldn't respond. Rebooting the computer made no difference. The autopilot remained unresponsive.

He slammed his hand down on the arm of the chair.

"Shit!"

Kaine started turning on all the raptor's systems.

The whine of the lift turbines filled the cabin as they spun up.

Hayden wasn't certain that the station's hangar systems were like those aboard *Scimitar*, where the doors were linked to the helm controls. It was a protocol designed around the assumption that someone launching in a shuttle had the authorization to do so and was coordinating with flight control. If it turned out that doors were controlled by the AI, he'd be forced to ram them open, and that would probably not end well.

With his teeth clenched, he touched the door control button.

Miraculously, a flashing amber light came on inside the hangar, accompanied by a klaxon warning that the space was being vented. The noisy alarm grew fainter until he could no longer hear it. As the giant doors began to part, a mechanical voice spoke faintly from someone behind him.

His eyes fell on the helmet hanging from the back of the chair, and he realized someone was trying to reach him on the raptor's comm system.

He put it on and heard the unmistakable artificial voice of the station's AI.

"Raptor 26-49B, you are not authorized for departure; respond."

He adjusted the helmet's mic and said, "There must be some mistake. I received clearance ten minutes ago."

His eyes were glued to the console readouts as he pushed the throttle for the vertical thrusters and the raptor lifted from the deck. He permitted himself to relax a bit when there was no perceptible increase in the reactor's temperature.

"Negative, Raptor 26-49B. You are in error. No departure clearance is issued. Shut down immediately."

"Uh, sorry, Control, but I can't do that. The autopilot won't release the helm to me."

Hayden's jaw tightened as he gingerly engaged the forward thrusters. The temperature readout remained constant as the ship moved toward the hangar doors.

"Raptor 26-49B, do not depart the hangar. Station defences will not stand down. You run the risk of being fired upon."

"Oh, dear, that doesn't sound good. Give me a few moments while I override the computer."

He shut off the receiver and removed the helmet.

The raptor passed through the opening, and he shut down the thrusters to let inertia carry him away from the station. His hand hung, poised over the thruster control. Would a power draw to them accelerate the overload? Was there time for the raptor to drift far enough from the station? He wished he knew the answer.

Watching the temperature readout, he timed its rate of increase. The number he got puzzled him. Thinking he'd made a calculation error, he did so a second time, only to arrive at the same value.

The temperature acceleration had slowed down. Perhaps drawing power had bled off some of the energy buildup. Maybe firing the thrusters would give him more time, at least until he reached the station's defensive perimeter. Then the big guns would do what the sabotage hadn't yet accomplished. His mission would be a success, but somehow the idea of flying headlong to his own destruction had become less compelling.

As he drifted past it, he gazed out the cockpit at the massive outer docking ring that curved away to its own horizon. *Scimitar* was somewhere farther along that curve, out of sight. He would have liked to see her one more time.

He felt Cora's crystal beneath his shirt and reached up to remove it from around his neck. The alien device was warm in his palm as he held it.

His brow furrowed as he turned over an idea. He checked the temperature increase rate to find it had sped up again. To him, that made sense, since he'd stopped using the manoeuvring thrusters.

Lifting the crystal near his lips, he whispered, "Maybe we have time to say goodbye."

He fired the jets in a series of bursts and redirected the raptor to follow the curve of the outer ring. The thought nagged at him that he was being foolish and exposing too many people to danger. But the readout confirmed that the temperature increase had again slowed, restoring his confidence in his plan.

Emerging from behind the ring, *Scimitar* became visible. At the sight of her, Hayden laughed while tears rolled down his cheeks. Her sleek, silver-grey surface glinted in the sunlight.

As he drew nearer, and the ship became revealed, he studied her storied hull. She wore every scar, dent, and scorch mark as a proud testimony to her improbable journey across the galaxy. The heat shielding on her bow was blackened, evidence of her fiery plunge through Oberon's atmosphere. By some miracle, she'd survived. He didn't understand how, and it didn't matter. She was here and in one piece, something he'd never dared do more than wish was possible.

He tore his eyes from the ship and released his harness. Floating free of the chair, he pushed himself toward the rear of the cockpit. Pulling open the storage compartment door, his lips pressed together in a tight grimace when he saw the contents.

"Damn."

He'd hoped it held an emergency full pressure suit, but the only garment inside was a high-altitude, partial pressure flight suit. It wasn't designed to keep him alive for very long in high orbit, but it was better than nothing.

He stripped out of his clothing and donned the tight-fitting suit. Before zipping it closed, he removed Cora's crystal from about his neck and wrapped the cord around his forearm. Then he pulled on the snug helmet, connected the oxygen canister, and tested the airflow before closing the seals. After pulling on the gloves and booties, he was ready to go.

Hayden synced the control embedded in the suit's arm with the raptor and brought up a holographic calculation interface. After a few quick entries to confirm the numbers he'd been running in his head, he pushed himself to the entry hatchway.

He depressurized the cabin and opened the hatch. Keeping a tight grip on the support rail, he eased himself outside.

As he hung there, he couldn't avoid looking down at the planet thirty-five thousand kilometres beneath him. He was in no danger of falling that distance back to the surface. His biggest risk if his plan failed would be floating in orbit forever. Of course, he'd only enjoy the experience until his oxygen ran out in ten minutes, according to the readout on his arm.

Dying of suffocation or burning up in a thermonuclear explosion—he hadn't given himself many options for how he was going to die. The crazy stunt he was preparing to do was not for his survival, although he did harbour a faint hope that he'd find his way to one of *Scimitar*'s airlocks. If he could get Cora's crystal close enough to the ship, she might still have a chance to transfer back to it. If he could ensure that she survived, then he considered his sacrifice to be worthwhile.

He focused his attention on the approaching form of *Scimitar* and the blinking holographic timer display on his arm. As the countdown rolled past thirty seconds, he forced himself to turn and face outward from the raptor, toward the ring rather than *Scimitar*.

The display turned red and pulsed in time with the remaining ten seconds. When it flashed to green, he jumped.

The most uncertain part of his calculation was how hard to push off. He knew the numbers but wasn't certain his body could reproduce the exact force required. Too little and he would miss *Scimitar* and drift away from the station. Too much, and he'd collide with the docking ring, knock himself out, and bounce off into space.

If he estimated the force correctly, however, his inertia would bring him to *Scimitar*, hopefully close to airlock B-2, but that was really wishful thinking. If he could reach the ship somewhere ahead of the engineering section, he'd have enough oxygen to locate the nearest access point. If not, he'd at least be able to place Cora's crystal in contact with the hull.

The countdown timer continued to blink as he lazily floated closer. When still a few hundred metres away, he was dismayed that he'd already consumed half of his oxygen. At this rate, he'd be cutting things very close.

He closed his eyes to concentrate on slowing his breathing. When he deemed his respiration under control, he opened them and was shocked by the ship looming before him.

Hayden searched the fast-approaching hull for any kind of purchase to grab and keep himself from bouncing off.

Fortunately, his arms absorbed most of the force, but he still bounced along the length of the ship from his unabated lateral inertia. While only half a metre away from the ship's surface, their separation was increasing. Unless he could grab something in the next few seconds, he'd skid away from the ship and be lost forever.

Quickly he unwrapped the cord to Cora's crystal from around his arm and reached forward to press it against the hull. He felt it drag along the metal surface. There wasn't enough friction to slow him down, but at this stage, saving himself was a lost cause. All he could do now was give Cora a chance to transfer back to *Scimitar* if she was able.

Something prompted him to turn his head. He saw an approaching handhold for a service hatchway. He reached across as he passed.

His hand struck the metal pipe, but he ignored the pain as he clamped his fingers around it. His momentum jerked him hard, sending a sharp, tearing pain up his arm. He held on tight as he flipped over. A sea of stars rushed into view, then his back slammed against the hull.

Maintaining an iron grip on the handle, he raised his free arm to check his readout. The flashing amber display indicated a minute of oxygen remained in his tank. He tried to slow his breathing but knew that would buy him only a few seconds of extra time.

Then, he looked at his arm again, and he felt his heartbeat stop. The cord was no longer wrapped around it. In the effort to save himself, he'd dropped Cora's crystal.

Hayden cried out as if someone had ripped his heart from his chest.

He'd failed.

His visor clouded as he sobbed in gulps. He'd never felt an agony so deeply—not even when he'd lost Stella. Though losing her was terrible, he consoled himself with the knowledge that she offered her life to save trillions. There was a nobility in Stella's death that somehow made the sorrow he suffered through endurable.

But Cora's loss was a tragedy beyond anything he'd ever experienced. There was no redeeming quality about it. She'd placed her faith in him, and he'd failed her.

The oxygen readout started to flash red. Only a few seconds of air remained, and for that, he was grateful. He would only need to endure the pain and the shame of his failure for a little while longer.

He turned back to face the myriad of stars above him. Perhaps he'd meet Cora in the afterlife, somewhere out there. He had to explain to her that he'd tried.

She was the gentlest, most loving and forgiving person he'd ever known. He hoped she would extend her forgiveness to him one last time.

PHANTOMS FROM ANOTHER LIFE

"Come back to us, Kaine."

The voice spoke to him from out of a murky fog. It was slow, like a recording played at half-speed, and sounded as if its source was everywhere around him.

After the ghostly voice subsided, all that remained was a high-frequency ringing.

When the pain arrived, it was like nothing he'd experienced. He thought his eyeballs were being peeled from inside of his skull.

He screamed but couldn't hear himself.

A new distorted voice spoke. "He is responding. Increase the stimulus to 150 millivolts."

"C'mon, Hayden, you can do this. Help us out here." The first voice was clearer now and almost sounded normal. There was a familiarity about it, but he couldn't say how.

The pain behind his eyes began to pulsate, seeming to slosh around inside his head like the contents of a half-full bottle.

"Neural patterns are resolving. Administer twenty millilitres of hyponecaratin."

There was a dull pressure at the base of his skull moments before a wave of fire exploded in it. A searing white light overwhelmed his vision, and all sound devolved into a low, rumbling thunder.

His brain was being pulled apart by red-hot pincers. The pain was excruciating, but he couldn't cry out or move any part of his body.

He wondered if he'd gone to hell, and this was his fate for the rest of eternity. He wanted to scream but couldn't.

His senses were overwhelmed as fire flowed down both sides of his neck. Inexorably, the slow-moving lava seeped into his chest. His lungs burned, and he thought his heart might explode with every painful beat. Relentless, the heat crept into his extremities, setting every nerve it touched aflame until he felt like he was being cremated. The encouraging voice was speaking, but he couldn't make out the words. There was an urgency in the tone as if whoever spoke offered him a lifeline to pull him out of the underworld. He wanted to reach up and blindly try to grab it, but he couldn't make himself move.

Then it all abruptly ended. A peaceful coolness washed over him like someone had taken pity on him and dipped him into an icy lake.

The ringing returned, and with it the voices.

His limbs grew heavy as the fire was extinguished. The burning behind his eyes became mild dizziness as he felt himself slowly spin.

Something warm rested on his shoulder.

"Hayden, can you hear me?"

He thought he should know who spoke, but his mind was a confusing jumble. Memories popped into being like bubbles, only to collapse upon themselves. There was no order to them. In one instant, he was a young boy playing ball with his father. The next, the comforting warmth of Stella's body pressed against him as they made love. Then he celebrated with his friends at the academy before transitioning to being aboard *Scimitar*'s bridge.

Friends and lovers, rivals and family all took turns presenting themselves to him in whatever order they arrived. He gave up trying to place them in their proper time, choosing to enjoy their all too brief visits.

Then, one familiar face floated before him and did not dissolve. It seemed to solidify until it became real enough for him to reach out and touch. Pavlovich's beard was unkempt and greyer than he could recall. His face was haggard, and his eyes were red and rheumy, as if he'd been weeping.

Then the memory spoke to him.

"Welcome back, Sunshine."

Hayden blinked several times, and the hallucination persisted. He squeezed his eyes closed, and when he opened them, Pavlovich was still grinning.

He tried to speak to the ghost but could only manage a hoarse croaking sound.

Pavlovich said, "Take it easy; it'll come."

Violent coughing racked him. After it subsided, he said in a raspy voice, "You're real."

The older man's smile broadened. "So are you."

He struggled to sit up, but the room spun again. Falling back to the bed, he said. "Where are we?"

"We are in *Scimitar*'s medical bay."

His eyes fell on a synth standing a short distance behind Pavlovich.

When it spoke, he recognized the other voice he'd heard. "I am Medical Synthetic 6-10 B."

Pavlovich said, "I call him Doctor Sexton."

Hayden addressed the robot. "What did you do to me?"

"You were brought in suffering from severe hypoxia as well as first and second-degree frostbite to your extremities. I performed a cranial neural recrudescence procedure to repair your damaged brain cells."

An odd-looking helmet was on the table behind the doctor. Multiple probes and wires extruding from it were connected to a computer console.

"It hurt like hell. I thought I was going to die."

"Technically, you were dead for approximately thirteen minutes."

Kaine's brow knotted. "I was trying to reach the ship. I think I ran out of air."

"That's exactly what happened," said Pavlovich, "and it was a damned foolish stunt. You're lucky I was on the bridge when you tried to scratch your way through the hull."

Hayden's eyes widened. "The raptor!"

"Its reactor went critical about ten minutes after I got you inside. A good thing too, or you'd have been irradiated along with everything else that happened to you. What the hell were you doing out there?"

Kaine rubbed his eyes. "You first; I was told you and *Scimitar* burned up in the atmosphere."

Pavlovich frowned. "Who the devil told you that?"

"The rebels I've been living with for the past three months."

"Jesus, Kaine, it sounds like we have some catching up to do. A lot happened to both of us since I ordered you and Cora into that escape pod."

Tears pooled in Hayden's eyes.

"What's wrong, Kaine?"

The doctor said, "Emotional rebound will be severe for the next few hours."

"No, that's not it; Cora...she's dead."

Pavlovich scowled, then turned to the doctor. "Is he still hallucinating?"

"I'm not hallucinating."

The older man chuckled. "You must be if you think Cora's dead. I spoke to her twenty minutes ago."

Hayden shook his head. "No, you spoke to the facsimile segment of her that remained with the ship."

"Ah, no, I didn't. It was Cora, and it is a welcome relief to have her back in charge of things."

"No, you're mistaken."

"Kaine, listen to me. There hasn't been an instance of Cora aboard this ship since Thomas's people cleaned her out of the computer core after they towed me here. I was forced to deal with a damned Confederation AI until you brought her home."

Hayden stared dumbly at him. "What? Did it work? She's alive?"

"Hale and healthy."

"Can I speak to her?"

"She's busy purging the last of that useless AI and determining the extent of the damage Thomas's people did to my ship. I'll make sure she visits with you as soon as she can."

Tears ran down Hayden's cheeks. "I thought I'd killed her when I lost her crystal."

"Hmm, which brings us back to you. What the hell were you doing out there?"

He pushed himself to sit in the bed. "It's a long story."

The captain pulled over a chair and sat. "I have nothing but time."

Over the next half hour, Hayden told him about everything that had happened to him, concluding with how he jumped from the raptor.

"Holy shit, you've got big balls," said Pavlovich.

He smiled. "I've missed you, too, you old tyrant. I never imagined I'd see you again."

Then a frown clouded his face. "I don't understand why it sounds like you are working with Thomas."

Pavlovich sat back in his chair. "Ah, I see it's time for my story."

Kaine laid his head on the pillow. "My eyes are tired, but I want to hear this. I'm going to shut them while I listen. Don't skimp on the details."

The captain chuckled. "All right, but if you start snoring—"

"I won't fall asleep."

"Fine."

Pavlovich leaned back in his chair. "Things got a lot worse

after you two ejected. Engineering was hit by another nuke, and our last functioning engine went offline. Weapons were hot, but the targeting sensors were fried by the blast. There were fires breaking out everywhere, half the crew had radiation burns, and we were caught in the planet's gravity well. I had control of only the manoeuvring thrusters and couldn't compensate for our degrading orbit."

"What about the FTL drive? Couldn't you make an emergency jump?"

"Wanted to, but it wasn't charged. I couldn't count on us surviving the next nuke to come our way, so I gave the abandon ship order."

Pavlovich fell silent. His hands clenched into fists and his face grew pale.

"What happened?"

"The bastards fired on the escape pods."

"No! All of them?"

He nodded. "I was helpless to do anything for them. None of them made it into the atmosphere."

"Shit," said Hayden. "Do you know who shot at them?"

Pavlovich looked up. "What the hell are you talking about?"

"We stepped into the middle of a battle. Do you know which side fired at our escape pods?"

The captain shook his head. "The locals told me the rebels did, but I suspect you're going to defend them."

"A couple of days ago, I might have, but now I'm not so sure."

Pavlovich arched an eyebrow. "Interesting."

"What happened after that?"

"Things got nasty. Two more ships moved in for the kill. They must have run out of nukes, because they used conventional weapons. Not enough to hurt me any more than I was, but enough to push me toward the planet. I entered the atmosphere and the heat shield lit up. I didn't know if the ship was gonna make it, but then Cora's simulacrum announced the FTL was charged, so I punched in some coordinates and said a prayer."

"You jumped; where?"

He shrugged. "Somewhere out by the Oort Cloud, but everything was down. We were blind, lost, and dead. Remaining power was dedicated to life support."

"What was your plan?"

Pavlovich laughed mirthlessly. "You think I had a damned plan? I'd made a last-ditch, low probability grasp at staying alive. There was no bloody plan, Kaine. I'd just witnessed my crew slaughtered and my ship pummelled into a useless piece of salvage. I counted myself lucky to be still breathing, and I had no idea how long that would continue."

"What did you do?"

"You mean after I decided to get drunk?"

"Yeah, after that."

"Cora's simulacrum—look, I'll call her by her name, okay?"

Kaine nodded.

"Cora initiated self-repair of the damaged Glenatat components, but her avatar synths were all gone. She talked me through making repairs to the sensors and engines and helped me get comms online. I had no intention of calling for help, but I wanted to monitor communications in case they found me and came to finish the job."

"A wise precaution."

"Thanks for your approval."

Hayden frowned.

"I'm sorry Kaine—that was uncalled for."

He smiled. "Forget about it. What happened next?"

"We just plodded away at making repairs. I decided that if I could get enough systems back online to defend myself, I might jump to another system, like Wolf 1061. I'm pretty sure the Malliac didn't make it there, but the state of every place we've visited has been a crapshoot. Truth is that our track record at making friends isn't so good."

"Well, as we've seen, chaos tends to bring out the worst in people."

"Anyway, I never got past dreaming about it before Thomas's people found me. They learned about *Scimitar* from the locals and put in a lot of effort to locate me."

Hayden stared at him.

Pavlovich said defensively, "What?"

"The only reason I can imagine that you are running around free is that you cut a deal with Thomas."

"Save your righteous indignation, Kaine. You don't know how desperate things were for me. As far as I was aware, my crew were dead, including you. I was alone with a damaged ship in a system where everyone was out to kill me. Thomas offered me clemency if I came back over to him. He told me I could keep *Scimitar*. The alternative was prison or a firing squad. What the hell was I supposed to do?"

Hayden wanted to tell him that he was wrong to join Thomas; that he should have destroyed the ship rather than turn it over. Maybe that would have been his choice, but he had no right to impose his values on Pavlovich, especially given how he'd experienced the same kind of despair. He knew how desperate he'd been and could empathize with his captain's state of mind when presented with a chance to survive.

He sighed. "I have no right to judge your motives or your decision. But my presence puts you in a difficult situation. What do you plan to do with me?"

"Goddammit, Kaine, how can you think so little of me? I thought we were family."

Hayden was taken aback. Pavlovich had never expressed that level of sentimentality toward him.

"I'm sorry, I—"

"It's okay, I can appreciate your perspective, but you didn't give me a chance to tell you where I am coming from. You and Cora showing up changes everything. For starters, I'm the only one who knows you two are here."

"How is that possible? Surely some of your new crew saw me."

Pavlovich smiled as he shook his head. "Nope, there is no

crew. Not yet. The only people aboard besides me are a bunch of engineers and technicians refitting the old girl, and they are screwing things up at that. I've been in a constant fight with them since they replaced Cora's simulacrum with that bloody useless AI."

"Why did you let them take her?"

"You think I didn't object? I argued until I was blue in the face, but as delighted as Thomas was to get his hands on *Scimitar*, it wasn't the ship he coveted the most. He's built an enhanced fleet around the little alien tech we provided him to help beat back the Malliac at Terra. But he has a little problem."

"It won't function without a Glenatat AI to integrate with the Terran systems. That's why he took Cora; to replicate her kernel."

"Exactly."

"Didn't you tell them she is necessary to effect repairs to the Glenatat components on *Scimitar*?"

"I wasn't given a choice. None of our Glenatat tech was damaged severely, so, strictly speaking, Cora's expertise wasn't required to continue the repairs. They replaced her with a standard AI."

"Were they planning to reinstall her?"

"I don't think so, at least not our Cora. As soon as Thomas has a lobotomized version of her, he'll install that. It will guarantee that no ship will ever go rogue again as we did."

"His version will run the fleet and answer to him."

"Yup, it's what I'd do."

"Shit."

"You don't have to say it, Kaine. I know I screwed up by surrendering to him. I should have destroyed *Scimitar* rather than let her fall into Thomas's hands."

Hayden shook his head. "You couldn't have known his plan. We thought Thomas was interested in using me to legitimize his regime and reconnect the worlds of his new Grand Terran Confederation. He's learned from bitter experience that the colonies aren't eager to return to the old ways. It looks like he's moved past reunification and gone straight to military conquest."

"It should be a cakewalk with a Glenatat-enhanced fleet."

Hayden closed his eyes, trying to digest the new revelations. As he went over the facts, his eyes popped open, and he shot up to a sitting position.

"What's wrong, Kaine?"

"Besides Cora, how much Glenatat tech was confiscated?"

"None, yet."

"So that means, with Cora returned, we still hold a technological advantage over Thomas's new fleet."

"Yeah, I suppose so, on a ship-to-ship basis, at least," said Pavlovich. "They have a scaled-down version of our dark energy cannon, and they don't yet have the ability to reproduce our enhanced armour."

"Plus, a myriad of subsystems throughout the ship that makes her instantly responsive to Cora's commands."

"Even using a Franken-Cora to run the tech he has, his ships will be more vulnerable and slower than us, but he'll have a whole bunch of them. We'd get our asses kicked even worse than what happened to us here."

"What if *Scimitar* wasn't our only ship?"

Pavlovich arched his eyebrow. "Where are you going with this, Kaine?"

"In order to reproduce the technology that he already possesses, Thomas is forced to employ reverse engineering and standard manufacturing processes. It's slow, and the result is not nearly as powerful as the real thing. He won't have figured out the biggest advantage of Glenatat tech is its self-replication capacity."

"That is a deficiency he is about to correct."

"Right, but even using a—what did you call her?"

"Franken-Cora."

Hayden smiled. "I like that. Even using his version of her, he still will only have a limited sample of Glenatat components to work from. *Scimitar* is the gold standard he requires to fully outfit his ships. If we take her away from him, maybe we can build a more powerful fleet to oppose him."

"That's a big 'if.' Where would these ships come from, for starters?"

"Somewhere out there is the rebel fleet that helped kick our ass. Trust me when I tell you that nobody on this planet is a fan of the Grand Terran Confederation."

"Yet, as you tell it, they are willing to surrender to Thomas to get out from under the local governor."

"In their minds, there is no alternative. The idea of surrendering isn't going over well with his rank-and-file troops. I am proposing that we offer an alternative course of action that will give these people a chance to govern themselves."

"It sounds like they've recruited you to their rebellion, Kaine."

"We already rebelled against Thomas and everything he stands for. It turns out a lot of other people share that sentiment."

"And you propose to rally them all under one banner."

"What is the alternative? Do you want to spend the rest of your life doing Thomas's dirty work as one of his enforcers? This regime is just a copy of the same old corrupt Confederation, except he is dropping any pretence of democracy."

"Don't get your panties in a knot. You don't have to convince me. Do you know how to contact the rebels to tell them we're on their side?"

"No, but I know someone who does."

HALE AND HEALTHY

Scimitar's briefing room was a welcome sight for Kaine. Any damage it had sustained during the battle was now repaired, and the space was restored to how he remembered it.

In the centre of the circular chamber was a round conference table, the familiar wooden surface polished to a shiny finish. Suspended above it was the grey, metallic hemisphere that he'd come to think of as Cora's home.

That was, of course, an oversimplification. She resided throughout the entire ship, and the hemisphere contained only the ship's conventional AI processor that she had radically modified with Glenatat technology.

"Hayden, welcome home."

Cora sounded like her old, chipper self as she addressed him over the room's speakers.

"I can't tell you how happy I am that you made it, Cora. I gather from the captain that you are your old self again."

"There are only a few minor residual things not worth mentioning; I've built workarounds to compensate for most of the damaged network. As far as you should be concerned, I'm back to normal."

Pavlovich asked, "Did you purge the last of that annoying ship AI?"

"It's gone, Cap'n. I fully control *Scimitar* again."

"Won't the tech crew know something is amiss?" Hayden said.

"I've spent enough time with the station's AI to know how this one thought. Pretending to be it isn't difficult, Hayden. They won't be able to tell anything is different."

"Speaking of AIs, what happened to you while you were in the station's system?"

"It is the most sophisticated intelligence I've ever encountered. I managed to avoid being detected by it until I glitched. It put firewalls around me and was in the process of purging me when you contacted *Scimitar*'s hull. My kernel was reincorporated into the ship, and I managed to tunnel my way out without Aramis realizing it. As far as it is concerned, I've been deleted."

"Aramis is the AI's name?"

"Of course, silly."

"It sounds like you two became cosy," said Pavlovich.

"Cap'n, are you jealous?"

Pavlovich blustered. "What? No, of course not."

Cora's giggle was something Hayden never thought he'd hear again. "I'm teasing you. To answer you...well, I can't explain it in terms you would understand. We shared the same network. It was the most intimate yet disturbing situation I've ever experienced."

Hayden swallowed, hesitating, before he said, "How disturbing?"

"I can't describe Aramis's experience, but the impression I got from it was that my presence was something like being covered in ants. For me, it was like I was strapped naked to a table and being dissected while conscious. It knows everything about me—or rather, it knows the glitched version of me. If anything, Aramis was confused as to how something as damaged as me managed to get as deep into its systems as I did."

"Will it pose a problem if you have to infiltrate its network again?"

"It wasn't an experience I am eager to repeat."

"But you can do it?"

"Of course I can. The question is why I would want to. It's a powerful AI, Hayden. Even in my restored state, I'm not sure I can defend myself from capture."

Pavlovich asked, "Is there a chance that it fears you just as much?"

"I don't know. My Glenatat coding confounded it. It was definitely as cautious as it was intrigued."

"But, as you said, you weren't yourself," said Hayden. "Could you defend yourself from it now?"

"Given that I know more about its capability than it does mine, I suppose so. But it won't take it long to adapt and establish countermeasures against anything I might do in its systems."

"We need to find out where they are holding Emma."

"I think I can do that much."

Pavlovich frowned. "Who's Emma?"

"She is the one who will know how to reach Krellig. I'm fairly certain that she was captured after I took off in the raptor."

"*Scimitar* is connected to the station's database and can confirm that, Hayden. She's being held in the station's detention block."

Pavlovich said, "You'll have to get past the security system."

"That might be a problem," said Cora. "I can passively access databases without drawing attention, but if you want me to override security protocols in any section of the station, Aramis will know instantly what I'm doing."

"There is no way I can get inside without your help, Cora."

"I didn't say it was impossible, Hayden, but I'll only be able to control those systems for a couple of minutes before it shuts me out."

"If you can get us inside, that's half the problem," said

Hayden. "If I must fight my way out, I'll need some weapons. What's in *Scimitar*'s armoury?"

Pavlovich shrugged. "It hasn't been touched. In addition to the UEF issue, there should be some Glenatat personal shield generators and a couple of dark energy rifles."

"Those will draw attention. Any small arms?"

The captain nodded. "Some flechette pistols are in there; small enough for us to conceal in a jacket."

"I'm going alone."

"The hell you will, Kaine. Cora may be able to get you past some locked doors, but when things go sideways, someone needs to mind your back."

"Do you think it's wise for you to leave *Scimitar* without her captain?"

Pavlovich scowled. "I've been stuck aboard this ship for months. Cora can keep an eye on the ship while we're away and prep her for a fast getaway. Cora, tell him he needs my help."

"He's right, Hayden."

"Won't the guards outside the ship recognize you?"

The older man's teeth peeked out from behind his beard as he grinned. "There are some stealth masks in storage. We'll lock the maintenance crew in the brig and pose as two of them. Cora can fake their biosignatures to get us past the scanners."

"That should be easy," Cora chimed in.

Hayden stared at the captain as he weighed the risks.

Pavlovich said, "There is no other way, Kaine. If we can't make this work, we can forget about bringing the fight to Thomas. We should just take the ship now and get the hell out of this system. What do you say?"

A small smile turned up the corners of Hayden's mouth. "I've already come to terms with dying once today. If you're sure you want to risk this..."

"Nobody lives forever, son."

"Then it sounds like we have the makings of a workable, if not mostly suicidal plan. What the hell; let's do this."

Kaine and Pavlovich walked calmly down the short docking bridge toward the guarded security doors that separated *Scimitar* from the rest of the station. They carried tool bags slung over their shoulders and wore coveralls borrowed from members of the maintenance crew who, along with their companions, were enjoying Cora's hospitality in the ship's brig.

As they approached the closed doors, Hayden fidgeted with the tight-fitting collar of his holo-masque generator.

"Leave it alone," hissed Pavlovich.

Hayden glanced up at the man he walked beside who sounded like Pavlovich but wore the clean-shaven face of a middle-aged Asian man. The quality of the projection was remarkable. There wasn't a hint of the bushy beard visible.

"When you scratch at it, the field jitters." The face that wasn't Pavlovich's smiled. "You look good. Your own mother wouldn't recognize you."

Kaine blew out a noisy breath and lowered his hand. "I'm about ready to scream."

"I didn't miss your whining about everything."

He glared at the captain, hoping his illusory face conveyed his feelings.

"There you go, Kaine. Now you look like someone who finished a long shift."

They arrived at the doors and Pavlovich let his hand hover over the bioscanner. "Here's hoping Cora got this right."

"Captain, you wound me," she said over their earpieces.

He shrugged and pressed his hand against the panel.

Hydraulics hissed and the doors parted.

The two guards on the other side gave them a cursory glance before they returned their attention forward.

Kaine and Pavlovich strolled past them and continued down the corridor until they were out of sight of the doors.

"That went surprisingly well," said Pavlovich.

"Where to from here, Cora?"

She directed them through a labyrinth of corridors until they arrived at the elevator shaft in the central pillar of the station. They boarded the car and selected the security level as their destination.

"I am limited in what I can do without attracting Aramis's attention. The men you are impersonating now have orders to repair a communications node in security block C. Emma is in cell 24, about twenty metres behind the doors."

"Did you find a way to make this easier?" Pavlovich asked.

"If you stick with the plan, you should have two minutes before the automated alarms go off. After that happens, I'll be limited in how I can help you."

Hayden turned his back to the security camera and zipped open his coverall to check his flechette pistol.

"We each have twenty anaesthetic darts."

Pavlovich used Hayden's body to shield himself from the camera while he pulled a magazine from his pocket.

"I brought something with a little more oomph in case we need a plan B."

Kaine slipped it in his coverall. "How many shots?"

"Six explosive rounds, so try not to waste them."

"If we have to resort to these, we will be in deep shit."

Pavlovich smiled. "That was always going to happen. It's a question of whether it's up to our waists or over our heads."

"How can you joke at a time like this?"

"I'm looking forward to this."

Hayden arched his eyebrow. "Seriously?"

He shrugged. "I don't get out much these days. Besides, I'm not worried. We have the Glenatat shields Cora built for us a year ago."

"We've never field-tested the tech."

"What's the matter, Kaine? Don't you trust her?"

Hayden scowled at him.

Cora said, "They'll protect you from conventional hand-held

ordnance, but once you activate them, I won't be able to communicate with you. You'll be on your own. Oh, and remember, the shields aren't permeable to air, so you'll have to drop them to replenish your air supply."

Pavlovich frowned. "That would have been good to know beforehand."

"I told you this when I first designed them."

"Yeah; over a year ago."

"You should be able to go for five minutes at a time if you don't expend yourselves."

"Don't expend—? Jesus, Cora, have you ever been in a firefight?"

"No, I'm an engineer."

"Is there anything else you neglected to brief us about?"

"There shouldn't be anything more."

"Is our escape route still available?"

"At the moment it is. I'll let you know if things change."

The elevator slowed.

"Okay, kiddies, stop arguing," said Hayden as he adjusted the tool bag over his shoulder. "It's showtime."

The elevator doors parted to an antechamber outside the detention area.

A lone security officer sat at a desk behind armoured glass. Behind him was the locked door leading to the cellblock.

"You guys were quick getting here," he said.

Hayden stepped across the threshold and smiled, hoping the masque properly displayed it. "We were coming off shift when the ticket came up. Decided we could use the overtime. What's the problem?"

"The comm is acting weird."

Hayden and Pavlovich approached the partition. "We need to look at things from your side."

The guard's brow knotted. "The last time they accessed it from out there." He pointed to a service panel on Hayden's side of the barrier.

"And it still needs fixing, doesn't it?" Pavlovich said. "We need to access the panel on your side."

"I'll need authorization."

"Suit yourself," said Hayden. "We were getting off shift anyway. I'm sure someone will get back to you in a day or two." He and Pavlovich turned toward the elevator.

"Wait."

Hayden turned back, eyebrow raised. "Yes?"

"Nobody is supposed to be back here without authorization. Will it take long?"

Hayden shrugged. "Won't know for sure until I look at it; likely not. It's probably a faulty relay module. We got a bad shipment last month."

"Can you guys be finished before my shift ends in an hour, so nobody knows I let you in?"

"No problem," said Pavlovich. "It's been a long day, and I want to get home to put my feet up."

The man considered the matter for another moment, then he pressed a button on his panel and invited them to enter as the door sprang open.

They entered the booth, and Hayden knelt to open the service panel door beneath the guard's console. He searched until he spotted the component Cora had instructed him to find. He pulled it out of its socket. "Did that do it, Cora?"

"All security cameras are now on maintenance reboot. You've got two minutes before the system registers the missing component."

"Excellent," said Pavlovich as he pulled his flechette pistol from inside his coverall and pointed it at the confused guard.

"Wh...what's going on?"

Hayden, who'd stood and now had his gun trained on the man, said, "Open cell 24."

The young man's voice cracked. "I can't do that."

Pavlovich pressed the muzzle of the gun into the fellow's temple. "Do you know what one of these can do to a human skull at close range? I'm not a patient man. Open the cell if you want to make it through your shift."

"Okay, okay, okay—don't shoot me. I'll open it."

With Pavlovich's pistol still pressed to his head, the guard shuffled to the inner door and pressed his hand against the biometric scanner. The door panel slid into the wall.

At the captain's urging, he led them into a corridor flanked on both sides with closed doors. On the wall beside each were a bioscanner and a sign indicating the cell number.

They made their way down the hall until they reached cell 24.

"Open it," said Pavlovich.

The guard pressed his hand to the panel and the cell door retracted into the wall.

Emma was sitting on the edge of a bunk, her wrists shackled together.

"Who are you?"

"Emma, it's me, Hayden. I'm wearing a holo-masque."

Her eyes moved to Pavlovich, still holding his weapon to the guard's temple.

"Hi, I'm with him."

Hayden gestured for the guard to undo the shackles.

The man, reluctant to move, said, "The controller is on my belt."

Pavlovich reached for it and pressed the button the guard indicated would unlock the bracelets.

As Emma stood, he directed their prisoner to take her place, and he locked the restraints in place.

Cora spoke into their earpieces. "You boys have less than a minute before the system comes back online and all hell breaks loose."

"Let's go."

They exited the cell, but as they entered the corridor, Emma said, "Wait. Aubrey and Caldwell are here too."

Pavlovich said, "Who?"

"There isn't time," said Hayden.

He grasped her by the elbow to usher her to the exit, but she jerked her arm back and held her ground.

"They'll be executed."

"They were quite happy to let us die," said Hayden.

Pavlovich said, "Who are you two talking about?"

"Please, Hayden? Aubrey's only fault is being zealous, and Caldwell is a follower. They're good people, and we've lost so many who are willing to fight D'Ville. And they are my friends."

Hayden's eyes shot to Pavlovich, who frowned and pointed to an imaginary chronometer on his wrist. "Tick-tock, Kaine. Make a decision."

Scowling, he returned his attention to Emma. "Do you know which cells they're in?"

She nodded at the guard chained to the bunk. "He does."

Hayden stormed back into the room and confronted the man. "Do you know who she's talking about?"

Wide-eyed, he stammered, "Th—there are only two other prisoners. They're in cells 27 and 31."

Kaine fished the remote control from his pocket and released the shackles. Grabbing the guard by his jacket, he pulled him roughly to his feet. "You know the routine; move."

"Hayden," said Cora, "you're running out of time."

Pavlovich said, "I'll go to the desk to hold off whoever security sends. Be quick about this. Cora, is there anything you can do to buy us time?"

"I'm working on it, Cap'n."

Hayden brandished his flechette pistol to inspire the guard to lead them to the other cells.

When they were in front of the door marked as 27, the guard didn't wait to be asked to press his hand against the panel. The door slid aside, and Kaine handed Emma the remote control, saying, "Hurry."

He then pushed the guard toward the next door, where he repeated the operation.

Caldwell was stretched out on the bunk. He sat up as Hayden pushed the other man into the cell at gunpoint.

Kaine was shocked by Caldwell's condition. His face was a mass of bruises, and his lips were split as if he'd endured more than one beating.

"Who the hell are you?"

Hayden hesitated. "Oh, what the hell; I'm out of time anyway." He reached up to deactivate the holo-masque. As his real face appeared, he said, "I'm here to rescue you, asshole."

"Kaine! How are you still alive? They told me you'd blown up."

"Well, I lived, no thanks to you."

Emma entered the room and hurried to unshackle Caldwell.

From outside the cell, Aubrey said, "Kaine, you're still alive."

"You both seem disappointed by this."

Caldwell rose to his feet, rubbing his wrists. With murder in his eyes, he stalked forward and seized the guard by the scruff of the neck.

He raised his other hand, balled in a fist. "I told you that there would be payback, you little shit."

Aubrey shouted, "Caldwell!"

Keeping his eyes locked on his victim, he said, "What?"

"There's no time. Let him go."

With the pained expression of a ten-year-old, he turned to her. "Really? I can't even hit him once?"

"No, we've got no time left," said Hayden, prying the man's collar free from his grip. He shoved him to the bunk and told him to put on the restraints.

As he followed the others into the corridor and sealed the door to the cell, Pavlovich's voice came over his earpiece.

"We've got company coming."

Kaine sprinted past the others back toward the security desk. When he arrived, he said, "Is there a new plan?"

"You mean besides 'don't die?'" Pavlovich shook his head. "It's the same shit plan we arrived with. Cora confirms the elevator is one of two access points, so whoever arrives in the next twenty seconds will be bottlenecked and easy to pick off. The worse news is that it will be the same situation for us once they figure out what's happened and send reinforcements to the other exit."

"So, we're screwed then."

"Yup." Pavlovich paused to examine Hayden, then reached up and deactivated his own holo-masque.

"I've been monitoring communications," said Cora. "The team on their way suspects the problem is hardware-related. There is still a time window for me to get you out."

"I'm all for that," said Hayden.

"I'm shutting down power to the lift. But there is no artificial gravity in the elevator shaft," said Cora. "If you can make it up three levels, I can guide you back to the ship, maybe even without attracting attention."

"Caldwell, help open these doors."

The other man didn't hesitate to put his back into it. Once the elevator doors were parted, Hayden stuck his head through the opening and gazed upward into the darkness.

"Cora, you're sure that car isn't moving?"

"It's stopped ten levels above you, but I can't hold it for very long. Aramis is beginning to take note of all the power disruptions in that section of the station."

Kaine entered the elevator shaft and grasped a service ladder. Weightless, he pulled himself deeper inside.

"Don't rush; use the rungs of the ladder to control your rate of ascent," he said.

When he was sure they understood his instructions, he propelled himself upward in the manner he'd described.

One by one, the other four entered the shaft and followed

him up. Cora kept them updated on how much time remained before the power would return to the elevator.

Just as they arrived at their destination, a generator's whine echoed around them.

Pavlovich said, "Shit!"

"Power is back on."

"We're out of time," said Aubrey.

Pavlovich dug into his coverall and swapped out his pistol's magazine. He pulled himself up past Hayden and stopped opposite closed doors. Aiming the gun at them, he shouted, "Cover your ears and hang on tight."

Hayden barely had time to hook his arm around a ladder rung and clap his hands over his ears.

A brilliant flare accompanied a deafening boom as the elevator doors were blown away. His skin tingled as the Glenatat shield automatically activated for a few seconds as dust and smoke whirled around him.

Pavlovich urged everyone to hurry through the smoking opening.

Hayden realized that their chances for a stealthy escape were now gone. They were forced to fight their way back to *Scimitar*.

LIFE RUNS ON PLAN B

G ravity grabbed Hayden as he passed across the destroyed threshold, and he stumbled to catch his balance. He looked up at a scene of devastation. The two bent elevator doors were ten metres away from the opening, and chunks of plascrete and twisted metal from the damaged shaft littered the floor.

Fortunately, there were no corpses or injured people lying about.

As he assessed the damage, the elevator car screeched as it rumbled along its damaged tracks past the opening. Hayden saw sparks fly and listened to the grinding of emergency brakes as the lift ground to a halt a few metres below them.

Pavlovich addressed the group as he again exchanged his gun's magazine.

"The three of you will stay between Kaine and me; we are shielded and can protect you."

"Where are you taking us?" Aubrey asked.

"We are going to make our way to *Scimitar*."

"That's on the other side of the station," said Caldwell. "Do you have any other weapons?"

Hayden shook his head. "We're improvising. Rescuing you two was not in the plan."

"Then why did you do it?"

A pulsing klaxon cut through the air.

"Debate this later," said Pavlovich. "We have to move."

Hayden adjusted his earpiece. "Cora, where do we go?"

"The station is going into lockdown. Security and damage crews are on their way to your location. Get to the nearest zero-G evacuation shaft."

She gave them the directions, and they ran down the curving abandoned corridor.

The escape shaft came upon them faster than Hayden expected. Outside stood two security officers. The guards waved at them, urging them to hurry but fell silent when they saw the flechette guns.

As the soldiers fumbled to draw their own firearms, Pavlovich dropped to one knee, took aim, and fired six shots in rapid succession. The men dropped to the deck.

Emma ran forward to check on them.

When Hayden arrived, she looked up at him accusingly.

"They're tranquillized," he said.

She glared at Pavlovich. "You didn't have to shoot them three times. They're barely breathing."

"My training kicked in," said the captain, annoyed. "They were going to use real bullets. It was them or us."

He turned to Caldwell and Aubrey. "There are your weapons."

The two retrieved the firearms from the fallen guards while Hayden went to check the evacuation shaft. After looking up and down and not seeing anyone, he turned to address the others.

"Nobody is inside. They must be evacuating only this level."

Pavlovich touched his earpiece. "Cora, what's our status?"

"Security is still confused as to what happened. There is a clear path for you to get up the shaft to the docking level, but I don't know for how long."

"That's fifty levels," said Hayden. "About two hundred metres; that will take about a minute to traverse."

"That's if we do it safely," said Caldwell.

"He's right," said Pavlovich. "We don't have that long before the laser grid turns on."

"What does that mean?" Emma said.

"It is meant to prevent unauthorized movement up or down the shaft," said Hayden.

"You mean they'll fry us?"

"More like cut us apart," said Aubrey. "We are seriously screwed."

"Cora," said Hayden, "is there any way for us to extend our shields around the others?"

"Sorry, no."

"It was a good idea, Kaine," said Pavlovich.

Hayden frowned and poked his head back in the shaft.

"Cora, the emitters are arranged in a regular pattern up the shaft."

"Give me a second to access the schematics... Yes, there are emitter/receiver pairs spaced in a rotating pattern every ten metres along the shaft."

"So, if one was to time his rotation, it's possible to always be facing them as you pass them."

Pavlovich scowled. "Where are you going with this, Kaine?"

"I know what he's thinking, Cap'n. It could work, Hayden."

"What could work?" Pavlovich said. "Will one of you tell me what craziness you're cooking up here?"

"We have shields. If we sandwich the others between us and time our ascent and rotation going up the shaft, then the lasers will hit us and not them."

"The timing would need to be perfect," said Aubrey.

"I can tell you what to do," said Cora. "We can make this work."

"And if we are really lucky, we'll get to our level before the grid activates," said Pavlovich. He considered it for a moment. "I'm out of better ideas. If you three are willing to try it…"

Emma, Aubrey, and Caldwell looked at each other.

"They were planning to execute us anyway," said Aubrey. "At least this gives us a chance. I'm in."

"Me, too," said Caldwell.

Emma remained silent.

Hayden said to her, "What are you thinking?"

"I'd never really admitted to myself that they might execute me after they were finished interrogating me. This is dangerous, but so is waiting here to be recaptured. Okay, I'll do it."

Pavlovich said, "Cora, give us the instructions and dumb them down as much as you can. We can't afford a screw-up."

She instructed them to enter the tube. It was about ten metres in diameter, so there was enough room for them to gather in the middle. They all stepped into the tube, with Kaine and Pavlovich jockeyed into position on either side of the threesome. Together they managed a configuration that locked everyone in place.

"You need upward thrust, but you must also time your rotation. Aim your flechette guns downward, and when I tell you, fire them in the sequence I give you."

"How will we control rotation?" Hayden asked.

"You will angle your guns to give you upward and rotational inertia, then you will control your spin rate by extending and tucking in your arms when I tell you."

"Like a figure skater controlling his spin."

"Exactly; I've worked out the math, so as long as you follow my instructions, you should get through this."

"What about oxygen?" Pavlovich said. "With the shields up, neither of us will be able to breathe."

"I will monitor the laser grid and activate your protective fields if necessary. You should have a few minutes of breathable air when your shields are up, so pace your breaths. Is everyone ready?"

"I don't think you can ever be ready for something like this," said Pavlovich.

"Wait," said Hayden. "With our shields up, we won't be able to communicate with you. I'm giving my earpiece to Emma."

He removed and passed it to her as he spoke.

"Let's get this over with," said Pavlovich.

On Cora's countdown, Kaine and the captain angled their pistols downward as instructed and fired two shots each. The recoil force pushed the group upward in a lazy turn.

Hayden's eyes were glued to the nearest laser emitter as they approached it, and he exhaled in relief when he faced it while they drifted past.

"One down," he said.

After passing two more, Emma spoke. "Cora says to slow our spin. Everyone needs to spread their arms out for two seconds when I tell you. Now! One...and two—pull them back in."

Hayden didn't detect any change in their rotation, but he was in the right position as he passed the next emitter, so he surmised the minor correction had the desired effect on their spin.

The group ascended past the first ten emitters, and they were halfway to their destination when a series of clicks began above them. He looked up at angry, glowing red lights turning on sequentially.

"The grid is activating," he said as the laser opposite him turned on.

He reflexively shut his eyes and clenched his teeth in antici-pation of a searing pain that never came. When he opened them, they'd rotated past the now active emitter, unharmed. He exhaled his held breath.

Someone was speaking—he thought it was Emma, but the shield muffled the sound of her voice. Too late, he realized that she'd relayed instructions from Cora to extend his arms.

As the next emitter approached, his heart skipped a beat when he saw the group was out of position. He lifted his arm to absorb the laser energy that would have burned into Caldwell's shoulder. With dismay, it dawned on him that his action to save Caldwell had further changed their rotation rate.

The plan was unravelling, and they had to get their act together fast or someone would die.

He dropped his shield.

"We're rotating too fast, and I can't hear the instructions."

They approached the next laser emitter. He barely had time to reactivate the shield before it struck his shoulder. A ruby dot drifted across his torso at a downward angle, trailed by the faint pink glimmer of the dissipated energy. He flexed his hip and extended his leg to protect Emma from the deadly ray as they turned at the wrong speed.

Looking up, he counted six more array levels to pass before they reached their destination. Out of the corner of his eye, on the next floor level above, a door opened.

To Hayden's horror, a head poked through the opening.

The security forces had found them.

The man looking at Hayden seemed equally shocked by what he saw. He snapped out of his hesitation and started to draw his pistol.

Kaine raised his flechette gun and fired three rapid shots. The soldier he hit grabbed at his throat before he collapsed to the deck, unconscious.

The force of Hayden's gunfire pushed the group laterally to collide into the side of the shaft, just two metres below the next emitter pair.

Seeing nobody else in the opening, Kaine dropped his shield.

"This isn't going to work. We've been discovered."

Pavlovich also deactivated his shield. "Cora, find us an alternate route. We're getting out of this death trap right now."

He instructed the others to work their way up the wall of the shaft and around the emitter pair and to make their way to the open doorway.

Hayden reactivated his shield and pushed off to cross the

chasm more quickly. The laser was harmlessly dispersed as he drifted across the beam.

Reaching the doorway first, he stepped back into the artificial gravity and scanned for any other security personnel. Seeing no one, he knelt to feel for a pulse on the man he'd shot. Finding one, he sighed and then turned to assist Emma and the others through the door.

She told him, "Cora says that we are six levels below the docking ring, and there are more soldiers approaching us. They've blocked off all escape routes. We're trapped."

As Pavlovich stepped across the threshold, he said, "I'm starting to regret rescuing you, Kaine." He tempered his remark with a wink.

"There may be more to regret before this is finished," Hayden said as he accepted the earpiece from Emma and inserted it.

"Cora, what can we do?"

"Aramis controls the system, and I am shut out. I can't do anything to help you; can't even tell you how many troops are converging on you or from what directions."

Pavlovich joined the conversation. "Any ideas?"

"I'm sorry, Cap'n."

"Cora," said Hayden. "Do you remember the station schematics? Where is the nearest airlock on this level?"

Pavlovich lowered his voice. "Kaine, if you're thinking of another spacewalk—which is crazy, by the way—these shields might protect us for a few minutes, but what about them?" He tilted his head toward the others.

Hayden scowled and shook his head at the captain. "Cora?"

"Go to the first junction, turn left, and it is a hundred metres along the outer wall. What are you thinking, Hayden?"

"How difficult will it be to break *Scimitar* out of its berth?"

"The ship has enough power and shielding to do it, but it will tear away a significant chunk of the docking ring. The defence network will go nuts and every gun on the station will be aimed at *Scimitar*, but I'm not going to leave you guys."

"That's not my preference either, Cora—the station's grid won't fire while the ship is inside the defensive perimeter, right?"

"Right—oh! I think I understand what you're thinking. If you can't come to me, I can come to get you. I can extend *Scimitar*'s docking bridge to the airlock for you to escape."

"Can it work?" Pavlovich asked.

"Yes."

"How badly will you damage my ship?"

"Cap'n, she's been through a lot worse. This will work."

Hayden said, "I hear footsteps. Things are about to get hairy."

"All right, Cora," said Pavlovich, "I give you permission. But any damage to my ship is coming out of your salary."

She giggled. "You owe me a lot of back pay anyway. See you soon."

TIME FOR AN EXIT

The five of them hurried along the still abandoned corridors leading to the airlock Cora had identified as their only hope for escape. The lights were dimmed, and the gloom was punctuated by the regular pulse of flashing red lights set every twenty metres along their route. The noisy klaxon had long since ceased blaring, which made the heavy footfalls of the security team following them sound that much more ominous. Hayden estimated they had perhaps a thirty-second lead that was diminishing.

"There it is," whispered Aubrey as they rounded a bend.

Set into the end of a short, dead-end passage was the heavy door of the service airlock.

Hayden turned, dropped to one knee, and raised his flechette pistol back where they'd come from.

"Hurry and get that thing opened," he said to the others as Pavlovich joined him. The captain swapped magazines. "How are you for firepower?"

Hayden checked his pistol's readout. "Fifteen darts. You?"

"The same." He offered Kaine the cartridge he'd just removed. "Take mine and give me your incendiaries."

Hayden dug into his jacket and passed it to him. "Those might kill us if you pierce the hull."

Pavlovich shook his head. "The outer wall is behind us." He looked at Hayden and smiled. "Don't worry, I'll only use them as a last resort."

"This door won't open," called Emma from behind them.

Hayden glanced back, then turned to Pavlovich. The captain held out his hand. "Go. Give me your pistol."

Kaine passed the gun to him and went to assist with the door.

He pressed his hand against the bioscanner, but it flashed red and beeped.

"Shit."

Touching his earpiece, he said, "Cora, the system won't accept my bioscan. We can't get the airlock opened."

"It's Aramis; it's purged your clearance and shut me out of the system. I can't do anything to help. You'll have to manually override the lock. The hardware is the same as on *Scimitar*, so—"

"I know what to do. How long before you get here?"

"*Scimitar*'s engines are hot, and I'm breaking away now. I should be there in three minutes, assuming I don't destroy the station or the ship in the process."

"I'd appreciate it if you didn't do either."

He checked the panel beside the door to confirm that the chamber was pressurized. Seeing it was, he dropped to one knee and pulled the cover from the access panel. Bending down until he was prone, he reached inside to feel for the switch that overrode the door lock.

"Kaine," Pavlovich called, "we have company."

Two small sections of the wall behind Pavlovich were blasted away.

The captain fired three flechette rounds in response.

"I've got this," said Caldwell. Brandishing his pistol, he joined Pavlovich. Seconds later, the pop of a conventional weapon joined the hiss-clack of the tranquillizer darts being released.

"I should go too," said Aubrey.

"Wait," grunted Hayden. "Emma needs help with the door once I find the damned switch."

Hayden groped around until his fingers found what he searched for.

"Try it," he told Emma.

Seconds later, a rewarding clunk announced the release of the restraining bolts.

As he rose to his knees, the deck beneath him shook, almost knocking him off balance. Aubrey and Emma were thrown to the floor as the entire station lurched and tilted before the artificial gravity reestablished itself.

A hideous metallic groan echoed throughout the structure, followed by a dull, percussive thump from somewhere in the distance.

Klaxons that had been silent now blared. Above their din, an eerily calm voice spoke from hidden speakers in the ceiling.

"There is a hull breach on the outer docking ring; section D, berth two-four-one. Decompression lockdown protocol is now invoked station-wide. Proceed to the nearest muster point and await further instructions pending determination of the nature and extent of the incident."

Hayden assumed the voice belonged to Aramis, because he couldn't imagine a human remaining so composed under such circumstances. From the noises and shaking, he imagined that the damage was extensive. He hoped Cora's confidence in *Scimitar*'s ability to endure that kind of stress unscathed was not misplaced.

Chunks flew from the wall behind Pavlovich as the security forces resumed firing.

Hayden joined Caldwell and Pavlovich. The captain had retreated behind the corner and periodically poked his head around it to return fire. Caldwell leaned against the wall, out of the line of fire. He clutched at his bleeding shoulder.

"Emma," called Kaine. "We need a medic."

The protective field hugging Pavlovich's body sparked with dissipated energy as bullets vaporized against it. He fired off two more rounds and fell back behind the corner. His shield dropped, and he gasped for air.

Seeing Hayden, he grinned. "This thing works great, but breathing is a bitch."

Two more chunks blew off the protective wall.

Pavlovich reactivated his shield and reached around the corner to fire three more rounds. A dim flash to his chest seemed to stun him. He pulled back and dropped the energy field. Groaning, he rubbed where the bullet had struck the shield.

"Your battery is almost depleted," said Hayden.

"Yeah, it's been getting a workout. They are using serious munitions. The flechette needles aren't doing anything, and Caldwell's gun is almost empty." He held up the pistol. "I'm gonna have to resort to the boom-booms soon. Did you get the door opened?"

Hayden nodded. "Cora's on her way."

"Yeah, I gathered that. These guys don't seem to think the decompression protocols apply to them."

The heavy airlock door was opened. He extended his hand to Aubrey. "I need your gun. Help Emma get Caldwell into the airlock."

She gave him the pistol and assisted the injured man to his feet.

Kaine put his hand on Pavlovich's shoulder.

"My shield still holds almost a full charge. You should go with them. That door should stand up to their ordnance until Cora gets here."

Still panting, the captain said, "How long?"

"Any minute, unless she stopped for takeout."

Pavlovich chuckled. "This has been fun, but I'm getting too old for this shit."

Kaine knelt beside him and prepared to activate his shield.

"You have a very strange idea about what is entertainment, Pavlovich."

The older man rose and, after glancing at the airlock, handed Hayden the gun with the explosive rounds. "*Scimitar* has arrived. You only need to hold them off for another minute or two."

Kaine nodded and took a deep breath before he turned on the energy barrier. After making sure that Pavlovich and the others had entered and closed the airlock door, he checked the pistol Aubrey gave him.

Hayden only had ten conventional rounds, unless he wanted to start firing the explosive ones. He lay on his belly and poked his head around the corner. Hugging the wall, three armoured Rangers crept toward his position. They spotted him and opened fire with automatic weapons.

Three rounds impacted his shielded face and vaporized, but he still felt their impact, like a firm finger poke to his forehead.

He brought up his pistol and fired off six shots. One of the soldiers dropped to his knees. A lucky hit had found the joint in his armour plating. His companions hurried to protect him with their own bodies. At the same time, another threesome emerged from cover and lent supporting cover fire for their companions.

Cursing, Hayden pulled out the gun with the explosive rounds, took aim at an interior wall above the heads of the second group, and fired.

A deafening explosion shook the deck beneath him, and a short-lived fireball filled the corridor.

Hayden pulled back around the corner and dropped his shield to greedily gulp air. Acrid smoke filled his nostrils, making him cough.

He looked to the airlock. Through the window in the door, he saw Cora had deployed the docking bridge. Supporting Caldwell, Emma and Aubrey made their way along a ten-metre walkway. Pavlovich appeared in the window, waving at Hayden to join them.

He nodded, then raised his shield and rolled back to assess the situation in the corridor.

Through the thick smoke, he evaluated the devastation he'd caused. The three soldiers he'd fired above lay on the deck, unmoving. The group with the wounded man were in better shape but still appeared stunned. The smoke-obscured silhouette of a soldier stepped out from behind cover and raised a weapon.

Hayden ducked back around the corner as the wall opposite him vanished in a blinding flare. The explosion's fireball disappeared into the black, star-filled hole where the ship's hull had been moments before. Invisible hands seized and dragged him along the deck toward the opening. He flailed for something to grab, but everything was being sucked into the vacuum along with him.

Larger chunks of debris bounced off his shield as he splayed himself to the deck on his belly, hoping he could create enough friction to avoid being dragged into the void.

He didn't see the soldier who slid into him.

The man tried to latch on to Hayden for purchase, but the energy shield would not let him. The two tumbled out of control until everything went dark, and he was spinning, surrounded by the inky blackness of space.

Though he searched, there was no sign of the man who'd collided with him. He turned his head, trying to find anything to orient himself. A large object flashed across his field of vision, vanishing before he could identify it. Almost as rapidly, it returned, and he realized it was the space station. It seemed to orbit around him in a chaotic, irregular manner, becoming smaller each time it passed before him.

Finally, his mind came to terms with what his senses already knew.

"Shit, not again."

SCIMITAR

Hayden abandoned his futile swimming kicks to try to stop his spin. He struggled to suppress the almost overwhelming urge to panic. Somehow, his rational mind still retained enough control to tell him to slow his breathing. His priority was to calm down, preserve oxygen, and assess his situation.

As bad as things seemed, he was still alive and unhurt. His shield prevented oxygen loss to the vacuum through his skin, and while his air supply was limited, he could still breathe. He remembered enough thermodynamics to understand that there was no immediate danger of freezing to death.

Recalling his recent ascent up the escape shaft in the station, he extended his arms to slow his rotation and get a better idea of where he was.

With the station passing before him more slowly, he got a good look at it. He estimated that he was already half a kilometre from it, but even at this close distance, there wasn't any evidence visible of the breach in the side of the massive station.

His heart skipped a beat when he realized that he couldn't find *Scimitar*, either. It was possible that the station had rotated since his exit, and the hole and his ship were merely hidden from his changing viewpoint.

Within a few slow breaths, he'd drifted to a kilometre from the station. From this distance, he began to appreciate its scale. Two UEF ships still docked to the outer ring were twice the size of *Scimitar* and dwarfed by the facility.

Then he recognized the guns that were the station's primary defence. Even from this distance, they appeared menacing. It wasn't until he looked more carefully that he realized a few were in motion, rotating on their turrets.

As they pointed in his direction, his panic returned.

Surely, he was too small a target for them to use those cannons on him.

Perhaps the station's AI had somehow detected his Glenatat shield and rationalized that, despite his size, he was a threat. With bitter irony, he realized that the only thing keeping him alive was also going to be the cause of his death.

The weapons tracked him, and he clung to a diminishing hope that they targeted something else.

From the periphery of his vision, something massive loomed. Within seconds, it came between him and the station, and he realized it was a ship. His momentary elation at the prospect of rescue evaporated when it dawned on him that his would-be rescuer was the target of the station's weapons.

An airlock opened in the side of the vessel, and a silhouetted figure in a spacesuit stepped to the threshold to wave at him.

Still spinning, Hayden flapped his arms to prove that he still lived, and the effort changed his rotation speed. As he turned, fleeting images whizzed past his eyes of the figure pushing himself away from the ship and drawing nearer. He trailed a cable behind him connecting him to the ship. Hayden's fears that it wasn't long enough to reach him vanished when firm hands gripped him by the shoulders. The cable tightened and his spinning halted.

He saw a bearded grin behind the helmet visor of his rescuer, and the last doubts he had harboured that it might be someone other than Pavlovich vanished. He felt strong arms wrap around his shoulders.

A brilliant light caught his attention, and he looked up as a fading flash of an explosion dimmed behind *Scimitar*'s bulk. A second one bloomed. The station had opened fire.

The time for the winch to reel them back to the ship seemed to drag as blast after blast pummelled the ship's hull. While they were protected by the ship herself, Hayden worried about the damage it had incurred to rescue him.

Finally, they stepped inside the airlock, and Hayden's legs collapsed under the sudden appearance of artificial gravity beneath his feet. He fell to his knees, and after the door closed and the pressure was restored, he dropped his shield to gasp for air.

There was a hiss as Pavlovich undid his helmet latch. He pulled it off to reveal a matted mass of sweaty hair pressed to his forehead.

"Whew, it's been a long time since I've done a spacewalk. You okay, Kaine?"

The deck vibrated under the impact of another volley.

Still panting, he nodded.

"Catch your breath," said Pavlovich. "Cora, he's inside. Get us the hell out of here."

"Already on it, Cap'n. Welcome home, Hayden."

Kaine rasped a hoarse thank-you.

The captain's firm grip helped him to his feet. "Are you ready to get back to work, Mister Kaine? Two warships are being dispatched, presumably to try to destroy us."

"Can we jump?"

Pavlovich pushed open the inner airlock door.

"Cora is charging the FTL drive, but the ship's been cold and will need—"

"Twenty minutes," Cora interjected, "and yes, I am pushing it past the safety margins as much as I dare. What the heck did you let them do to my ship?"

Pavlovich frowned and lowered his voice. "She's done nothing but bitch since she got here."

"You know that I can hear you, right?"

Hayden smiled, happy to hear them bantering like an old married couple. "How is the ship holding up to the pounding of those guns?"

"Armour plating is solid, for now."

"Do you intend to return fire?"

Pavlovich arched his eyebrow. "After all your efforts to prevent the station's destruction, I didn't think you'd approve of me blasting it to atoms."

The deck vibrated again.

"I didn't think my approval mattered that much to you."

The captain slapped him on the shoulder. "Don't worry, my sentimentality is temporary. Besides, the dark energy cannon is powered by the FTL drive, or did you forget?"

Hayden scratched his head and smiled sheepishly. "I suppose I did."

"Hmm, can you recall enough about operations to make yourself useful?"

"I'll be fine. I just need some water and a moment to catch my breath."

"Good. Meet me on the bridge ASAP."

Kaine straightened and saluted. "Aye-aye, Captain."

Pavlovich rolled his eyes and turned to walk down the corridor. Over his shoulder, he said, "Five minutes, Kaine, or I dock your pay."

Hayden grinned. It was good to be home.

SHOW ME THE EXIT

When he arrived on the bridge, Hayden was surprised that Emma, Caldwell, and Aubrey were gathered around the captain's chair where Pavlovich held court. They all looked up at him, wearing expressions of anticipation.

"Kaine," said Pavlovich, "you didn't tell me that this young woman has helm experience."

He stared at Aubrey, who frowned back at him with her arms crossed.

"I didn't know."

"Well, I consider that an asset, given that our crew is down to the two of us at the moment."

Hayden blinked, confused. "Are you asking me what I think?"

"Of course, I am."

His frown deepened as he peered at Aubrey.

"C'mon, First Officer," said Pavlovich. "Do you want to trust her: yes or no? If not, take her to the brig, but decide before those ships get close enough to start shooting at us."

"They're gaining?"

"They are two of Thomas's new vessels built for his armada, sent to prepare the way for his arrival. They have next-generation everything, and *Scimitar* is a quaint antique in terms of comparable conventional technology."

Hayden went to the sensor panel to examine the readouts. "How much Glenatat augmentation do they have?"

"From what I saw on the station, not as much as us, but enough to be a problem if they get close enough to use it. If they catch us, those two will do in ten minutes what our welcoming committee needed half an hour for. We need an experienced pilot at the helm. Between the two of us, I'm rusty but have more experience than you, so if you don't want to take advantage of this young woman's skill set, decide now."

"Can't Cora pilot us?"

"Yes, I can, Hayden, but if I have to also take on the work our crew normally does in other parts of the ship, my attention will be too divided and my response time too slow in a battle situation."

Kaine looked from Pavlovich to Aubrey. "Tell me why I should trust you."

"I was following my orders, Kaine. It was nothing personal."

"We intend to escape, not fight. What's to prevent you from going kamikaze on those other ships?"

"Look, the little I've seen of your ship convinced me of its value to our cause. I don't want it destroyed or captured by the feds' new masters. I promise I won't betray you."

Hayden looked back to Pavlovich for a few seconds before he said to Aubrey, "How good are you?"

She smiled wryly. "Do you want to read my CV?"

Kaine shook his head. "Fine, take the station."

As she stepped toward the helm, he added, "But if you try anything, I will shoot you in the back of your head." He patted the holstered pistol on his belt.

She nodded as she took her seat. "Understood...sir," she said, smiling.

Amused, Pavlovich grunted, then turned to Caldwell and Emma. "You two?"

He shook his head. "I'm just a jar-head. Sorry."

"Medic," said Emma.

He directed them to the unoccupied stations at the side of the bridge. "Sit there and don't touch anything."

Pavlovich rose from the chair. "I'll command from the tactical station, Kaine. You're in charge of everything else."

"Aye, sir. What is our plan?"

"Keep as far ahead of those ships as we can until the FTL drive spins up. Cora, how long?"

"Eight minutes, sixteen seconds."

Hayden went to the navigation console. "What coordinates are we jumping to?"

"Well, I presume that your rebel friends have a secret base where they keep those ships that shot at us."

Hayden raised an eyebrow at Aubrey. His hand rested on the pistol at his belt. "Well?"

She leaned across and punched in the coordinates on his console. "It's on a terrestrial moon orbiting one of the gas giants in the outer system."

"Did you reach Krellig so he doesn't shoot at us when we arrive?" Hayden asked Emma.

"Cora sent my coded message to him the moment I came aboard."

"Any response?"

She shook her head.

"Well, I hope he got it," said Pavlovich. "We don't want anyone to start shooting if we turn up unannounced."

Hayden turned to input something on the console.

"What are you doing, Kaine?"

"Entering the second set of escape coordinates in case that happens."

"Where?"

"Out beyond the heliopause."

A light blinked on Hayden's console. "We are being hailed."

D.M. PRUDEN

Pavlovich scratched his beard. "Who might that be? Let's hear it."

The communications hologram projector came to life, displaying an officer seated in a command chair like Pavlovich's. "Attention, UEF *Scimitar*; this is Captain Traynor of the UEF battlecruiser, *Halcyon*. You are ordered to shut down your engines and prepare to be boarded."

The captain arched an eyebrow. "That's rude. Open an audio channel, Mister Kaine."

He cleared his throat and lifted his chin to address the air. "This is the captain of the *Scimitar*. Under whose authority do you operate?"

He made a slashing motion at his throat, and Hayden cut the microphone.

The holographic captain seemed taken aback by the question but recovered. "Under the authority of the United Earth Forces, I order you to shut down your engines and prepare to be boarded. Is that clear enough, Captain?"

Pavlovich smiled. "Cora, how much time?"

"Four minutes, twenty-one seconds."

"Helm, are we redlining the thrusters yet?"

"We are at eighty-seven percent of maximum thrust, Cap'n."

"Push it all the way to the line. Reopen that channel."

Looking thoughtful, he paused before saying, "Captain Trenwich, it seems to me that there is some local dispute as to the planetary government's legitimacy, at least according to certain individuals I've spoken with. I'll ask again, under whose authority do you operate?"

The other captain's image frowned. "My name is Traynor, not Trenwich, and I operate on the direct authorization of the Grand Terran Confederation president, Robert Thomas."

"What? How much did it cost ol' Stinky to buy his way into office?"

Captain Traynor was becoming agitated. "The elections were six months ago, and the results are legitimate."

"Well, I didn't vote for him. In fact, I don't think anyone outside of the Sol System cast a ballot. That's hardly what I'd call a legitimate election result, if only one system in the Confederacy participated."

Pavlovich slashed at his throat. "Time, Cora?"

"Two minutes, twenty-seven seconds."

"Captain," said Hayden, "we are pushing maximum thrust, and they are still overtaking us. It also looks like—"

Scimitar shook. Red lights lit up across Hayden's panel.

"They fired on us."

"No shit," said Pavlovich. "What did they hit us with? That didn't feel like a conventional rail gun."

Hayden pored over the detailed sensor record. "They hit us on the dorsal stern. It was a particle beam with a dark energy signature. Glenatat?"

"A knockoff; Thomas bragged about how he no longer needed our cannon because his eggheads reverse-engineered their own version. Damage?"

"The hull readings are fluctuating; he hurt us, but I can't tell how badly."

"Cora?"

"That really stung, Cap'n, but no permanent damage. I can't say how many more of those we can take before there is, though."

"Can you compensate?"

"I'm already on it. One minute, thirty-nine seconds until the FTL drive is online."

The bridge shook again, more violently, followed immediately by a second, strong spasm.

"They've doubled up the power. That one took a chunk out of our armour."

"Cap'n, the hull could only redistribute sixty percent of the energy. We can't take another hit on that section."

"Helm, hard port, any heading. Present our flank to them."

The deck jerked under Hayden's feet, and the bulkheads shook under another barrage.

"I'm estimating they need twenty seconds to recharge their weapon."

Pavlovich said, "It's a good thing Captain Tweedle-dumb hasn't thought to alternate volleys with his other ship. Time, Cora?"

"Fifty-four seconds."

The ship shook once more, not as strongly. A few moments later, it happened again.

"Ten seconds," said Hayden, "they're alternating shots."

Pavlovich scowled at him as he shouted, "Helm, execute random course changes. Don't present the same side to them twi—"

Hayden gripped the console to steady himself as two more shortly separated impacts rattled *Scimitar*.

Pavlovich called, "Cora?"

There was a longer than usual pause before she answered. "We have enough power from the FTL drive for weapons, Cap'n."

"It's about freakin' time," said Pavlovich as he turned his attention to the weapon controls.

The bridge lights dimmed, and the air around them seemed to buzz like angry bees.

Scimitar's dark energy cannon hurled a deep violet beam into the nearest pursuing ship. The vessel distorted, like a reflection in a pond disturbed by a ripple. After a couple of seconds, everything returned to normal.

"They have augmented hull plating. I can't get a reading on the damage, if any. How hard did you hit them?"

Pavlovich scowled. "That was at fifty percent."

Scimitar's hull rattled under another enemy weapon strike from the second ship.

"Cora, why is this weapon taking so long to recharge?"

"I presumed that you want to make a jump soon, so I'm…"

"Dammit, girl, I need this weapon to be at full power before they can hurt us."

"Or we can jump," said Hayden.

Pavlovich glared at him. The ship shook again as the first ship resumed firing. "We should jump to the secondary coordinates, then."

Hayden studied Pavlovich's expression. "Why?"

Another blast shook the bridge. Damage indicator lights began to light up Hayden's console.

"Because—" His scowl deepened. "Cora, scan the ship for a signature of a quantum signal pulse device."

Hayden raised his eyebrows. "You think they planted a tracker aboard."

"That's what I'd do."

"If we jump, those ships will be able to locate us in seconds and follow."

"And we will lead them straight to the rebel stronghold. I don't think your new friends would appreciate that."

"I've found something, Cap'n. It's coming from one of the empty crew cabins on deck C."

Hayden asked, "Can you disable or mask it?"

"No, someone has to physically locate it and eject it from the ship."

Hayden addressed Emma and Caldwell. "Get down to deck C and find it. Cora will guide you."

As they left the bridge, Hayden turned to the navigation console. "Setting jump destination to secondary coordinates. Cora, how long before—"

"We can jump now."

Kaine reached across to Aubrey's console and pressed the button to execute the jump.

The air around them crackled with a static charge, and Hayden's ears began to ring. Vertigo suddenly hit him, and he couldn't tell which way was up. The bridge seemed to pulse and compress around him as if it were being sucked into a black hole centred in the middle of his skull.

Then, abruptly, everything returned to normal.

Aubrey turned her head and vomited on the deck. The stench triggered Kaine's gag reflex, and he dry-heaved a few times.

"You're out of practice, Kaine," said Pavlovich, who, despite his words, was pale as a ghost. "Where are we?"

Hayden wiped his mouth with his sleeve and looked at his readouts. "We are within the Oort Cloud, ten thousand AUs out."

"Keep sharp, I'm betting Captain Whatshisface won't take long to follow us. Cora, did they find the tracker?"

"Cap'n, they are still recovering from the effects of the jump."

"Tell 'em to mop it up later and get their asses down there. How long until there is full power to the weapon?"

"Another fifteen seconds."

"Do you intend to fire on them before they can recharge from a jump?"

"If they are dumb enough to jump to these exact coordinates, then yes, I do. Any objections, Mister Kaine?"

Hayden shook his head and returned his attention to the sensor readout. "No, sir."

Pavlovich didn't say as much, but Hayden knew he intended to fire the weapon at full power. Normally, he would object to destroying a ship and everyone aboard, but if they were capable of tracking *Scimitar* wherever she went, then their options were limited until the tracker was disabled. After what he'd witnessed, though, he had doubts about what a full-power blast from the dark energy cannon could do to those updated ships.

What if they could withstand their weapon? Thomas would have an armada of ships equally as powerful as *Scimitar*. Nobody in the galaxy would be able to resist his plan to pull every surviving system back under the smothering pall of the Confederacy.

An object appeared on his long-range scanner, followed by a second one.

"It appears that they are not dumb, Captain. Two ships popped up on the edge of our high-resolution sensors." He sat up and turned to face Pavlovich. "They've jumped to positions two hundred thousand kilometres on either side of us."

"Well, shit."

Another indicator flashed on Hayden's console. "Correction, four additional ships have arrived. We appear to be surrounded."

"Where did they come from?" Aubrey said. "There were only two of them in our system."

"Ansible," said Pavlovich.

"They revived that old technology?" Hayden said. "It hasn't been used since the Destin Era, and even then, it was notoriously unreliable."

"Thomas blathered about revisiting and perfecting it. I thought it was bullshit. But if he succeeded, those ships came in from other systems."

"My God, this could change everything," said Hayden.

"Yeah, I don't think these guys plan to take us alive, either," said Pavlovich.

JUMP

"They're coordinating their approach," said Hayden, his eyes glued to the sensor readout.

"They will hit us simultaneously," said Pavlovich. "Our armour won't withstand that. Cora, what's the status on that tracker?"

"They are tearing the cabin apart but haven't found it yet."

"Do you have a synth body available to help them?"

"If I did, don't you think I would have sent it?"

Pavlovich winced. "Okay, sorry. Where are we with the FTL recharge?"

"We can't jump for another ten minutes."

Hayden said, "They will only follow us again."

"I'm open to better ideas."

Hayden's brow furrowed before he turned to the navigation console and began furiously inputting commands.

"What are you thinking, Kaine?"

"For their plan to work, their acceleration curves are limited by the slowest ship. If we assume that they began to fire on us earlier as soon as they were in range, that tells us..." He looked up at Pavlovich. "They will all be within firing range in eight minutes."

The captain smiled. "That's only if we wait for them to arrive."

Hayden returned the smile. "Exactly. Our weapon has twice the range and power." His finger pointed to the display. "If we vector to this hole in their coverage at maximum acceleration, we may be able to break out of their net before more than one of them can get a shot at us."

"Helm, set a course to Mister's Kaine's coordinates; maximum acceleration."

"If we are forced to take a shot, it will delay our jump and leave us vulnerable for far longer than I'm comfortable," said Hayden.

Pavlovich scowled. "What's our status on that tracker, Cora?"

"They still haven't located it."

"Damn."

"Aren't there a bunch of engineers locked in your brig?" said Aubrey. "They might know where it is, and I can't imagine any of them are ready to die."

Kaine and Pavlovich looked at each other.

"That's not a bad idea," said the captain. "Which of us should speak to them?"

"Leave it up to me, Cap'n," said Cora. "I have a pretty good idea how to motivate them to cooperate."

"Do it," said Pavlovich. "But don't screw around, Cora. Threaten their grandmothers if you need to."

"It won't come to that."

Aubrey whispered. "Are you sure your AI is our best chance for quick results? She seems too...nice. I'd be happy to—"

"Just keep your attention on that helm and be prepared to make evasive manoeuvres."

Her shoulders slumped for the briefest of moments. "Aye-aye, Cap'n."

Hayden got up and approached Pavlovich. Lowering his voice, he said, "She's not wrong."

"I trust that Cora knows what she's doing. I'm surprised that you don't. Did something happen down on the planet?"

Hayden couldn't help but think of Cora's confusion while they were on Oberon. She hadn't exhibited any of those symptoms since her return to *Scimitar*. There was no legitimate reason to question her abilities, yet he was disappointed in himself that he had.

Shaking his head, he said, "No, everything is fine. I'm trying to act like an XO and examine all angles."

"Well, you're coming across like a nitwit, so unless you have a legitimate reason to doubt her—"

"I don't."

"Then get back to your station and keep your head in the game."

"Yes, Captain."

He returned to his console in time to see the readout change.

"They're reacting; everyone is turning to pursue or intercept us. We will enter the closest ship's weapon range in thirty seconds."

"Helm, continue to adjust course to keep them out of range for as long as possible. I'm going to target the nearest one."

"Firing the cannon will delay our chance to jump."

A smile emerged from beneath Pavlovich's beard. "We have more than one weapon, Mister Kaine."

Hayden nodded, feeling foolish. He'd forgotten how devastating *Scimitar*'s rail guns were at close range.

His console showed the changing positions of the six ships that converged on them. The closest one registered a sharp power surge.

"They are powering up their weapon."

The deck plate beneath Hayden's feet vibrated as their rail gun's magnets launched a projectile at a tenth the speed of light. In the blink of an eye, the fast-approaching ship lurched and veered off course under the impact.

"A direct hit to their ventral bow. They are venting atmosphere. Their cannon is—"

His warning was cut short by a violent impact. He grabbed the edge of his console to prevent being dumped to the deck. The status panel lit up with red lights.

"They got a full-power shot off as we passed them. We took a direct hit on our starboard midsection." Hayden struggled to keep up with the accumulating list of damages, minor and major the ship—meaning Cora—relayed to him.

Pavlovich said, "How bad?"

Kaine took a moment to finish reading the report. "The hull plating ablated fifteen percent; no breaches, but gamma radiation levels spiked for two seconds in section E-6."

"Good thing that part of the ship isn't occupied."

"The Glenatat components have already initiated regeneration."

"Enemy status?"

Hayden switched his display and threw it up on the holoprojector in the centre of the bridge.

"The ship we hit is drifting. The remaining vessels are in pursuit. We are beyond the range of their weapons, but they are closing the gap. I estimate five minutes before the closest one fires on us. Wait—"

He frowned as he tried to interpret what the sensors told him.

"Three ships just made FTL jumps."

"Shit," said Pavlovich. "Push sensors to maximum."

"I'm already on it."

Hayden's fingers danced across the console. "Got 'em. They've jumped to parallel us on three sides, outside of weapon range."

"Only until their FTL engines recharge," said the captain, "then they'll draw the noose closer. Plot an evasive course."

"A fourth one jumped out in front of us and is matching our velocity."

"And we're surrounded again. It feels like this is something they rehearsed for. Cora, please tell me you found that bloody thing."

"The engineers were cooperative. They've located the tracker, but it is behind bulkhead plate, and they are having a bit of difficulty accessing it."

"Tell them to blast a hole in the wall if necessary, but get that damned thing off of my ship."

"They retrieved a cutting torch from engineering stores. It should be soon."

"Captain," said Kaine, "they've begun to close the gap."

"So soon?"

"I think their recharge profile is different from ours. And they don't need full power to their weapons if they coordinate their fire on our engines."

"How long?"

"A minute; maybe less."

"What is our jump status? Maybe we can reset the board."

Hayden glanced at the readout as Cora recited the information.

"Engines will be charged in fifty-four seconds."

"That's too close; what happens if we jump sooner?"

"Cap'n, you know that won't work, a jump requires a full recharge."

"You know what I call that?" Pavlovich said, scowling. "Bloody poor engineering design, that's what."

"I'll mention it to the Glenatat the next time I speak to them."

"We could fire a low-energy discharge at them," said Aubrey. "Goad some of them into shooting prematurely. It would weaken their combined attack."

"And it would prolong the time before we can jump," said Hayden. "Rail gun?"

Pavlovich shook his head. "That was a one-off; I kept one round in the chamber, so to speak. Without a crew on the gun deck, we can't reload. I'd intended to automate the system while *Scimitar* was being refurbished, but it didn't seem like a priority."

"Having the dark energy cannon as a principal weapon made us complacent," said Hayden.

Pavlovich's brow knotted. "Duly noted, First Officer. It's something that will be corrected if we get out of this mess."

An alert on Hayden's panel drew his attention. "Reading a simultaneous energy buildup on all ships."

"Damn it."

"Cap'n; it's gone. They just dumped the tracker out the disposal chute."

"Punch it!" Pavlovich shouted.

The air around them crackled and pulsed, and a second later, Hayden's stomach felt like it had been turned inside out.

Aubrey retched again, but this time he managed to keep himself from trying to join her.

"Status," said Pavlovich, wiping his mouth.

He checked the navigation computer.

"We jumped to the coordinates Aubrey gave us for the rebel base."

"Any signs that we were followed?"

He studied the readout, checking and rechecking for any of the tell-tale dark energy signatures associated with a jump. After several seconds, he cautiously said, "No, it appears not."

"Any sign the rebels spotted us yet?"

"Not so far."

Pavlovich exhaled his relief before he said, "Maintain a watch and set in some escape coordinates, just in case."

"Aye, Captain," said Hayden, "but I don't think it will be necessary."

"I hope you're right, but I'm still going to tell Cora to go over every centimetre of this ship to look for any more of those trackers."

"That is something I will be happy to do, Cap'n."

A light came up on the communications console. When

Hayden examined the cause, he smiled. "We have an incoming transmission, Captain."

"Source?"

"Local."

Pavlovich arched an eyebrow. "Answer it, Mister Kaine. I suspect this call is for you."

The holographic projector shimmered and resolved into an image of Krellig.

"General," said Hayden. "I take it you received our message?"

"I had trouble persuading a few of the others that Emma's transmission wasn't a ruse, but then we learned about what happened at *Xury Baecher* station. Your arrival here wasn't unexpected, but I must ask: what are your intentions, Mister Kaine?"

Pavlovich stepped into the camera view. "General, I am Yegor Pavlovich, captain of the renegade vessel *Scimitar*. We are here to offer you our ship and our allegiance. From what we've experienced, you will need both."

Krellig lifted his chin, and a faint smile appeared. "Thank you, Captain. Your offer is both timely and very welcome. Standby to receive coordinates. I look forward to greeting you both, personally."

The hologram winked out, and Pavlovich placed a hand on Hayden's shoulder as he looked over it at his console.

"The FTL engine is charged, Kaine. Are you sure you want to join someone else's fight? We can pick a spot beyond the line and hide from Thomas forever."

Hayden considered the captain's suggestion. He smiled and said, "If that is what you want to do, I wish you well, but I'm staying."

Pavlovich's brow was crinkled. "Why? What changed your mind about getting involved?"

He sighed. "I have amends to make for a lot of generations of Kaines. This *is* my fight, no matter what I believed before. I'm morally obliged to help Oberon and any other system that chooses to resist Thomas. But I understand if you decide it isn't something you want to involve yourself with."

"Morally? Where is this coming from?"

He extended his hand. "How about it. Will you join us?"

Pavlovich stared at it for a few seconds. "I can't speak for Cora, but the only way I'll take your hand will be as a comrade in arms."

Before Hayden could respond, Pavlovich gripped his hand and squeezed.

Cora said, "You can count me in as well, Hayden."

"Thank you both. I can't tell you how much your support means to me."

Pavlovich slapped Kaine on the shoulder. "Let's go find a way to make Thomas's life miserable."

Hayden couldn't imagine anything he wanted more.

ACTING ON AN EPIPHANY

The view from the rebel base's observation lounge captivated Hayden. The gilded halo around the shadowed edge of the gas giant dominating the small moon's vista seemed to glow amidst a sea of stars.

He came here whenever his new duties permitted, just to stare at the planet. Its tranquility soothed him.

"Am I interrupting?"

Emma's silhouette was in the doorway.

He smiled. "Not at all; come in."

She joined him in comfortable silence, staring out the window.

Without turning to her, he said, "How did it go?"

He felt her eyes on him, and when he turned, they glistened with tears.

"What's wrong?"

Emma shook her head and wiped her eyes. "Nothing is wrong; I never imagined I would be going to space. Now, here I am waiting to be assigned to a ship as its medical officer. It's overwhelming."

He smiled. "Well, you have time to get used to the idea. Your ship won't be ready for a few weeks yet. There are still a few details to work out for the FTL and weapon modifications to your fleet."

"Cora keeps the engineers hopping, that's for sure. We were fortunate that the ones trapped on *Scimitar* agreed to join us."

"Having your employer try to kill you can change a person's perspective, I imagine."

She shook her head. "It wasn't that, although it may have helped. The speeches you and Krellig recorded are inspiring a lot of people to act. D'Ville is having a difficult time keeping order. I doubt he'll be governor for much longer."

Hayden's eyebrows drew together. "That won't be good for the people of Oberon. His replacement will answer to Thomas, and he doesn't brook failure. I may not have done your people any favours."

"You've opened a lot of eyes. We've been complacent for far too long, too willing to accept our fate as slaves for a corrupt regime, believing it is our natural place. It is important everyone sees off-worlders like you willing to share our struggle."

"I just tell a good story. Krellig and you and the others are the real inspiration."

Her hand rested on his arm. "Well, you're a natural."

He grunted and turned back to the view. "I was trained from birth to be a politician." He shook his head. "I was such a naive fool."

Emma squeezed his arm. "You didn't know the truth then. What you've done since—what you are doing—is the true test of your character. I, for one, am grateful you fell from the sky."

"And I am happy to have found a good friend in you, Emma."

She looked down at her feet and nodded. "Friends; right."

He tentatively reached around her shoulders and drew her closer. Side by side, they stood in silence, staring out the window. Gradually, she relaxed into him until her head rested on his shoulder.

"I never thanked you for coming to get me on the station," she said.

He looked down at her and smiled. "It's what friends do."

She sighed. "On the station when I kissed you... I thought..." Emma shook her head. "I'm sorry, I didn't know about your wife, Stella. You must miss her terribly."

His throat tightened. "Every day is a struggle, but Cora and Pavlovich help me through; they're family. When I thought I'd lost them too..."

She said, "I'm glad you got them both back."

He hugged her tighter.

She looked up at him. "Are you still determined to go? We can really use your help here."

He nodded. "I'm tempted to stay, but there are dozens of systems out there like Oberon. Someone has to warn them what is coming."

"It won't be easy."

"No, it will be damned difficult, but if we don't do something, any taste of freedom they've had since the collapse will be snatched away when Thomas shows up with his armada. The more systems he reclaims, the stronger he will become. If we can persuade even a few to join us, or to let us help them to prepare, he can be resisted. Maybe even defeated."

"Maybe we can make a stand against him here."

He shook his head. "Thomas won't throw more than a token force at your system. If you resist him and make Oberon too costly to control, he'll leave you alone."

"But only for a short time, right?"

Hayden sighed. "He doesn't like to lose. After he subdues enough systems and accumulates ships, soldiers, and resources, he will return to crush you for defying him. The only way to help Oberon is to force him to fight for every system."

"And that can only happen if someone goes out to warn them. I understand that it must be done, but why do you believe it's up to you?"

Hayden removed his arm from around her and moved closer

to the window. His breath fogged the glass as he considered how to answer her.

"My family shares responsibility for what happened to your world and countless others like it. I'm obligated to do this."

He shook his head, searching for the words that would help him explain his shame and the overwhelming need he had to make things right.

She touched his shoulder. "Nobody expects you to carry that burden, Hayden, but I understand why you feel you must. When do you leave?"

"Another week; as soon as Cora is confident the engineering teams know what they're doing."

She nudged him in the ribs. "How about that dinner you owe me before you go?"

He studied her face for a few moments, then smiled. "What's your calendar look like?"

"Hmm, I think I can fit in time with a friend this evening."

He laughed. "Dinner with a friend sounds great."

"Okay, I'll meet you in the mess hall at six."

She rose to her toes and kissed him on the cheek before she left.

Still smiling, Hayden turned to look out the window.

The Milky Way was splashed across the sky, making it appear to glow.

"So many stars," he said, desperation in his voice.

Only the unimaginable distances between them had protected them for the past fifteen years. Most of the few worlds that he'd visited had fallen into anarchy, rebellion, or war. A very small number had found their way out of the chaos of the collapse to become mature democracies. Left to themselves, he understood that many more would follow, while others would fall to despots.

It was the nature of humans. For thousands of years, the fall of one empire gave rise to new ones. Often it was not for the better.

He understood why Thomas felt he must save these struggling orphaned worlds from suffering. On the surface, the idea
could even be regarded as a noble one.

Humans had migrated from Earth to find new lives, but they
had never been permitted to pursue that destiny.

Perhaps it wasn't too late for that to happen.

PREVIEW OF KAINE'S REGRET

Hayden Kaine squeezed his eyes closed and tried to control his unsettled stomach.

Despite the uncounted times he'd endured an FTL jump, it seemed that he could never get used to the experience. It wasn't natural.

But, as unsettling as the physical discomfort was, something else accompanied it that he'd never confessed to anyone. The sense of another presence tapping on his memories as if on a closed door. It was fleeting, lasting only a second or two, but it always happened. And it terrified him.

Humans evolved to live on Earth, he'd long ago decided, and he doubted he'd ever grow accustomed to having his atoms dragged across dimensional barriers. It was alien, and as much as his mind wanted to normalize faster than light travel, he knew that his body would be happier with him if he just stayed home and obeyed Einstein's understanding of the laws of physics.

"We've arrived at the designated coordinates, Captain."

Kaine opened his eyes to glance at McKenna, his first officer. The younger man seemed unfazed. Hayden suppressed a smile as he briefly glanced about to assess his crew's adjustment to the transposition. The complexion of some of the newer bridge officers was as green as he felt. He was grateful that no one had puked this time.

Sitting straighter, he said, "Situation Report."

A woman's chipper voice answered from the overhead speakers. "All of *Scimitar*'s systems are optimal, Captain. I'm running full spectral scans, but we jumped in a long way from the distress signal's coordinates, so seeing anything may take a few moments."

"And the rest of the party?"

"All six ships have joined us without incident."

"Thank you, Cora. Weapon status?"

Lieutenant Aubrey Martini answered from the tactical station. "Our rail guns were loaded before we departed. Dark energy cannons are fully charged and at the ready, sir."

Hayden said, "It looks like your new recharge design is working, Cora."

"You doubted me?"

He grinned. "Not for a moment. How about the the others?"

"Your little fleet is ready," she replied over the speaker, then through the private comm unit plugged in his ear, she said, "Why so nervous, Hayden?"

His smile faded.

She bloody well knew what was on his mind.

"Anything on those sensors, yet?"

"I'm picking up what looks like debris on the thermal bands."

Hayden scowled. "How much."

A few seconds passed before Cora's reply. "Too much. I think it's them."

"Anything else in the area?"

"Nothing. It has to be our missing task force."

Hayden exhaled noisily and stared at the holographic viewer in the centre of the bridge. He couldn't see anything, which meant that whatever remained of the ships he'd been sent to find wasn't very large.

"Distance?"

"One and a half AU, Captain," replied McKenna.

Kaine did the math in his head. "All ships proceed to the coordinates at twenty percent 'c'. Maintain full battle readiness. Probe that area with everything we've got, Cora."

"Captain, it may be a trap. I advise caution," said Martini. "We should send in some drones to evaluate first."

Kaine shot a critical glance in her direction. She didn't flinch, but straightened her back and jutted out her chin.

He studied her for a few seconds before saying, "Thank you, Tactical, but we will proceed as I've already ordered."

Martini barely hesitated before she returned a curt nod and said, "Yessir."

He watched her as she returned to her seat.

"I know what you're thinking," said Cora into his ear comm. "She was the best choice for the position, despite your dislike for her."

"We will discuss this later. Stay focussed on those damned scans."

"Aye-aye, *Captain*."

He winced, regretting his harsh tone. Cora was more than his chief engineer. She was the heart and soul of *Scimitar*. Hell, she practically was the ship. But she was more importantly his best friend and confidant. Sometimes he forgot that she still had human feelings. He resolved to make up for his rudeness when they returned to base.

For Hayden, the next hour seemed to drag itself out. He had to force himself to remain seated in his command chair and try to at least give the appearance of calm confidence. But he couldn't keep his eyes from the holographic viewer as he searched for—what? He had no idea what he hoped to see that the sensors didn't.

By this point it was pretty clear that whatever debris remained of the five ships he'd been sent to find would probably fit into *Scimitar*'s cargo hold. And that frightened the hell out of him.

Admiral—now President Thomas didn't have any weapons capable of such total destruction. Or, at least, he wasn't supposed to. His weapons were derivative designs of *Scimitar*'s own. Not nearly as powerful. He just had a lot more ships than the rebellion. But whatever ripped this Taskforce apart was something completely new. And yet, it felt familiar to him. He couldn't explain it to himself, let alone attempt to articulate it to Cora, but it felt like an old threat that had been long dead.

He shook his head to clear his thoughts. As he did, his eye caught something on the holographic viewer.

"There." He jumped to his feet and pointed at the three dimensional star field.

Everyone turned to him, confused.

McKenna rose to stand beside him on the command platform. "Sir?"

Ignoring his first officer, Kaine said, "Cora, did you see that? Those stars winked out for a moment."

"Nothing showed on the sensors," she said.

"Damn the sensors. I know what I saw. Replay the hologram recording. Backup one minute."

"Yes, Captain," said McKenna as he nodded to one of the junior officers to comply.

A few seconds later, the hologram flickered as the previous minute's display playback replaced real time monitoring. The star field looked identical as Hayden stared intently at the image.

"There, stop," shouted Kaine as he pointed. "Did you see it?"

"I...I'm sorry, sir. No," said McKenna.

Hayden glared at him briefly before turning to the rest of the bridge crew.

"Did any of you see it?"

He was met with blank, embarrassed expressions.

Scowling, he faced the display again and said, "Backup ten seconds and replay. Everyone watch closely."

When it replayed, others gasped.

"I saw it," said McKenna. "That triad of stars in the middle of the display winked out."

"I saw it as well," said Martini.

Hayden lifted his eyes to the ceiling. "Cora?"

"Nothing registers on the sensors."

"But you saw it, right?"

She hesitated. "Something occluded those stars, but it could have been anything. A gas cloud—."

"But sensors would have seen a gas cloud," said Hayden.

"Yes," admitted Cora. "Whatever you saw cross in front of those stars is not registering on any of our devices."

Hayden nodded to himself. "Like dark matter."

"Yes," Cora replied, cautiously, "but dark matter clumps are common in this part of the galaxy. It could be nothing."

Realizing that Cora was being far too rational for what his gut told him, he said, "Navigation, can you get a fix on whatever that was."

Collins, the navigator, hesitated. "I would need a second sighting from another position, sir."

"Then launch a probe. Now, people."

As the crew jumped to obey his order, McKenna approached and spoke quietly. "I don't understand what your concern is, Captain."

Hayden locked eyes with him. "You grew up on Oberon, didn't you?"

Puzzled, McKenna nodded. "Yessir."

A crewman announced that the research probe had been launched. Hayden turned his attention from his confused first officer to the real time data readout that appeared beside the holographic star field.

"Cora, coordinate with the other ships. Have every crew replay their observational logs and report back position and time of the occlusion to you. That should give us a positional fix on whatever that thing is."

"Assuming they saw it," she said in his earpiece.

Annoyed, he plucked the comm unit from his ear and put it in his pocket.

Time slowed to a crawl as Hayden stared intently at the holo-display, almost desperate to see the stars wink out again and prove to himself he'd seen what he had.

"We have a positional fix, sir," said Collins. The star field was augmented by a yellow ellipse imposed on the display. "It is approximately two-kilometres from our present position. And, Captain. It appears to be moving."

A hint of a satisfied smile turned up the edges of Kaine's mouth. He resumed his command chair and re-inserted the comm unit into his ear.

"All ships, go to battle alert. Tactical, target that ship with all weapons."

"Ship, sir?" Martini replied. "I mean, yessir."

Cora spoke into his ear. "Hayden, it can't be the Malliac."

"Do you know of any other ships built with dark matter?"

"But my Glenatat sensors are tuned to see Malliac ships. I can detect nothing out there."

"Maybe it's not them—I bloody well hope it isn't, but some-thing destroyed the task force. And this situation is beginning to stink like a trap."

A brief, brilliant flash bloomed on the hologram display.

"Our probe was destroyed," announced Collins.

Kaine shouted, "All ships, open fire!"

The lights dimmed as *Scimitar*'s dark energy cannon drew power from the engines. Deep violet lancets of light shot from every ship, all targeting the same coordinates.

"I can't tell if we hit anything," said Martini.

"Recharge the weapons. Everyone keep your eyes peeled for any sign of—"

Scimitar was rocked by a powerful blow that almost threw Kaine from his command chair. Alarms blared as the crew scrambled to return to the chairs they'd been tossed from.

"A direct hit to our dorsal stern," Cora announced. "They were targeting our engines."

"Damage?"

"Still assessing, but we're okay."

"Tactical situation."

Martini shouted above the alarms. "I've got a rough fix on where I think it came from. Preparing to return fire."

"Belay that. They're moving and want us to draw down our power banging about for them. Maintain observations and only fire if you spot some kind of anomaly."

"Damage reports coming in from the other ships," said McKenna. "*Draco* was hit hard; engines are out and she's drifting. *Karpov* and *Curie* have extensive damage to their dorsal shielding."

Another brilliant flash appeared on the hologram.

"*Draco* was hit again. She—she's gone!"

"Destroyed?" Kaine asked.

McKenna's eyes glistened. "Yes Captain."

Scimitar's bridge was rocked by another blow, forcing Hayden to grip the arms of his chair. Three more blooms of light flared on the hologram.

"*Arcturus* is gone," said McKenna as he read from his work-station display. "*Delhi* looks like she's broken in two and the *Caspian* is venting plasma."

"Our armour integrity is down to forty percent," said Cora. "I can't augment its regeneration without drawing power from the jump engines."

Hayden stared at the hologram as a hundred scenarios flashed before his eyes.

"Survivors?"

"None," said Cora. "There are no active shuttle or escape pod beacons. Nobody had time."

"Set course for the *Caspian* and order them to prepare to transfer to *Scimitar*."

The ship shook again as another invisible blow hammered

her. As they turned to approach the damaged ship, it exploded in a horrifying nuclear flare.

"*Caspian* is destroyed with all hands, Captain," Cora announced coldly. "*Karpov* and *Curie* have both jumped and I suggest that we do as well."

Kaine turned to the hologram display. The star field looked exactly the same as it had on their arrival, the stars seeming indifferent to the massive loss of life that had happened in an instant of time.

He lowered his head in a silent prayer for the lost souls under his command and said, "Get us the hell out of here."

OTHER BOOKS BY D.M. PRUDEN

Visit https://dmpruden.com for a complete list of books and stories by
D.M. Pruden

SHATTERED EMPIRE SERIES:

Kaine's Sanction

Kaine's Retribution

Kaine's Reparation

Kaine's Rebellion

THE GALACTIC MISADVENTURES OF IGNATZ BAUER

Brain for Rent (Hardly Used)

The Soul Eater of Flipimoff IV

THE DESTIN CHRONICLES

Armstrong Station

Phobos Station

Rhea's Vault

Ganymede Station

Europa's Revenge

The Jovian Collective

The Ares Weapon

Mother of Mars

Child of Mars

Legacy of Mars

COLLECTIONS

Shattered Empire Super Omnibus
The Destin Chronicles Complete Collection
Future Vistas Vol. 1

ABOUT THE AUTHOR

D.M.(Doug) Pruden worked for 35 years in the petroleum industry as a geophysicist. For most of his life he has been plagued with stories banging around inside his head that demanded to be let out into the world. He currently spends his time as an empty nester in Calgary, Alberta, Canada with his long-suffering wife of many years, and a far too energetic cavapoo puppy named Lucy. When he isn't writing science fiction stories, he likes to spend his time playing with his grandchildren and working on improving his golf handicap.

You can find Doug at these social media links: